Sisters
of Cain

—⧋—

To Ursula —

September 2000

SISTERS
OF CAIN

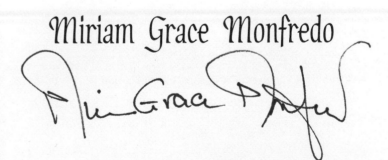

Miriam Grace Monfredo

BERKLEY PRIME CRIME, NEW YORK

SISTERS OF CAIN

A Berkley Prime Crime Book
Published by The Berkley Publishing Group,
a division of Penguin Putnam Inc.,
375 Hudson Street
New York, New York 10014

The Penguin Putnam Inc. World Wide Web site address is
http://www.penguinputnam.com

First edition: September 2000

Library of Congress Cataloging-in-Publication Data

Monfredo, Miriam Grace.
Sisters of Cain : a Seneca Falls Civil War mystery / by Miriam
Grace Monfredo.
p. cm.
ISBN 0-425-17672-X
1. United States—History—Civil War, 1861–1865—Fiction. I. Title.
PS3563.O5234 S5 2000
813'.54—dc21
99-089770

PRINTED IN THE UNITED STATES OF AMERICA

10   9   8   7   6   5   4   3   2   1

To
the former
fourth-, fifth-, and sixth-grade school members
of Rochester, New York, Girl Scout Troop #125.
With whom, in the autumn of 1975,
I began a journey into our uncharted past.

ACKNOWLEDGMENTS

I would like to thank the following:

Betty Auten, Historian of Seneca County, for generosity and invaluable assistance; Mike Brennan, Natural Resources Management Specialist, National Parks Service, for an impromptu and informative walk along a now quiet battleground above the James River; Jared Bryson, Alexandria Archaeology Museum and Laboratory, for pointing the way; Wanda Dowell, Director of the Fort Ward Museum and Historic Site, for her gracious assistance; Mazie Fobbs at the Urban Forestry Division of the Parks and Recreation Department in Richmond, Virginia; Rachel Monfredo Gee, for finding elusive answers; Kevin Heinicke, my brother and a former navy man; David Minor, the Time Master of Eagles Byte Research; and Simon Pontin of Rochester's Public Radio, for his eclectic taste in music that led to the pigeons.

And especially Frank Monfredo, for many things, among which was guiding the Sisters down a very long road.

For Miriam Grace Monfredo's Web site, visit
www.miriamgracemonfredo.com

AUTHOR'S NOTE

—⚹—

Sisters of Cain is based on an actual historic event, the Virginia Peninsula Campaign of 1862, which was the largest single campaign of the American Civil War. Intelligence information, or the lack of it, figured heavily in the outcome. On the eve of this campaign, four Union espionage agents assigned to Richmond were arrested, and a fifth mysteriously disappeared into the historical unknown.

The major characters in *Sisters of Cain* are fictitious, but actual historic figures frequently appear. The lives of some of the lesser-known figures are described in the Historical Notes at the end of the novel. Although *Sisters of Cain* is a work of fiction, recognized historical facts have not knowingly been altered.

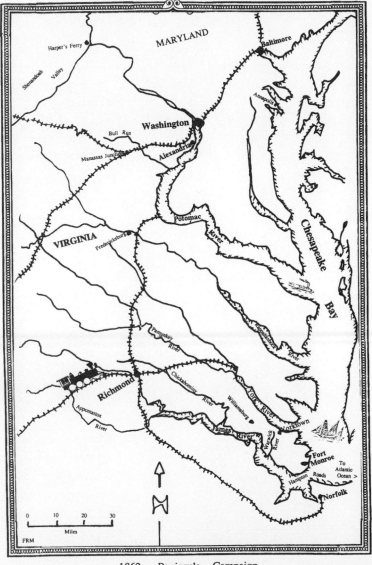

1862   Peninsula   Campaign

Word over all, beautiful as the sky,
Beautiful that war, and all its deeds of
  carnage must in time be utterly lost,
That the hands of the sisters Death and Night
  incessantly softly wash again,
  and ever again, this soil'd world

—Walt Whitman, "Reconciliation," 1865

1

Too much attention cannot be given to spies. . . . they are as necessary to a general as the eyes are to the head.

—Marshal Saxe, 1756
(Hermann Moritz, comte de Saxe)

FEBRUARY 1862
Richmond, Virginia

*I*t was too quiet.

The abrupt silence, while occurring in a seldom used hallway outside the hotel room, had now lasted far too long to be anything but ominous. Hattie Lawton had been carrying medication across the room and had stopped midway to listen, praying that the footsteps she had heard a minute earlier would continue past the door. The footsteps did not continue, and the silence stretched.

Suddenly, like a clap of thunder, came the bang of a fist striking the door.

"McCubbin, chief of police!" a voice barked.

Hattie drew in her breath and glanced toward the bed where Timothy Webster lay helpless. The pupils of his eyes, long dulled by pain and the small amount of opiates Hattie could smuggle into the hotel, now glittered with alarm when he mouthed at her, "They've found us."

Hattie gathered in her long skirt and rushed to the bed, where she bent over him, whispering, "Tim, we don't know that yet."

Timothy, his once-sturdy frame racked with inflammatory rheumatism, winced as he shook his head, murmuring, "They've come for us. You have to get away."

Another blow struck the door. "Open up! Now!"

"I won't leave you here," Hattie said, under her breath,grasping the sick man's wrist and lifting his hand to hold it against her cheek.

The Federal government and Chicago detective Allan Pinkerton were dependent on this man for intelligence information from the Confederate capital, but if captured, Timothy Webster might be abandoned by both.

Two harder thumps rattled the door.

"We won't answer," Hattie said, while Timothy strained to pull himself upright in the bed. "If we don't respond," she told him, her lips pressed to his hair, "they might leave."

He struggled to an awkward, half-seated position, and his voice held despair when he urged, "Get away, love! Please, leave by the window. Then go to the others."

"I can't, Tim. The two agents Pinkerton sent to contact us have been arrested. And that new man you just hired has disappeared. Unless . . . oh, God, could he have betrayed us?"

The sick man hesitated before answering, "It's possible, but I checked his background myself. And who could be more loyal than a—"

He was interrupted by a determined battering against the door.

"Those agents might have broken under questioning," Hattie said softly. "And if they did?"

She jumped at a crash of splintering wood. The door burst open, and two uniformed men strode into the room.

Her mind racing over their cover story, Hattie felt a cold

thrust of fear when she recognized them. The first one, silver-haired and heavyset, was General John Winder, Richmond's provost marshal and prison commandant. The man behind him was Captain Sam McCubbin, the recently appointed chief of police.

"Well, now," said General Winder, his mouth curving in a smile that did not include his small shrewd eyes. "And what have we here? A love nest?" The smile vanished. "Or more to the truth, a nest of vipers." It was not a question.

"You have no right to break in!" Hattie objected, remaining beside the bed as she faced the Confederate officers. "This is a very sick man, as surely you can see."

" 'Fraid he's going to get a whole helluva lot sicker," McCubbin stated, pulling a cigar from his pocket. "What's your pleasure, Webster? You want to tell it to us here, or would you rather do it in a cell? Won't matter none, 'cause one way or t'other you're goin' to swing. We don't much cotton to Yankee spies."

"You're badly mistaken," Hattie said icily. "How could this man be acting as a spy? He's been here in this bed for weeks."

"That won't work," retorted McCubbin, striking a match and waving it in dismissal. "We got word about your two Pinkerton friends. When we picked 'em up, they spilled the beans. *All* the beans!"

"This is absurd," Hattie protested, desperate to keep his attention from veering to Timothy, who, to protect her, might confirm McCubbin's claim. And when he had said "We got word," did that mean she had been careless and revealed their whereabouts? Or had she and Timothy been betrayed? If the latter were true, no one could help them.

"Funny you don't know those fellas," McCubbin said, lighting the cigar, then tossing the match to the floor, " 'cause they sure do know y'all! Now we got ourselves four Pinkerton spies"—he grinned at Hattie, baring tobacco-stained teeth—"and we sure as hell don't have to worry about that fifth one!"

Before she could stop herself, Hattie glanced with dread at Timothy, wondering if he'd caught the insinuation of treachery. His drawn face expressed nothing but resignation. To cover her lapse, Hattie reached down and smoothed his blanket, her fingers lingering on his before she thrust her hand into a skirt pocket.

"Miss Lawton," said General Winder affably, "I'd say you best cooperate. We have enough to keep you in prison for the duration. You follow me? When we picked up your two contacts, one of them was totin' a carpetbag. Guess he was either too dumb or too rattled to get rid of it like a good agent should. And what do you s'pect was in that bag?"

Because Timothy looked as if he were about to reply, Hattie answered quickly, "I have no idea, since I've never met the man."

"No! That won't do," Winder growled. "We know damn well that you Yankees are schemin' to do something down here—maybe even have a mind to try takin' Richmond! And your friends confirmed it."

"That's a lie!" Hattie scoffed.

"It's no lie," Winder replied. "That bag held reports on the whole eastern section of Virginia—fortifications, number of troops here, the whole shootin' match. Even had the launchin' schedule of our new ironclad ship, which is more'n *I* had!"

He turned to Timothy Webster. " 'Course *you* knew it, 'cause you're the one snooped 'em out. Now, none of this will reach your Mr. Pinkerton, but you can't be allowed to just saunter off with all that information. You follow me?"

"This whole thing's nonsense!" Hattie insisted, and heard the tremor in her voice giving lie to her protest. She glanced again at Timothy, afraid he would break if he felt she was in danger, and she would have to live with the knowledge that she'd sent him to his death. Her own life would mean nothing then.

"Don't bother denying it," Winder said to her, and his voice held a confidence that terrified Hattie more than his words. "We've got everything we need to hang you. Maybe you didn't know we have our own friends," he went on, the smile back in place. "But you, Webster—and your lady, too—won't be sending any more reports to Pinkerton or Washington."

Hattie again began to protest, but Timothy stopped her by saying to Winder, "This woman's no threat to you. She's simply been nursing me. Let her go."

"Can't do that," Winder answered, while McCubbin began to randomly search the room. "She's a spy same as you—though not near as dangerous—so's I can't just let her go. You follow me? Besides, you say she's your nurse, and that's fine, 'cause we can't let anything happen to you, Mr. Webster. We need you healthy so's you can make that gallow's walk."

Hattie turned toward the bed to conceal her movements, waiting until she thought McCubbin's attention was occupied with yanking out drawers of a bureau and dumping their contents on the floor. But he must have seen her from the corner of his eye, because he leapt across the room just as she pulled the derringer from her skirt pocket.

He grabbed her wrist, attempting to wrestle the pistol away, and Hattie, struggling in his grasp, could only sink her teeth into his forearm. At the same time, Timothy managed to slide off the bed. Before he could gain his footing, a blow from Winder's fist knocked him to the floor as McCubbin, now yelling in pain, swung his free hand across Hattie's face. Cigar ashes and sparks scattered as the derringer discharged to send the bullet flying into the ceiling. Hattie collapsed to the floor beside Webster, throwing her arm protectively across his shoulders.

"Like I said," McCubbin panted, standing over them and

vigorously rubbing his forearm, "you're goin' to hang. Only now maybe it'll be both of y'all swingin' from those gallows!"

A cold winter rain had begun to spatter against the windows of the Monument Hotel and into the large, horse-drawn phaeton awaiting General Winder, when four figures, one of them hunched over and leaning heavily on another, emerged from the lobby onto the cobbled thoroughfare. Street vendors were scrambling to cover their wares as shoppers hurried for shelter, and none seemed to notice the odd little parade crossing to the carriage.

A fifth figure, instrumental in the capture of Timothy Webster, had concealed himself behind a column supporting the hotel porch. He stood observing the scene with narrowed eyes, attempting to overcome his unease by fingering the pouch of silver and gold coins in his frock coat pocket. At that moment the coins weighed heavy, but he assumed he would learn to carry them without a pang of conscience, as this was, after all, only his first payment. He had earned it. Preventing the North from learning the launch schedule of the Confederate's ironclad *Merrimack* had alone been worth the price.

Some distance below the hotel, the rain joined the James River as it tumbled and frothed in its twisting course to the Chesapeake Bay. The observer remained in place, watching the rain and the river until Winder's carriage rumbled away. Then, forcing a leisurely gait, he ambled down the deserted street toward the Richmond telegraph office. He would wire a report to Washington, and no one there could question that Timothy Webster's illness had caused his uncommon lack of caution. It was close enough to the truth; Webster's undoing had been his uncommon lack of distrust.

The coins in the man's pocket jingled seductively against his thigh, their weight becoming lighter with every step.

2

There is one evil I dread, and that is their spies. I wish, therefore, the most attentive watch be kept.

—George Washington, 1776

Baltimore, Maryland

Bronwen Llyr refused to dwell on the danger. It would disturb her concentration and she could not afford it, since her most immediate enemy was time.

Shadows of the late-winter afternoon were lengthening beyond the library room window, making it nearly impossible to read the crabbed handwriting of Dr. Worth, not without narrowing her eyes to a squint. Bronwen rubbed them with the knuckles of one hand and continued to write with the other; even a brief pause would put her at risk. To bring about this small opening of opportunity had taken weeks of tedious surveillance, and now time was relentlessly ticking away with each swing of the desk clock pendulum.

The young woman groaned softly as she flexed her cramped fingers, and glanced with longing at the kerosene desk lamp that sat just inches away. She didn't dare to light it. The window's open draperies made it foolhardy to even consider, and to draw them would be the mistake of an amateur. They might be noticed by someone on the street outside, or even by the returning owner of the house, if she forgot to open them again before she left. In any event, she should be nearly finished.

A few dozen or less pages to copy and then she could leave the treacherous Dr. Worth's library. Who would have guessed that his papers held not only evidence of the counterfeiting activity that Treasury suspected, but the names of secessionist agitators who, amid other deviltry, were plotting to further sabotage the single Northern railroad line that ran into Washington City? Leaping off the pages at her were references to the Baltimore and Ohio Railroad, the Brooklyn Navy Yard, and the *Monitor,* whatever that might be. It appeared the activities of Dr. Worth and his cohorts included several recent train derailments. One the month before had killed five Union solders and two civilians, and injured scores of others.

Bronwen had also found a page bearing cryptograph for which there was time only to duplicate it as written. It would have to be decoded later by the Treasury Department. But the evidence she could read was damning enough that, after she'd put it in the appropriate hands, it would see the good doctor imprisoned for treason and possibly murder. With him should go some of his cohorts, labeled with what must be bynames of "Vandyke" and "Bluebell."

As Bronwen filled each page of her notebook, she detached and tightly rolled it, then placed it into a small leather pouch. This done with one ear cocked toward the long corridor outside the room, although the Worths' manservant Thomas, a Treasury agent plant, would warn her if their carriage approached. For the tenth time Bronwen glanced at the clock. The Sunday-afternoon musicale at the Maryland Institute, which the doctor and his wife attended once a month, should just be ending; what with a reception following the concert, and then a fifteen-minute carriage ride home, there should be enough time.

Only a few additional minutes had passed when there came a sharp rap on the library door. Startled, Bronwen jumped to her feet as the door flew open and Thomas rushed into the room, his round, usually ruddy cheeks blanched as he announced tensely, "They're back. Coming up the drive right now."

"They can't be!" Bronwen protested, but immediately began grabbing the files spread on the desktop. "It's too early, and I haven't finished. Weren't you watching the road from an upstairs window?"

"I was looking for their gray carriage, but something must have happened to it," the young man told her as he helped with the files. "A hansom cab has brought them—the horses had already turned into the drive before I realized it carried the Worths. The front door's locked, but you need to get out of here fast!"

It was a short few minutes later when both heard the hard, metallic clunk of a brass door knocker.

Baltimore, under occupation by Union troops, was a volatile, dangerous city, and Bronwen knew Worth carried a revolver. After weeks of observing and following the man, she doubted that he would hesitate to use it.

While she and Thomas were slinging files into the cabinet, she asked him, "If you don't answer the door . . . I assume he has his key?"

As Thomas nodded, Bronwen glanced toward the window. *Always have an alternate escape route;* it had been drummed into her during her earlier Pinkerton training. She had entered the house by the kitchen door, but if Worth and his wife came into the front entry, which now seemed likely, and imminent, she would be caught red-handed.

She was just tossing the last files into the drawers when she heard the front door opening, followed by Dr. Worth's demanding, "Damn it, boy, where are you?"

"Go!" Bronwen whispered to Thomas, giving him a shove. "Keep them in the front rooms as long as you can."

As he hurried into the corridor, she quickly closed the door behind him, then grabbed the leather pouch and rushed to the window. While tugging at its bolt, she could just barely hear Thomas excusing himself, while Dr. Worth dressed him down. Then, although he continued to lambaste Thomas, Worth's voice became more audible, as if he was starting down the hall.

Under her breath, Bronwen cursed in fury—and what was wrong with the bloody damned bolt? She had tested it when she first entered and it worked perfectly, but now she couldn't budge it. In the meantime, the volume of Worth's voice made it clear he was drawing closer. There was no way other than the window to get out, and no good place to conceal herself. Worth would surely notice that things were not as he had left them.

She grasped the bolt anew and gave it a strong jerk. It didn't move. She tried jiggling it, then jerked it again. Nothing worked.

In desperation she slammed the heel of her hand sideways against it, and the bolt shot back so smoothly she was thrown off balance. With Worth now sounding as if he was almost at the door, she regained her footing and pushed up the window frame, then hoisted herself to the sill. After drawing up her knees, she pivoted and thrust her trousered legs outside, at the same time tossing the pouch into the shrubbery below.

Her awkward perch on the sill made her attempts to haul the window back down futile ones, and after several frantic tries, and since she heard the library's doorknob rattling, she had to concede there was nothing more she could do. She dropped from the sill, landing in tall, spiny barberry shrubs.

Her wool jacket was snagged by thorns, but untangling herself would take time she could ill afford. Wincing, she ripped herself free and, after retrieving the pouch, crouched against the stucco wall, then edged along sideways between the shrubs and the house. It was not a swift process, but she couldn't risk standing upright, fearing that if Worth noticed the open window, he would go to it and look out. As it was, the shrubbery should conceal her. When she reached the corner, she crept around it, her eyes scanning the grounds and road beyond for passersby. She did not need any witnesses to her trespass, and neither did poor Thomas.

After Bronwen readied herself for a sprint to the road, a carriage came clattering into view, and she forced herself to crouch there, nervously waiting with the growing sense that at any second she would hear gunshots from the house.

"Come on, come on!" she muttered at the carriage that seemed to be taking forever to pass. She wiped a scratched, bleeding hand across her forehead, wondering how, if she were spotted, she could explain away her appearance.

When at last she judged the way to be clear, she made an open dash across the grounds for the shelter of trees along the property line, while from the tail of her eye, she caught a curtain moving in the second story of the house next door. Anticipating an outcry, she flinched in dread, but reached the trees in silence.

Still hearing nothing from either house, she cautiously edged out onto a road of the quiet neighborhood, which, despite its conspicuous affluence, had by its isolation protected itself. An explanation, perhaps, for why Dr. Worth had felt secure in holding such ruinous evidence.

Now Bronwen could only hope that Thomas had kept his wits and invented a plausible reason why the library window would be raised on such a frigid March afternoon.

They must believe she was a spy. And a Pinkerton spy at that, Bronwen decided three days later while walking rapidly down Charles Street, resisting the urge to glance over her shoulder. But if those shadowing her thought she was with the Pinkerton Agency, they would be wrong. Not that it would matter much if she had been marked. Whether employed by Pinkerton or the United States Treasury, a Yankee spy would be a Yankee spy, period.

Detective Allan Pinkerton, however, had fired her for insubordination over a year ago, and she was now employed by the detective unit of Treasury. The unit had been formed to combat the growing threat of counterfeit money, that, by most estimates, now constituted upwards to a third of the Federal monetary supply. Treasury had managed to track one counterfeiting cabal to the Baltimore area, the reason Bronwen had been sent there.

After she'd had time to think about it, she wondered if Dr. Worth and his secessionist friends, given their involvement in sabotage, were using their counterfeit funds to purchase weaponry from the North, a practice that would not be unique. Lincoln's naval blockade was beginning to take effect, and while the flow of smuggled weapons into the South had diminished, it had not altogether ceased.

She had discovered her shadows while pausing to relace her boot in front of a store window, some blocks from the Calvert Street station of the Baltimore and Ohio Railroad. The reflection in the plate glass had clearly displayed three men standing across the cobbled street. At first they had appeared to simply be loitering, and if she hadn't already been uneasy, and trained by Pinkerton to always credit such uneasiness, she might not even have taken note.

One thing that had made her suspect the three men of something less innocent than loitering were their distinguishing characteristics: there were none. They might have been triplets. All three stood about the same height, all wore dark overcoats with the collars turned up, concealing the lower halves of their faces, and three slouch hats concealed the upper halves.

The only thing that hadn't jibed with her suspicion had been the presence of a black-haired woman leaning on a silver-handled, ebony walking stick, while speaking to one of the men.

Their conversation had been inaudible, until the woman turned, asking, "It's that way?"

She must have been asking directions, because she had then limped off in the general direction of the waterfront.

Bronwen, still hoping she might be mistaken, had casually pulled up the hood of her dark green cloak over her red hair. She had moved slowly down the street, making a show of peering with interest into each shop window. Being a cold afternoon, there was little foot traffic, and she could watch the men, pausing when she did, walking when she did. They weren't particularly skillful, otherwise she might not have spotted them, but because of the previous Sunday's activity, she'd had cause to be wary. Not that any of this was particularly reassuring.

On Monday, two days before, she had gone as usual to the afternoon rendezvous. She was required to make contact with another Treasury agent, twice weekly, at a prearranged time and place. No exceptions were permitted.

Toting the leather pouch and its hard-won contents, she had arrived at the courtyard of St. Paul's Church on Charles Street with minutes to spare, and had waited. And waited. There had been a wintry chill to the air, and she'd kept moving to stay warm, circling the church and its courtyard. Her contact had never appeared. When darkness threatened, she had finally gone back to her residential hotel and awaited some explanation. None had come.

Yesterday afternoon she had repeated the procedure. Again no contact appeared, and again she had returned to the hotel. And then today, just an hour ago, a telegram had been delivered. When deciphered it read: AUNT BEVERLY FAILING FAST. COME HOME WITH ALL DUE HASTE. MOTHER. Which meant she should return to Washington immediately.

The wire had been sent by Treasury chief detective Rhys Bevan, addressed to her assumed name of Belle Lyon. But why would Belle Lyon now be the object of a surveillance? And by three men, which number was definitely excessive. Her stiletto, always stowed in her right boot, lent small comfort against such odds; she was good, but not so good she could fell three with one throw.

Bronwen, trying to ignore the obvious, along with the hard

knot forming in the pit of her stomach, was forced to consider the operation at the Worth house. Could she somehow
have been exposed and traced? Thomas might have been
found out and forced to disclose his affiliation with Treasury,
and with her.

The knot in her stomach grew harder.

A harsh wind off the Chesapeake gave her an excuse to
slow and pull her cloak more tightly around herself, making
sure it concealed the pouch hanging from its drawstrings
around her neck, and confirming in a shop window that she
was still being tailed. And now, giving her a nasty turn, she
observed that the men had conspicuous bulges beneath their
overcoats. Since revolvers were not the standard accessories
of a routine shadowing operation, presumably shadowing
was not all they had in mind. It must be the contents of the
pouch they were after, because nothing else made any sense.

For the first time that afternoon, Bronwen felt real fear.
She made herself keep a steady pace. Every instinct screamed
at her to run, but that would immediately signal that she was
aware of the men, when what she needed was time to think
through an escape.

In one of the many taverns at Fell's Point there was supposed to be a Treasury contact, but one in deep cover, to be
used only if in the most dire straits. She believed her present
straits should qualify.

When she turned east onto Pratt Street, she could see the
harbor basin ahead, but the cold had made the Fell's Point
streets less bustling than she had expected. The warehouses
fronting the harbor, and the long piers jutting out over the
water, held more seagulls than humans. Fear told her she had
only one path open.

If she located the contact at the waterfront tavern, she
might be able to turn over the pouch. The problem with this
plan was that she did not even know the contact's name. It
could be anyone; deep cover meant exactly that. Which now
seemed to her an absurdly useless arrangement.

It was, however, all she had.

After slowing her pace slightly, and forcing her shadows to also slow, she made three fast turns, in and out of an alley, then into another. When a glance showed no one directly behind her, she pulled up her skirt and dashed perilously over the uneven cobblestones before swerving onto Eastern Avenue. Ducking into an entryway, she bent over and whipped out the sheathed stiletto. It would be better than nothing.

Ahead of her at last was the waterfront and its numerous taverns, in front of which, despite the cold, stood clumps of sailors and dockworkers. At the tavern entrances lolled what could charitably be called ladies of the late afternoon. It abruptly occurred to Bronwen that, God forbid, one of them might be her contact.

Hanging in front of one tavern swung a decrepit sign bearing the name of Anchors Rest. It sounded familiar. Then, to no earthly good purpose, the words of her Aunt Glynis came to mind: "Respectable women do not go into taverns. Not if they value their good reputations." Since Aunt Glynis herself had been known on one occasion to breach this commandment, Bronwen quickly concluded that a bad reputation was preferable to no reputation at all.

Before she hurried forward, she unsheathed the stiletto and concealed it in the folds of her cloak. When passing the first group of men, she heard comments that she was glad her mother could not also hear, and when several of the men reached out to fondle her, only with effort did she resist the urge to flash the knife. Instead, she slapped their hands away, bringing boisterous guffaws from their companions.

From behind her came a shout of "Stop, thief! Stop her— that thieving woman in the cloak!"

Bronwen didn't dare take time to look, but dashed for the Anchors Rest entrance. After pushing herself through the women lounging there, she yanked open the door and lunged into a smoke-clouded barroom, so dimly lit that the raucous noise, the shifting, packed bodies, and the pungent odors of beer and tobacco made her light-headed. Before thrusting herself into the gloom, she paused to take a breath, and reached into the leather pouch to extract a large gold coin with the Treasury seal. She held it up between her thumb and forefinger, willing the unknown contact to see it before someone else snatched it away.

Since the tavern was two-storied, there must be a stairway . . . but where was it? Then she felt a sudden surge of cold air, and could only assume that her pursuers had followed her inside. She plunged blindly forward, immediately stumbling into the bottom step of a staircase.

Pinkerton's warning roared in her head: "When threatened by seizure, never go *up*! You'll be trapped. Always go *out*!"

Out *where*?

A hand seized her shoulder. Bronwen, struggling to raise the stiletto, wrenched around to see kohl-lined eyes surrounded by tangles of frizzy orange hair, and smelled perfume as strong as bedbug repellent. Lips smeared with bright red rouge whispered, "The room at the end of the hall. Straight ahead!"

At the same time she heard yelling from the direction of the front door, and ducked her head to plow through the crowded barroom. When she reached the rear she saw an empty, lantern-lit hallway and gathered her skirts to run down it. At its end she came up against a closed door, and as she stepped forward to jerk it open, a long, dark-sleeved arm shot out in front of her. She looked up into eyes the glacial blue of ice.

"Can't go in there," said the broad-shouldered man in a navy uniform, an ample smile warming his winter eyes. "And I can't imagine why you'd want to. Your likely customers are back there!"

He jerked his thumb in the direction she had just come, his other hand grasping a beer tankard.

Since a muscular body filled out his well-tailored coat, it would be folly to try elbowing him aside. Bronwen tossed back her hood and drew herself up to somewhere below his smooth-shaven jaw, glancing at three gold stripes on his sleeve before saying, "Do I look like a woman who needs customers, Lieutenant?"

She held up the Treasury coin.

The lieutenant's eyes flared with surprise, although the smile remained. "What *do* you need?" he asked.

Since the harsh shouts coming down the hall now distracted the man, Bronwen yanked open the door before he could stop her, and flung herself into another smoke-filled room.

Chair legs grated against a bare floor and earthenware beer tankards clattered as the half-dozen men seated around a circular table leapt to their feet, scattering ashes of cigars and cigarettes and clutching their playing cards tightly against their chests. A quick scan of the room's occupants, and the blue jackets slung over the back of their chairs, told Bronwen they were all navy men, probably from nearby Annapolis. If her situation hadn't been so desperate, she would have found their expressions hilarious, like those of cats caught munching canary bones.

She said hurriedly, "I'm being chased by three men."

The six stares directed at her changed from chagrin to annoyance. Undoubtedly they believed she deserved to be chased because she was a pilfering trollop.

Whirling to the officer who had followed her into the room, Bronwen said with frustration, "Please, Lieutenant— shut the door! At least give me a chance to explain!"

She thought her voice sounded remarkably strong, as if she were playing a starring role with standing-room only, instead of pleading for an audience.

"You'd better explain fast!" the lieutenant told her. He was no longer smiling, although he did close the door on what were now increasingly loud voices in the corridor.

Bronwen answered quickly, "I have no idea what those men want, but they have been following—"

The door burst open. Followed by a crash as the overturned table hit the floor. The tankards shattered, spraying
beer and shards of pottery, while the navy men appeared to
be diving under their chairs. *The wretched cowards!* thought
Bronwen angrily, hefting the stiletto in her right hand. At
the same time, another tankard had shattered on the floor
beside her, accompanied by an odd scraping noise. But her
eyes were fixed on the first man through the doorway, since
when he stepped into the room he brought a revolver up level
with her chest. The other two followed him, their revolvers
aimed at the men behind her.

Bronwen rocked slightly on her feet, poised with the stiletto ready to hurl the instant she heard the click of a cylinder
falling into place. Incredibly, she heard nothing, and could
sense no movement in the room at all. Everyone there must
be cast in place like bronze statues.

Breaking the silence, the lieutenant beside her announced
crisply to the first man, "You can lower that gun, my friend,
or you can lose a hand and maybe more. It's your call."

Bronwen watched in disbelief as all three revolvers descended, and she risked a sideways glance. The lieutenant
grasped a raised sword, its two-foot-long blade gleaming in
sinister splendor above its brass grip. Drawing the blade from
its scabbard must have made the earlier scraping noise she
had heard.

The three men stood motionless, the revolvers now at their
sides, which seemed to her an unusually meek capitulation.
Three guns versus one sword? She risked another glance, this
one over her shoulder. Then she spun all the way round to
see six crouched navy men with six revolvers trained
squarely on the trio in the doorway.

She swallowed hard against a bubble rising in her throat,
deciding that laughter, even if hysterical, would not be well
met by her stern-faced heroes.

"Well, Miss Braveheart," the lieutenant said to her, "what

shall we do with these scoundrels? Shoot them or decapitate them?"

"Is that my call?" asked Bronwen, bestowing upon him the lavish smile she reserved for only the most favored of men.

"Your call, milady."

An hour later she was on the Chesapeake Bay, southbound for Annapolis aboard a frigate with a brisk wind snapping its sails. The three thugs, she had been assured, resided in the brig. They would be taken to Washington, as Bronwen assumed that Rhys Bevan would want to interrogate them. Thus far the men had refused to say anything, but they must have been hired by someone who knew her, or knew of her. Which was a disquieting thought, and even had she not been recalled by Treasury, the sooner she left Baltimore the better.

For her to take the Baltimore and Ohio Railroad to Washington was out of the question. There might be others hired to watch the station, and she was relieved that she had trusted her instincts and not gone there when she'd first realized she was being followed. To reach the capital by ship, though, meant sailing down the Bay to the mouth of the Potomac River, and then northwest to the city, which amounted to a considerable time and distance. Rhys Bevan's wire from Treasury had said to return immediately.

Before the ship cast off from Fell's Point, the lieutenant, who had introduced himself as Alain Farrar, gallantly offered himself as her escort for the journey by water.

"Not such a terrible sacrifice, Miss Braveheart," he had said, smiling down at her as they waited on the pier.

Just behind Farrar hovered his solemn young aide, Oliver Evans, who stood balanced as if ready to spring at the slightest request. This slender, quick-witted ensign, Bronwen learned, had been one of those at the tavern's poker table. Evans had held a spectacular, winning hand, the reason that Lieutenant Farrar had gone to fetch his own beer.

"And I couldn't abide the smoke," he had explained, "makes me cough like I had consumption. Needless to say," he had added, "poor Evans lost that legendary hand in the fracas."

For this misfortune Bronwen, after thanking Evans for his valor, had apologized profusely. The sober-faced ensign had replied courteously, "My pleasure, Miss Llyr," a response that was nonetheless accompanied by an expression speaking volumes about remorse.

"Thank you for your offer, Lieutenant," Bronwen answered Farrar, "but it's only thirty miles overland from Annapolis to Washington, and I can easily take a train. I'm anxious to see my sister Kathryn. She's a nurse," Bronwen added, which was the truth but irrelevant in the extreme, except that she felt a sudden affection for her sister.

"I believe Kathryn might be reaching Washington today," she elaborated, which was a lie, although not an outlandish one, because at some point soon her sister would be coming to Washington. Then Bronwen wondered if perhaps she should not have mentioned Kathryn's calling. Female nurses, what very few existed, were viewed by most with disapproval, and by some as even less acceptable than actresses.

On the other hand, she had needed an excuse, since she had been unable to disclose the real reason she required swift transport, having learned—painfully learned—to trust almost no one. This included attractive naval officers. Even one who was clearly the Fell's Point contact for Treasury, assisted by the orange-haired wife of the tavern keeper.

Lieutenant Farrar looked crestfallen, saying emphatically, "But the railroad bed at Annapolis was only recently dug! And the track just laid—a wooden one and it's rickety."

He seemed to be watching for her response, and when she gave none, he persisted, "It's not much of a train, either. Just used to haul military supplies. It's old and not too sturdy, although you don't seem to go out of your way, Braveheart, to avoid hazards," he added with a grin.

Bronwen shook her head. The fact was that even now, in the second year of the secession war, the Federal capital still held Southern sympathizers. For her to arrive there with a United States Navy officer in tow could jeopardize an anonymity that might later be needed by Treasury. Rhys Bevan would expect her to enter Washington as she had left it. Alone.

When she again refused Lieutenant Farrar's offer, she smiled at him with what was genuine regret. And that was to be the last she would see of him.

Shortly after the ship cast off, he gave her a backward wave as he strode toward the cabin of the frigate, trailed closely by his dutiful aide.

3

*It is certain that if I had the information, I should
have given it. I should consider that I was performing a holy duty to my friends.*

—Rose Greenhow, Confederate spy

Washington City

$\mathcal{B}$ronwen hurried along the edge of Lafayette Park, which
looked untidy and forlorn under a bleak, cloud-strewn morning sky. A sky matching exactly in color the uniform of
Confederate officers. Not an observation, she supposed, that
she should point out to just anyone.

"Clear the way!" bellowed the driver of an army supply
wagon rumbling toward her. Bronwen scurried to the roadside as the horse-drawn wagon clattered past her over the
cobbled thoroughfare, followed by others that churned up grit
to rain down in their wake.

Although the hour was early, she could hear the tinny roll
of snare drums beating the cadence for troops that marched
through Washington in seemingly endless drill. The entire
city, it often seemed, had become a noisy, dirty, jumbled
garrison. Brawling in the streets was now a common pastime,
especially at sundown when the saloons overflowed, and just
recently the grounds of the august Smithsonian had been con-
fiscated for target shooting.

Over the snare drums, Bronwen could hear the thumping and pounding of construction work at the Treasury Building. This labor was meant to maintain and enlarge the massive granite structure as an impregnable fortress—as if, she thought, it wasn't already akin to the Rock of Gibraltar. Due to the war effort, the work proceeded by fits and starts; the war being, paradoxically, the reason Treasury was fortified to the hilt in the first place.

The erratic pace of construction grew out of the current attitude in Washington, where half the residents, transient politicians, and military believed the war would end next week, while the other half believed the Confederate army would storm the city at any minute. All behaved as if their beliefs were indisputable.

The result was that nothing begun had been completed in a city paralyzed by those tugging in opposite directions. Unfinished structures littered the landscape, one such being the Capitol, which sat cocooned in scaffolding. The Potomac River ran muddy and smelled foul, the old city canal had become an open sewer. Marshes and swamps breeding countless swarms of insects had not been filled, not even the more odoriferous ones near the Executive Mansion. Thoroughfares for the most part were still dirt roads along which cattle and swine frequently meandered, and bridges were by and large unfit to cross. The capital city of the Federal government stood firmly entrenched in limbo.

There were as yet, in the second year of war, Southern sympathizers operating in Washington; some were even employed by an ungainly bureaucracy which seemed not to know how to rid itself of them. Thus security was, in a word, lax.

After Bronwen went through the Fifteenth Street employee entrance of Treasury, she turned over her signed pass to the guard stationed in a wood and glass cubicle. He checked it against her signature and that of her immediate superior, both of which were kept on file. She thought this a pretty feeble attempt at surveillance. If outsiders wanted to gain entrance badly enough, they could bribe an insider to plant bogus signature cards in the file. Nor were the guards immune to distraction.

When she reached the main staircase to the second floor, she found one of them standing at its foot; a paunchy, uniformed man, who looked to be more or less on duty.

"Can't go up," the guard informed her and gestured to the stairs, punctuating this with a yawn wide enough to dislocate his jaw. "They're workin' on the windows up there."

"I'm employed *up there!*" Bronwen told him. "How would you have me get to the second floor—sprout wings and fly in through those windows?"

"No need to get frisky, miss. Just tellin' you what was told me."

"And were you also told of an alternate route?" she asked in exasperation, while trying to hold her tongue and temper in check.

"I s'pect if you want, you can take the back stairs," he replied, yawning again like a zoo hippopotamus.

Already barely on time, Bronwen cursed under her breath as she hurried down the detour route of an unfamiliar hallway. When she reached another set of stairs and paused to hoist her skirt, she glimpsed a plaque hanging on a nearby door: OFFICE OF THE U.S. SANITARY COMMISSION, FREDERICK OLMSTED, EXECUTIVE SECRETARY.

She recalled reading in the *Evening Star* that the Sanitary, as it was inelegantly called—and thus evoking images better left unimagined—had received authorization from President Lincoln to conduct observations and forward its recommendations to the Army Medical Service. Bronwen made a mental note to tell her sister about this office when she arrived. Kathryn intended to apply for work in a Washington hospital, but Bronwen had heard enough about the supervisor of female nurses, Dorothea Dix, to believe that her sister might not pass muster. Miss Dix was reputedly insisting that only older, "plain-looking" women would be accepted. If it were true, Kathryn didn't stand a chance.

As soon as Bronwen entered the fair-size office of Chief Detective Rhys Bevan, she saw that his mood seemed singularly grave. The penetrating, lucid blue eyes were clouded and underlined by dark smudges, and while this was not sufficient to detract from his sleek good looks, his grim appearance did not bode well. She began to feel uneasy.

He gestured to the chair in front of his desk, and said briskly, "Sit down. We have only a few minutes, and since you've been in Baltimore for some time, I need to bring you up to date quickly. So hear me out and please don't interrupt."

The brusque request, although delivered in his pleasant Celtic lilt, sounded ominous to Bronwen as she wordlessly sank into the chair. He, meanwhile, had swiveled to face the window.

"There is bad news all the way round," he began, and steepled his fingers under a firm, clean-shaven chin. "First, the Baltimore situation. The police there did not arrest your Dr. Worth—"

"They *what*?" Bronwen broke in, rising from the chair. "But how could they not? Or are they so infiltrated by secessionist—"

"What the Baltimore police are, or aren't, is beside the point," he interrupted, "because the fact remains that Worth is gone. By the time your telegram arrived from Annapolis, saying you had the goods on him—for which I took your word—and the Baltimore police had been wired the orders to arrest him, he'd already managed to disappear. His wife said she didn't know when or where he'd gone."

"Well, she *would* say that, wouldn't she? What did Thomas have to say about it?"

Rhys Bevan had swung around to stare at her. "Agent Llyr, are you deaf? This is urgent business and I asked you to hear me out. Now, allow me to finish. And sit down!"

Bronwen sat, and clamped her lips together. This was a side of the normally sanguine Rhys Bevan she had not seen before. Why was he so edgy?

But he did answer her question, stating, "Thomas couldn't say anything. Last evening Mrs. Worth, ostensibly looking for her husband in the carriage house, found Thomas's corpse. He'd been shot in the head."

Bronwen jerked forward, sucking in her breath. Thomas was dead? Then with horror she remembered the window in Worth's library. The window she had failed to close.

"Not only that," Rhys went on, plainly choosing to ignore her distress, "but it was evident that before his death Thomas had been interrogated, and none too gently. There's no way of knowing how much he told whoever questioned him. And, unfortunately, there's more."

Bronwen moaned, resisting the impulse to clap her hands over her ears.

"Your contact in Baltimore," Rhys went on, "the one you said failed to rendezvous, was found yesterday morning, his body washed up on the Fell's Point waterfront. It's possible, I suppose, that he'd been trying to reach the tavern and was killed near there. The wire I received said his body had likely been in the water several days, and he also died from a bullet in the head."

Rhys stopped and studied her for a moment, then said less harshly, "We've decoded the page of cryptograph you delivered to the cipher room last night—the one you copied at Worth's—and it contained still more disagreeable news. It confirmed, as we suspected, an intelligence network that is connected to the Confederate Signal Corps. Clearly it's part of an underground link between the Washington-Baltimore area and Richmond. Looks as if there are numerous espionage and counterespionage agents operating along what Worth's document refers to as the 'Secret Line.' If that's true—and there's no reason to believe it isn't—we now have solid evidence of an established Confederate spy unit."

Bronwen, overwhelmed by the fate of her colleagues, had no trouble being silent.

"Since your contact was one of those named on that page, you may also be known. The upshot of it," Rhys added, "is that I can't send you back there. Which, at least temporarily, gives me no agents in Baltimore."

She knew him too well to take this as a callous remark. No matter how it sounded, it wasn't a lack of agents in Baltimore that had so disturbed him, but their violent deaths.

She asked cautiously, "Is anyone else dead?"

"None I've heard about, not yet," he replied.

Bronwen, staring at the floor and wishing it would swallow her, knew she must admit to her part in Thomas's death. Rhys Bevan was one of a very few whose opinion mattered to her, and while he might overlook occasional disobedience, he would never tolerate dishonesty.

"I . . . I left the window open in Worth's library," she told him, "when I had to exit through it. He must have seen it and . . . and knew it implicated Thomas. Especially if Worth discovered that his files had been rifled."

Rhys was regarding her with a steady gaze, and when he answered she heard understanding as well as compassion.

"There will always be details we can't control, Bronwen. Always. There is no perfect plan. And no one ever told Thomas, or any other agent, that there wouldn't be risks."

His expression indicated she was not the only one he was trying to persuade that those unspoken words would grant absolution.

Bronwen added in misery, "But I exposed the agent at the tavern, didn't I?"

"What you did was sensible under the circumstances. Note that you, at least, are still alive." He drew a long breath and straightened in his chair, saying, "In any event, the tavern keeper's wife is secure. Or I hope that she is."

"And Lieutenant Farrar?"

"He's been promoted—it's Lieutenant Commander Farrar now. And he wouldn't have stayed long in Baltimore in any case. He's being transferred to Alexandria, as is a substantial portion of the naval force at Annapolis. You'll learn why later. But that, in a roundabout way, brings me to the next item of bad news."

Just when she had somewhat begun to recover. Not that she would ever forget the consequences of that open library window.

"When you worked for Pinkerton," asked Rhys, "did you know an agent named Timothy Webster? Or a Hattie Lawton?"

Bronwen nodded. "Both of them. I met Hattie a few times, but didn't know her well. Webster's the best there is, so I imagine Pinkerton has him assigned to Richmond. Why?"

"Webster's in Richmond all right. He's imprisoned there at Castle Godwin. Lawton's in prison also."

"Webster was *caught?* No, he was too careful to be caught! Someone must have betrayed them," she murmured. "What other Pinkerton agents are down there?"

"Two others, names of Lewis and Scully, who were arrested a few days before Webster. Know them?"

Bronwen shook her head.

"What about someone who goes by the initials H.J.K.?"

Again shaking her head, she asked, "Why?"

"Because neither we nor Pinkerton knows the actual identity of this H.J.K. He was recently hired by Webster, according to Pinkerton—who has been unsuccessful in making contact with him—but he's apparently now gone underground. Under the circumstances, one can hardly blame him."

"Webster will be released, though, won't he?" she asked. "The Confederates wouldn't hang him."

"Oh, yes, they would."

Bronwen saw from his expression that his comment was in earnest. "Can't something be done?" she insisted. "Maybe an exchange of prisoners? Allan Pinkerton must be frantic."

"He is that!" Rhys agreed. "Pinkerton was in the field with General McClellan when the news came through, and he asked the general to intercede. McClellan refused—his grounds being, rightly or wrongly, that it would be tantamount to admitting that Webster and the others *were* spies. And that they might all be summarily executed. Pinkerton has rushed back here, asking the president to request what you mentioned—a prisoner exchange. It would not be unprecedented."

"But Richmond's just been placed under martial law," Bronwen recalled. "Would that make an exchange less likely?"

Rhys didn't answer.

She sank back into the chair. If Webster could be caught, anyone could. *Anyone.* She had more or less considered this surveillance activity as a kind of game; a serious one to be sure, but a game nonetheless, like hide-and-seek with the neighborhood boys in Rochester's Mt. Hope Cemetery. In those days she had always won the game; once hidden, she had never been found. But neither until now had Timothy Webster.

"We don't have much more time," Rhys said, "because linked to the disastrous arrests in Richmond are new circumstances of which you're not aware, and I've had to recall two Treasury agents in addition to yourself. They and others will be arriving shortly."

"What others?"

He ignored her question, saying instead, "The face of war is changing. Much of it is due to new weaponry, and the North and South are both currently racing to construct ironclad ships. It's feared these ironclads will render all wooden ships obsolete. If that's true—and we don't know yet that it is—among other things jeopardized will be the Union blockade of Southern ports and the defense of our own East Coast ports, as well as the rivers that flow into them. These new ironclad ships could well be pivotal factors in the war. How much the South's espionage network will involve itself in this race is unknown, but we do know they have struck once at the Brooklyn Navy Yard, where the Union *Monitor* is being fitted out."

Bronwen sat on the edge of her seat, recognizing the name *Monitor* as having been in Dr. Worth's library files and wondering where Rhys was going with this alarming monologue. She did not have to wonder long.

"To combat the Confederate's network," Rhys told her, "Treasury has been assigned the responsibility of training a special intelligence unit. The need is especially urgent now, because the president is considering a campaign to bring the war to the South—"

He broke off as the outer office door opened, and immediately got to his feet. Bronwen also rose, while Rhys went to the door. He opened it to five people, three of whom she did not recognize.

Before someone else had the same idea, she went to perch on the windowsill. And this window was already open, she thought with another pang for the dead young Thomas.

While the others filed in, she looked them over.

The two she recognized, Dan Morrow and Ward Nolls, had been in place when she had come to Treasury. Men in their late thirties, both Morrow and Nolls had years of experience in counterfeit detection, and, ironically, some of those years had been spent in Richmond. Since Bronwen knew they were sorely needed in the field, the fact that Rhys had recalled them made it abundantly clear—if she hadn't already been given fair warning—that the need here must indeed be urgent.

The last three entering the room were a surprise. She experienced a stab of disappointment, or, more accurately, jealousy, that one was a woman. Until now, Bronwen had assumed herself to be the only female in the detective unit, and realized she had become possessive of her singularity.

This woman must be eight or ten years older than she, and was, Bronwen had to admit, quite attractive in a full-blown way. Rhys greeted her as Harriet King, while he drew out his desk chair for her to sit upon—something he had never done for Bronwen. She decided she did not much care for Harriet.

One of the two unfamiliar men was introduced merely as Mr. White. Bronwen wondered if Rhys had found the rough-looking man in a Washington saloon. White looked to be older than the rest, but was so bewhiskered and unkempt it wasn't possible to reckon his age. He did not acknowledge the others with even a grunt and, after withdrawing a half-smoked cigar from a pocket of his soiled overalls, he seemed to be fumbling for a match. Harriet King wrinkled an aristocratic nose, and pulled in her skirt, as if afraid it might be defiled. Bronwen refrained from smiling.

The other man, still poised in the doorway and scanning the room as if debating whether he wanted to enter, was introduced as Kerry O'Hara; blond-haired, slim but wiry-looking, with regular features and eyes of vivid turquoise, O'Hara had a square, short-clipped beard that followed his jawbone, and must be older than the adolescent he appeared. He now agilely maneuvered around the others to lower himself to the floor beside the window, giving Bronwen a suggestive wink.

"Well, how do *you* do, Red!" he greeted her, too loudly for anyone to ignore.

He really fancied himself, Bronwen thought, not bothering to reply, and decided she did not care much for him either. And if he thought he could call her "Red," he had another think coming.

Rhys Bevan stood in front of the door he had just shut, then crossed his arms over his chest and stood there surveying the six. They were packed into the room like sardines in a tin. In addition, the man named White, evidently set on making their cramped quarters as repulsive as possible, had lit his cigar. As the smoke rose, Harriet King put her hand over her mouth and gave a delicate cough.

Bronwen turned to shove the window up higher, just as Kerry O'Hara said to White, "Hey, that damn stogie stinks to high heaven. Stow it, will you?"

White turned very slowly to look at O'Hara, then took a long step toward the young man and exhaled a mouthful of smoke directly at him. O'Hara leapt to his feet, moving so fast that Bronwen saw only a blur before he had assumed an aggressive stance.

Ward Nolls quickly inserted himself between them, and Rhys Bevan said in a level voice, "Put out the cigar, White. Sit down, O'Hara. And do it now."

White shrugged, but proceeded to take his time squashing the cigar in the desk ashtray. In the meantime, O'Hara had squared his shoulders, hitched up his blue denim trousers, and with the cocky attitude of a bantam rooster, reseated himself on the floor.

Rhys continued to stand with his arms crossed, and Bronwen could sense the tension in the newcomers, since they didn't know that Rhys could do this all day long. He was, she knew from experience, taking everyone's measure.

Finally he said, "All right, people. We need to get down to business."

" 'Bout time," muttered O'Hara.

Rhys, if he heard this remark, ignored it, saying, "First, you need some background."

He briefly related the tragedy befalling the Pinkerton agents in Richmond. "The consequences of those arrests," he concluded, "may not be readily obvious. Not unless you know that the Pinkerton Agency was, for all intents and purposes, the extent of the Union's intelligence operations in the Confederate capital."

This sent a ripple through the room. Rhys glanced around, and apparently satisfied that everyone was listening closely, he continued, "For a number of decades, a Federal intelligence-gathering network was looked on as unnecessary. An expensive burden to be avoided and, some claimed, too dangerous a tool for the government to possess. So, at this point, the Federal government has no intelligence information coming out of Richmond—or anywhere else, for that matter. President Lincoln and the War Department are extremely concerned. Rightly so."

Ward Nolls, a solid, alert-looking man, now sighed heavily, fingering his short beard before he commented with the trace of a British accent, "So we're supposed to make up the lack of operatives? That will take some doing, Chief. Not to mention some time."

"We don't have time," Rhys replied. He turned as if checking the door, and said, "Agent Llyr, please close the window."

Bronwen twisted on the sill and gave the window a tug. It wouldn't budge, instantly returning her to the nightmare of Baltimore. She had just slid off the sill to get a better grip, when O'Hara suddenly sprang to his feet and encircled her with his arms. She heard the window behind her come down with a thump. O'Hara, though, didn't release her, but stood with his face inches from hers. Strangely enough, he smelled like chocolate.

"See, it takes a man, Red," he told her with an insolent smile that bared even, white teeth. "Looks like you might need one."

Bronwen, aware that the room had grown quiet, stared at him coldly. "I'll tell you what I need, Mister Rooster," she said. "I need you to move—or in less time than you can say cock-a-doodle-doo, you'll be one very sore capon!"

Nolls and Morrow were both grinning.

"Sit down, both of you," Rhys Bevan ordered, but with a note of indulgence. O'Hara leisurely stepped aside to stand against the wall, his thumbs hooked over the belt of his trousers.

"If there's been sufficient comic relief," Rhys said, "we need to continue. In a very few weeks, the Army of the Potomac will be on the move. General McClellan has submitted a plan to the War Department that is now being studied, and while the details are not yet final, the proposal involves an invasion of Virginia, and the capture of Richmond."

This news was received with prolonged silence. Ward Nolls at last broke it by inquiring, "How does McClellan mean to get there, Chief? Rebel troops are concentrated just southwest of here at Manassas. And last time I looked, that's right smack in the path to Richmond."

"There are ways," Rhys equivocated, "to bypass the Confederate force in northern Virginia."

"Then how does McClellan figure to move the army?" O'Hara unexpectedly piped up. "That's thousands of men we're talking about, along with their horses, artillery, food wagons, and all the rest. What's he plan to do—send 'em down there by balloon?"

This interesting question surprised Bronwen, coming as it did from a lout. But Rhys must have checked the man for brains before now.

He smiled and shook his head at O'Hara. "I doubt McClellan will take to the air, but that's the point—we need information before these issues can be addressed. Which is one of the reasons you're here."

Bronwen shifted uneasily on the sill, having decided that the situation must be even more desperate than Rhys had earlier stated. While Nolls and Morrow were experienced agents, their focus had been counterfeiting, not espionage, and she'd had Pinkerton's training in surveillance, but not as a spy in the field. If anyone needed an example of how dangerous this activity could be, they didn't need to look further than Pinkerton's best agent—who had just been caught and might well hang. Along with three others.

Rhys was now saying, "We need to act immediately, because there's a compelling factor I haven't yet mentioned. Last October the Federal government approved plans for an ironclad ship. Its construction is nearly complete."

O'Hara leaned forward to say, "Is that the weird-looking thing described in *Scientific American?*"

Bronwen could hardly believe her ears. This character could, and did read?

Rhys, seemingly not surprised, said, "Yes, and the publicity created by that magazine article was unfortunate, because it alerted the Confederates to our time schedule. But go on, O'Hara."

"That ship's got close to two hundred tons of iron plates covering it," O'Hara immediately answered. "A revolving turret that houses two big guns. Most of the ship rides below the water line, and it's supposed to be impenetrable to heavy shot." He shrugged as if this did not greatly impress him, and added, "Sounds like a crazy idea to me."

Bronwen had changed her position on the sill to study O'Hara through narrowed eyes and didn't like the scornful dismissal she saw in his expression.

Rhys said dryly, "President Lincoln must not think it's too crazy an idea, O'Hara, since he approved it. The Union *Monitor* is due to be launched soon—very soon. We don't know exactly how far along construction of the Confederate's ironclad is, but its presence in the Chesapeake Bay would, among other dangers, clearly threaten any plan of McClellan's to invade Virginia. To neutralize that threat, the success of the *Monitor* is crucial. Even after its launch, additional acts of Confederate sabotage may be planned, and they must be uncovered and thwarted."

He stopped momentarily and glanced at each of them, as if to gauge their reaction to this implicit order. No one, not even O'Hara, said a word. And what *could* they say? thought Bronwen. Just how did one go about protecting a mostly submerged ironclad ship? Where was it vulnerable, if at all? Protecting it seemed an absurd expectation.

"What you are going to receive," Rhys said, abruptly switching topics, "is training in espionage—concentrated, rapid training. For want of time, some of it must be done in the field. Obviously this is not the ideal way to proceed, but it's what we have been handed, so we will do it."

His voice carried a determined ring that Bronwen had heard before. They would do it, all right, but at what cost?

As if reading her seditious thoughts, Rhys added, "I can't promise it will be free of discomfort, or of some risk."

With this last he held everyone's riveted attention, and he quickly added, "I believe the risk can be kept to a minimum—" he paused, and Bronwen thought he probably saw her skepticism "—at least for most of you. Your pay will be good. As good as I can get."

This brought from O'Hara a snort of satisfaction. And the ceiling-reading Mr. White momentarily lowered his gaze to look vaguely interested. Bronwen glanced around at the other faces, which were absent of alarm, and wondered why. Was it only she who feared that when Pinkerton had lost his agents, Rhys Bevan had lost his mind? On-the-job espionage training? But then, Morrow and Nolls might never have been chased through the streets of Baltimore, and maybe these new recruits didn't know danger when they saw it staring them in the face.

"There are no manuals, no instruction booklets for this," Rhys told them. "To make things tougher still, this war is unlike any other that's been fought on our soil. Contrary to what our Southern brethren believe, we're all Americans, so we can't identify the enemy just by looking at him. He looks like us. No red coats and no bagpipes . . . I pray! We can't tell who he is by listening to him either, because we've got a stew of languages, regional accents, colloquialisms . . ." He stopped, and smiled. "For that matter, we've even got Welshmen who call themselves loyal Americans."

Bronwen smiled along with the others, knowing that Rhys Bevan, besides being a Welshman, was a showman who could play his audience. He had always been persuasive.

"Any one of you can choose to bow out now," he said. "You can not be ordered to participate. But once you've committed—and this is the time to decide—you are obligated to see it through, and it could be a long haul. Is that clear? Everyone?"

No one made a move to leave. But Bronwen wondered if Rhys had calculated that none would have the nerve to publicly back out. If so, he may have miscalculated.

"Just what does this 'concentrated, rapid,' in-the-field training involve?" she asked, making everyone's head swivel toward her. "I think that I—that we—have a right to know what we're getting into before we commit to it."

"Some big-game huntin', Red," answered O'Hara, a swagger in his voice. "Think you can do that? Without a man to take care of you?"

"O'Hara, I didn't ask you," Bronwen retorted. "Unless you're an expert in espionage—which, given your lack of discretion, I doubt—keep your mouth shut."

In response, O'Hara grinned at her like a sassy delinquent.

"That's a fair question, Agent Llyr," Rhys conceded, "but I can't wholly answer it. I did some intelligence work for Britain during the Crimean War, but this is a new and different landscape."

Bronwen realized, as she had a number of times, that she knew very little about Rhys Bevan. She did not, for one thing, know he had previously been involved in espionage, although given his Treasury position, he must have proved prior experience, or he would not have been hired. She did not even know how old he was; the Crimean War had ended about six years ago, but that didn't tell her much. It hadn't mattered to her before, and she supposed it shouldn't matter now.

He had moved on, telling them, "Some training can be done right here in the city—learning to read maps and memorize them, and even to draw them. You will need to learn

Morse code in order to operate the telegraph. Know how to use a compass. Learn regional accents . . . and I should mention here that only one or two of you will ultimately be sent to Richmond. That's no place for a novice. Most will be assigned to other locations in the South—New Orleans, for example—and undoubtedly to the West as well. Clearly more agents will need to be recruited, but you six, if you prove qualified, will constitute the core."

"What else," persisted Bronwen, "do we pioneers-on-probation have to learn?"

If she was irritating Rhys, he didn't show it. He merely answered, "Some of it you already know, Agent Llyr."

"You mentioned the president," she said. "Has he been told about this intelligence unit?"

"He has some knowledge of what is being discussed," Rhys answered in what sounded like evasion. "And he's well aware that without knowledge of what the enemy is doing, we are—to put it crudely—more or less shooting blind. Lack of that knowledge has already cost us dearly. Witness the catastrophes at Manassas and Ball's Bluff."

If it was Lincoln who had requested this special unit, that fact alone would make Bronwen's decision, and she suspected that Rhys knew it. On the other hand, if she found it was not to her liking, was he prepared to shoot her for desertion?

She turned to gaze out the window, while hearing behind her restless fidgeting. When she turned back, she found Rhys watching her, and she sent him a brief nod.

An expression that might have been anything from relief to satisfaction flashed across his face.

He picked up the loose papers he had earlier placed on the desk, and scanned them momentarily. "I've decided," he said, lowering the papers and rolling them in his hands, "that the most efficient way to handle this is to pair those who have some experience with those who do not. Plus, since you each have talents in specific areas, I have kept those in mind when assigning you in what we are calling the Special Intelligence Force of Treasury."

"Or SIFT," deadpanned O'Hara, his quickness another surprise to Bronwen. And everyone there smiled, straightened, and looked more alert, which was difficult given the soporific effect of the stuffy room.

Rhys first turned to Harriet King. "Since you already have a natural ear for languages, along with certain other advantages, you can pass for a well-to-do Southerner. I'm sending you to Baltimore with Dan Morrow—who at least knows how to behave like a gentleman, whether he is one or not."

Bronwen did not join in the smiles. She suddenly had a sense of having failed in Baltimore, at least in Rhys Bevan's eyes.

Rhys added, "We need to uncover the active secessionists in that city and we need it done quickly. That's one of our directives. I'll mention the others in a minute."

With this, he glanced at Bronwen, who deliberately turned away to stare out the window. She supposed she should get down on her knees and thank him for not being returned to Baltimore, but instead she felt . . . punished.

"You should be able to blend into that atmosphere without much trouble," Rhys went on to tell Harriet, "and through the city's loyalist politicians, we can pave the way for you."

Bronwen began to fume. This seemed like another slap in the face. Miss Well-to-Do would not be spending many cold, lonely surveillance hours, that was obvious. So just whom would she herself be teamed with—the cigar-smoking Mr. White? Surely on no one's list as a gentleman. Then another possibility, even more unpleasant, rose in her mind. But Rhys wouldn't do that to her. He would probably give her a solo assignment.

"Another thing all of you need to know, and know backward and forward," Rhys was saying to them, "are the offices of the Confederate government and who holds them, and the chain of their military command. Nothing makes a 'foreigner' easier to spot than ignorance of local politics. Our colleague Mr. White here knows all there is to know about that."

The quiet of surprise had descended, and they all turned to take another, longer look at this unlikely expert. Mr. White, however, continued to study the ceiling. Bronwen wondered whether the man was mentally sound. And indeed, O'Hara sat upright, saying to her impudently, and again too loudly, "Bevan's joking, right?"

She had the satisfaction of watching Rhys swing to O'Hara with a merciless stare. "Mr. O'Hara," said the chief in a wintry tone, "either you curb your unfortunate tendency to churlish behavior, or I'll do it for you." His tone changed when he said, "I expect all of you to avail yourselves of Mr. White's knowledge."

While they all availed themselves of gaping—Bronwen being no exception—White brought his gaze back to earth and said to Rhys, "The Lord will repay ye a hundred times over, me boy."

Rhys looked vaguely amused, and Bronwen decided there was surely more here than met the eye. Obviously Rhys didn't intend to enlighten them, and White himself was again gazing at the ceiling.

Bronwen had noticed, however, that both Nolls and Morrow were eyeing White dubiously. Nolls glanced up and caught her eye, and quickly looked away. It made her suddenly wonder if White might be a known counterfeiter—no, of course not. Rhys would hardly employ a criminal. Would he? Maybe if he needed forged documents, like passports to enter Richmond, he would.

"We're nearly finished," Rhys announced. He turned to Ward Nolls, saying, "For the moment you and White will remain in the Washington area. One of our objectives is to identify Southern sympathizers who are still employed in government positions. And since you're familiar with Virginia, Ward, if McClellan's proposal is approved, you will probably be sent there."

Although Ward Nolls nodded placidly, Bronwen thought: Poor, doomed Ward.

Rhys had unrolled the papers in his hand, and while appearing to study them, he said abruptly, "One of our most immediate assignments is to access the Confederate army's intention. To that end, Agent Llyr, you're going down to Northern Virginia. Not too far down, only to the Confederate lines at Manassas Junction. Your Pinkerton training in railroad operations will stand you in good stead."

Bronwen jerked forward to the edge of the windowsill. *What* had he said?

Rhys, not raising his eyes from the papers, continued, "We need information on the condition of the railroads there. Would they be vulnerable to sabotage and, if so, where? Find out if the Confederates have laid a telegraph line along the tracks, and if that line connects with Richmond. Primarily, keep in mind that our War Department needs information about a potential shift of Confederate troops, while it's evaluating the feasibility of General McClellan's proposal. Any questions so far?"

With this last, Rhys finally looked up at her.

Bronwen stared back at him in stunned anger. *Manassas?* If he wanted to be rid of her, why not simply send her back to Baltimore and the tender mercies of Dr. Worth and his cohorts?

He glanced again at the papers before saying, "I also need to know the Confederate troop strength at Manassas. Do they have sufficient food supplies and a reliable supply route— again the railroad question—or are they hungry enough to begin retreating? I don't expect an exact figure, only the closest estimate that can be made."

Rhys paused, presumably waiting for her response. She could only stare at him dumbly.

He leaned over to put the papers down, and after straightening, he said, "To this purpose, Agent Llyr, with you will go a numbers expert. A gambler by trade and, without even pencil and paper, a wizard at calculation. Thus I give you good luck and Godspeed—and Kerry O'Hara."

"Chief! No!"

Ignoring her outcry, and while O'Hara stood grinning like a fool, Rhys opened the office door and motioned for the others to leave. When there remained only Bronwen, mute with anger, and O'Hara, still grinning, Rhys closed the door and said, "This is an important assignment we have been given."

"Then why," Bronwen asked, "are you jeopardizing it by including this ass"—seeing Rhys's expression, she quickly rephrased—"this asinine O'Hara?"

O'Hara obviously intended to retort, but Rhys cut him off with, "I'm not interested in any petty squabbling between you two, and it needs to be put aside. Right now!"

He waited until O'Hara bobbed his head and Bronwen gave a short, unwilling nod.

"All right," Rhys said. "Secretary of War Stanton is insisting that General McClellan move against those Confederate troops encamped at Manassas. Stanton wants an estimate—as close as you can get it—of their numerical strength. Again, this assignment is important, and to *all* of us. There are those who have strenuously questioned—I should say *objected to*—the formation of this new intelligence unit. And have even more strenuously objected to certain of those who have been chosen as fledgling members of it."

With this he sent Bronwen a look, the meaning of which she could guess; either her own capability had been brought into question by her nemesis Allan Pinkerton, or there had been blanket disapproval of females being included, period. Her anger rose a notch higher.

"Understand," Rhys went on, "that your performance will be closely observed. A great deal is riding on this, so if you both want to continue with Treasury—and with this intelligence unit—you had best show results!"

"No trouble. Nothing to it," said O'Hara, a cocky smile accompanying his swagger to the door.

"O'Hara, wait just a minute!" demanded Rhys. "There's something else. You must be back here within four days from now. *Four days at the most!* Any later than that, and you needn't bother to come back at all!"

4

Be my brother, or I will kill you.

—Thomas Carlyle

Coast of Maryland

The sharp wind sliced across a narrow promontory of land, roiling the Chesapeake to chop at an already jagged shoreline. Two men, illuminated by a stark white moon, walked briskly over ankle-high marsh grass as they headed toward a copse of sheltering pine. One of the men swung a kerosene lantern. Its pallid amber glow lent them only a phantom warmth, but the cold and the desolation suited the men's purpose.

If seen from a distance, the two men would appear to be similar; both were of average height, both clean-shaven, both slim and vigorous in motion. Both also wore overcoats, but the overcoats were not similar.

"Bitter night," said the one named Norris in a pleasant, drawling voice, his frosted breath snatched by the gusting wind. "Damned cold for March." The color of his coat was cadet gray.

"You're thin-blooded," replied the other, words more clipped, voice somewhat deeper, coat so dark a wool it blended into the night. "Spend a winter along the North Atlantic—then you'll see what cold is!"

Norris bent down to place the lantern on the grass between them, as if to mark a line over which the other should not step, and then straightened to stand facing him across the flickering light.

"Your communication insisted it was urgent we meet," said Norris. "Do you have something?"

The other bit off the words, "Yes, and you might want to take it to Richmond fast. But don't trust the telegraph, even if the message is coded. Send it by courier."

"Let me worry about that. If it has to travel quickly, the telegraph is more convenient and—"

"No! It's my neck I'm concerned with, not your convenience. And Lincoln's got himself some good cipher-operators. Send it by courier. Agreed?"

He waited until Norris gave him a brief, reluctant nod. Then, speaking rapidly, his words clipped even more closely than before, the man said, "Your ironclad ship is ready for immediate launch from Norfolk. It's the Union's old wooden *Merrimack,* covered with an armor of iron plates and its prow fitted with an iron ram that looks like an eagle's beak. The Confederate government has rechristened it the *Virginia,* but nobody other than the Virginians are calling it that."

Norris laughed softly, his nod more willing now.

"But there's bad news with the good," the other told him. "The Union ironclad *Monitor* is also ready."

"So soon?" Norris looked unpleasantly surprised. "One of our agents infiltrated the Brooklyn Navy Yard, but was discovered after he placed a grenade in the blacksmith's shop. The grenade worked—the delaying tactic didn't. The Yard got around to tightening security after that, so we've not had much luck there lately. This *Monitor* is said to look like a tin on a shingle, or a cheesebox on a raft. Is it any good?"

"I saw only the early stage of construction, but it was designed from scratch by naval architect Ericsson, so chances are it's a good ship. Or I should say a good 'battery,' because at the center of the hull it's got a revolving gun turret."

"So I've read," said Norris. "How many guns and what type?"

"Two eleven-inch Dahlgren smoothbores. They're probably all the ship needs."

"What's its draft?"

"Not much—maybe ten or eleven feet, half that of *Merrimack*'s. Plans call for launching *Monitor* from Long Island any day now."

"You think it's a better ship than the *Merrimack*?" asked Norris, his face passive, but his tone demanding.

"I'd say so."

"How much better?"

"Better enough," said the man with a faint smile.

Norris did not return the smile, saying, "Does the North plan to construct more of these ironclads?"

"That's what I've heard."

Norris stroked his chin, staring down into the lantern's flickering light as he commented, "But this *Monitor* can't be completely indestructible!"

"By conventional means?" the man asked him.

After receiving a curt nod from Norris, the other looked off toward the water, and answered, "The *Monitor* might be in trouble if it were hammered by shore batteries. But there's nothing else that could do it much damage. Theoretically it could navigate the James River all the way to Richmond, because of its shallow draft."

Now it was Norris who looked off at the water before he asked, "What about internal damage to this ironclad? Or shall we say, intentional damage?"

The man's eyes narrowed. "If you mean, 'Is the *Monitor* vulnerable to sabotage?' then yes, I think any ship is. But that could mean heavy Union casualties, and—"

"This is war," Norris interrupted, "and the rules of the game have changed since our fathers' time. Just think what a loss of the Union's vaunted ironclad would mean—the demoralizing effect it would have on the North. And if the loss were to look like the result of an accident—as for instance, because of an inherent flaw in the ironclad design—it could certainly delay, if not permanently halt future Union production of these ships. Yes," he went on, thoughtfully, "this is definitely something worth exploring. And who better than you to do it?"

The other's shoulders twitched in a slight shrug. "I can attempt to look into it."

"I'd prefer that you do more than simply attempt."

The other nodded, then repeated his earlier warning. "If the Confederacy intends to keep control of the James River— and the Norfolk naval base along with it—you tell the folks in Richmond they need to move damn quick with *Merrimack*."

"That should provide an interesting spectacle," Norris said. "An iron-plated behemoth ramming the Union's wooden frigates. Could produce a lot of matchsticks."

"And maybe hold the James for you," stated the other. "I'd say that's crucial. You lose the river, you could lose Richmond. So you had better act."

Norris again nodded and rubbed his hands together, then cupped them around his mouth, guarding his breath. "Anything else?"

"The arrest of the Pinkerton agents in Richmond is known, so the U.S. Treasury Department is forming a special intelligence force of undercover operatives. I don't have any more on it yet."

Norris seemed to find this item of as much interest as the first. "Well, well—although I've been expecting it before now. All right, I would like the operatives' names, descriptions, their assigned locations. Most important, find out how many will be sent to Richmond. I need to know who, and how soon."

"My inside contact, as you know, isn't free to come and go at will—at least not yet—so it could be difficult."

"What isn't? It wasn't easy trapping Timothy Webster either, if you recall. It's never easy. Now, let me know when you have something in regard to that earlier matter. And I would like to know soon."

Before the two men moved back toward the mainland, Norris reached into the pocket of his overcoat to withdraw a bulky envelope and handed it to the other.

"Until next time, then," he said, and picked up the lantern.

As both men strode off into the night, the chill wind followed, flattening the marsh grass behind them as if a fleet of ghost ships rode in their wake.

5

The fight continued with the exchange of broadsides
... the distance between the two vessels being not
more than a few yards.

—S. Dana Greene, U.S. Navy, executive officer of the
Monitor, 1862

Washington City

The U.S. Military Telegraph Office was located in the War Department building, only a short stroll down a well-worn path from the White House. David Bates, the young office manager and cipher-operator, sat slumped over a large desk, chin in his hands, elbows propped on the desk's scarred, cluttered surface. Bleary-eyed, he stared with frustration at the stacks of books, manuals, and cipher notebooks on the shelves overhead. Hours of searching them had finally convinced him there was no answer to be found.

The first-floor room was large and brightened by two windows overlooking Pennsylvania Avenue. Despite the impersonal nature of the faded floral carpet, several tables, a second desk which contained the cipher drawer, an ever-changing number of chairs, and innumerable immense rubbish baskets, David had come to feel the room was more of a home than the one in his boardinghouse. At least this was usually true. Today it felt more like a funeral parlor.

During the past year, David had become accustomed to the daily appearance—and occasionally the extended company—of a tall, lanky visitor. And now, on a dismal Sunday afternoon, Mr. Lincoln was seated quietly in a chair beside one of the windows, the president having for many hours provided an eye of calm in the hurricane that was Secretary of War Edwin Stanton.

Earlier that morning, Stanton had been galvanized—as had everyone else—by a telegram that carried devastating news. This telegram had originated the day before in the form of a dispatch from General Wool, commanding officer at Fort Monroe, stating that the Confederate ironclad *Merrimack* had successfully attacked three Union frigates harbored some seven miles above his Chesapeake fort. One of these ill-fated ships had been rammed and sunk. Another had gone down in flames. The third, while trying to escape the monster, had run hard aground, and although the ironclad's assault had been interrupted by approaching darkness and ebbing tide, the hapless wooden ship had every expectation of being finished off early the following morning. Which meant *this* morning.

Upon arrival of this catastrophic information, David had found himself caught in a maelstrom, where he struggled to keep from drowning in the eddy of Secretary Stanton's feverishly dictated telegrams; among the many recipients of these were the governors of three coastal states, advised to immediately take whatever measures necessary to block their harbors. Following this action, Stanton had rushed to the windows and delivered himself of a chilling prophecy.

They would soon see the *Merrimack,* the secretary had announced, steaming up the Potomac River to briskly demolish the Union fleet anchored at Alexandria. After which it would train every one of its twenty guns on Washington, reducing the capital city to rubble. It would then proceed, unsinkable and unstoppable, to annihilate New York City and Boston. Followed by the Union's Atlantic coastal forts. And then, by way of their rivers, the Northern inland cities.

The secretary, quite naturally, demanded that something be done.

Lincoln had rushed to the Navy Yard for consultation. A short time later, Secretary of the Navy Gideon Welles had attempted to persuade Secretary Stanton that, because of the *Merrimack*'s deep draft and the relatively shallow waters of the Potomac, his apocalyptic vision of Washington laid waste was highly improbable. If not altogether impossible. The Welles Theory had the effect of reassuring the president, but did not soothe Secretary Stanton. Instead, he had then aimed his frenzied anxiety, again quite naturally, at the navy secretary.

"Do you realize what this means?" Stanton had demanded of Welles, his sparse beard quivering in high dudgeon. "Our entire Union navy has been rendered obsolete. Doomed to extinction. We now have nothing more than a fleet of antiquated wooden ships—as impotent as ghosts against this iron monstrosity! Which is undoubtedly spawning others like it even as we speak."

"We have the ironclad *Monitor*," replied Welles with admirable calm. "I have every confidence that it is superior to the Rebel ship."

"Yes, yes, so you've been assuring us. But where *is* this expensive savior? It was supposed to have been ready weeks ago," Stanton charged. "If the *Monitor*'s as good as you insist, Mr. Secretary, it should by now have attacked Norfolk's naval yard and destroyed the Rebel ironclad while it was still in dry dock. Instead, we now face Armageddon!"

Secretary Welles suggested they wait for more information before predicting the end of the world.

That information soon came in the form of a Virginia secessionist newspaper which, trumpeting the *Merrimack*'s triumph over the Union navy, predicted a swift end to the war. The stunned Federal secretaries and cabinet members, who had congregated in the War Department telegraph office, tensely awaited what could only be more very bad news.

There had then occurred an untimely break in the telegraph line.

A frantic search had determined that wherever the break in the line had taken place, it was not accessible to repair. Gloom had descended like a coffin cover.

David, attempting to inject a note of optimism, had said, "This happens fairly often, so I think the telegraph line will be restored. I'd even say the chances of it are moderately high," he added in answer to the unspoken question on everyone's lips. He recognized that his age probably did not inspire much confidence in these men, most of whom were old enough to be his father. Or his grandfather.

All that would be needed to seal the doomsday casket, David decided, was the appearance of General George Mc-Clellan. Ironically, the general was the one most responsible for bringing the telegraph to the War Department. But since then, David had transcribed enough communiqués to make him worry that the general might believe the broken telegraph line—and possibly the attack of the *Merrimack,* too— was part of a conspiracy by those determined to scuttle the general's own ship. Those being his "host of enemies" in the government; those who were plotting to strip him of his position as general-in-chief of all the Union armies, leaving him in command of only the Army of the Potomac.

Shortly thereafter, General McClellan had arrived.

To David's relief, and undoubtedly everyone else's there, the general's state of mind concerning the *Merrimack* had not appeared to be as disturbed as Secretary Stanton's— which indeed would have been difficult to match. The general had, however, indicated that the Rebel ironclad, if looming in residence at the mouth of the James River, cast grave doubts on his ability to invade Virginia. "It may very probably change my whole plan of campaign," he had said, "just on the eve of execution."

Perhaps noticing the president's doleful reaction to this

comment, the general had hurriedly left for quarters unknown, after sending couriers racing off with suggestions to
the commanders at Annapolis and Fort Monroe for defending
themselves.

The lugubrious others had then adjourned to the White
House. Mr. Lincoln, though, remained in the telegraph office,
and had for some time stood gazing out the window. At last
he had walked to the bookshelves, withdrawing his large volume of Shakespeare, whose work the president greatly ad-
mired. Indeed, when things were slow, he often read whole
passages aloud. When Mr. Lincoln had then asked David if
he had a favorite play, the young man answered without
hesitation, "Yes, sir, *Henry the Fifth.*"

The president's shaggy brows had lifted, indicating familiarity with the intrepid Henry, and David wished he'd had
the presence of mind to say instead *Much Ado about Nothing,* or better yet, *All's Well That Ends Well.*

And thus he now sat helplessly watching the telegraph, as
if, he chided himself, his focused gaze could somehow hasten
its recovery. Behind him, Mr. Lincoln was sprawled in a
chair, his feet up on a table, and David could hear the familiar voice frequently murmuring lines from *Henry* while
he read, the most recent recitation being: "*I would give all
my fame for a pot of ale, and safety.*"

David suddenly heard another familiar voice, this one elec-
tromagnetic. The president quickly got to his feet, and hov-
ering near David's elbow, inquired, "Is that what I think it
is?"

"Yes, sir," David replied, "the line must be repaired! A
message is coming in from Fort Monroe."

"Son, let's just keep this to ourselves a mite longer—before we advertise for a full house."

"Yes, sir!" David gratefully agreed, and fell to work, tran-
scribing to a sheet of yellow foolscap the Morse code of what
proved to be a very short message. All the while, the president stood peering over his shoulder. Mr. Lincoln soon began

to chuckle, and David smiled himself even before he completely absorbed what it was he had written:

> *Fort Monroe*
> *March 8, 1862*
> *Secretary of War: The iron-clad Ericsson battery* Monitor *has arrived, and will proceed to take care of the* Merrimack *in the morning.*
>   *John L. Wool, Major-Gen'l Com'd'g*

"See the date, sir? It must have been composed last night," David told the president. "But now that the line is working, there should be other messages coming in straightaway."

And indeed, messages began pouring in as fast as he could translate them. In the course of this, he learned that during the day a new cable had been laid between the eastern Chesapeake shore and Fort Monroe. And that the *Monitor* had very nearly been lost in a violent Atlantic storm, encountered on its maiden voyage to the Chesapeake. Which news was not reassuring.

The office was quickly packed to the rafters with men nervously awaiting word. At last it came: the two ironclads had joined in combat. And while the *Merrimack* had not been destroyed—the outcome of the four-hour battle having been seen by those who reported it as something of a draw—the monster had prowled back to its watery Norfolk lair. Its threat had, at the very least, been neutralized.

Several hours later, David again found himself alone with Mr. Lincoln. For some time the president had been seated quietly in the chair, and David, himself groggy with fatigue, wondered if he could be asleep. Although if he was, it would be unprecedented. But soon, unfolding his long length slowly, the president got to his feet, saying, "Reckon I'll go on home now, young man. You've done some fine work here this day, and I'm much obliged."

"Thank you, sir."

Mr. Lincoln nodded as he plucked a gray plaid shawl from the top of the door where he had earlier draped it. As he started to leave, David asked, "Mr. President, do you think the *Monitor* arrived down at Fort Monroe from New York when it did—on the very edge of doom so to speak—simply by accident? Or do you believe, sir, that it was the hand of Providence?"

Mr. Lincoln turned round in the doorway to say, "Don't ever question good fortune, lad. She comes calling seldom enough, and when she does, we can't have her thinking she's not appreciated."

6

Soon the slopes . . . were swarming with our retreating and disorganized forces, while riderless horses and artillery teams ran furiously through the flying crowd. All further efforts were futile.

—Colonel Andrew Porter, U.S. Army,
Battle of Bull Run (Manassas), 1861

Northern Virginia

$\mathcal{I}$t was the smell that warned her.

At first it came so faintly on the chill wind that Bronwen wondered if she might have imagined it. When she rode some distance farther, the odor gradually grew more distinct, until finally there was no mistaking it.

She stood in her stirrups to sniff the wind coming from the southwest. The rolling land made it impossible to see any great distance, but now her roan mare had begun to toss its head and whinny softly, so the animal must smell it too. It was definitely the odor of charred meat. And now when she looked up she saw traces of smoke ahead, drifting on high like long blue streamers that the ground winds could not snatch.

"Why are you sniffing like that?" asked Kerry O'Hara, riding beside her on a chestnut gelding. He rode well, very well, something that Bronwen hadn't expected from a self-described "city boy."

Grinning at her, he added, "You look like one of those coon dogs we saw earlier."

"O'Hara, keep your voice down," Bronwen said to him for probably the hundredth time, urging the reluctant mare forward.

When she reined in, it was near a stream swollen by recent rains and overflowing its banks, but even so, after consulting her map, Bronwen gazed down at the muddy water with astonishment. This was *it*?

Hard to believe that the previous summer this commonplace creek called Bull Run had given its name to a humiliating Confederate rout of green, undisciplined Union troops, near an equally commonplace railroad town called Manassas Junction. The creek had rambled beside her and O'Hara ever since they had entered the sparse woodland of mostly saplings and scattered stands of pine. Bronwen deliberately stayed clear of heavily forested terrain. She needed to see behind her and to either side, as well as ahead.

After dismounting, she threw the reins over a sapling and looked up at O'Hara. "We'll leave the horses here," she said in a low voice. "Come on."

"Why leave them? And what were you sniffing?" This while his gelding had begun tossing its head and snorting, no less skittish about the odor than the mare.

"Quit arguing," Bronwen told him, "and get down from that horse."

"Would you stop ordering—"

"I swear to God, O'Hara, if you don't shut your mouth for more than one minute at a stretch, I'm leaving you here. And you won't get very far on your own, city boy. Now get down!"

O'Hara looked about to protest again, then grinned instead, and swung down from the gelding. "You know, Red, you sure aren't much to look at when you're snarling."

Bronwen ignored him. It wasn't easy. He made himself known.

After glancing around, she opened the pack stowed behind her saddle, and loosened its drawstring, then pulled out a telescoped spyglass. Although she preferred field glasses, they would be too bulky and were not as accurate for distant viewing; above all else, Rhys Bevan wanted accuracy. A spyglass was also easier to conceal. What Virginia farmgirl—her current persona—would be wearing a necklace of field glasses?

Bronwen elongated the spyglass as O'Hara sniffed the air.

"Yeah, now I can smell something!" he announced in a voice that should carry throughout Virginia. "What the hell is it? And look at that smoke! Must be some big bonfire the Rebels made to roast pigs. A lot of pigs. What're they doing, having themselves a picnic?"

"It smells like more than pigs," Bronwen answered, craning her neck but unable to see anything other than the blue smoke. "I'm going to climb that rise over there to higher ground. You stay here with the horses. And be quiet about it!"

"Stop giving me orders." He withdrew a spyglass from his own pack, and began to climb the rise.

"O'Hara, get down! Fast!" Bronwen hissed in exasperation. "You're walking big as life straight into a Confederate bullet."

O'Hara grinned, but lowered his head and kept going. Just where, Bronwen wondered as she followed him, did Rhys Bevan ever find this character? It wasn't the first time she'd wondered if O'Hara had been recruited in one of the newly popular poolrooms, which would account for some of his bad habits, although not for his incessant talking.

Words ran from O'Hara's mouth like water from a primed pump. But while he argued constantly, he seldom took permanent offense at anything she flung back. He also maintained an uncalled-for cheeriness. At least he had stopped the suggestive remarks and lecherous glances; a threatening flash of her stiletto seemed to have discouraged him. The one and only advantage she saw in having him along was his surprising strength. Even though he was wiry, she hadn't expected the ease with which he hauled, tossed, or lifted nearly anything. Just what exact purpose this might serve in future she didn't know, but she had begun to fear that too much of his muscle lay between his ears.

Earlier, she'd tried to correct his pronunciation of Rhys Bevan's name. "It's not *Rise,*" she had said. "It's pronounced *Reese.* Rhymes with *peace.*"

"What kind of weird name is that?" he had asked with some scorn.

"Happens to be Welsh, O'Hara. As 'Bronwen Llyr' also happens to be."

"Welsh! Well, no wonder. They're Brits."

"You can refrain from nasty remarks about the British."

"Can't do that. Being of the Irish persuasion, I can't pass up a chance to bad-mouth Brits. It's an obligation."

Bronwen gave up.

Now, directly ahead of her, O'Hara crouched just below the top of the small rounded hill. He glanced back, swinging his arm for her to come forward—and for once he was not yelling.

Bronwen went to crouch beside him and O'Hara inched forward, pointing straight ahead as he peered through his spyglass. She raised her own glass to see below her, about a quarter mile distant, a haze of smoke, through which she could make out a half-dozen men putting torches to the edge of already smoldering pyres of rubble. Tongues of blue-and-yellow flames licked around charred mounds as large as hay stacks, and what must have recently been tons of meat.

"Bacon!" pronounced O'Hara, inhaling deeply. "That's fried bacon perfuming the air."

The only things moving that Bronwen could distinguish were the six or seven figures. Since there were horses tethered nearby, not harnessed to wagons, she guessed the men might be cavalry. Probably cavalry rear guard, because she couldn't see another living soul. The Confederate infantry had evidently withdrawn, and not long ago from the look of it.

"I don't know about you, but I'm hungry," O'Hara announced. "Shame to let all that bacon go to waste. Think those cavalry would mind if two starving farmers were to forage?"

"We can't go anywhere, O'Hara, until those men have left." Bronwen swung the glass to the south. "I need to think about this. We have a time schedule, remember?"

"What do you need to think about? The Rebs are gone. Turned tail and hied it for home."

She shook her head. "Why burn all that meat? It can't be a diversionary tactic, so how could they afford to sacrifice all those supplies? Besides, the Orange and Alexandria Railroad's there, and the Manassas Gap Railroad, too, so why not transport it by rail? And look over there, beyond the fires."

O'Hara trained his glass in the direction she indicated. "So? There's nothing but . . . wait a minute. Are those guns? Artillery pieces? Batteries?"

Bronwen crept back down the hill a few feet while she speculated. "It's been raining plenty the past week, so maybe the roads are too muddy for moving anything as heavy as those guns. I can't believe they just left them behind."

Haste could be the only explanation for the destruction of food and recklessly abandoned equipment. But why, and to where had the Confederate brigades of infantry, artillery, and cavalry, camped here for months just twenty-five miles from Washington, gone in such hurry?

"We'll wait until those cavalry leave," Bronwen told O'Hara, "then take a closer look. And if we run into anyone, be careful what you say. We're supposedly farm people, but you don't sound any more like a Virginia farmer than my horse does. Do you understand?"

"I understand you sure are the most high-and-mighty, bossiest female I ever had the displeasure to meet," he answered, the grin as usual drawing the sting from his words. She guessed he had traveled far on that grin.

"If you recall," Bronwen told him, "Rhys Bevan put me in charge during this assignment. Now, once again, do you understand?"

"Yes, sir! Your word is law, sir, and I am just a low-down toad. Sir!"

The cavalry men had long since disappeared over a far rise when Bronwen and O'Hara reached the former Rebel camp. There was more of the same thing they had seen by spyglass, and not only charred food stores and cast-off debris but personal gear, soldiers' baggage, and even trunks that had unquestionably been discarded in haste. By this time, Bronwen was no longer baffled.

As they had ridden toward the camp, she decided that word must have leaked about General McClellan's plan to advance on Richmond. This should have come as no shock; it was common knowledge that Southern sympathizers were firmly ensconced in Washington offices and among the garrisoned Union troops. Thus the Confederates camped here might have been ordered to move quickly toward their soon-to-be threatened capital.

"Hey, come 'ere!" O'Hara yelled from a far edge of the torched area, his call loud enough to lure a moose from Canada. "Take a look at this!"

After a quick glance at the horizon with her glass, Bronwen hoisted her gingham skirt to her knees and sprinted to where he stood, pointing at some odd-looking objects. "O'Hara, your yelling could raise the dead. Or bring back that cavalry. Now, it's the last time I'm saying this. Keep your voice down, or I'll use your shirt to gag you. Or better still, I'll use my stiletto. Take your pick."

"You're not only bossy, you're vicious. Not an attractive feature in a woman."

"Do you hear me?"

O'Hara shrugged, and turned to point again at the strange objects. "What do they look like to you?" he asked, his voice, if not soft, at least not a trumpet blast.

Bronwen stepped closer to them. "They look like wagon wheels," she said, frowning in bewilderment, "and stove-pipes."

She glanced at O'Hara and found him grinning from ear to ear. "All right, what's funny?" she asked.

"Those are," he said, starting to chuckle and gesturing at the pipes. "Remember back there on the hill, when I thought I saw batteries? Well, here they are! Stovepipes of different sizes. Or—for the Rebels' purpose—supposedly different caliber. Mounted on old wagon wheels."

By this time he was laughing.

Bronwen saw it now. "The Confederates camped here all winter with stovepipes mounted on wagon wheels to look like batteries of guns?"

"Whole batteries!" O'Hara repeated between gusts of laughter. "Why, there's enough guns here . . . *ha, ha!* . . . to blow Washington straight into the Potomac! Hell, straight into Chesapeake Bay!" At this he pounded his thighs, chortling merrily.

Bronwen did not find it amusing. Several months before, when Mr. Lincoln had suggested that someone might take a closer look at the Confederate troops camped at Manassas, McClellan adamantly disagreed. He had, he lamented, too few seasoned troops, because his boys were not yet ready. Also because, he knew without doubt, more than one hundred and fifty thousand Rebels sat waiting out here on the city's doorstep.

But . . . had there really been that many troops?

After once again checking the horizon, Bronwen left O'Hara's hilarity, and walked toward a small clump of trees, where she had earlier seen scores of black muzzles pointed east toward the Federal capital. And indeed, there they were, wedged between wagons and tree trunks, black and deadly looking. But less deadly looking as she walked closer.

Behind her, a crash like breaking pottery made her jump, and O'Hara's voice, still brimming with laughter, called "Sir Red! Come look what else I found."

"No," she said, "you come here."

O'Hara loped toward her with something brown in his hand. He stopped some yards from her, eyeing the black muzzles. Then he took several steps forward, saying, "Are those what I think?"

"It depends," Bronwen said. She reached out to run her fingernail down one of the muzzles. "If you think these are long guns, O'Hara, you'd be wrong. On the other hand—" she paused to hold up her blackened fingernail "—if you think maybe these are peeled, young tree trunks painted black, you'd be right!"

O'Hara was again roaring with laughter. "Trees!" he gasped. "Whole damn Union army . . . *ha, ha!* . . . kept from marching twenty-five . . . puny little miles by . . . trees! I can't stand it!" He rocked from side to side with gales of infectious laughter.

Bronwen had to succumb, laughing as she sank onto one of the bogus guns.

"Watch out now, Red!" O'Hara laughed. "One of those dangerous things . . . it might fire!" He got up and stumbled toward her to pose behind one of the painted trunks.

"Hey, over here, General Napoleon McClellan!" he yelled. "Come on over, you blue-coated devils—take a look at my big guns!"

Bronwen swiped at her eyes—smarting as much from laughter as from the receding smoke—and while telling O'Hara to quiet down, began to cough. She abruptly received several thumps between her shoulder blades, then found a dark object thrust into her face. With irrelevance, she noted that O'Hara still carried the smell of chocolate.

"Here, have some," he offered.

"What's that?" Bronwen asked. "Looks like a whiskey jug."

O'Hara began to laugh again. "Well, yes, I agree—it does look like a whiskey jug. But seein' as how around here things aren't always what they look like, I think I'd better investigate!"

He tilted his head back and took a large swallow.

"Well?"

O'Hara said solemnly, "It's the real thing! Authentic gen-u-ine whiskey."

"Where'd you find it?"

"There," O'Hara answered, pointing. "I tripped over about a dozen half-full jugs of it, and some charred decks of cards, too, just lyin' on the ground next to the . . . the . . . artillery!"

Convulsed with laughter again, he dropped to the ground and pounded his fists against the dirt.

"O'Hara, you're a bad influence. This is serious business, and we don't have time for tomfoolery. Now enough!" As Bronwen spoke, she scanned the area with her glass. She had a sudden, unpleasant sense of being watched, and although she could spot no one, the sensation persisted.

"You're right. Sir."

"We obviously need to inform Rhys Bevan of this . . . this camp, and quickly. No, don't start again! If anyone else finds this place, McClellan will be made a laughingstock."

"He deserves it," O'Hara argued. "Spends the whole damn winter parading around, while all of Washington City is held hostage by tree trunks and stovepipes!"

"I think that's overly harsh," Bronwen said, not lowering her spyglass. "And in some quarters that kind of talk would be considered treasonous. After all, McClellan couldn't have known—"

"Well, of course he couldn't have *known*," O'Hara interrupted, "if he never got close enough to use his bloody eyes!"

"I suppose, though," Bronwen went on, "that no one will pass this way soon, so we can probably wait until we get back tomorrow to tell the chief."

"Damn good thinking, sir."

Bronwen couldn't help but notice that O'Hara's command of himself had improved dramatically with a few swigs of Southern whiskey. For some reason, this did not add to her peace of mind.

"Besides, it's not McClellan I'm concerned for," she told him. "You know who will ultimately be given the blame for this."

O'Hara stared at her, and she could nearly see his thoughts revolving. He had a better brain, she admitted, than she had earlier credited him with. And she felt another twinge of uneasiness.

"Yeah, well," he answered, "you could be right. But somebody should tell the president what kind of clown he's got for a commander."

"McClellan had no way of knowing," Bronwen persisted. "But it's Mr. Lincoln who will be the one most embarrassed if this reaches the newspapers. Which reminds me, other than the telegraph line laid along the railroad tracks, I haven't seen any other cable, have you?"

"No, but if I had, it'd probably be fake. Something like dead snakes tied end to end. You have to admit, Red, this was pretty damn smart of those Rebels. They just moseyed around here all winter, defended by their phony artillery, drinking their whiskey, and playing cards. Hey, bet you don't know who was in command of the cavalry here."

"Are you testing me, O'Hara?"

"Yeah, I'm testing you. It's one of the things we're supposed to know. Do you?"

"I did know, but I can't remember," she confessed.

"It was Colonel—nope, he got promoted—it was *General*

James Ewell Brown Stuart. Jeb, to his friends."

"How do you know that, O'Hara?"

"I pick up things here and there."

"From where?"

After a slight pause, he said, "If you mean where is General Stuart from, how would I know?"

All at once recalling his curious and timely knowledge of the Union's ironclad *Monitor,* Bronwen asked him, only half in jest, "You mean you didn't read about Stuart in *Scientific American*?"

He gave her a disgusted look, and Bronwen, although she guessed his response was an act, let it drop.

"Be sundown in an hour or two," he said, glancing at the sky. "You reckon we should head back to the city tonight?"

"No, I don't reckon that. We have an assignment."

"Yeah, to count troops who aren't here."

"We should find out where they're heading."

"You mean follow them?" He looked reluctant. "That could take time we don't have. And Bevan didn't suggest it."

"This camp wasn't emptied all that long ago, O'Hara, if the fires are still smoldering, and that many men certainly won't be hard to track. I'm going to risk the time. But you don't have to come."

"Not come! And miss more of these Rebel magic tricks? Besides, Bevan wants a count and now I do, too. I'd like to know exactly how many big, bad men were holding off the Union army here. I'd be willing to bet it wasn't any hundred and fifty thousand!"

"Allan Pinkerton, among others, made that estimate," Bronwen reminded him. "It's hard to think that McClellan would have accepted that figure unless there was some convincing evidence."

"How much?"

"How much what?"

"How much will you bet there were fewer troops?"

"I forgot, you're a gambler. O.K., I'll bet you one whole hour of silence. But I don't think you can manage that, O'Hara."

"You're on. But if I win . . ."

"What?"

"I'll think of something.'

"I bet you will."

"How much?"

After retrieving the horses, they didn't travel far before learning the railroad had not been used by the troops. The wide swath of litter left behind by thousands of marching men continued on well past the railroad depot where Bronwen and O'Hara had reined their horses.

"The tracks here are in good shape," Bronwen said, after dismounting to look at them. "No reason for them not to use the trains . . . unless the troops are heading straight south. The Orange and Alexandria line runs west to Culpeper and Charlottesville."

"What about Fredericksburg?" asked O'Hara, after jumping from the gelding.

"There's no train that runs from here to there. And since Fredericksburg is due south, that's where they must be bound. They could pick up the line that begins just above Fredericksburg and runs straight into Richmond—the Richmond, Fredericksburg and Potomac line."

"That's good, Red. Impressive. Pinkerton the one taught you that?"

"O'Hara, what are the chances that you'll voluntarily stop calling me 'Red'?"

"About a million to one."

"That's what I thought. So maybe a threat would—" Her voice broke off.

"What's the matter?"

"Don't you hear that?"

O'Hara spun on his heels to look toward the depot. Coming around the squat structure, one by one, were a line of pale, gaunt figures.

When Bronwen saw them, for a brief moment she experienced a certainty that the figures were ghosts; phantoms of the men, Union and Confederate, North and South, who had fallen here months before, joined in death as they could not be in life. How had she found laughable any aspect of this haunted place?

Breaking the spell, O'Hara asked, "Who do you think they are? Not troops, that's for damn sure."

Bronwen watched the people straggle toward them. "They look like farmers," she answered. "But then, we do too, so let's hope that's all they are. And remember your Virginia accent—the one that doesn't exist."

"Very good, sir."

Bronwen sighed heavily. And for the first time realized why this was such a frequent response by her Aunt Glynis; some things just were not worth any more effort.

"Evenin,' sir," she said to the first of the strangers, a spare, bearded man who preceded the others.

He nodded civilly enough, but the thin woman just behind him eyed Bronwen and O'Hara guardedly.

Another man, behind the woman and also too thin, proved somewhat more forthcoming. "So they've gone. All of 'em."

"The troops?" Bronwen inquired. "Do you mean the soldiers have gone?"

"That's what I mean," the man answered, giving her close scrutiny. "Haven't seen you in these parts before."

"No, you wouldn't have seen us, because we're just riding through. We're on our way to—"

"Fredericksburg," O'Hara inserted. "Goin' to Fredericksburg."

Bronwen, concerned about what he might be hatching, turned to give him a warning look. He was, naturally, grinning, and since he seemed about to enlarge upon his inspiration, she said quickly, "Yes, we have kin there."

"Wouldn't go there now," offered another man just joining them, along with a number of others who were now coming forward.

"Why is that?" asked Bronwen, with a glimpse of what O'Hara intended.

The bearded man snorted. "You want to follow them soldiers, that's your business, I s'pect."

Another woman, her frazzled gray hair standing out like a nimbus around her head, said in an angry voice, "Just look at that! All that wasted food. They *burned* it! Never asked nobody if they wanted it, did they now?"

"Been here all winter, they were," said the first woman, "eatin' away, and now they burns what they couldn't stuff in their mouths."

"Not kind," murmured O'Hara.

"You're right, boy!" said the gray-haired woman. "Not kind, 't all."

"When we seen all that smoke," the bearded man offered, having apparently decided that "kin" in Fredericksburg was endorsement enough for strangers, "I told mother here, they's puttin' the torch to all thet meat! Looks like I was right," he added, with more satisfaction, Bronwen thought, than the situation merited.

"Lotta meat there," said O'Hara, giving Bronwen a significant look.

"Yes," she agreed, and asked the gray-haired woman, "How many soldiers were here, that they needed so much food?"

"Thousands!" the woman answered, watching as most of the others begin to drift toward the rubble.

"That many?" prodded Bronwen, in what she hoped sounded like sympathy.

"More," said the woman.

Bronwen felt a poke in her ribs. She turned to O'Hara, who was unaccountably jerking his head at the lowering sun.

What on earth was he . . . oh.

"When did they begin to move on?" she asked. "That is, my . . . my brother and I wouldn't want to . . . to accidentally run into them."

The bearded man gave her a long look. "You sayin' these soldiers aren't gentlemen?"

Now that, Bronwen thought, was an interesting response. Here was a man, he and his wife and neighbors obviously not well-fed, prepared to defend the honor of troops who had just destroyed food enough for a dozen families.

O'Hara gave her another poke. "Oh, no," she said, "I didn't mean that. I just wouldn't want, well, to get in their way is all."

The gray-haired woman gave a short, unhappy laugh. "Don't worry yourself 'bout that. There's so many, they couldn't tell if they tripped over y'all. 'Sides, they started leavin' yesterday, so they's ahead of you by some. Our farm's over that away"—she pointed to the west—"and we seen 'em at their supply depot in the mornin', the soldiers grabbin' everything they could lay hands on, 'fore they started the fires. Smoke was so thick yesterday, couldn't breathe for it."

"How many would y'all say there was of them soldiers?" O'Hara asked, sounding credibly like these farmers, and with the look of a wide-eyed youngster.

"We heard tell there was 'bout a thousand," offered a younger woman who had just joined them. "Oh, no, I mean a thousand eighty times over," she corrected herself, sending O'Hara an exceedingly friendly smile.

"That so?" O'Hara said, sending back a friendlier smile. He walked over to the young woman and said something Bronwen couldn't hear, but the woman laughed, and when O'Hara began to move away from the others, she moved with him. It was done so smoothly that it looked innocuous, even to Bronwen, and in the past she had done much the same herself when she wanted information. But O'Hara was supposedly a novice.

As the farmers scavenged through the rubble, she wondered how many times in the coming months this scene would repeat itself. She supposed an army on the move could hardly be expected to issue invitations to the surrounding countryside. But what a waste!

Suddenly O'Hara was coming toward her at a fast pace.

"C'mon, sister," he announced, snatching her arm and pulling her toward their horses. "We need to skedaddle!"

"What happened?"

"Nothing much. Just a father who didn't like his daughter talking to strangers. He seemed to feel strongly about it."

"Considering the stranger," Bronwen said, "I can hardly blame him."

The setting sun was taking with it any remaining wind, and the air had grown warmer, holding the balmy softness of early spring. Bronwen, again astride the plodding mare, and watching the dark red ball drop toward the horizon, tried to pinpoint why she felt nagged by uneasiness. She couldn't seem to shake it.

The most ready explanation was all those troops ahead, but they were a known danger, pure and simple; she would be dimwitted not to worry about them. The other explanation, not so pure or simple, was the man riding beside her. While she had to admit that she rather enjoyed O'Hara, she also had begun to view him with some mistrust. It was small things that were making her wary, but there was nothing she could tell herself with real conviction: That's why.

She also still had the unnerving sense that she and O'Hara were being watched; from where and by whom she could not see, even though she constantly scanned with the spyglass. The fact that O'Hara did not appear to share her misgivings was something she did not find comforting.

"You think those Confederate troops have camped for the night yet?" O'Hara asked her, abruptly switching his topics. He had for some time been expounding on the designs of regimental flags, not a subject of profound interest to Bronwen, but one she expected would be useful to know.

"I have no idea," she replied, "but keep your eyes open. They'll surely have rearguard cavalry watching for anything behind them."

"They're probably not too worried that McClellan might be chasing them."

She didn't bother to look; she knew he was grinning.

While the Confederates' trail was easy enough to follow southward, Bronwen had pulled out her compass, merely so she could report to Rhys Bevan that she had actually used it. Marching feet passing over the earlier muddy ground had left their marks deep and wide. In some places furrows had been plowed, and debris was strewn as far as the eye could see. She now saw a few muddy overcoats.

"Let's collect those," she said, pointing to two cadet-gray coats that looked like those of infantrymen. "Never can tell when we might need them."

"They're optimistic," she guessed aloud, after they had rolled up the coats and stuffed them into their packs. "Probably figure they might as well lighten their knapsacks, since they won't need these overcoats again. I wonder, though, if they truly believe this war will be over before next winter?"

For some time, they had been riding just west of heavy forest. It began to thin as they rode up the long rise of a hill, and reaching its crest, O'Hara exclaimed, "Look there! Straight ahead. Must be the Rebel camp."

Dots of lantern light had begun to appear, scattered at first like the stars just emerging overhead. The dots rapidly multiplied until they merged into a vast field of pale yellow light.

"There's hundreds—thousands of them," Bronwen said, feeling increasingly unsettled. Listen to your instincts, she told herself. And they were not due back in Washington until tomorrow night.

"O'Hara, we're close enough. It's getting dark, and we don't need to meet cavalry on patrol! We'll camp there in that woods and get some sleep. Just keep in mind that I've got my stiletto, Don Juan. And I'll use it."

The glow of a hanging lantern reflected off the canvas walls of the tent, but still gave little enough light to the luxuriantly bearded Confederate officer bent over a map spread on a camp table. He turned quickly at the sound of a horse being reined in just beyond the tent.

Its rider dismounted and asked permission to enter.

"C'mon in, Captain," the rider was told. "You got something on those two?"

"Yes, sir. Seems as if they've camped for the night in the woods back there. And they're dressed like farmers, sir."

The bearded officer nodded. "That's what our informant told us to watch for. Man look like the description we were given?"

"He was wearin' a slouch hat, sir, so I can't be sure. 'Bout the right height, and lean but not scrawny."

"Could be him. And the girl?"

The captain shook his head. "She had on a hat, too. Couldn't see any red hair."

"They didn't spot you, did they?"

"No, sir. Don't think so. Do you want them brought in?"

"No," the officer answered, "don't want them to suspect anything beforehand. If they've camped, mornin' will be soon enough, 'cause nobody, not even U.S. Treasury agents, could be fool enough to wander round in the dark with a countryside full of enemy troops. No, that's all, Captain. Get some sleep now."

"Very good, sir."

7

*How can any man decide what he should do himself
if he is ignorant of what his enemy is about?*

—Jomini

Northern Virginia

"I'd trade my horse for a mug of coffee," O'Hara declared
the following dawn, while they stowed their blanket rolls
behind the saddles and chewed on tough, saltless biscuits.

"We can't risk a fire," Bronwen told him. "And we need
to move fast."

"You're right, sir!"

She had promised herself to ignore his petty needling, and
merely said, "We should return to that high ground quickly,
do what needs to be done, and head straight back to Washington. We can guess the Confederates' destination, and I'm
not comfortable this close to all those troops."

"Why not? We look harmless enough."

Bronwen shook her head, saying, "Let's get on with it.
And remember, we're farmers, O'Hara."

The sun was just appearing and the air was still misty
when they left the forest. Gradually the mist evaporated,
gone by the time they again reached the crest of the hill they
had climbed the night before. Bronwen drew in her breath
at the sight below. Spread over an immense area, less than

a mile distant, was the Confederate camp. It seemed so near, she could almost smell the coffee.

The troops looked like gray birds skimming over a field, and they were obviously preparing to move out. There must be every type of tent ever made down there, but she recognized only the shelter and dog tents, and the ones that resembled teepees. Moreover, the tents were swiftly disappearing.

"O'Hara, they're breaking camp down there. I hope we're close enough for you, because I'm not going any farther."

Surprised at receiving no insolent remark about cowardice, she looked around. O'Hara had already dismounted and was sprawled on his stomach, spyglass methodically scanning back and forth over the camp.

"Seeing as how you aren't bossing me around at the moment," O'Hara said, eyes still trained on the camp, "want to get the pencils and pad of foolscap out of my pack?"

When she returned with the items, Bronwen handed them to him, saying, "O'Hara, we need to hurry, and I thought Rhys Bevan said you could figure without pencil and paper. Besides, your lady friend back there at Manassas said eighty thousand."

"You willing to trust that? I'm not, although it's something to check against my own numbers. I need to write these down for Bevan, anyway. Be quiet for a few minutes, will you, Red?"

Bronwen, astounded at this request—of all people to be asking for quiet!—walked away and watched the troops below with her spyglass, looking mainly for telegraph cable; she hadn't spotted any since leaving the railroad junction in Manassas. Every now and then she glanced at O'Hara. He would scan for a minute or two, write some numbers on the cheap, yellow lined paper, then scan some more. Occasionally his lips moved silently before he jotted down more columns of figures.

When the first ragged lines of soldiers began to file southward, the flags of their regiments hanging limp in the windless air, O'Hara still appeared to be counting. Just what he was counting, Bronwen couldn't tell, but she sincerely hoped it was not individual men. They needed to start back to Washington.

She asked him, "What have you got?"

O'Hara grunted incoherently and continued to figure, some of it on paper and some apparently in his head, while he chewed the end of a pencil.

Bronwen left him and went back to her scanning position, but when she raised the spyglass again, she received a nasty shock. A pair of men on horseback had pulled away from the camp, and for some unknown reason, they were coming on hard toward the hill.

"O'Hara! We have to move!"

"Give me another minute. I'm just recounting the flags and—"

"We don't have a minute!" she broke in. "Look down there," and she grabbed his shoulder as she pointed.

"Ease off, Red." He didn't look up from the paper. "Nobody knows we're up here."

"Has it occurred to you, chum, that if we can see them, they just might be able to see us?"

O'Hara glanced up, grabbed his spyglass and held it to his eye, then scrambled to his feet. "Let's get the hell out of here!"

He grabbed the pad and pencils, and they dashed to the horses, where O'Hara stuffed the writing implements into his pack. As Bronwen was mounting the mare, she glanced around with a feeling that she had overlooked something, but since she could now hear the hoofbeats of galloping horses, there was no time to think about it. She looked over her shoulder, and with a jolt realized the two horses were already coming up the rise.

"O'Hara, those horses are faster than ours. We can never outrun them, and we'll look guilty as sin if we try."

To her surprise, O'Hara said nothing. He just nodded, and raised his spyglass—as if he couldn't see the approaching figures with his naked eye! She had expected him to put up an argument, and though she would have ignored him, it bothered her that he did not even attempt it.

"Dammit to hell!" he swore, which seemed to Bronwen a seriously delayed reaction, and when he swung to face her, his grim expression startled her. He looked ten years older as he said rapidly, "I know one of those men—"

"You *what?*"

"No time to explain. Red . . . Bronwen . . . you're going to have to trust me."

"O'Hara, what are you raving about? Pull yourself together and talk sense!"

"There's no time! When those men get here, let me do all the talking. Just go along with whatever I say. I mean it!" The riders were less than a quarter mile away when he muttered, "Unless you want to spend the next ten years of your life in a Confederate prison."

Bronwen could only stare at him, unable to make sense of his gibbering. They had known this might happen, and had planned to say they were farmers looking for more land to work. So why was he acting as if this was unexpected? In numb confusion, she turned to watch the men riding toward them, her stomach cramping as if it recognized imminent disaster even if her brain did not.

O'Hara suddenly rose in the saddle and yanked off his hat, waving it back and forth like a semaphore, yelling, "Hey! Hey there, over here!"

The two riders were close upon them, but the only thing Bronwen could make out clearly were their slouch hats. She could only wait, dumbfounded and terrified by O'Hara's inexplicable behavior.

Shortly, the two men reined in beside them. The first thing Bronwen saw was the double row of buttons on one's belted, gray frock coat. His horse was in splendid condition, its

sweating coat gleaming like satin in the early, slanting sunlight, so unquestionably these were Confederate cavalry, and
the one nearest to her was an officer. His bright eyes glittered
at Bronwen, and when he swept off his slouch hat, its plume
fluttered as he bowed low over the saddle. A full curly beard
nearly grazed the horse's withers.

"Mornin,' miss." His smile flashed and his bold eyes remained on her when he said over his shoulder to O'Hara,
"And to y'all, too, sir."

O'Hara prodded the gelding forward a few steps, and with
a voice mercifully restored to composure, said, "Mornin' to
you, Jeb."

Bronwen's stomach clenched as her memory tossed up the
fragment *it was General James Ewell Brown Stuart. Jeb,
to his friends.*"

The cavalry officer had turned sideways in visible aston-
ishment. "Well, I'll be . . . O'Hara! O'Hara, what the hell—
Beggin' your pardon, miss!" He shifted to smile briefly at
Bronwen.

She lowered her eyes demurely, and the officer turned
back to O'Hara, saying, "What're y'all doin' out here, you
no-account cardsharp?"

"Watchin' you, Jeb," answered O'Hara with breathtaking
candor, his grin broad as the side of a barn. "And what are
y'all doin' out here?"

"Breakin' camp, is what. Headed south."

"Where to? Goin' home?"

The man's eyes narrowed. "Not yet. Thought I spied the
sun glint off a glass on the hill here, and my horse and my
aide needed some exercise."

The other man inclined his head, but said nothing.

"Never expected to see you, O'Hara! Now, you weren't
ever much in the manners department, but when are you
goin' to introduce this fine-lookin' young lady?"

O'Hara chuckled, and winked at Jeb, saying, "Allow me
to introduce Miss Belle Lyon."

This chilled Bronwen as much as anything he had said so far. How would O'Hara know her Baltimore alias? Or had Rhys Bevan for some reason told him?

The plumed hat was sweeping aside again as the man said, "Jeb Stuart, at your service, Miss Lyon."

Bronwen struggled simultaneously with anger at O'Hara and with fear of what his familiarity with a Confederate cavalry officer might mean, but she clenched her teeth and managed to nod. She had no problem not speaking, since the battle raging in her head left her speechless. Not so O'Hara, who, since the arrival of Jeb Stuart, had developed a letter-perfect Virginia accent. Or had it simply been restored?

"O'Hara, the last time I saw you was on an anchored Mississippi riverboat," Stuart said, laughing. "Holdin' a full house against me and a handful of Annapolis navy men on leave. Lady Luck was surely lookin' after you that night!"

"Indeed she was," O'Hara said, still chuckling. "And to answer your question, me and my lady friend here are just takin' the mornin' air, so to speak." He winked at Stuart again.

But Stuart, whose sharp eyes Bronwen thought probably did not miss much, was now eyeing the bulging packs behind their saddles. She took a quick mental inventory of the damning items, starting with the spyglasses, the compasses, the maps, the . . . the gray Confederate overcoats! Those were what she had neglected earlier—she should have gotten rid of them. If Stuart demanded to look at the packs, just how was O'Hara going to explain those coats?

Maybe he wouldn't have to explain. Not if, as she was now forced to consider, he was involved in the treacherous activity of a double agent: a spy who served two enemies, each thinking he was spying only for them, while he spied *on* them. Did he really think she was so simpleminded she wouldn't detect that? Well, two could play this charade.

"General Stuart, sir," she asked, spreading as much honey

in her voice as she could in the midst of fury, "just where-all did you first meet our Mr. O'Hara?"

From the corner of her eye, she caught O'Hara's frown and the barely visible shake of his head. To the devil with him!

"Where'd we meet?" Stuart repeated, his eyes moving from the packs to her and radiating mischief. "You mean the scoundrel didn't tell you, Miss Lyon?"

"No, sir, he did not," she answered, smiling and holding his eyes.

"Now, Jeb," protested O'Hara, "she doesn't need to know all that."

"Why not, Kerry darlin'?" she asked, smiling stupidly at O'Hara. Seeing his alarmed expression, she almost enjoyed herself when she said, "If we're goin' back to Culpeper with all your earthly goods—" she gestured to the packs "—so's you can meet my mama and papa, then I s'pect I should know 'bout your colorful past. My word, a Mississippi riverboat?"

For a moment, O'Hara looked so startled she could not imagine that he would recover—or even trouble himself to—and she had a sudden vision of a southern prison. Did they hang women in Virginia?

O'Hara, though, found his voice remarkably fast. "Jeb, I s'pect my misspent youth is finally catchin' up with me. 'Course, I didn't know," he turned to Bronwen with a don't-say-anymore look, "that we were goin' to Culpeper for the particular purpose you just now mentioned. In fact, I was goin' to ask General Jeb here if he had time for a round of poker."

"Why, Mr. O'Hara," said Bronwen, "that's not what y'all told me last night. Said you were intendin' to ask my papa—"

"Say now, Jeb," O'Hara interrupted her, "I s'pect you got better things to do than listen to a lady's chatter, no matter

how beguilin' she is." He sent Bronwen a look that demanded silence.

Stuart, grinning at O'Hara's apparent discomfort—real or
feigned—looked over his shoulder at the disappearing camp
below, then turned back saying, "I can catch up with them
anytime. O'Hara, sounds like y'all been up to your old tricks,
boy. And this pretty lady, she deserves the truth."

O'Hara employed his grin.

"Miss Lyon, I tell you true," Stuart said to her, "this Vir-
ginia boy is a bad one. Drummed out of the U.S. Military
Academy, he was, for gamblin' and drinkin' and whor—
Beggin' your pardon, miss."

"I see," said Bronwen, afraid that she did.

O'Hara gave a forced laugh, saying "Jeb, you never did
get over losin' all that money to me that night, did you?"

"No, sir!" Stuart responded. "But I surely do feel better
'bout it right now!"

"General Stuart, sir?" ventured the aide, gesturing toward
the grassland below. "They're movin' out fast down there,
sir. And General Longstreet will be expect—"

"Yes, Captain," Stuart interrupted. "O'Hara, it has been
most satisfyin' to see you again. Worth the trip up here,
'cause now I am a whole lot happier 'bout that last hand of
cards!"

O'Hara, naturally, grinned. Bronwen prayed.

"Been a great pleasure makin' your acquaintance, Miss
Lyon," Stuart said, returning the feathered slouch hat to his
head with a flamboyant gesture. "And don't believe a word
this boy says, you hear?"

That would not be hard to do, she thought as she nodded
and smiled. She was too angry to speak.

The two men wheeled their horses around, and Stuart
called over his shoulder, "Y'all want to lose some of that
money, O'Hara, you come on down to Fredericksburg—I
s'pect we'll be there a spell. And anytime y'all change your

mind about the army, let me know. Can always use a good poker player!"

In what seemed like moments, the horses were thundering down the slope, grass and clumps of mud tossed aside by their pounding hooves.

Bronwen sat watching them, the questions so many she didn't know where to begin. Did General Stuart knowingly play a part in O'Hara's charade? And did O'Hara realize she had figured it out? But how could he not?

The safest thing to do, she decided, was to act oblivious. She certainly could not confront him, not alone here, and not in the face of the strength he possessed. Double agents were not noted for their kindness. And if O'Hara planned to carry through his deception, and thought for even a minute that she might stand in his way, he would never allow her to return to Washington. As it was, she might not make it back in time.

At the foot of the hill, Stuart brought his horse to a slow canter, and glanced over his shoulder. "Now, that was good work, Captain. Seems like Richmond really does have itself an inside contact."

"So she was the one?"

Stuart nodded. "Shame, though, 'cause she's a mighty fetchin' gal. See those big green eyes? Just like a cat's. But don't you ever turn your back on a huntin' fe-line, Captain, or you won't live long 'nough to regret it."

"The man, O'Hara—you told him we're headed for Fredericksburg."

"No harm in tellin' a man what he already knows, Captain. O'Hara's a shrewd sonofabitch, a whole lot smarter than he looks. No need to worry 'bout him, the cheatin' rascal, 'cause you scratch that hide and you'll find a Virginian under it, no matter what color coat he's wearin'."

•   •   •

They rode northeast toward Washington City for some time before the uncharacteristically silent O'Hara said, "Aren't you going to ask anything?"

"About what?" Bronwen replied, looking straight ahead.

"C'mon, Red. I figure you've got to have a few questions."

"All right. How much money did you win from Stuart?"

"Won a lot, as a matter of fact. But that's not what you really want to know."

"O'Hara, I don't care whether you knew Stuart in the past—that's your business. So, how many troops did you calculate were there?" Although she wanted the answer, she wanted even more to divert his attention.

"I'd put them at somewhere close to half what McClellan and Pinkerton estimated. Which means the Confederates, who were supposed to be such a threat to Washington and McClellan's army all winter, were outnumbered about two-to-one!"

"That much?" Her surprise was genuine.

"That much. 'Course it doesn't take into account all that dangerous artillery they left behind."

Bronwen made herself smile.

She could feel O'Hara's gaze on her, and feared if she did not exhibit some curiosity it would look suspicious. The place to start might be the most obvious; she could hardly forget, and surely neither could he, her frequent reference to his deficient Virginia accent.

"Were you born in Virginia?" she asked.

He nodded without hesitation. "Just south of Wheeling."

"And you went ahead and let me make a fool of myself."

"I didn't think telling you was important."

Not important? If they hadn't met up with Stuart, who would have known? But now that she thought about it, he must have been aware they might run into Stuart's cavalry unit. Then she remembered the reluctance he had displayed about following the Confederate troops.

She pulled her attention back to him, because he was saying, "Look, Red, I didn't set out to embarrass you, or to deliberately deceive you. But you just kept nagging at me about the accent, and I thought it would be fun, at some point, to surprise you."

"Oh, you certainly did that!" she responded. "Well, was it fun?"

"As a matter of fact, yes. Yes, it was."

Anger was a good excuse to be silent. And if he did not let the subject rest, it would just make her more suspicious.

"What do you know about western Virginia?" he asked.

"Is this another test, O'Hara?"

From the tail of her eye, she could see him grinning. "Yeah, it's a test. You're supposed to know Southern history."

"Then why don't you just tell me what I'm supposed to know."

"O.K.," he answered. "The western part of Virginia never voted to leave the Union. And when the rest of Virginia did vote to secede, the politicians from the west hightailed it back to Wheeling and drew up their own state constitution—even elected their own governor of what they're calling West Virginia."

"I didn't know that," Bronwen said. Which was true, and if her admission kept him off guard, and thinking she hadn't caught on to him, it might see her safely to Washington. She was more afraid than she wanted to admit even to herself, although her anger at being duped helped to dilute the fear.

"It was the truth, though," O'Hara went on, "what Stuart said about the military academy. I was thrown out. But the reasons that—hold up!" he said, his voice quieter than she had ever heard it. He slowed the gelding and Bronwen's hand slid down her thigh toward the stiletto in her boot.

"What's the trouble?" she asked him, her fingers finding the sheath, then the stiletto's handle.

"Thought maybe I felt the ground shake some."

"You're on a moving horse, O'Hara. Of course the ground shakes some."

"That's not what I meant. Listen."

Then Bronwen heard it, too, and leaned forward to catch the distant *thump, thump, thump.* She withdrew her hand from her boot and prodded the mare forward until they were at a gallop. Faster and faster they went until, if O'Hara tried to shoot her, he would have to contend with a wildly shifting target.

The sound of thousands of marching feet gradually became more distinct. So did the drums and the fifes.

"What in hell is that?" yelled O'Hara, his voice coming from behind her.

Risking a backward glance, she saw no weapon in his hand, but did not dare to hope quite yet. She urged the mare toward the nearest high ground, aware that O'Hara was right behind her. When she reached the crest of a small hillock, she reined in and looked down, not entirely believing what she saw. In the distance, not more than a mile and a half away, were long dark lines.

After drawing out the stiletto, Bronwen waited until O'Hara slid from the gelding, then pulled the spyglass from his pack. She waited still longer to see if he would take out the revolver. When he did not, she dismounted and, with the stiletto concealed under her arm, fumbled nervously with the drawstring of her own pack. She finally managed to yank out the spyglass. While she gripped the knife in one hand, with the other she raised the glass to her eye.

The long blue columns stretched as far as she could see until her view was interrupted by a hill that, like a sleeping green dragon, appeared to be constantly disgorging more marching men. On and on they came, the regimental flags waving bright blurs of color above the troops, the steady rhythm of the fifes and drums clear even at this distance, and the sight and the sound of it made her skin tingle.

"It would appear," O'Hara beside her said, "that the Army of the Potomac is at last on the move."

Bronwen, feeling less apprehensive, slowly lowered her glass. O'Hara was a good rider, but she was better. She might, with a head start, even reach the front line of the troops. If he attempted to kill her, at least there would be plenty of witnesses, but she doubted he would do anything now that earlier could have been done more easily. It would be stupid of him to chance it, and she had already made the mistake of underestimating his intelligence. She would not do it again.

"But where are those troops go—?" O'Hara's voice trailed off.

Bronwen didn't answer, although she was fairly certain she knew where those troops were bound. A minute later O'Hara apparently did, too. She cautiously turned to look at him when he said incredulously, but laughing nonetheless, "They're going to Manassas! Now that the Confederates have finally withdrawn, McClellan is bringing out the whole damn army to capture Manassas!"

By the time he had lowered the spyglass and was looking around, Bronwen had jumped astride the mare. And before O'Hara had time to so much as mount the gelding, she was racing toward the Union troops.

With luck, she might even make it to Washington before Rhys Bevan's deadline expired. Although it was already too late to stop McClellan's useless foray.

8

We have spies in Washington & Maryland, and they no doubt have them here—some are perhaps cheating on both sides.

—Judah Benjamin, Confederate Secretary of State

Coast of Maryland

The drawing-room ceiling was spanned by massive cypress beams, its walls wainscoted with black-grained oak, and its sofas and chairs upholstered in rich brown leather. All of which made the setting resolutely masculine, but also made it as dark as the inside of a cave. Flames in the fireplace were the sole source of light, giving the faces of those standing nearest them a decidedly sulfurous cast. Which might be appropriate for the hellish business they were about this night, observed a man deliberately seated well away from the flames and thus cloaked in shadow.

"I've told you repeatedly, I don't know how much she found in my library!" The agitated voice of Dr. Elias Worth was in marked contrast to his usual, carefully modulated tones.

Worth, a short, courtly-looking man, pressed his temples with spidery fingers as he paced up and down the length of a Persian carpet. "Her accomplice unfortunately died while being questioned," he further explained, "before your men,

Norris, could learn how much she'd uncovered. Did they have to kill him?"

"These unpleasant things happen in war, Dr. Worth, and in any case, it was remarkably foolish of you to keep those damning files," answered Major William Norris. He also stood some distance from the fireplace, and his affable tone belied the seriousness of the charge when he added, "And in your own house, no less. Were you planning to frame them to hang on your costly walls? Mount the counterfeit plates as avant-garde neoclassic sculpture?"

"You needn't be sarcastic," retorted Worth. "I hardly expected my home to be vandalized."

Someone gave a muffled laugh.

"You can't recall seeing this woman anywhere?" questioned a third man, whose short, slightly pointed beard had earned him the byname of Vandyke.

"No, I've never seen her. Why?"

"Damn it, Worth, you've put us all at risk! And some of us have more to lose than others. What was in those files?" demanded Vandyke.

"Various . . . ah, personal items," Worth equivocated.

"The hell they were!" continued Vandyke in heightened anger. "This 'vandalism,' as you call it, obviously required planning, and since the counterfeit plates and the incriminating files couldn't have been something she just happened to stumble over, she must have had reason to search your library. And have been following you for some time. How else could she have known the house would be empty at that hour?"

"As I have twice explained, the manservant was a plant!" Worth snapped defensively. "That much Norris's thugs said the man admitted, and that he and she were working for the U.S. Treasury."

"So they were already suspicious of your counterfeiting connections. And now we're *all* jeopardized, because of your arrogance—"

"This is all rather pointless, isn't it," interrupted a woman stepping forward from the shadows.

Her tightly laced corset lent her fashionable contours, and her thick hair, so black it held a sheen of blue, had been elaborately coifed. The overall effect was only slightly diminished by the bandage wrapped round her ankle. She held at her side an ebony walking stick.

"I thought the reason for meeting at this late hour," she said, "was to delegate future assignments. Not to cry over spilt milk."

Whether the woman's intention was to simply express impatience, or to divert attention from the doctor's error in judgment was unclear.

Norris nodded and moved into the firelight as he said, "Trust our Virginia Bluebell to go straight to the crux of the matter. And it's plain the ankle injury has not clouded your mind, because you're right, Bluebell. We need to proceed, although it's true"—he nodded at Vandyke—"that most of you may have been exposed. Which means you are in danger if you remain in Baltimore."

"Since it was your men who killed that Treasury agent, that would include you, Norris!" responded Worth, the bitter note in his voice unmistakable.

"Oh, I would not be staying in any event," answered Norris, while he poured into a tumbler a thimbleful of bourbon from one of the bottles readily at hand on a pier table. "I had planned to leave this announcement until later, but given your last remark, Worth, I think I'll do it now. The Confederate War Department has named me director of the Signal Corps and Secret Service Bureau. It might be well to keep in mind, doctor, that as of this evening, I am no longer simply your immediate contact, but your immediate superior."

Worth looked as startled as most of those there, who were, in addition to Norris, four men and the woman. The doctor's expression held surprise, and possibly disappointment, but since he had just been cautioned, he wisely refrained from comment.

"Tomorrow I move on to Richmond," stated Norris, his voice now more authoritative than affable. "But before that— given the doctor's lapse, and several new developments— you will all need to be reassigned. Which is why I brought you in this evening." He turned to the woman, saying, "As you see, Bluebell, this wasn't calculated to deprive you of beauty sleep. Not that you need it."

Since his announcement, the woman had been gazing at Norris speculatively, and now took the opportunity to give him a prolonged and suggestive smile.

In return from Norris she received a curt nod.

"All right, Maddox—give us the good news from Richmond," Norris directed, settling himself in an oversized chair and gesturing with his tumbler at a muscular man who had hitherto been standing in silence.

Most would agree that Joseph Maddox more resembled a pugilist than the successful businessman he purported to be. "Reliable word has it," he said, leaning back against the table and crossing his arms, "that the last of Pinkerton's Richmond operatives have been ferreted out. With the arrest of Timothy Webster, they're all four presently enjoying General Winder's renowned hospitality."

"I assume that means they're imprisoned," confirmed Bluebell. "What's planned for them? A prisoner exchange?"

"No, I expect Webster at least will hang," Maddox answered indifferently. He glanced at Vandyke, who gave a brief nod of agreement.

"Can't we assume those Pinkerton agents will be replaced?" asked Bluebell, after declining an offered snifter of brandy from Dr. Worth, who appeared to need it more than she.

"I doubt it," Maddox replied. "Certainly not in the foreseeable future. Richmond's been placed under martial law, so who's going to get in there, and how? Not novice Pinkerton agents—and who else is there?"

"What about that Treasury agent?" she persisted.

Maddox's reply was cut off by Norris, who said, "We'll get to that later. Right now—" he paused and turned to the figure still seated in shadow "—we need to discuss something closer to home. Let's hear from our guest. The floor is yours, my friend." Norris's last words carried a hint of sarcasm.

The man did not come forward, and when he spoke his voice seemed to come from the far side of a chasm. "It appears," he began without preliminaries, "that the Union's General McClellan may finally be intending to use his army for other than display purposes, although you may have heard about his brief foray to Manassas in Northern Virginia. The newspapers have succeeded in making McClellan look a fool, outfoxed by Confederate resourcefulness and their so-called Quaker guns—nothing but painted tree trunks."

"Lincoln is the fool for keeping McClellan," the woman remarked in a sour voice.

"Perhaps," said the man.

"Well, well," said Maddox. "Is that what finally succeeded in building a fire under Young Napoleon?"

"Partly. The story making the rounds is that Lincoln is supposed to have said, 'If General McClellan does not have use for his army, I wonder if I might borrow it?' "

Norris and Maddox laughed. The other three looked disgusted.

"In any event," the man in the shadows went on, "McClellan has proposed a campaign to invade Virginia, its goal being the capture of Richmond."

This news was met by pregnant silence. The only sound came from beyond the room's leaded windows, that of water slapping against an unseen shore.

The stillness was broken by Maddox. "How does McClellan propose to get there? A substantial number of Con-

federate troops are now at Fredericksburg, so they stand
between Washington and Richmond—or have McClellan
and his army suddenly grown wings?"

"The word is he intends to go by water."

"How?" Vandyke asked. "We control the James River all
the way to Richmond, as well as the Norfolk naval base at
its mouth. Which, I might add, is the residence of the ironclad *Merrimack.* It may not have sunk the *Monitor,* but it's
still a threat to the Union's fleet of wooden ships."

"This plan of McClellan's is still under consideration,"
said the man, "so details haven't been discussed yet. But yes,
the *Merrimack*'s threat will undoubtedly prevent McClellan
from using the James River—even though the *Monitor*'s the
better ship."

Maddox's expression remained skeptical. "Are you saying
that Lincoln is actually giving thought to approving this new
scheme?"

"That's what I'm saying, although the plan is McClellan's
through and through. Lincoln had a different idea—and his
might have worked—but he was talked out of it. He hasn't
got his bearings yet, and the commanders still intimidate him.
Remember, the majority of them now are McClellan's men."

"So are we to learn this proposal's details?" asked the
woman. "And if so, isn't that a little beyond our scope?"

Ignoring her question, Norris inserted, "McClellan is an
extremely cautious man. He won't take an army to Virginia
without establishing a plan for retreat. And if we can hold
the Norfolk naval base, the *Merrimack* will continue to be a
factor, so that should narrow his field of opportunity."

The man in the shadows nodded his agreement. "Experience says that McClellan will take the safest route possible."

"Don't anyone underestimate McClellan," Norris said. "He
did, after all, rank second in his class at West Point, and he
served laudably in the Mexican War. Granted, he is essen-
tially an engineer, but a brilliant one. Also keep in mind that

Lincoln has become increasingly impatient, as have his countrymen, to begin field campaigning. So the question is—" Norris turned to the anonymous man "—will Lincoln's eagerness make him approve a large military campaign, under a relatively untested commander, even if all the necessary pieces are not in place?"

"I don't make predictions," said the shadowed man, a flash of white teeth the only indication he might be smiling. "I just report the facts."

"All right!" said Norris, in an abruptly commanding manner. "We need to move on. These are the assignments. Maddox, given your Northern connections, you'll proceed to Washington. For the time being, continue your smuggling activities, or 'commercial dealings' as you call them, and learn what you can about this invasion plan. I'll be in touch after I have talked to Richmond."

Maddox smiled and nodded. "Fine with me," he said, reaching for a whiskey bottle on the pier table, apparently intending to top off his half-empty glass.

Vandyke also stepped to the table, but looked around as Norris addressed him.

"Vandyke, you will go to Virginia—" Norris smiled faintly "—if that can be coordinated with your other . . . obligations."

"How do I contact you from there?" asked Vandyke.

"For the time being, you don't. It's risky and your position is too valuable to jeopardize. You did a good job handing Timothy Webster to us, and—"

"Just why," interrupted Dr. Worth, "isn't he reporting to me as usual?"

"That should be obvious," answered Norris bluntly. "Given your most recent gaffe—which was not your first, I might add—you've compromised your usefulness here. You must realize you cannot stay in Baltimore."

"I don't agree—"

"Don't interrupt, Worth! You should easily be able to obtain a position in a Washington hospital. Those places are veritable founts of information, particularly from wounded soldiers, as well as naive, talkative doctors."

Worth, clearly recognizing the demotion, seemed about to protest, but then demanded, "What about that agent—the one who broke into my library?"

"Yes," the woman unexpectedly agreed. "I think Dr. Worth has grounds for concern. It has occurred to me that if this Treasury agent was tailing him, she may have seen us together."

"Which should teach you to be more discreet in your affairs, Bluebell." Maddox grinned, adding, "You, too, doctor."

Dr. Worth began to retort, but the woman broke in with, "Don't be so dismissive, Maddox. A name on a list is one thing. Recognizing a face is quite another! And I'm not likely to be the only one she can identify."

Norris glanced at the man in shadows and received a slight shake of his head. Whether Norris interpreted this signal correctly would have to be resolved later.

"As it happens," Norris said, "we have a man in the construction crew working on the Treasury Building, and we can keep track of her Washington activities. She did slip out of the city for several days, but we learned in advance that she would be in Northern Virginia."

"You know who she is?" Worth asked eagerly.

"We do. A contact in the Federal Post Office intercepted a letter from this young lady—I use the term 'lady' loosely— mailed to her aunt who is located in a small town in New York. By a quirk of fate, British intelligence agent Colonel Dorian de Warde, our valuable friend in Canada, is acquainted with both women, so we now know this agent is one Bronwen Llyr. And Colonel de Warde advises we should not underestimate this sturdy Yankee lass."

"According to her male colleague, she's little more than an adolescent!" said the middle-aged Worth with scorn.

"Apparently," Norris went on without missing a beat, "this

'adolescent' is quick-witted and resourceful. And willing to take risks, possibly because of her youth, doctor—although you would certainly know more about risk-taking than I. At any rate," he said, disregarding Worth's sharp rejoinder, "we did try to stop her in Baltimore, but she sailed past us."

"So use more efficient means!" demanded Worth. "She can identify at least two of us."

"Then stay out of her sight. That's not too complicated to grasp, is it? And you're not likely to run into her at a hospital."

Worth shook his head, objecting, "I think she should be dealt with now."

"Not yet!" said Norris sharply. "For the moment we will keep eye on her, as she may prove to be more useful to us alive. When that's no longer the case, we'll take measures. Naturally, should she leave Washington again, she'll become too great a liability, and will need to be disposed of immediately."

Ignoring Worth's evident dissatisfaction, Norris turned to the woman. "As I earlier mentioned, Bluebell, you are assigned to Washington and Alexandria. Our people there are expecting you." He paused as if mentally calculating, and then said cryptically, "I have further instructions for you, but I'll give them to you later."

The woman's forehead wrinkled slightly, but after an odd glance at Dr. Worth, she nodded.

Norris, if he saw the glance, chose to ignore it and addressed the others. "We have a good intelligence network under way, and our line already stretches from Baltimore to the Washington area, and south to Richmond. Thanks to Colonel de Warde, it will soon reach north to Quebec. And from there to our potential European allies."

"Any word yet on when, and if, they will recognize the Confederacy?" asked Maddox.

Norris shook his head. "It's still under discussion, but the negotiations look promising. And all in all, we are in far

better shape than the North—who, remember, has no intelligence network. Not at the moment. But we know that Treasury is forming a special espionage unit. Since it will take
time to train agents, we don't need to worry about that just
yet. And there are distinct advantages to warring on one's
own soil. Any questions?"

Norris, however, did not wait for responses to this before
saying, "That's all, then. Good evening."

He then turned his attention to the stack of papers lying
on a handsome mahogany desk.

Sensing his impatience, the agents prepared to leave. Bluebell moved with surprisingly agility, and although limping
slightly did not use the walking stick. When she passed his
desk, Norris stopped her and, after waving on the others,
spoke a few quiet words to her. She seemed about to argue,
but then simply commented, "Yes, I see your point. I'll take
care of it."

"Good," was all Norris said before turning back to his
desk.

Bluebell and two of the men went out into the chill, misty
night, leaving Maddox with Norris and the figure in darkness.

Maddox walked rather unsteadily toward the pier table,
evidently intending to set down his full tumbler of whiskey,
but he tripped over a corner of the Persian carpet. In catching
himself, he staggered sideways, losing his grip on the glass
and drenching the shadowed man's trousers along with the
leather chair.

The man leapt to his feet with a short curse, then at once
lowered himself into another, nearby chair, taking care to
remain in darkness. But perhaps the damage had already
been done.

"Sorry," Maddox apologized, after regaining his footing.
"Clumsy of me! Here let me help."

Norris raised his eyes from the papers only briefly, and
while Maddox was grabbing a fistful of linen napkins from

the table, the outside door opened. Vandyke reentered, almost as if he had been summoned.

"Forgot my coat," he told them, "but not for long. It's damn cold out there—what the hell happened?" he asked, seeing Maddox swiping at the chair, and the other man blotting his trousers. Vandyke laughed as he went toward them, pulling a large cotton handkerchief from his pocket to assist, and saying, "You never could hold your liquor, Maddox!"

Maddox appeared to smile good-naturedly, and offered the man another apology, this time receiving in return a nod of acknowledgment.

"C'mon, Maddox, let's get out of here," Vandyke said, "before you do any more damage. Good evening, gentlemen."

Vandyke took his coat from a clothes tree beside the door, and the two men went out. Norris then looked up from his papers, watching their departure with narrowed eyes.

The remaining man delayed his leave-taking, as Norris had suggested, waiting for some time to be certain no one lingered outside the door. Although his wariness had been only recently acquired, he now knew as well as anyone that disloyalty could be bought.

Norris went to the door and locked it. Then he returned to the desk, and lifted the papers and a blotter, revealing another sheet of paper on which had been drawn a rough rendering.

"Did you have any difficulty?" Norris asked the man.

"Not much. But I had to work fairly fast, so it doesn't include a great amount of detail."

"I see here—" Norris paused and leaned forward to study the rendering "—that you've circled something. What is it?"

"The gunpowder magazine."

9

We had threats of being driven away, threats of fire, and threats of death.

—Elizabeth Van Lew, 1862

Washington City

"So you *knew* O'Hara was from Virginia?" demanded Bronwen. "That he went to military academy with General Jeb Stuart, and heaven knows how many other Confederate officers?"

"Yes, I knew," Rhys Bevan responded with customary aplomb. "Why don't you sit down?"

"But you neglected to tell me?"

"I chose not to tell you. I wanted you to take him at face value."

"And is that how you take him?" she stormed. "At face value? Isn't that a little dangerous at this particular time?"

"Agent Llyr, you are fast exceeding my tolerance for melodrama. Now sit down!"

He leaned forward in his chair, glancing at the clock on his desk. "We don't have much time before Secretary Chase arrives, and there are several important items you need to think about."

Bronwen unwillingly lowered herself into the chair opposite his desk. "You're just ignoring my suspicions. If that means you are actually going to keep O'Hara, I want it clear that I am never to be assigned with him again."

"That may be impossible to accommodate. Regardless of your . . . reservations, you two seemed to have worked well together."

"Who said so? That fountain of lies, O'Hara?"

"Results are the measure of success."

"Despite the fact that I was scared witless of him half the time?" When she saw the answer in the upward curve of his lips, she retorted, "It was not amusing!"

"Forgive me," Rhys said, without a trace of contrition, "but I find it inconceivable that you were 'scared witless' of anything, much less of Kerry O'Hara."

"You weren't there!" But seeing that she was getting nowhere, she tried another tack. "Why is it you trust him? How do you know O'Hara isn't a double agent? A mole planted here by the Confederate intelligence network?"

"I don't know. Nor do you know that he is."

"But I told you," she protested, "about the encounter with General Stuart. About O'Hara admitting he had been tossed out of military school."

"Those are circumstances that have already been checked, and O'Hara appears to be clean. It's all that can be said about anyone—even you. His familiarity with men who are now in Confederate command positions will undoubtedly be useful, and that is all I care to say on the subject of O'Hara. I mean it!"

"I don't trust him."

"That's all, Bronwen! As it is, we will have to discuss these next items quickly, so I'll ask you not to interrupt. First, the matter of the Pinkerton agents."

Still angry, but knowing when Rhys Bevan could be pushed no further, Bronwen said, "I trust you're not planning to offer me up for Timothy Webster in a prisoner exchange."

She assumed he would recognize it as a flippant remark,

resorted to because she was upset, and that he would unbend and smile.

He acted as if he had not heard her, saying, "As I have told you, in addition to the four Pinkerton agents who were arrested in Richmond, we learned of another still at large, one Webster had recently hired and referred to only as 'H.J.K.' Pinkerton doesn't know the identity of this agent, and he hasn't yet been located. As you also have been told, there are at present no known Union operatives in the Confederate capital. This lack has become increasingly serious, and we've been much in need of intelligence from there. That need has now grown even more urgent."

Bronwen experienced an unpleasant sensation in the pit of her stomach, but said nothing.

"Richmond is under martial law," Rhys reiterated, "so it's not easy to get a man in and out of there."

Bronwen pressed against the back of her chair, positive she had heard an emphasis on the word "man." She managed to keep her mouth closed only because of her regard for Rhys. "What is needed," he went on without seeming to notice her discomfort, although she knew he missed very little, "is someone who knows Union loyalist Elizabeth Van Lew— and who is trusted by her. That woman is the best source of information in Richmond we have right now, but often we don't receive that information timely enough to act on it. Her network is, of necessity, cautious and therefore very slow."

Elizabeth Van Lew belonged to a respected and wealthy Richmond family and for years had helped to spirit escaped slaves out of Richmond by linking them to the Underground Railroad. She had appeared to Bronwen as nearly fearless.

"I've met the woman only once," Bronwen reminded him. "*Once*. And not under the best of circumstances." She remembered vividly the night, a year before, when she had sought refuge at the Van Lew mansion.

Rhys appeared to discount this and went on, "Also needed is someone who's familiar with Richmond. Who's observant and can move around without arousing suspicion. Who can travel in and out without being noticed, and who knows how to encode and transmit information. All of which you are capable of doing."

He stopped there, and sat appraising her with eyes like cool blue glass.

"I don't believe I would care much for a Richmond assignment," Bronwen responded.

"That's not particularly important," Rhys said. "I would rather not ask you to do it, but that's not important either."

"Then what, I'd like to know, *is* important?"

"That's a childish response. As you are most certainly aware, this is not a juvenile game!"

Since she had recently reached the same conclusion herself, she had no ready comeback.

"Those are the basics," Rhys said. "When Secretary Chase gets here, you'll learn more, but I wanted to prepare you and I think when you have heard the whole story, you may react differently. Understand, you have a choice here. No one can force you to do this—"

"I'm glad to hear it," she interrupted.

"—but if you don't, you will be discharged from Treasury and the detective unit. And you will know, forever after, that you abandoned your country and also your president—"

Bronwen broke in angrily, "That's not a choice!"

Rhys looked at the clock, then sat back in his chair and studied her. "What's really wrong here?" he asked. "This isn't like you. Usually you jump on a new assignment, and while this is not an everyday surveillance, I think it can be done without placing you in excessive peril. So what is it?"

"Because in Baltimore, and in Northern Virginia, whether you believe it or not, I was scared. *Really* scared."

Rhys expelled a sigh, and looked relieved. "Is that all?"

"*All?*"

"Every agent has fears now and again. I don't, after all, employ idiots. But scared or not, you kept your head. The

Manassas assignment was also something of a trial run."

Bronwen rose from her chair. "Are you saying that you sent me out there alone with that deranged turncoat O'Hara as some stupid *test*?"

"We needed the information," Rhys said as if that made it acceptable, "so no, it wasn't entirely a test, but there were those who needed assurance that you could handle as serious an assignment as Richmond will be. And sit down."

"Just who wanted to know?"

"You will be told all in good time," he answered. Bronwen remained on her feet, debating whether to walk out. "Besides," Rhys went on, "I'll be more confident if you have learned some caution. You've been reckless on occasion."

"You never accused me of that before."

"It's not an accusation. It's a fact, and something I have tolerated, trusting you would outgrow it. Now, do we have that out of the way? If so, sit down."

Before she could respond, he went on, "When Chase arrives, be prudent in what you say. As you're aware, he holds espionage in low esteem unless it concerns counterfeiting and money. In fact, the secretary opposed the formation of the special unit." Rhys added, "He was, however, overruled."

"Ah yes," she said, lowering herself back into the chair, "we mustn't forget the treasury secretary's money! The one true essential."

"And forgo the sarcasm! Especially, Agent Llyr, if he brings up the subject of women—or, for that matter, men either."

"Which reminds me," Bronwen retorted, "you've never said whether you questioned those three men."

"What three men?"

"You know, the thugs who followed me in Baltimore. Who were—"

A rap on the door stopped her. Rhys rose and came round the desk as Salmon Chase stepped through the doorway with his usual solemnity. At all times, the treasury secretary carried himself like a flagship.

One of his eyes had a peculiar cast to it, but the most prominent feature on an otherwise ordinary face was a remarkably high forehead, and this not altogether because he was balding. Giving her a stately nod, Chase said, "Good day, Miss Llyr."

"And to you, sir," Bronwen replied, starting to rise. Chase waved her back into the chair while he went to seat himself at his chief detective's desk.

"Have you informed Miss Llyr of the present circumstances?" he asked Rhys Bevan, his inflection plainly conveying distaste for the subject.

"As much as I felt at liberty to do," Rhys answered, leaning against the closed door with his arms folded across his chest. He succeeded with uncommon grace in appearing as if this were exactly where he preferred to be, despite the presumptuous occupancy of his desk. He added, "I think she needs to be better informed before she can assess the risks."

The secretary's bushy eyebrows rose. "I would think the risks are ours to assess."

"We are not being assigned to Richmond," Rhys responded with an engaging smile.

"Well, no," Chase conceded, to Bronwen's surprise. She should not have been surprised, though; Rhys Bevan could, if he chose, persuade a lion to purr.

"Has the president approved General McClellan's proposal?" Rhys asked.

"He has given tentative approval," answered Chase, "and with the same reservations we have all voiced. I saw him last evening, but some of that time was spent on the Webster trouble." Chase shook his head. "An unfortunate thing to have happened just now. Most unfortunate indeed."

He managed to make it sound, Bronwen thought, as if Webster should have had the decency to be imprisoned at a more convenient time. Although irritated, she straightened in her chair when she realized Chase was addressing her.

"What are your questions, Miss Llyr?"

"I don't know enough yet to have questions, sir," she answered, which was certainly the truth.

Chase looked at Rhys, who merely said, "I thought that was your prerogative, Mr. Secretary."

"Very well," the man said, turning to Bronwen. "You should have some background on this matter before you see the president."

Bronwen's heart sank. If it were Lincoln requesting her to walk into hell—which was about what assignment to Richmond right now would mean—there was no question she would do it. And she wagered Rhys Bevan had counted on that.

"Before you are actually assigned, Miss Llyr, the president has insisted upon speaking with you," said Chase, sounding exasperated. "Inasmuch as you are an employee of Treasury, I don't believe it at all necessary that he do so, but, of course . . ."

His voice trailed off as if the matter of the president's whims was too tiresome to recount.

Bronwen suppressed a frown. It was common knowledge that Chase was often exasperated by Lincoln, although the president seemed to ignore it, just as he frequently ignored the attitude of superiority expressed by some of his Cabinet members. The attitude rankled Bronwen, and she suspected that it also rankled Rhys Bevan. But then, she and he had a somewhat unusual history with Lincoln; a history begun shortly before he became president. She glanced at Rhys with impatience while they waited for the secretary to rally. Rhys only gave his head a brief shake, his expression impassive, but tapped his fingers on his crossed arms.

"Miss Llyr," Chase said, regarding her with grave eyes, "I trust you do not need to be reminded of the oath you took when you became a member of this department. One of sworn silence on any subject that may be discussed."

"No, sir, you do not need to remind me," she said. For the hundredth time, she thought.

"I am gratified to hear it," he declared, as if he had never heard it before.

The man's pomposity never failed to irritate her, especially since it was so unwarranted. His position as treasury secretary had been a political appointment, forced upon Lincoln because of promises made by others during the Republican presidential convention. The secretary's political experience had come as governor of Ohio. He did not even have a background in finance.

"Now, without further ado," he said, as though she had been the one delaying his weighty statement, "General McClellan proposes to transport by water a substantial portion of the Federal army to the peninsula east of Richmond. He plans to land his troops at Fortress Monroe. This campaign is to be initiated in the very near future with its final objective, surely needless to state, the capture of the Confederate capital. Thus ending this deplorable secession conflict."

Bronwen pulled herself up straighter in the chair, while her mind raced ahead. She now clearly saw the dilemma that Rhys Bevan had earlier broached: the arrest of all the Pinkerton agents in Richmond just before the launch of a massive military campaign. How would information about the enemy's intentions be gathered and transmitted to McClellan?

And to start this invasion from Fort Monroe? The Virginia terrain alone gave reason for concern. To the east of Richmond it lay riddled with creeks and streams, tangled woodlands, impassable swamps and treacherous bogs, forested slopes and deep ravines. It was not a place for an army to invade blindly. She could understand now why Rhys Bevan had been so relentlessly grim.

"Do you comprehend what I'm saying, Miss Llyr?" asked Chase, a weary note in his voice suggesting that if she did not, it would be too tedious to further explain.

She wondered if *he* comprehended it—had even the slightest notion of what this undertaking would require.

As if reading her mind and fearing she might actually voice the thought, Rhys Bevan said quickly, "I'm confident that Agent Llyr is capable of grasping the implications here. Perfectly confident," he added, sending her a warning look.

She swallowed her annoyance and smiled at Chase. "I understand, Mr. Secretary," she answered, "that it would be . . . ah, be incautious"—she had nearly said stupid—"to proceed with a military campaign on such a scale without reliable intelligence."

She smiled at him again, but mostly because of Rhys Bevan's amused expression of approval. She felt like a performing seal.

Chase, however, looked dubious. "Perhaps so," he said, equivocating. "As you may be aware, I have grave reservations about the use of Treasury for such activity. The military should be charged with whatever espionage is needed. If it is needed. However," he added with distinct regret, "mine is not the final word on the matter."

At this, Bronwen didn't dare look anywhere but at the floor. As Rhys Bevan had pointed out in that first meeting of the special Treasury unit, the lack of good intelligence had already been a factor in the past year's failed campaigns.

The Confederate spies had shown themselves to be more effective than the Union's fledglings. An example of this was Rose O'Neal Greenhow, a beguiling and notorious secessionist spy living handsomely in Washington. She had effortlessly gathered information about Federal troop strength and movements from her besotted admirers. These admirers were said to include a high-ranking military officer, and the U.S. senator Henry Wilson, who was no less than chairman of the Military Affairs Committee. Greenhow had given what she had collected to Confederate general Pierre Beauregard before the Union army's catastrophe at Bull Run. How much of it had been accurate was open to speculation. The results of the battle were not.

Pinkerton had finally caught up with Rose. But members of her spy ring had been alerted by his staggering blunder of merely putting her under house arrest, which did not dissuade the determined widow Greenhow. She simply began using servants to courier information, reportedly concealing messages on scraps of paper tucked into the elaborate, upswept hairdos of her maids. Greenhow had at last been confined in Old Capitol Prison, but Rhys Bevan suspected she was still at work, undoubtedly using her wiles to bribe the prison guards.

Breaking in on her thoughts, Secretary Chase pronounced solemnly, "No, this matter is unfortunately out of my hands."

Bronwen brought her head up with a jerk when she realized that Chase was speaking to her.

"While I may be thought old-fashioned," he said loftily, "I remain unconvinced that young ladies such as yourself should be exposed to such unpleasantness."

Bronwen wondered if Chase believed it better for young ladies to be exposed to the unpleasantness of brothers and fathers being killed in war under military commanders who were ignorant of what the other side was doing. She stifled the thought, recalling that Rhys Bevan had forbidden sarcasm.

It suddenly occurred to her that Lincoln might be insisting on intelligence capability before giving final approval to McClellan's plan, thus throwing a monkey wrench into the heretofore autonomous workings of the Treasury Department. To say nothing of diminishing the authority of Secretary Chase.

He, glancing at the clock, now rose from the chair. "We should be on our way. The president will shortly be expecting us."

As the secretary went toward the door, he abruptly turned, saying to Rhys, "I fear Secretary Welles will insist on bring-

ing his latest concern to the president's attention. I intend to
state, however, that I think it inappropriate for Treasury to
become involved in security measures for the navy's ironclad
ship."

Bronwen saw the look of frustration on Rhys's face, and
although he did not directly contradict his superior, he responded, "Since McClellan's proposal calls for use of the
Chesapeake Bay when transporting the army to Virginia, that
could make Secretary Welles's concern more compelling."

Chase was passing through the doorway so Bronwen heard
only "Nevertheless . . ." and missed the rest of his reply. But
what, she wondered, could have prompted that initial comment from him?

It was said that the *Monitor* was patrolling the lower Chesapeake, guarding the Union navy's wooden ships against attack from the *Merrimack*.

It was also said that the *Monitor* was virtually indestructible.

10

I will hold McClellan's horse, if only he will bring us success.

—Abraham Lincoln, 1862

Washington City

Bronwen sat waiting, restless and bored, in the anteroom of the president's office, while from the floor above her came the thumps of running feet and the high-pitched hollering of a young boy. Tad Lincoln, no doubt, who must be recovering from the death of his older brother the month before. Not so, his mother.

After suffering for weeks, twelve-year-old Willie had been claimed by typhoid fever, and Mrs. Lincoln, overcome with grief, had not been seen in public since his death. Willie was the second young son the Lincolns had lost, and Bronwen wondered if they would ever mend. The president had not been able to withdraw, and a country at war had given Willie's father small time to mourn.

A husky, white-coated Negro man now emerged from the president's office, looking remarkably complacent for someone who was balancing an oblong silver tray nearly the size of a canoe. It was laden with used cups and saucers. Bronwen, glad for any activity, jumped up to add her empty cup to the stacked dishes, and in so doing dribbled coffee dregs down the folds of her long, dark green skirt.

"Blast and corruption!" she breathed, snatching a napkin from the tray.

"Need another one, miss?" the servant asked her as she blotted furiously, the laughter in his rich baritone voice rumbling like a distant train.

"No, thank you," she replied, reseating herself with an already short supply of patience strained to its limit.

Secretary Chase had instructed her to wait there in the anteroom until, he had said, "we gentlemen have finished certain weighty items of business in which you have no part. In due time you will be summoned."

Making it sound as if a blast from Gabriel's horn was imminent, alerting St. Peter to consider her chances of passing through his gates.

The door to the office swung open, and Navy Secretary Gideon Welles came through it. With his large protuberant eyes, beak-shaped nose, brown wig, and full white beard (wig and beard mingling to look like a variegated ruff of feathers), the secretary resembled a parrot. He gave Bronwen a quick appraisal as he passed her, trudging toward the outer door of the Executive Mansion. She would have given a great deal to know what discussion of the *Monitor* had disclosed.

Next through the door came a slim, even-featured man with receding hairline and impressive brush mustache. She didn't recognize him, but, to her surprise, he paused in midstride, then came to stand in front of her. "Miss Bronwen Llyr?"

"Yes, sir," she answered and got to her feet, assuming he must be some ranking government official.

"Gustavus Fox, Miss Llyr."

He had bright alert eyes, and when taking Bronwen's extended hand he did not mask his frank scrutiny of her with even a smile, although lines radiating from the outer corners of those eyes indicated that he smiled fairly often. She supposed she should be offended by this close examination, but his name had registered and she knew who Gustavus Fox was: Gideon Welles's assistant navy secretary. While she wondered what had prompted this attention, clearly he was not going to enlighten her, because after a brisk nod, he released her hand and made for the outer door.

The door to the president's office had remained open, and she caught a glimpse of some of the men inside: General George McClellan, Allan Pinkerton, and Secretary of War Edwin Stanton. Stanton had been confirmed little over a month earlier, and although Bronwen had never seen him before in person, the short thick neck and stance of a bulldog had been described to her. No one had mentioned the peculiar graying beard, which, sprouting just below his lower lip, resembled a strand of Spanish moss.

She moved closer to the window as several of the men approached the door, the first being General McClellan, the handsome, dark-haired man responsible for the interminable drilling of Union troops. Even though the soldiers joked and complained about their endless practice maneuvers, they seemed to be devoted to the dashing, if exacting, McClellan. Unquestionably it was because the general had given these men self-respect; or, perhaps more accurately, because he had built a formidable army in which they could be proud to serve. This had been no small feat. McClellan had been appointed shortly after the Union's inglorious performance at Bull Run.

Bronwen had met McClellan in Cincinnati a year ago, when he was still president of the Ohio and Mississippi Railroad, and then only a politically appointed leader of the Ohio volunteers. Thinking he might remember her, she now stepped forward. But the general marched through the door as if on review, shoulders thrown back, head held straight, looking neither right nor left as he made for the entrance hall. His expression appeared to be one of profound disgust.

While Bronwen stood looking after him, pondering a possible reason for this disgust and deciding it could not be her, Edwin Stanton came through the doorway, followed by Allan

Pinkerton, whose short beard quivered with some strong emotion. She guessed it likely that Timothy Webster's arrest had been discussed. How could it not have been?

Bronwen turned away, ostensibly to gaze out the window, since she wasn't anxious to revisit the mutual antagonism that had led Pinkerton to fire her a year before. With luck he would be too engrossed in talking to Stanton to be aware of anyone else. When she turned sideways to watch him, she noticed his twitching fingers in search of his usually omni-present, but now notably absent cigar. He began to vigor-ously pat his jacket pockets, then, glancing round him as if expecting a cigar to materialize in mid-air, he found Bron-wen.

There seemed little point in slighting him, so she gave him what she intended as a courteous, if cool, nod of her head. The look he returned could have frozen the Gulf of Mexico. She swung round to confront him eye-to-eye and received an even colder glare before he stalked off.

She stayed at the window, angered and at the same time puzzled. Was Pinkerton's response to her just his usual dis-like grown stronger, if that were possible, or had something regarding her Richmond assignment been mentioned in the president's office?

She heard someone behind her and turned to see the pres-ident himself step into the anteroom.

She hadn't seen Lincoln since she had left for Baltimore at the turn of the year. The furrows in his face had become more pronounced, his frame more gaunt, his dark, deep-set eyes more distant, as if looking around himself too closely might prove intolerable. Despite these bleak signs, she trusted that behind his eyes, no matter how aggrieved the man they reflected, lay a fierce, lucid intelligence, and a shrewdness that many—mistakenly or deliberately—would not credit.

She put her hand into the large one he offered, and said

the first thing his appearance brought to mind. "Mr. President, I am so sorry about Willie."

Immediately after the words left her mouth, she feared having made a brutal error, and Lincoln's forehead creased in visible pain as he gazed off toward the window. Once again her sentiments had run ahead of her sense, and she stood there stricken, wishing she could fall on a convenient sword.

After a pause, and returning his gaze to her, he said, "I'm much obliged for that letter you sent. And I reckon you got it right about Willie and his tin soldiers, likely making the heavens a mite uneasy by all that marching."

When his wide mouth stretched into a slow smile, her rush of relief brought with it gratitude. His voice then dropped to a barely audible undertone. "Miss Llyr, you surely are a sight for sore eyes. I've been trapped in there for hours with a pack of hound dogs who'd rather bark than hunt."

Smiling, Bronwen gestured toward the window. "Maybe it's the rain, sir. My family had a terrier who sat inside at the window and howled at every drop that came down. Of course he never got wet, but I guess just the prospect of it set him off."

Lincoln's own smile remained as he nodded, saying, "And that is the truth of it!"

He stood aside while she went through the doorway, and her face straightened when she saw Chase's expression of displeasure.

The president seemed to disregard his treasury secretary's vexation and went to stoke the logs burning in the fireplace. What happened next might have seemed spontaneous to those who did not know him, and as if he had just realized that Chase was still there when he said over his shoulder, "Mr. Secretary! I expect you're a busy man with things to do, so I'd best let you go do them. And I thank you for coming by, sir."

Chase's expression turned to one of surprise. He seemed

about to protest his dismissal, but must have thought better of it, and sailed sedately from the room with his face holding ill-concealed annoyance.

"Well, now, Miss Llyr," said Lincoln, going to stand behind his desk, "you just sit yourself down there and we'll talk."

As Bronwen was settling herself in the indicated chair, he startled her by saying, "I hear you've a hankering to go on down to Richmond. That right?"

At the edge of her sight, Bronwen glimpsed the unusually quiet Rhys Bevan shifting his feet, and she felt a spurt of anger. He had known bloody well she wouldn't embarrass him in front of the president by snapping *"Who's* hankering?"

She was aware that Lincoln was watching her, and he was another who didn't miss much.

"Mr. President," she answered, "I can truthfully say that I will do anything you ask of me."

She could almost feel the chief detective's relieved satisfaction, while Lincoln's expression showed that he understood exactly what she had said. He didn't press her further, even though she suspected he had deliberately provoked an unguarded response to his question. While his long frame sank like a folding accordion into the desk chair, he said to Rhys, "I do mightily wish I could hear that from everybody who comes in here!"

Rhys said nothing, but his dry smile must mean that Lincoln's comment was a frustrated reference to his general and Cabinet members.

"Our Mr. Chase," continued the president, "allowed as how he failed to see what a young lady could accomplish that the military could not. But I told the honorable secretary," and his voice took on the accent of a disingenuous backwoods man, "that I'd seen this par-ticular young lady in action, so I had to most respectfully disagree with him. And I reckoned as how he'd just have to 'bide by that."

Bronwen could imagine how well that comment had been received by Chase. She wondered if it had been just before she'd entered, when Chase had been alone with Lincoln and Rhys, or, given Pinkerton's glare, if the other men had still been present. Not that it mattered now, but it could make a difference down the road. Then, remembering the attention she'd been given by Assistant Secretary Fox, she had to assume it had been mentioned earlier.

"Tell me, Miss Llyr," Lincoln asked her, "do you happen to be acquainted with a fellow by the name of Quiller? Jim Quiller?"

"I don't believe so, sir. Should I be?" She glanced at Rhys, who seemed to be going out of his way to ignore her.

"No reason for you to," answered Lincoln, "but Jimmy's an old crony of mine. He publishes railroad and steamship guides. Publishes maps and ocean charts, too, and he draws tolerably well. Thought you might know him—I hear you do some bit of map drawing yourself."

Bronwen sat forward, listening closely. Given the president's reference to maps, she decided that Rhys—the only one who could have told him—probably knew where these comments were leading.

As casually as if he were describing the weather, the president explained, "He's a businessman of sorts, Jimmy Quiller is, and he does a fair amount of traveling. Even calls on our Southern family members in their . . . seclusion. Draws maps of places he's seen, and he's got a good memory—like a pup who's once met up with a porcupine, he never forgets."

Bronwen smothered a smile at his play on the man's name, and Lincoln's voice held a trace of humor when he went on, "So Jimmy's good at recollecting faces, like the ones of our European cousins who come calling down South. Jimmy said he can't help but wonder if those French and British folks have a notion to visit more often, maybe even take up residence."

At this, Bronwen didn't stir an inch, but sat glued to the

chair. Lincoln was studying her, and she gave him a quick nod to indicate she understood.

"Last time I visited here with Jimmy was about four weeks past," continued Lincoln, "and he said I might not see him again anytime soon. Told me he was having trouble with his eyesight, kept thinking he saw somebody watching him. Couldn't tell if the somebody was a man or a woman, so he figured it must be his eyes failing, and sure enough, I haven't seen him since."

The president sat back in his chair, and staring toward the fire, he appeared to be reminiscing. Bronwen waited, and when no more was forthcoming—not that she believed for a minute he was lost in reverie—she ventured cautiously, "I believe, sir, that I just might know something of your friend after all."

"That so?"

"Did Mr. Quiller happen to mention," she asked, "where he thought his eye trouble had developed?"

"He did. Told me it was down Richmond way."

Still cautious, she said, "I thought as much."

"I expect you did," he replied.

Bronwen glanced again at Rhys Bevan. He got up and went to stoke the fire, as if trying to remove himself from the conversation while still making his presence known. And the president must have wanted him there, or he would have been dismissed with Chase.

Lincoln shifted his legs to stretch them out alongside the desk. "Jimmy allowed as how his eyesight always got worse whenever he was down along the river by the Richmond iron foundries. You know of those foundries?" he asked Bronwen.

"Yes, sir, the Tredegar Iron Works."

"You aware that's where the plates were made for the Virginia ironclad?"

He didn't wait for an answer, but turned to Rhys Bevan,

asking, "Did you tell Miss Llyr about that dustup over at the navy shipyard?"

"No, I thought you wanted to do that, sir."

Lincoln nodded at him, and turned back to Bronwen. "Seems as if Navy Secretary Welles, and most particularly Assistant Secretary Fox, both of whom have good eyesight, are fretting about some shipyard fellas who don't. Seems as if these same fellas, a morning or two ago, couldn't find a set of plans they had for the *Monitor*. Looked and looked, they said—and they got the Secretaries into a lather about it—but then, a few hours later, that set of plans just popped up right where it was supposed to be. Now, I can't help but wonder if all this eyesight trouble just might be catching. What do you think, Miss Llyr?"

Bronwen, whose spine had tingled the whole time he had been talking, rubbed the back of her neck. She looked at Rhys, who was staring purposefully into the fire, but from the way his jaw had clenched, she guessed his thoughts were running along the same track as hers.

"I think, Mr. President," she said, "that these troubles might have a common source, and possibly unfortunate consequences."

"I believe you could be right," he agreed. "And I reckon they should be looked into right about now."

Bronwen was sure she grasped what he meant, but wondered why Rhys didn't comment. Or was this conversation, its meaning lying between and around the spoken words, never to have taken place? In which case, Rhys Beven would not have heard it, should he be asked. In which case, why was he there at all?

She asked Rhys that as they left the White House, dodging scattered raindrops and several goats that were exercising squatters' rights to the road.

Rhys had stopped at the road's edge, and appeared to be deliberating about something, and then, as if making a decision, he swerved away from the path that led to the Treasury building. When they started down the road he finally answered her question, but not before taking a quick look around. "I expect the president wants someone—trusted by both of you—to know what you're engaged in. It's for your protection."

Bronwen also looked around. "You mean he doesn't trust . . . the secretary?" she asked, satisfied they were beyond the earshot of any eavesdropper. She recalled Pinkerton saying, "Get rid of bad habits. Such as assuming you can't be overheard, or, if you can, that nobody would be interested. In this work, habits can be deadly."

"It's not necessarily a matter of distrust," Rhys said. "But he's aware that anything you report—officially report—will have to be shown by me to my superior."

Meaning Secretary Chase. "You knew about this beforehand, didn't you, Chief?" said Bronwen, glancing around again.

"The president was emphatic that he wanted to measure your response himself. Your conversation with him, as far as others are concerned, never took place. I'm certain you understand that."

She nodded. "But why? Who does he have doubts about?"

"Again, it's not as simple as that. He wants to be kept apprised—separate and distinct from his Cabinet—so he can assess whether information is being withheld from him. The reasons for withholding it don't have to be sinister ones, but they could be politically motivated ones."

Since the rain had stopped, Bronwen paused at the edge of Lafayette Park. Restraining the urge to look around yet again, she said under her breath, "Could I be suffering from eye trouble, too? Or have Baltimore and Virginia just made me skittish?"

He stopped walking, and while he didn't turn his head, Bronwen could see him scanning the park. "I don't know," he said finally, "but we tend to develop a pretty reliable sixth sense about this, so if you think we're being followed, don't discount it. Just act as if we're out for a stroll."

He took her hand, tucking it under his arm, and began walking again.

"Why, my dear Mr. Bevan," she said, joking to cover her uneasiness, "I had no idea!"

"Don't be impudent. Now, in answer to your earlier question, think of the contentious forces Lincoln has surrounding him, all vying for his attention, pressing their own agendas, jockeying for power. It must be next to impossible to assess the information they give him. Secondhand information that's been filtered and edited by others—and he's a man who likes to be in control."

"He must like it. I can't imagine why else he would want to be . . . where he is."

"Don't be too charitable," Rhys responded. "He is an astute politician. While he's not naive, in the past year he has learned the hard way that he is not an expert on military matters. At least not yet. He may become one, but it will take time."

He put a sudden pressure on her hand, saying, "Don't look around. I begin to think perhaps we do have an interested observer."

"Where?"

"Some ways behind us. It could be nothing, but in case it isn't, we'll take a roundabout way to where we're going. Be ready to follow my lead."

They had turned onto a deserted side road before she said, "The *Monitor* plans—the ones that went missing? That sounded disturbing."

"Secretary Fox was the one most worried," Rhys said, "but even he had to admit there might simply have been a mix-up—that the men who thought the plans were gone became overly agitated before searching for them thoroughly enough. Shipyards can be pretty disorganized areas. Still, I could see that Fox wasn't happy with that explanation."

"Surely the navy has more than one set of plans."

"Yes, and the architect Ericsson has several more. Those specific ones were being used frequently, though, because there are more ironclads now under construction and the original design is being modified. Fox wants to use larger guns than the *Monitor*'s eleven-inch ones."

"The president was bothered enough to mention it, and I don't think it sounds like simply a mix-up, do you?"

Rhys shook his head. "I'm uneasy about it."

"The plans were found to be missing in the morning?" Bronwen asked. When he nodded she said, "So they could have been taken sometime the night before."

"That's the way it looks. Security there at the yard can best be described as . . . relaxed."

"So there would have been enough time to draw a rough copy of the plans," Bronwen said. "Not in great detail, but whoever took them—if they *were* taken—might only have been looking for something specific."

"And the readiest explanation is that *Monitor*'s architect is not available to the Confederacy," Rhys said.

"But if it was the design that was wanted, why not just take and keep the plans? Why 'borrow' them and then return them?"

"You tell me."

"Because whoever took them did not want it known the plans had been used . . . for something. And didn't realize before putting them back that their absence had been discovered."

"All right," Rhys said, "but why?"

"You and O'Hara, always testing me! I don't know why, unless . . ."

"Yes?"

"Isn't the *Monitor* supposed to be indestructible?"

"If I understand your question, I doubt any ship is indestructible against a deliberate act of sabotage," Rhys said bluntly.

"You suspect that's what this may be about?"

"Don't you?"

She nodded, reluctantly.

"So does Gustavus Fox," Rhys said. "He took me aside in the president's office, while the others were being served coffee, and he said as much. Fox is quick and sharp. He was a naval officer—unlike Welles, who was a practicing lawyer—and then a successful businessman before Lincoln tapped him for this navy appointment. He has been an enthusiastic promoter of the ironclads, and he's concerned about this incident. His instincts seem sound, so I take his concern seriously."

Bronwen, given that criterion, didn't think too hard about whose concerns he might not take seriously. "Fox is surely observant," she commented, and told Rhys about her brief meeting with the man. "I was surprised he made the effort to introduce himself."

"I expect Lincoln mentioned something to him," Rhys told her. "Fox knows that there is no organized intelligence unit other than Treasury's—or if he didn't know it before, he knows it now. But we have somewhat of a tightrope to walk here."

"Why a tightrope?"

"Secretary Chase doesn't want Treasury involved in what he believes are solely military matters."

"What does he think the intelligence unit is for," Bronwen blurted, "gathering secret recipes for the White House chef?"

She expected Rhys to reprove her, but he said only, "Chase has his reasons. And since the president needs to keep everyone reasonably content and cooperative, he has some sidestepping to do, too. Thus, as far as investigating a possible threat to the *Monitor,* Agent Llyr, it has to be an unseen, unheard activity. Involving you and me, maybe a few others, and some birds."

"What?"

As Bronwen gaped at him, Rhys slowed his pace slightly.

"And now I think we need a change of course," he said. "Stay with me."

He suddenly swerved and, with her hand still held under his arm, they went at a fast clip between two brick houses, passed through a courtyard, and, after the quick turn of a key she'd not known he had ready, went in the back door of another brick house. It faced a road parallel to the one they had just left, and the room they entered was completely empty of furniture. It reminded Bronwen unpleasantly of the Baltimore carriage house where her fellow agent Thomas had been murdered.

Rhys closed the door behind them and went to a window overlooking the courtyard. For a time he stood there watching while Bronwen waited by the door in impatient silence. Then, not turning, he beckoned her forward and directed her gaze to a woman coming into the yard.

"Ever seen her before?" Rhys asked.

Bronwen squinted. "I can't tell," she answered, "not with that big hat she's wearing, and those long ostrich feathers fluttering over her face. Which just may be intentional."

"There are plenty of large hats in Washington."

"But they're not usually topped off with an even larger parasol," Bronwen observed, craning her neck to find a better vantage point.

"Come again?"

"Chief, have you no sense of fashion? My Cousin Emma— the one who owns a dress shop—would have heart failure if she saw that woman. Even I can see she looks absurdly overloaded."

Rhys leaned forward to peer out again and muttered, "These days I think women deliberately make themselves look absurd. That hoop skirt must be three yards across."

The woman had paused and was now glancing around from under the feathers and the parasol. At last she turned, and with a slightly uneven gait that made her hoop skirt swing like a lop-sided bell, she walked back the way she had come.

"No, it doesn't fit," Bronwen stated with conviction.

"What doesn't?"

"Pinkerton insisted that one should always question the unusual amidst the usual. Anything that's out of place."

Rhys pulled back from the window, and Bronwen saw his amused expression.

"I'm not joking, Chief. That woman was dressed in the most stylish gown, in the most currently stylish color, with satin slippers dyed to match. The blue silk fabric alone must have cost a king's ransom. With the glaring exception of that hat, she was, as Cousin Emma would say, *à la mode*. Or something like that—I never paid much attention in French class. But you see my point?"

"I'm not sure I do."

"Well, to begin with, who, in this muddy swamp of a city, would take a long walk in soft-soled, satin slippers? And those mammoth hoop skirts are supposed to be worn with tiny bonnets no bigger than handkerchiefs. I have it on the very best authority."

"Your cousin."

"The same. I think the hat was worn to do exactly what it did. Hide the woman's face. And her long stroll hadn't been anticipated. When we left the White House, there was every reason to assume we would return to Treasury, not even a block away."

"I applaud you for being observant, but the woman may simply have bad taste," Rhys commented dryly. "Which doesn't necessarily translate into evil intentions."

Bronwen shrugged. "Maybe. Maybe not. But for all we know, Mr. Chief Detective, that woman could have been concealing a sword or a musket under her hoop skirt. Even a clipper ship or two," she said, smiling up at him, "and you wouldn't even have noticed."

"I have always said," Rhys remarked, "that women make

valuable spies. Male ignorance in the mysterious matters of female dress is one obvious example of why. Because you are quite correct—I wouldn't have noticed."

He returned her smile and drew her away from the window. "We need to go. There's someone waiting for us. No, don't ask—you'll learn soon enough. We'll use the side entrance to leave and take some back alleyways. Just in the event your gauche woman has a cannon readied under her petticoats."

In spite of his teasing, Bronwen observed that he took another lengthy look out at the courtyard.

But what had he said earlier about *birds*?

11

Their ships are as fast as a bird.

—Homer

Washington City

Rhys Bevan proceeded to take such a swiftly zigzagging course that Bronwen was hard-pressed to match his pace. After they had veered onto yet another dirt road, and his silent response to her query as to destination had discouraged her from repeating it, she asked, "Who else from the Treasury unit will be going to the South?"

"I can't say. Unless two agents are assigned together to the same territory, no one in the unit will know exactly where anyone else is working. It's safer for all that way."

The weeds poking through the road's surface made it appear seldom traveled, and alongside it several hobos lay among strewn jugs and overturned wine bottles. Bronwen avoided looking down.

"Where are we?" she asked, glancing back over her shoulder, and recognizing they were not that far from the city, since she could see the unfinished dome of the Capitol.

"As you've noticed, we have come to this unfashionable neighborhood by a circuitous route," Rhys answered. "We're only about a mile from the Treasury Building, but I wanted to make sure we weren't followed here."

"Where is here? And who would want to follow us to this place?"

"No one I know. I'm concerned about the ones I don't know."

They turned again, this time into a muddy pathway leading to several tenement houses, standing side by side and displaying broken windows, peeling paint, and sagging roofs.

"Ah, Chief, this community looks less than respectable. Should I ask if your intentions are honorable ones?"

"It's a little late to be questioning my intentions. All the same, you needn't worry. You're too young for me."

More's the pity, thought Bronwen, as occasionally she did. He led the way into one of the buildings that appeared vacant, and pointed straight ahead to a dark staircase. What little light there was struggled through grime-streaked windows.

"Go on up," he directed.

Hesitating, Bronwen wrinkled her nose at a faint but familiar odor. "It smells like a henhouse in here."

"Up!"

Gathering her skirts calf-high—who knew what might be garnishing the steps?—she started climbing. When she paused at the first landing, he shook his head and pointed to another flight of stairs. Reluctantly, Bronwen went up them, with Rhys following. At the top, she was confronted by a small landing with two doors, one of which he opened, and then stood aside for her to pass.

When she walked out onto a flat roof, she immediately saw a row of what looked to be cages, but the sounds she heard did not resemble those of chickens. A closer look disclosed that what she had taken to be cages were, instead, good-sized wooden coops. The coops were immaculately clean, and they held not chickens but pigeons. Unusually sleek-looking pigeons.

Bronwen, with growing bewilderment, wondered why Rhys had brought her to a dovecote.

She started to turn and ask him this, but saw someone moving at a far corner of the roof, and a voice she would recognize anywhere said, "So, how do you like the aviary?"

She stood in astonishment while the young man came striding toward her. "Marsh? Is that you?"

"Who'd you expect?" he answered. Tristan Marshall had stopped within a few feet of her, and she stared at him with disbelief.

"Well," she answered when she had found her tongue, "I didn't expect *you!* What are you doing here?"

He glanced over her shoulder and said to Bevan, "You didn't tell her?"

"No, I thought I would enjoy seeing the reaction."

"And are you enjoying it?" she asked in irritation. He was entirely too free with surprises today.

"So far, I am."

She looked back at Marsh. His face was as she remembered it, including the pugnacious thrust of his jaw. His fair hair appeared to be somewhat darker, as if it had not seen much sun lately, plus he had grown a short beard that followed his jawbone, and he was a few pounds heavier. Which was just as well, because the man with whom she had sailed the Chesapeake Bay—under perilous circumstances—had been too spare and then some.

For no reason she could imagine, the sullen look Marsh was giving her implied that he held a grudge about something. This was not a new feature, as she recalled he often seemed sullen for no specific reason. He had never been that easy to get along with, much less to understand, and the tension between them now felt awkward. To be fair, she supposed he possibly felt awkward, too, but his moods were so mercurial, this was only speculation.

To conceal her discomfort, she peered into the nearest coop. A shining dark eye regarded her, the pigeon's neat rounded head cocked to one side, its iridescent neck feathers shimmering even in the gray afternoon light. It puffed out its chest, then bobbed forward a few steps, and Bronwen started to stick her finger between the slats. Marsh leapt forward and pushed her hand aside.

"What's wrong?" she asked, "will it bite?"

"Where have you been today?"

"I beg your pardon?"

"Have you been around chickens that might have the pox?"

"Of course! I spend all my days with flocks of poxed chickens! Are you serious?"

"Not so quick, Agent Llyr," said Rhys with an indulgent smile, as if, Bronwen thought, she and Marsh were two squabbling children. And they probably did sound that way, exactly as they had probably sounded the first time they had met. Rhys added, "While Marsh may be overly protective, those are valuable birds."

She swallowed her annoyance and said to him, "Why are they valuable? They look like plain everyday pigeons, and those aren't usually found in the most sanitary of places." She glanced at the one in the nearest coop, and then admitted, "Except they do look healthier."

"That's because they're not sick with pox!" Marsh retorted.

"Obviously," said Bronwen.

"And they're trained. To home."

"Oh . . . they're homing pigeons?"

"That's what I said."

She turned to Rhys. "Can they carry messages?"

"They can, and they are completely trustworthy," he said, smiling. "An ancient and noble bird, the pigeon."

He slid open one of the coop doors on its grooved channel. The pigeon inside walked onto his hand, making a soft cooing sound when Rhys ran a finger down its breast. "They're especially useful for carrying messages when human couriers can't travel freely, or for long distances."

"Like during wars," Marsh specified, unnecessarily, because Bronwen had immediately understood the implication.

With the pigeon still perched on his hand, Rhys removed the cover of a nearby tin pail and scooped out a handful of barley to coax the bird back into its coop.

"You will use these birds to send coded messages to me from Richmond," he told Bronwen, "because obviously you won't be able to trust the Confederate telegraph lines. And make sure that you use them if you need to relay information meant for Assistant Secretary Fox. He and I prefer that it not go though the normal channels that involve the War Department telegraph. I assume you understand?"

Bronwen nodded and looked again at the nearest pigeon. Actually, it did appear a trifle noble, she decided, once she had bypassed the memory of its scruffy-looking relatives in Lafayette Park.

After she had voiced this opinion, Rhys chuckled, and even Marsh began to smile; as Bronwen now recalled, it transformed his face utterly. He looked so attractive and likable, until he stopped smiling.

A short time later they were seated on two small sofas in a comfortable room across the landing from the dovecote. The windows of the room were remarkably clean, allowing in the late-afternoon grayness, and Marsh, after lighting several lamps, pulled a bottle of wine from a pine cabinet.

"How did you come to be here?" she asked him.

He shrugged. "Why not here?"

Rhys, seated next to her on the sofa, was more forthcoming. "When I was a child in Wales, my father owned pigeons—pigeon racing is still a popular sport in Britain. Since I'm rather fond of them, I acquired a few and kept them here with a caretaker—he's on holiday while Marsh learns the routine. Those birds you just saw are offspring of my original pairs."

"Don't they have to be trained to home?"

"Yes, but it's not difficult. You take them short distances

at first, then farther away, then farther still. They learn quickly, because like many birds, pigeons instinctively return to their birthplace. By now the ones out there on the roof have successfully flown back here from as far away as New York City."

"When you first got them," Bronwen asked him, "did you plan to use them as messengers?"

"It was probably somewhere in the back of my mind," he answered, then added, "No one else knows about them other than the caretaker and Marsh, and now you. I want to keep it that way."

Which explained the excessive caution he had used in coming here. But what role was Marsh playing in this? He must be a member of Treasury's intelligence unit, but why hadn't he been at that first meeting, if Rhys trusted him here? It might mean there was someone in the unit whom Rhys was not yet completely sure of—someone like O'Hara? Despite what he had said to her earlier today?

"And now," he announced, getting up from the sofa and refilling their glasses, "we need to get to work."

Bronwen glanced at the small clock sitting on the cabinet. They had been thrashing out plans for nearly two hours, having taken time out only to eat; thick slabs of cornbread with cold chicken, at least Bronwen trusted it was chicken and not pigeon she'd been given. Marsh had also handed her a bowl of dried figs—apparently he had remembered that she loved them. When she had thanked him, he smiled more amiably, his black mood evidently lifted after he learned of her Manassas jaunt and her active dislike of Kerry O'Hara.

At last Rhys announced, "I think we have covered as much as we can at this stage. Let's go over the main points one more time. Marsh?"

Marsh picked up a fig, tossing it between his hands as he said, "Next week I leave with a wagon and the pigeon crates.

Move south through the Shenandoah Valley, then head into Richmond from the west—"

"Being cautious," Rhys interrupted, "to avoid the Confederate force there in the valley."

"Doesn't bother me—it's a big valley," Marsh said laconically. "Ole Stonewall can't be everywhere."

"General Jackson is a man to avoid," Rhys warned sharply. "Go on."

"When I reach Richmond," Marsh said, "I head for Church Hill, contact Miss Van Lew, and then lay low with the pigeons until she"—he glanced at Bronwen—"gets there."

"And don't let it be known in the neighborhood," Rhys told him, "that you have dealings with Miss Van Lew. She could be under surveillance by General Winder—he's the one who arrested Timothy Webster and the other Pinkerton agents. Van Lew sent us word of those arrests, but by then we had already been told by Pinkerton. Her couriers are anything but swift, because they are mostly loyalist farmers who simply pass word by relay along the James River to Fort Monroe. But avoid Winder! That includes you, Bronwen. Let's briefly cover your assignment."

"Find out if one of us, or Miss Van Lew, can gain access to Webster in Castle Godwin prison," she said. "But I still think Pinkerton will have already tried that."

"You're not Pinkerton," Marsh interjected. "The prison guards are a lot more likely to let *you* see Webster than they would that cigar-puffing jackass."

Bronwen didn't attempt to hide her amusement.

"That might be true," Rhys agreed. "We need to know if Webster, or the others who were arrested, have identified to Winder that unknown fifth agent—the H.J.K. whom Webster hired. It's important to locate this man and learn whether he holds information that he has been unable to smuggle out of Richmond."

Bronwen nodded doubtfully.

"Go on," Rhys directed.

"Gather information about the city itself and the area east of it. Find out if Union loyalists there can be counted on to support a military seizure by the Union army. What might be the attitude of diehard secessionists—would they continue to resist by using guerrilla warfare, such as sabotaging the railroad lines. Doesn't that cover it," she asked Rhys, "other than the president's business?"

"Which is?" he prodded.

"Find what became of this Jim Quiller."

"Remember, too," Rhys reminded her emphatically, "that Lincoln wants to know if Britain and France are continuing to send emissaries to the Confederate government. Be resourceful, because there's almost nothing that is more important to the president right now. If they, especially the British, decide to recognize the Confederacy . . ."

"We could all be working the cotton fields for Queen Victoria," Bronwen said. "I'm suppose to look into the incident of the *Monitor*'s missing plans, but I don't know where to start."

"Listen for whatever you might pick up," Rhys told her. "And remember to relay by the pigeons *any* information for Secretary Fox."

As Bronwen nodded assent, she noted that this was the second time Rhys had told her to bypass the military telegraph if she needed to communicate with Fox. There must be some imperative reason. A suspected mole in the War Department?

He added now, "There will also be others working on the *Monitor* problem—"

"Who?" she interrupted, afraid one might be O'Hara.

Her answer was a shake of his head before he asked, "Any questions from either of you?"

"When does Bronwen leave here?" asked Marsh.

"She'll go on one of the ships transporting the army to Virginia. We're not certain when McClellan will begin this operation, but it will be soon—probably within the week.

Needless to say, the campaign will be an enormous undertaking, and it will take time."

"I still can't believe the scale of it," Marsh commented.

Bronwen, once she had heard what it entailed, could not believe it either.

Confederate troops, in addition to occupying areas in the rugged terrain of the Shenandoah Valley, were now massed around Fredericksburg. Which meant they stood between Washington and Richmond, capital cities that were only a hundred miles apart. To avoid these troops, McClellan intended to send tens of thousands of men, plus the artillery, horses, supplies, and road- and bridge-building equipment, as well as edible livestock, steaming down the Potomac to the Chesapeake, then south to Fort Monroe. The plan sounded either brilliantly conceived, or monumentally insane.

"I'm sure," Rhys said with a wry smile, "that the world has never seen the likes of it. A nineteenth-century version of the Spanish Armada. But the size of an invading army does not necessarily mean it can win a war—one hopes that was learned from the American Revolution, or what my former countrymen still call the 'colonial uprising.' "

After a few moments of silence, while they considered this quaint phrasing and its implications for the present day, Marsh exclaimed, "Wait a minute! How can Bronwen go with the army if it's landing at Fort Monroe? That's on the coast, and a mighty long way from Richmond."

"Thank you for your concern," Bronwen said, although she was not sure whether it was concern or doubt of her ability that prompted his question. "I think I can find my way to Richmond, especially given all the time I've recently spent with maps."

The Virginia peninsula was formed by two rivers, the James and the York, and at its tip stood Fort Monroe, seventy-five miles from the Confederate capital. McClellan would be forced to use the York River to supply his army on its move up the peninsula, because the ironclad *Merri-mack* still posed a threat at the mouth of the James, and the Norfolk naval base there was in Confederate hands.

Further inland there were railroad lines that ran west into Richmond, so it should not be too hazardous a trip, Bronwen had reassured herself several times in the past hours.

Rhys got to his feet, saying, "We've covered the gist of it. If anything more immediate comes up, I'll be in touch with you," he told Marsh. "Just stay on here until I give you the signal to leave."

Marsh nodded, and reached for a remaining chunk of corn-bread. "It was bad luck," he remarked, "all of the Pinkerton agents being picked off before this campaign. Or maybe it wasn't luck," he muttered darkly, echoing Bronwen's own fear.

"Well, there's still Pinkerton himself," she said, also rising from the sofa. "How does he plan to continue gathering in-formation without agents in Virginia?" she asked Rhys. "Did he say? It must have come up in the meeting with the pres-ident."

"It came up," Rhys answered. "Pinkerton claimed anything that needed to be known could be obtained from deserters and captured Confederate soldiers."

"Pinkerton's planning to rely on deserters? And prisoners of war? That's foolish and dangerous! They can be planted to deliver false information."

Rhys, looking as if he agreed, said nothing.

As Marsh drained the last of the wine, she asked Rhys, "How did you choose Marsh for this assignment?"

"I like birds," responded Marsh.

Rhys answered, "Mr. Marshall and I have kept in touch since his days as a fugitive from the state of Alabama."

Making both Marsh and Bronwen wince at the memory.

After she and Rhys had returned to Treasury, Bronwen asked, "In that meeting with the president earlier today, was my name mentioned?"

"Several times," Rhys answered, standing behind his desk and shuffling through a stack of papers and telegrams.

"I suppose Pinkerton wasn't any too complimentary?"

"You could say that." Rhys kept tossing items into various baskets. "Naturally, Pinkerton wants to keep his position with McClellan secure. You should be able to understand that. He and McClellan were less than sanguine when Secretary Stanton brought up the matter of Confederate troops at Manassas."

Bronwen assumed this referred to O'Hara's estimate of the Confederate troop strength there as being half what McClellan had believed. No wonder he and Pinkerton had earlier acted as though she—and likely all members of the Treasury unit—carried the plague.

"I put the best slant on it that I could," Rhys said, "but I think we can expect some ill will there. Especially since— and you may not know this yet—McClellan has been relieved as commander of everything except the Army of the Potomac."

"Because of the Manassas fiasco?" Bronwen asked. She received a shrug. "I suppose," she went on, "it didn't help that there were newspaper reporters traveling with McClellan on his heralded foray. But that wasn't our fault."

Rhys looked at her across the desk. "You do understand that in Virginia you are to stay clear of both McClellan and Pinkerton."

"Pinkerton will be with the army?"

"That's the plan. Meaning you need never cross his path. In that meeting today, the president cut off objections to Treasury's presence in Virginia by insisting he needs intelligence concerning the political situation in Richmond. That's outside Pinkerton's purview, so there shouldn't be any conflict between you—and you make absolutely certain there isn't."

"I just don't want him breathing down my neck," Bronwen said. "You know how he craves applause. He tries to take credit for everything, or rather, everything positive."

"Ignore him!" Rhys said with unusual harshness. "I mean it! This assignment is too important to be undermined by some running feud between you and Allan Pinkerton. Bronwen, do you understand that?"

"I'll keep out of his way. Gladly."

"Good! And again let me emphasize that it's possible Lincoln may still be searching for some means of compromise with Jefferson Davis and the secessionist states. He will need to search hard if it appears that Britain intends to enter this war on the side of the Confederacy. And to do that, he needs information."

While Rhys went back to scanning the papers, Bronwen said, "I'm starting to understand what a calamity it would be if Britain—"

"Wait," Rhys interrupted, "here's something you need to know." He tapped a finger against the telegram, saying, "In an unfortunate coincidence, this informs us that one of our more slippery British opponents has resurfaced."

Startled, Bronwen began to ask who, then exclaimed, "Not *de Warde?*"

"I'm afraid so. This wire says," he now read, " 'British espionage agent Colonel Dorian de Warde arrived Baltimore this date.' "

Bronwen groaned, and took the wire Rhys handed her.

"Since the Confederates hold Norfolk," Rhys said, "de Warde must have slipped in by way of the Chesapeake to avoid the Atlantic blockade. I'd be willing to wager that by this time he's on his way to Richmond, unless he is up to some prolonged deviltry in Baltimore."

He paused to give her a troubled look. "De Warde would be likely to recognize you, wouldn't he?"

"I met him by way of a freak accident when I was still with Pinkerton's," she said slowly, "so yes, he might well recognize me. Plus I wonder what he might learn about me in Baltimore. Damnation! On top of everything else, de Warde is all I need right now!"

Abruptly Rhys leaned forward, his hands flat on the desk, and demanded, "Agent Llyr, have you read William Shakespeare?"

Bronwen stared at him. "At the risk of sounding insubordinate, sir . . . have you lost your mind?"

"You might give old Will a look sometime," he answered, "just to see how little things have changed over the past several centuries. For example, hear this line: 'When sorrows come, they come not single spies but in battalions.' "

12

I think my duty lies near the Military Hospitals for the present.

—Dorothea Dix

Washington City

The large house, its ground floor having recently been converted to offices, smelled of fresh paint, turpentine, and lye soap. Kathryn Llyr stood alone in the main hallway, where she could hear the murmur of feminine voices coming from behind a closed door. At eye level on this door had been hung a large and impressive bronze plaque which read: SUPERINTENDENT OF WOMEN NURSES.

When she reached for the brass doorknob, Kathryn felt her pulse accelerate and could almost hear her heart pounding. She paused, making herself take several deep breaths while smoothing the folds of her long muslin skirt one more time. And checked again that the brown leather folder with its letters of recommendation was still tucked securely under her arm. Then she reached again for the knob.

Before she could turn it, the door was yanked open from the inside. She stumbled forward, barely catching herself in time to keep from sprawling headlong into the room. At the same time a young woman, who looked to be close to Kathryn's own age, came rushing past her through the doorway, weeping into a handkerchief. Kathryn glanced inside to see if anyone would go after the unfortunate woman, but since the dozen or so other women seated there seemed to be gazing intently at their shoes, she backed into the hall to ask if she could be of help. By then the young woman had already disappeared through the outer door, leaving only an echo of her sorrow.

Kathryn, her nervousness now coupled with bewilderment, stepped into the room.

A slight woman with dough-colored skin was standing just inside, wearing a brown bonnet which resembled a pancake and whose color matched the remaining dark strands in her graying hair.

Hesitantly Kathryn asked her, "What happened to that woman who just left, do you know?"

The other lifted her shoulders in a sturdy shrug. "Poor thing got turned down, I 'spect. But she should have known she would. Too young."

Kathryn must have looked as confused as she felt, because the woman explained herself by saying, "Have to be over thirty years. Says so right up there on that sign over the front desk."

When several women's heads swiveled to look at Kathryn, she nearly turned and bolted back through the doorway. She managed to restrain the urge, recalling what her aunt had once told her; her aunt who also suffered the curse of shyness.

"When I'm in a situation from which there is no escape," Aunt Glynis had said, "I try to concentrate only on what needs to be done, rather than on those who are watching me do it. I also take a good many deep breaths."

Kathryn found herself breathing rapidly, but knew from her training that too much of this would make her lightheaded. *Concentrate only on what needs to be done.*

She lowered her head, murmuring "Excuse me, please," to the women she passed on what seemed a very long walk to the front desk. When she reached it, the ample, pleasant-faced woman seated there did not look up from her work, but recited, as if she had said it hundreds of times, "You'll need to fill out an application, and return it to me before you can be interviewed. There will be rather a long wait."

With that, the clerk waved at a stack of forms on the near corner of the desk. Kathryn took one just as the woman happened to glance up at her.

"Young lady," she said, her expression becoming troubled, "I do hope you aren't here to apply for a nursing position?"

"Well, yes, I am," Kathryn replied, by now unable to speak louder than a whisper.

She took the folder from under her arm, intending to place it on the desktop, but before she could, the clerk stated, "I'm sorry, miss, but there are rules here that you must not be acquainted with. Please read that," she directed, gesturing at a printed sign on the wall behind her. Then her brows knit, and she asked sympathetically, "Oh, perhaps you can't read?" Her expression indicated this would explain everything.

"Yes, I can read," Kathryn murmured, trying not to imagine that she was the focus of every eye in the room. The clerk's face resumed its doubtful cast before she bent again to her work. Kathryn could feel chill beads of perspiration breaking out on her forehead while she stood and read.

NO WOMAN UNDER THIRTY NEED APPLY TO SERVE IN GOVERNMENT HOSPITALS. ALL NURSES ARE REQUIRED TO BE PLAIN LOOKING WOMEN. THEIR DRESSES MUST BE BROWN OR BLACK, WITH NO BOWS, NO CURLS, NO JEWELRY, AND NO HOOP-SKIRTS.

Below this, written in a precise hand, was the signature of Dorothea Dix.

Kathryn suppressed the impulse to clutch at her seed-pearl earrings to see if they had unaccountably mushroomed. Even so, they should be hidden by her hair, which she did not curl, and although her blouse was a spotless white linen, her skirt was black with no bows nor a hoop. Her age, then, remained the only obstacle, but she prayed the years she lacked would be offset by her experience. Nonetheless, her meager store of confidence was dwindling.

While she stood there, wondering how she might best state her qualifications, to her immediate right an office door opened. Into the waiting room came a tall and rather frail-looking woman, gowned in glossy black silk, with dark hair skinned back into a bun.

The woman went to the desk and reached for the top application form on a far stack. It must have been a completed one, because she stood for a moment, her eyes scanning the page, then turned with it and started for the inner room. In the meantime, Kathryn had become aware of a reverent hush that had descended over those waiting. This tall, elegant woman must be Dorothea Dix.

Miss Dix deserved reverence. In the past decade, she had done more to reform insane asylums—most of them no better than brutal storehouses for the mad—than had any other ten persons combined, and hers had been a tireless voice for those who had none of their own. Kathryn felt for her an admiration clearly shared by the others there.

Miss Dix now turned back to the clerk, saying in a pleasant, low-pitched voice, "Miss Turner, how many more applications are there to—"

Her question broke off, and Kathryn realized with a start that the woman's gaze was directed at her. Miss Dix, her prominent jaw jutting forward, asked, "My dear girl, how may we help you?"

Kathryn swallowed before answering, "I hope . . . that is, I would like to apply for a nursing position."

Dorothea Dix's sable eyes widened as if in surprise, and Kathryn, having heard an emphasis on the word "girl," feared that her application might be rejected out of hand. It seemed to be speak now, or never.

"I've just read your notice, Miss Dix, and have learned that . . . that I'm younger than you would prefer," Kathryn began, feeling even more shaky, because the woman's attention already appeared to be ebbing. "But I've done a year of training at the Infirmary for Women and Children in New York City, and have spent the last year nursing at a hospital in western New York—"

"Just one moment, my dear," Miss Dix interrupted. "There are sound reasons for my requirements. Surely you cannot think that caring for women and children would be at all similar to caring for wounded men?"

Kathryn, in the stark silence that followed, searched for an answer. The idea simply had not occurred to her that there might exist an unbridgeable chasm between the suffering of men and that of women and children. Those who needed care . . . needed care.

Aware that her silence would further jeopardize her application, Kathryn anxiously cleared her throat and ventured, "Miss Dix, I have letters of recommendation—" she paused and held out the folder "—from five physicians. Two are from those I trained under, Drs. Elizabeth and Emily Blackwell, and—"

"Women doctors?" Miss Dix again interrupted, not only ignoring the folder, but speaking in a tone that carried unmistakable irritation. "You trained with females, and you now expect to work with male physicians? Surely not."

"But I *have* worked with male physicians," Kathryn said, embarrassed by, but unable to control, the pleading note in her voice. "Miss Dix, if you will please just look at these letters, you'll see that two are from men."

Kathryn instantly saw that she had gone too far. The woman's eyes narrowed to dark slivers of disapproval, and she turned toward her office, saying briskly over her shoulder, "You must excuse me."

Then she stopped, and turned again to retrace her steps while giving Kathryn a warm smile. "You shouldn't fret, my dear," she said, and with slim, white fingers that bore several rings, she patted Kathryn's cheek. "Someone as lovely as you does not need a nursing position to find a husband."

Dorothea Dix pivoted forcefully on her heels, reentered her inner sanctum, and closed the door.

"It's not for nothing she's called Dragon Dix!" observed Bronwen, stretched to lie full length on her bed.

The boardinghouse attic room was a large one, but held few lamps, and since it was now late evening, Kathryn had drawn up a rocking chair beside her sister's bed. But it might have been less distressing, she thought, to have told Bronwen of the humiliating episode with Dorothea Dix while concealed by darkness. Even now she could feel her cheeks burning with embarrassment.

"The only thing I can take any comfort in," she said, "was that I managed to leave without weeping. If I'd ever started, I would have flooded the nether world of that waiting room like the river Styx."

"Dousing the Dragon's fiery breath forever?" Bronwen suggested.

Kathryn tried without success to force a smile. She pushed the rocking chair back and forth with her stocking feet, saying, "I wanted a nursing position more than I've ever wanted anything, but I couldn't possibly have done more wrong than I did."

In any event, it was now beside the point. She had succeeded in destroying her only chance of serving in a Washington hospital. Miss Dix was in charge of all female nurses placed in them.

"Maybe Dix was so effective at insane asylum reform," Bronwen muttered, "for very good reason. I'd say those requirements of hers suggest an unsound mind. For instance, that 'No one under thirty'! I would think she'd *want* young

women, as many as she could get. After all, nursing is not
something that everybody cares to do. It's not something I'd
care to do—no offense meant, Katy. But emptying bedpans?
Not me!"

Bronwen's familiar teasing on this subject made Kathryn
shake her head, again unable to smile, although she knew
what her sister was trying to accomplish; brooding was not
something that Bronwen herself found useful.

And that 'plain-looking' women business," Bronwen continued, "is the worst yet! How can a woman's *looks*—either
plain *or* ravishing—predict whether she'll be a competent
nurse? Did anybody question the ability of General McClellan
to serve because he happens to be handsome? Or the ability of
Navy Secretary Welles because he resembles a parrot?"

Kathryn managed a wan smile, saying, "You're beginning
to sound like Aunt Glynis."

"Well, it's true! Just because a woman has been born
good-looking," Bronwen went on, clearly gathering steam,
"doesn't mean she's also been born a bungling idiot. Or a
Jezebel . . . aha! That's it! That's what Dix thinks you have
in mind for wounded soldiers—tempting them in their sick
beds!"

"Bronwen, I probably took Miss Dix's rejection too personally, because she did, after all, post her rules. She must
believe that only older women have the needed dedication.
That younger women would be more . . . more easily distracted."

"No, I think I'm right," Bronwen insisted. "What's afoot
here is that the woman's fixated on the potential for temp-
tation. But what are you going to do now, Katy? You won't
give up and go home, will you? You shouldn't do that."

Kathryn sighed. "I'm not sure what to do next. But thank
you again for letting me stay here."

"Stay long as you like. Besides, I'll be leaving soon on a
long assignment."

"I have to say, Bronwen, that being a Treasury agent is

not something I'd care to do—no offense meant." Kathryn smiled. "But then, I've always been fainthearted."

"No, you haven't," Bronwen objected. "You went to New York City alone, don't forget that, and spent all those weeks of training there. Learning how to empty bedpans," she added with a faint smile that opened into a yawn.

"I've kept you up too late," Kathryn said with apology.

"No, and before I forget to tell you, the Office of the Sanitary Commission's secretary is in the Treasury Building. I've forgotten the name on the door, but you should see him."

"*Him?* You think I should try giving my application to a man? After what happened with Miss Dix?"

"Yes, you should at least try," Bronwen declared. "Maybe he has more sense than Dix." She stretched like a limber cat, saying sleepily, "But don't worry about tomorrow until it comes. I'm not going to. For instance, if I'm ordered to work with an agent named O'Hara, I'll have to think of some way out of it. Or if Bevan fires me, I can always pilot observation balloons, or drive mule teams, or stow away on a ship—" Her voice broke off, and she jerked herself upright.

"Katy, you read everything! Did you see the newspaper stories about the ironclad battle—the one between the *Monitor* and the Rebels' *Merrimack*?"

Startled, Kathryn stopped rocking, and said, "Well, yes, I did see some. Why do you ask?"

Bronwen crawled to perch on the edge of the bed. "Because I only scanned those stories myself. Since the so-called battle was something of a draw, I didn't pay much attention, but you're a careful reader, so let's compare notes here."

"Bronwen, why?"

"I can't tell you. What did the stories say about the *Monitor*?"

"I didn't read them very closely either—I'm afraid I don't have a consuming interest in warships. Do these questions have something to do with Treasury?"

Bronwen hesitated before she said, "Sort of, yes. I know you're discreet, or I wouldn't tell you even that. Now, try to remember what you read. Was the *Monitor* described—how it looked, what made an ironclad different from wooden ships, et cetera?"

Kathryn began to smile. "Yes, it was described as being 'clad in iron.' Surprised?"

"Katy, don't joke. This is important! Were there drawings of it?"

"I can't remember."

"Try. How much detail about the ship did the news articles include? For instance, how big it is?"

"Not very big, I gathered. Not relatively."

"Relative to what?

"The *Merrimack*." Kathryn frowned in concentration, saying slowly, "You know . . . I did see a drawing of the *Monitor* somewhere. Yes, because I recall thinking at the time that it looked like an oval metal tray with a squat tin can set in its middle, and not much else."

Bronwen was staring at her, her green eyes narrowing as if too bright a lamp had been lit. "Oval metal tray," she repeated. "Strangely enough, I just saw a tray like that at the White House, and your description is a good one. Now try to think hard. In this drawing, did it look as if most of the *Monitor* would be *under* the water?"

"Yes, that's what I meant when I said there wasn't much to see other than the tin can—I think it was called the gun turret. And I assumed that was the point of the *Monitor*'s design—to ride low in the water so most of the ship couldn't be hit by enemy fire."

Bronwen was nodding and said, "You're exactly right. Now the question is, how is it boarded?"

"If you want a spin on it, Bronwen, why don't you just ask your Treasury—"

"*I* don't want to, but what if someone else did? Someone who wasn't familiar with the *Monitor*'s design? This person or persons would need to know how to gain access, and where the engine room is, the pilothouse, the crew's quarters. How would someone get into the turret and the guns and . . ."

Bronwen stopped and stared toward the window, while Kathryn could feel herself growing uneasy. She protested gently, "I don't know enough about ships to be discussing this, Bronwen."

"We're not discussing it!"

"But—"

"We never had this conversation. You can't mention it to anyone. Not even under sentence of death!"

"Bronwen!"

Her sister ignored her and went on, "So, if someone needed to learn the sections of a ship, and for some reason or another would be denied permission to board it, the most logical course would be to look at the architect's plans."

"I think this is something I don't need to know," Kathryn insisted.

"I think so, too," her sister responded, obviously thinking about something else.

Kathryn sighed. "I have the frightening sense that you're trying to figure out how someone might go about—"

"Don't say it, Kathryn! Don't even think it! Just put any ideas out of your mind, because I'm only . . . curious."

Kathryn felt fairly certain this was a lie, but Bronwen simply flopped backward on the bed to lie flat, gazing at the ceiling.

Astonishingly, her eyes closed, and almost immediately Kathryn heard her breathing slow. How could she just fall asleep after that conversation? Although, it wasn't really a surprise; Bronwen had always been able to catch her sleep anywhere, anytime. Perhaps she really had been merely curious about the ironclad. And curiosity from Bronwen should not come as any surprise either.

Kathryn rose and went to a dormer window overlooking the road three stories below. A few closed carriages were rumbling past, the breath of the horses rising like plumes of frosted smoke. At least the cold might lessen the number of diseases she had heard were rampant in Washington. They occurred mostly during the summer and fall, but no one knew why this was so. There were some who insisted that warm weather brought more insects—flies and ticks and mosquitoes—and those might spread the diseases. They could sweep through an army regiment in a matter of days.

Their brother Seth—who had left Oberlin College to enlist six months ago, much to their mother's distress—had already been stricken with a debilitating fever. He wrote home to say that he was sicker when he checked himself out of a hospital than when he went in. Some of the other soldiers, he had said, guessed the fever might be caused by the army's indifferent approach to cleanliness; latrines were dug next to camp kitchens, or on the slopes above rivers and streams from which the soldiers took their drinking water.

Seth had also written that if a mother or two were to see the camps they would be cleaned up fast.

But lacking mothers on the battlefield, the army would soon urgently need nurses. Kathryn knew she was a good nurse, and since the wintering armies should shortly be on the move, she had thought she would be given a position quickly. Only by sharing Bronwen's room had she been able to come to Washington, and she was glad of the opportunity to spend some time with her sister. While growing up in Rochester, they had never been particularly close.

Bronwen had spent most of her younger years with their brothers and the neighborhood boys, playing mumblety-peg with pocketknives, or racing ponies along the Erie Canal towpath, or stalking one another in games of hide-and-seek in the cemetery across the road from their house. Kathryn had frequently watched them from her bedroom window, where every free moment of her own time had been spent in reading.

But what was she going to do now?

Had she possessed even just half her sister's confidence, she would attempt to see the Sanitary Commission secretary as soon as she could. But was he, like so many other men, opposed to female nurses? She doubted she could survive another humiliation like the one undergone today in Dorothea Dix's waiting room. She was not bold like Bronwen. And courage had never been something she could call her own.

Kathryn found a cotton comforter and spread it over her sister before returning to the rocking chair.

13

———ᗰ———

The organizing genius of Mr. Frederick Olmsted made the Sanitary Commission what it became—a great machine running side by side with the Medical Bureau wherever the armies went.

—Katherine Prescott Wormeley

Seneca Falls, New York

Before she sank onto the parlor sofa, Glynis Tryon gave the wooden cradle another swing with her hand and wondered if she dared to hope. The infant had finally stopped squalling and should have worn himself out, but he was still punching the air with tiny hands balled into fists, clearly fighting to keep his eyes open. Somewhat worn-out herself, Glynis smiled down at the blinking eyes of as-yet indeterminate color, although probably destined to become brown.

When she had settled herself on the sofa, she nudged the cradle gently with her foot to keep it moving, then turned up the lamp wick and reached for a half-opened envelope on the side table—an envelope she'd started opening earlier but had to abandon at the insistence of her young charge.

He had been with her off and on for nearly a week, since a raging typhoid fever epidemic had made it unsafe for his mother to keep him with her at the Women's Refuge. The typhoid was suspected to have arrived by way of a returning soldier, and had spread with such stealthy purpose that the few doctors in Seneca Falls had been caught unawares. When the mayor became convinced the village should be placed under quarantine, he had insisted that "every place of business must be closed which is not essential to life itself . . . or to the war effort." This statement gave pause to those who thought they recognized a paradox when they heard one.

Public gathering places had also been shuttered, including Glynis's library. The isolation the quarantine brought felt similar to being entrapped by a winter blizzard, she thought, withdrawing several sheets of ivory stationery from the envelope. Except that typhoid could be far more deadly than any storm.

She recognized the graceful handwriting of her niece Kathryn, and settled back against the sofa cushions to read. Like Glynis herself, Kathryn was an insatiable bookworm, and her letters were written with an eye toward her reader's taste.

Washington City
March 24, 1862

Dear Aunt Glynis,
    First, Bronwen and I are both fine, since I know that will be your main concern, and she intends to send you a letter soon. In the past days she has been busy learning Morse Code, and sketching map sections that appear to me to show the roads and rivers and railroad lines of Virginia. She copies these from scraps of paper that have come, I would suppose, from Union loyalists in the South. (While Bronwen jokingly says the maps were likely scribbled with porcupine quills, something she muttered made me wonder if they might have passed through the president's hands.) In any event, she has taken to calling herself a neophyte cartographer. This is a new word

*being used, she says, to describe one who drafts
maps.*

Glynis, stopping to reread the last several sentences, was
amused by "neophyte"—a term she would never before have
associated with Bronwen. And Kathryn's mention of loyalists in the South reminded Glynis of her friend Chantal Dupont, who lived just outside of Richmond. Her last letter to
Chantal had gone unanswered. Even more troubling were the
newspaper reports of harassment and even arrest of loyalists
in Virginia. There was known to be a small but staunch core
of Union supporters in Richmond, and the president of the
Confederate States, Jefferson Davis, fearing subversive acts
by this group, had recently appointed a provost marshal to
investigate those known to be loyal to the Union. So while
the lack of response from Chantal could well be due to the
threatened suspension of mail service, Glynis hoped it signaled nothing more ominous.

She sighed deeply and, after a glance at the now sleeping
infant, went back to Kathryn's letter.

*The troops here are combining their daily marching
drills with what look like preparations for a large campaign. Teams of horses, and mules, and oxen pull wagons in miles of snaking columns that move south from
Washington by way of Long Bridge over the Potomac
River. It is my guess that they are bound for the
Federal-held harbor at Alexandria. Considering Bronwen's map work, I am also guessing the campaign will
take place somewhere in lower Virginia. She will not
(or cannot) say, although I am almost certain she
knows.*

*In my last letter I related the humiliating experience
with Miss Dix. I'm ashamed to say that I have to report
another embarrassing incident. But before that, the
good news.*

*Several days ago I went to see Mr. Frederick Olm-
sted, who is the executive secretary of the U.S. Sanitary
Commission. (You may have heard of him, because he
was the architect for New York City's Central Park).
His office is in the Treasury Building, which, as you
know, is where Bronwen's employer Rhys Bevan is located. This is not such a coincidence as you might
think, because I believe Bronwen was responsible for
my visit there, although she won't admit to it. Nonetheless, just a few days after she met with President
Lincoln, I received Mr. Olmsted's invitation.*

*The "visit" was in truth an interview, and I'm glad
I didn't know that beforehand, or, after the episode
with Miss Dix, I might have been too nervous to go
through with it. As it was, Mr. Olmsted (a calm and
frail-looking yet commanding gentleman) read my letters of recommendation and then asked me several
questions. After which he told me I had the qualifications to be included in a group of nurses the Commission is sponsoring for an assignment in the near future.
He did not say what or where this assignment might
be, only that I would be fully informed in due time.
Although I know you will be curious, I cannot tell you
more. (Needless to say, I am curious myself!)*

*I could scarcely credit my good fortune, and was so
elated that when I left his office in unseemly haste—
lest he should change his mind—I collided with a man
standing just outside the door. I careened into him with
such force that we both staggered. (And since he was
no small man, you can tell how hard I must have struck
him.)*

*I was so embarrassed that at first I didn't dare to
look at him. After a few moments of complete silence
that felt like a year's worth, I heard a quiet laugh. I
glanced up to see quite the most interesting-looking
man I have seen in Washington. I was even more em-*

*barrassed, though, when I also saw that he wore a
dark blue Army frock coat with captain's stripes and
the long, emerald-green silk sash that designates a
doctor.*

*You are the only one, Aunt Glyn, who will under-
stand how I felt! My face was burning, so I must have
been blushing like a schoolgirl. He surely thought me
the world's clumsiest person, but he behaved as if
nothing unusual had occurred (so perhaps he is run
into by women every day), and helped to pick up the
Sanitary's forms I had scattered in the collision. Although he introduced himself as Gregg Travis, I was
so flustered that I nearly forgot my own name when he
asked it. I could hardly find the breath to apologize.*

*Fortunately, I am unlikely to see Dr. Travis again,
and so can quickly forget the whole incident and how
foolishly I behaved.*

*I hope this finds you well, and I pray the typhoid
victims in Seneca Falls are recovering. It is a fearsome
illness, and I have heard that a number of soldiers here
in Washington died of it last summer.*

I will write again soon.

Your loving niece, Kathryn

Glynis refolded the pages and tucked them back into the
envelope. She had smiled at Kathryn's account of her meeting with the "interesting-looking" doctor, but also felt keenly
their shared millstone of shyness. She had learned to manage,
perhaps even overcome, her own and hoped that in time
Kathryn would, too.

And Bronwen? Heaven only knew what she might be involved in now. Rhys Bevan, whom Glynis had met when he
investigated a counterfeiting ring in western New York, had
promised he would lend a hand of restraint, but Bronwen
was difficult to anchor in one place. Like a clipper ship under

full sail, she frequently just ran with the wind, leaving prudence foundering in her wake.

Incredibly, the infant had begun to fuss again. Glynis rose from the sofa, intending to pick him up, when she heard the front door open. A moment later, Dr. Neva Cardoza-Levy came into the parlor. She looked tired and pale, and had the worried expression she'd worn since the epidemic had taken hold. With one glance at the baby, though, Neva's fatigue seemed to fall away.

Her step buoyant, she hurried to the cradle, asking, "So, how is my son?"

"Oh, about the same," Glynis answered evasively.

"Which means," Neva said, while lifting him from the cradle, "that he was demanding. I'm sorry, Glynis, I can't imagine where that trait might have come from—although it's undoubtedly from Abraham's side of the family!" Her grin belied any of this statement's sincerity.

"Undoubtedly." Glynis smiled at the swiftness of Neva's recovery. "How are those at the Refuge?"

"No new typhoid cases—for the third straight day," Neva answered as she unbuttoned her bodice and put the now loudly complaining infant to her breast. "Perhaps the worst is over. But losing three of the Refuge children to the fever has been unspeakably tragic. And almost as tragic is little Annie Pearson, who because of it has lost her sight. I'm afraid it's a permanent loss."

Glynis sank into the sofa cushions. "I know Annie well. She often comes . . . came to the library to read. Neva, she's only nine years old."

They sat in sad silence for a time, and then Neva's face brightened somewhat when she said, "I've heard from my absent husband. Abraham said in his letter that he may be home within the week."

"I'm glad, Neva. Where is he now?"

"Out of Washington, I hope! And when he finally gets here, I intend to chain him to the house so he can't go off again. Really, Glynis, you'd think the Sanitary Commission could do without a new father when equipping their relief wagons. To say nothing of Abraham having to leave his hardware store. But my own Cousin Ernestine was the one who forwarded his name to the Sanitary directors in Washington."

Ernestine Rose was active in the Women's Central Relief Association in New York City, formed by Dr. Elizabeth Blackwell upon her return from England and her meeting there with Florence Nightingale. Now women in other Northern cities had started their own relief societies, funneling contributions of food and clothing to Union soldiers through the Sanitary Commission. Although the commission had grown directly out of these women's efforts, all of its directors were male.

"Neva, I know you've missed Abraham," Glynis said to her, "but he's had experience in ordering equipment and working with suppliers, and it must be difficult for Sanitary to find men outside the military who are willing to volunteer."

With obvious reluctance, Neva nodded and shifted the baby. "This war is affecting all of us in one way or another. The typhoid for instance—in my experience we've never had that in Seneca Falls before."

The war was indeed being felt here in the North. To Glynis's distress, Seneca Falls constable Cullen Stuart had spoken of possibly joining Seneca County's 33rd Regiment, stationed just south of Washington in the Union occupied portion of Northern Virginia. What had prompted Cullen's disturbing comment was the rumor that a large campaign would soon take the 33rd farther into Virginia. Glynis suddenly wondered if the troop movement described by Kathryn might give truth to this rumor. But surely, she tried to reassure herself, the army would not take Cullen, a man in his forties and responsible for the policing of an entire village.

Breaking into her uneasy thoughts, Neva said, "According

to Abraham, there are long columns of wagon trains leaving Washington loaded down with supplies and equipment. What do you suppose is going on down there?"

Glynis, now more dismayed than she wanted Neva to know, said only, "A letter I received today from Kathryn mentioned the same thing."

"And what else do you hear from her?"

"She's been accepted as a nurse by the Sanitary Commission."

"Well, I should think so!" Neva retorted. "She certainly has more qualifications than most."

"Apparently a friend may have arranged for her to see Frederick Olmsted," Glynis said, purposely not naming the president, whom Neva blamed for intensifying the war. "Thus managing to circumvent Dorothea Dix."

Neva shook her head, saying, "The unmitigated stupidity of placing a martinet like Dix—who among other things has no administrative talents—in charge of female nurses defies explanation. Those women are going to have a hard enough time being accepted by male doctors without the added burden of Dix's prejudices."

"Well, poor Kathryn was certainly bruised by the treatment Miss Dix gave her application," Glynis replied, and added, "It does seem very shortsighted to take only older women."

"I shudder to think what awaits those nurses," Neva said with vehemence. "And every other member of the medical personnel, because no one—*no one*—in Washington seems to have the vaguest notion of what to expect if there's a large engagement. Abraham wrote that the Army Medical Bureau doesn't even have its own ambulance wagons—they have to be requisitioned from the Quartermaster's Department. Now, if that isn't the most idiotic situation!"

"How on earth can the number of casualties—and the number of ambulances that will be needed—possibly be predicted before a battle?"

"They can't, of course," answered Neva. "And you'd think, after the lamentable situation following Bull Run, that both armies, North and South, would have learned. Wounded men were left stranded on the battlefield, and many died not from their wounds but from lack of the most basic care. There were nearly five thousand Union and Rebel casualties at Bull Run. Men who were fathers, sons, brothers, husbands. *Five thousand!*"

Glynis flinched, the number too staggering to grasp. It was greater than the entire population of Seneca Falls.

"But isn't the Sanitary Commission pressing for reorganization of the army's Medical Bureau?" she asked, searching for some reason to hope, and thinking that Cullen simply could not join this growing nightmare.

"Yes," Neva said angrily, "but only because that incompetent Surgeon General Finley is as old as Methuselah and refuses to die. And only after thousands of men have been lost."

Glynis thought the picture Neva painted was too bleak to be borne. Curiously, none of her anger seemed to disturb in the least her infant son; having finished nursing, he gazed up at his mother with soft, placid eyes. Abraham's eyes.

"The Army Medical Bureau is not prepared for huge numbers of casualties," Neva went on, "while the army keeps insisting this war will be over tomorrow and just ignores the looming catastrophe. In the meantime, disease is killing more men than combat is."

"But disease is just what the commission plans to address," Glynis offered quietly, trying to find an optimistic note, and now concerned for her nephew Seth. "Especially since it's been modeled on the British Sanitary Commission."

The United States version was an attempt to avoid the horrors visited upon British soldiers during the Crimean War. The determination and compassion of Florence Nightingale, along with her skillful use of the press, had aroused the British public, and the ensuing outcry had forced politicians and the military to address the thousands of casualties from disease.

"The question," Neva stated, "is will the army listen? The commission has no power, no real authority. It's a volunteer organization, and can only make inspections and recommendations. And it was your friend the president, Glynis, who called Sanitary a fifth wheel to the coach."

"That will change," Glynis said, finally having to protest. "Lincoln signed the approval for Sanitary's formation, and also agreed to an overhaul of the Army Medical Bureau. He's an intelligent man—he'll be quick to see the need if things become as grim as you're predicting."

Neva groaned. "Trying to change the military will be like pushing an elephant uphill."

She hoisted her son to her shoulder, saying, "I can tell you this, though. Young Aaron here will never go to war! Over my dead body will some army use my son as cannon fodder."

Glynis expelled her breath in a long sigh, as she tended to believe Neva's intent. And the futility of it.

She herself had come to the disheartening conclusion that while wars were not necessary evils, they were very likely inevitable ones. Humans did not seem capable of avoiding them.

But then, she thought with sadness, they were, after all, the children of Cain.

14

*I shall soon leave here on the wing for Richmond—
which you may be sure I will take.*

—General George B. McClellan, 1862

Alexandria, Virginia

Kathryn stood at the foot of a long shallow hill sloping
down to the Potomac. Spread before her lay a mile-long waterfront and its wharves, teeming with activity, while on the
broad river itself, ships of every conceivable design were
pouring in and out of the Alexandria harbor. It was exactly
as Bronwen had predicted: the launch of a colossal armada.

At the piercing sound of a steam whistle, Kathryn glanced
over her shoulder at the small brick town built on the hillside;
the site that since colonial times had marked the farthermost
point of the Potomac's deepwater navigability. The whistle
she had heard came from yet another train rumbling down
the hill from the Orange and Alexandria depot.

She and Bronwen had arrived at the waterfront several
hours before, and the trains had been chugging continuously
to the warehouses, one unloading its freight and pulling out
as another approached. With each locomotive came the smell
of burning wood, metallic steam, and acrid cinders. Their
whistles and screeching brakes were among the few individual sounds she could make out over the clamor of men and

animals and vehicles. Added to this were three military bands simultaneously playing three different marches. Only on occasion could Kathryn hear the bells of Christ's Church perched halfway up the hill.

Bronwen's transport ship had been scheduled to depart at four P.M. As she and Kathryn had first walked slowly in the direction of its wharf, Bronwen had glanced toward the slope and then abruptly stopped, muttering, "What's *he* doing here?"

Kathryn had gathered, from what her sister then added, that the man she subtly pointed out was a member of Treasury's intelligence unit, one blond-haired, short-bearded Kerry O'Hara. Bronwen bore him a particular dislike, although Kathryn could observe no signs of the portrait her sister had drawn: "O'Hara is a lying, rotten schemer." Kathryn thought his facial expression was remarkably cheerful and carried an elfin mischievousness despite the firmly set jaw. Perhaps that was the problem.

"Will he recognize you?" she had asked, since Bronwen was disguised as a dockhand. Because of her slimness, it had taken little to accomplish; she simply wore a loose, unbleached cotton shirt and overalls, the straps holding a bib strategically over her chest. The black leather boots covered all contingencies.

Her red hair had been braided, then pinned atop her head and tucked under a cap, although Kathryn could frequently see loose strands beneath the cap's small front brim. Bronwen had lost what had apparently been a long-standing skirmish with Rhys Bevan over this hair when he arrived at the boardinghouse that morning, and Kathryn had been introduced to a far more attractive man than Bronwen had ever described.

"Agent Llyr, you might as well be flying a red flag," Rhys had objected. "I told you—in fact, *ordered* you—to cut that hair and to dye it! I even purchased the dye myself, with no small embarrassment."

"I didn't have time," Bronwen had answered unconvincingly, "and it's too late now. I'm due at the harbor."

"I'll hold the ship!" Rhys said, also somewhat unconvincingly, as Kathryn guessed the flotilla waited for no man, much less for a woman.

"Damn it, Agent Llyr!" Rhys swore, in what Kathryn later learned was a rare display of temper. "Sporting that hair is like waving a red cape in front of a bull. I should dismiss you on the spot for insubordination."

"But you won't," Bronwen countered, donning the cap and giving it a rakish tilt. "I am not only indispensable to you and Treasury, but am also in the service of our president. Who, incidentally, has never once complained about my hair!"

"Correction—you are *not* indispensable," Rhys told her sharply. "I can replace you with O'Hara, immediately if necessary."

Bronwen gave him a look of stunned disbelief as he continued, "The transport ship will have a barber, and you are to see him directly after boarding. Is that clear?"

Bronwen seemed about to protest again, but finally nodded with obvious reluctance.

Kathryn, agreeing with Rhys, retrieved the dye from a bureau drawer. Before stuffing the small box into her sister's duffel bag, she had glanced at its label, and shuddered: *WARREN'S HAIR DYE—Lime, white, and litharge, to be mixed with water to dye black, or with milk to dye brown.*

"The next time I see you, Agent Llyr," Rhys had warned, "I do not want to also see red."

In response, Bronwen had simply pulled the cap down over her ears.

As they had continued walking down the waterfront, she had answered Kathryn's question, saying, "Yes, O'Hara probably recognizes me. He has very sharp eyes. Also, he's seen me before in overalls and likely expects me to be dressed as a dockhand, but I have no intention of acknowledging him."

Bronwen had been looking straight ahead, and Kathryn, glancing over her shoulder, had received a nod and an unmistakable wink from the eagle-eyed O'Hara.

Beside the Alexandria wharves, Long Island side-wheelers had belched steam as they backed and filled, and Bronwen named scores of vessels that Kathryn had never before seen, or even imagined. Tugboats, navy gunboats, mortar-boats, ammunition and artillery barges, Philadelphia ferryboats, canal packets, Hudson River excursion boats flying colorful banners, and a vast flotilla of ships under sail. And those were only what claimed the water. What claimed the land defied inventory.

Bronwen had pointed to a wharf some short distance away. "Look at that! Those horses can't be any too pleased."

Kathryn, following her sister's line of sight, had watched as three steam-driven derricks hoisted massive draft horses, suspended in what looked like slings, onto the bed of a transport ship.

"Those horses are huge," she had said to Bronwen, "I've never seen the like."

"That's why no one's fool enough to try sending them up the gangplanks," Bronwen had told her. "They're artillery horses, and they have to be huge to haul the cannons. They must weigh thousands of pounds."

"Which, the horses or the cannons?"

"Both!" Bronwen said, laughing.

All the commotion had not fazed her; if anything, it seemed to energize her. Kathryn did not share her sister's enthusiasm for crowds, but she had to admit that despite the jumbled disorder of people and vehicles—to say nothing of the cavalry horses, and sheep and goats and pigs being herded onto the ships—the turmoil could have been much worse than it was. In fact, the degree to which utter pandemonium had been avoided seemed nothing short of miraculous.

It had been while watching the horses that Bronwen had exclaimed, but in a low undertone, "Another agent! Is everybody in the Treasury Department here?"

Prompting her comment had been a sturdy man who stood intently observing the loading of an artillery barge.

"That's Ward Nolls," Bronwen had said, smiling, obviously less annoyed than when she had spotted O'Hara. "I guess a few agents have come to make certain I really leave town! Or maybe Rhys Bevan asked them to, since he couldn't come himself—he told us, remember, that he had to attend an emergency meeting called by Navy Secretary Fox. Or it could be O'Hara and Nolls simply wanted to see this extravagant show for themselves."

"And someone must be directing it," Kathryn had replied, "because eventually you can sense an overall design. It's not really as chaotic here as it seemed at first glance."

"You're right, there is a sort of method to this madness. The one in charge is John Tucker, who's the assistant secretary of war. What an assignment! He obviously had to round up transport ships from all over the Northeast. Just look at those excursion boats."

Kathryn had readily agreed that Secretary Tucker must be a magician.

But then, this was supposed to be one of the operation's final days. Presumably much had been learned during the previous two weeks of delivering to Fort Monroe over 120,000 soldiers and 15,000 animals, plus supplies of food for them all, in addition to cannon carriages, battery and ambulance wagons, and untold tons of equipment.

Something not even a magician could control was the noise. Added to that on the land and the water, in the sky above the harbor gulls screamed, circling against thick clouds the forbidding color of gunmetal. Rain had been threatening all afternoon.

As they had walked, Bronwen continued to scan the waterfront and sometime later said in surprise, "I just cannot understand this! Over there, standing on that far jetty and staring into the water, is the eccentric Mr. White."

Some distance farther, Bronwen had jerked her thumb over her shoulder, saying, "And there's Dan Morrow!" Frowning, she had added, "I thought Morrow was supposed to be in Baltimore with Harriet King. But she's here, too. I saw her on the road a few minutes ago climbing from a carriage."

Then, as they had neared a wharf where a group of navy men were congregated, her sister had laughed. "Now there's a more welcome sight! It's my gallant Lieutenant Commander Farrar and his ever-present aide Evans. I met Farrar in Baltimore last—"

Her next words had been lost in the blast of a steam whistle from one of the departing ships.

Now, after having at last seen Bronwen aboard a converted excursion boat named the *Alhambra,* Kathryn sought shelter from the impending rain under a clump of trees, mostly willows and oaks, growing along one of the harbor's side access roads. Surprisingly, it was the most secluded spot she could find close to *Alhambra*'s wharf. In fact, the ship was near enough that even without the small opera glasses Rhys Bevan had loaned to her, she could see Bronwen standing near the stern, relatively alone, waving her arms.

Kathryn returned the wave, determined not to show her concern. It should be reassuring, she supposed, that Rhys Bevan had assigned two novice undercover men—masquerading as scruffy-looking dockhands—to accompany Bronwen to Fort Monroe. It would have been more reassuring to Kathryn had the two men planned on staying in Virginia; instead they would return immediately with the transport ship. Bronwen had insisted that the mammoth fortress—at a third of a mile across, the largest coastal fortification in America—would be the safest place from which to begin her overland journey west to Richmond. A journey she would undertake alone.

Kathryn had been made to swear she would not disclose her sister's destination, or even that she had a sister.

"The Sanitary Commission might be part of this campaign," Bronwen had announced the night before. "The Army Medical Bureau doesn't much care for the idea—it thinks civilians will only be in the way—but War Secretary Stanton and Mr. Lincoln were impressed with the proposal Frederick Olmsted submitted, and rumor has it that Sanitary will go to Virginia."

"Do you suppose it's true?" Kathryn had asked, thinking this might well be the assignment Mr. Olmsted had mentioned.

"Could be," Bronwen had said, shrugging. "But the point is, Katy, that you cannot so much as breathe my name, or anything at all you might have overheard or guessed about Richmond. Or anything you imagined—mistakenly, of course—that I was suggesting about the *Monitor,* either," she had warned. "Not to anyone!" And had added with melodramatic flourish, "Not even under threat of torture or death!"

Kathryn had felt this demand to be excessive. "You're being unreasonable, Bronwen. It's not as if the people of Alexandria—and, we can assume, nearly everyone else in Northern Virginia—have not already gathered that General McClellan has something more serious in mind than a stroll through their countryside."

"It doesn't matter what they've gathered! You are not to say *anything,* if for no reason other than my safety may depend on your silence."

Bronwen, in an uncharacteristic gesture, had caught her sister's hand and held it tightly while she said, "Listen to me, Katy, because this is important. If McClellan does what he says he intends to do, this war could be over soon! But they—McClellan and the president—need eyes and ears in Richmond, or it will all be for nothing!"

After this, Kathryn had not further objected, but wished she knew less than she did. Bronwen had also seen fit to thoroughly alarm her by recounting a dangerous Baltimore assignment, and a vague hint of what she would be doing in Virginia. Her sister's candor had surprised Kathryn, but the more she thought about it, the more alarmed she became; it was as if Bronwen had felt the need to explain all this now— and to a trusted family member—in case something dire prevented her from doing so in future.

Kathryn looked again at the ship her sister had just boarded. It wasn't by any means full, and it seemed to be carrying mostly men wearing the dark blue frock coats, epaulettes, cocked hats, and gold lace stripes of naval officers. Bronwen had been intercepted at the foot of the gangplank by one of these officers and had stood for a minute talking with him. He could have been the Lieutenant Commander Farrar she had earlier seen, because this officer had appeared very attentive to a mere young dockhand.

Kathryn felt a few sprinkles of rain as she leaned against the stout trunk of an oak and gazed up the hill. The narrow streets that ran down to the waterfront had at one time been crammed with spectators, but as late afternoon approached and the sky continued to darken, the crowd of onlookers had dwindled. Now there was hardly anyone left within shouting distance of her. She had seen few other women on the waterfront, except those peddling fruit and flowers, and occasionally a well-dressed woman waving a departing officer on his way. Earlier, one such woman, face buried in a handkerchief, had hurried toward a large closed carriage waiting on the roadside, her hoop skirt swaying unevenly in a gait that bespoke the distress of parting with a loved one.

Since it looked as if the rain might increase at any minute, Kathryn saw with a mixture of relief and sadness that the mooring lines of her sister's steamship had been cast off. Water foamed through the clacking paddle wheels as the ship began to inch away from the wharf.

Bronwen still stood alone near the stern, but for some reason she had stopped waving and was holding field glasses to her eyes. Kathryn wondered if perhaps she couldn't be seen, which seemed unlikely, but she stepped away from the oak and waved her arm. Her sister now began pointing at something to Kathryn's right.

When Kathryn glanced about her, she spotted nothing that could have caught Bronwen's attention. All she could see was a slightly built man, some distance away, who appeared to be simply crouching on the shore while he watched the ship's departure. But when she looked again at her sister, Bronwen was gesturing at him.

Kathryn turned to study the man more carefully. He wore a long black overcoat and, she now noticed, his slouch hat was pulled forward as if to deliberately conceal his features, something which made her watch him with growing unease.

He suddenly reached into a side pocket of the overcoat. When he withdrew his hand, it held a revolver. He raised the gun with both hands, inexplicably training it on the only figure standing near the stern of the ship.

Kathryn drew in her breath, for a moment unable to credit what she was seeing, but the gun was unmistakably real. Her first and only thought was that he must be confusing Bronwen with someone else. "No!" she cried, "No, you're making a mistake! That's my *sister*. Don't shoot!"

The gunman rose from his crouch, pivoting on his toes like a dancer as he brought up the revolver, its black muzzle pointed directly at Kathryn.

She heard the click of the gun's cylinder and at the same instant was given a powerful shove that hurled her to the road. Immediately followed by a heavy weight falling over her as the gun cracked.

Her forehead was pressed into the sandy dirt, and she gasped for air while struggling to free herself. In another instant the weight lifted. Strong hands gripped her shoulders, slipped under her arms, and dragged her back behind the oak.

Kathryn pushed away the hands and, wiping dirt from her eyes, got to her knees. And looked up into the face of Dr. Gregg Travis.

He said quickly, "Are you all right?"

"Yes. Yes, I think so, but . . ."

He was already sprinting toward the spot where the man with the revolver had been. In the meantime people had begun to gather, casting curious glances at her, but the gunman had disappeared.

Clambering to her feet, Kathryn rounded the clump of trees to see the excursion ship swinging toward mid-river. She could not see Bronwen, but several men in navy-blue uniforms, their hands shading their eyes, were staring back at the wharf.

Kathryn, looking desperately about for her purse, which held the opera glasses, saw it on the ground where she had been thrown, and she rushed towards it just as a barefooted boy in ragged trousers darted forward and scooped it up. With a practiced gesture, he tucked the purse under his shirt and was turning to run when Kathryn reached him. She caught hold of his tattered sleeve and pointing at the hump beneath his shirt, said, "That's mine."

The boy tried to squirm away, but by now Kathryn had a grip on his thin arm. Speaking in as calm a voice as she could muster, she said to him, "Thank you for finding my purse."

With a startled jerk, the boy's head reared back, hazel eyes large in his small, pinched face. Kathryn took advantage of his surprise to seize her purse, and still holding him firmly with one hand, said hastily, "Let me reward you for your trouble."

Releasing him, she hurriedly rooted in the purse, found some loose coins at the bottom, and thrust them at the boy.

His mouth dropped open, but he had enough presence of mind to snatch the coins. After taking several unsteady steps backward, he turned and dashed off, while Kathryn yanked the glasses from her purse. She whirled with them toward the receding steamship, and crashed into the man who stood just behind her.

"We seem fated for violent encounters, Miss Llyr," said Dr. Travis, his eyes on her face as dark as the bottom of a well.

Kathryn was too alarmed about Bronwen to respond, and, raising the glasses, she scanned the transport. A few fearful moments of searching the stern of the ship, now more populated than before, found her sister. Without thinking, she started to lift her hand in a wave, but then realized that Bronwen was also looking through glasses, hers trained on the shore. Since enough unwanted attention had already been paid to them both, Kathryn dropped her hand, reasoning that although her sister must have witnessed the gun incident, she would see that Kathryn was still whole. And Bronwen was by now flanked by the two erstwhile dockhands.

"So where were they before?" Kathryn murmured to herself, in her relief forgetting she had a listener.

"Where were who?" Dr. Travis asked.

Kathryn's shoulders slumped with fatigue. She backed up against a tree trunk, and with Bronwen's emphatic warning leaping to mind, said only, "Did you find that man?"

"No. He'd already disappeared behind those warehouses."

Although she had assumed as much, she looked toward the buildings, and suddenly glimpsed one of the Treasury agents Bronwen had earlier pointed out. At least Kathryn thought it was an agent; the man was loping up a hillside road, thus only his profile was visible. She could not recall his name, but wondered if he had witnessed the attempt on Bronwen. If so, he would know it had not been successful.

Dr. Travis, also looking around, observed, "We appear to be drawing a crowd here. Why don't we walk somewhere, while you tell me why someone would want to shoot you."

He was studying her so intently that Kathryn could feel a flush rise into her face. She did not reply and remained rooted to the spot, seeking a way to keep faith with her sister without lying to this man.

"Are you feeling unsteady?" he asked. "Although I can't imagine why you would be." This last said with a faint, sardonic smile.

"No, I'm perfectly well," she answered, already shading the truth. "But of course you're right. It's not every day that someone aims a gun at me."

"He did more than aim. The bullet is lodged in that oak." Dr. Travis reached for her arm, and drawing her forward none too gently, said, "Come along. There's no need to entertain half of Alexandria."

Kathryn felt she had little choice. He seemed determined and his grip on her arm was firm, but he would surely question her again, and what could she tell him?

Actually, Dr. Travis, I wasn't the one that man planned to shoot. His intention was to kill my sister, and I simply got in his way. Why would he want to kill her, you ask? Perhaps because he had somehow discovered that she is a U.S. Treasury agent whose destination is Richmond.

No, true though it might be, she could not say that.

Dr. Travis released her arm and asked her nothing as they walked. Kathryn was aware of his glancing down at her, undoubtedly coming to the conclusion that she was simpleminded, unable to respond to anything as complicated as a two-part question consisting of "who" and "why."

Or maybe he thought . . . what? Probably that she had been targeted by a man who wanted to rid himself of a demanding mistress, because Dr. Travis had already glanced at her bare ring finger and would know she was not a wife. Thus he might be thinking exactly what she feared. Or perhaps he . . . no! She was letting her imagination run wild. But what could she tell him? Possibly she could deflect his questions altogether, having just realized, to her sincere dismay, that she had neglected to voice her gratitude.

"Dr. Travis," she began, "I am very grateful for your . . .

your intervention back there. And I apologize for not thanking you sooner. Please forgive me."

He stopped walking, and his face held a curious expression. She noticed again the darkness of his eyes, nearly as black as his hair—it was tousled probably as a result of his rescue effort—and the strong, aquiline features. They made him interesting-looking, but also gave him a slightly dangerous cast, much like the appearance of a raptor just before it swooped. A quality not overly reassuring in a man of medicine. And now the bemused half-smile he wore seemed forced and incongruous on an otherwise grave face so apparently unaccustomed to smiling.

The smile had become a sardonic one when he said, "No need to thank me. I was merely playing the role of an officer and a gentleman. Neither of which comes readily to me."

Kathryn found this an oddly intimate disclosure, but tried not to show her surprise.

"Moreover," he went on, "I doubt you needed much in the way of heroics. You seemed very self-possessed."

"That's not quite as I remember it, Dr. Travis. I was very *frightened!*"

"You didn't appear to be. *Purposeful* is the word that jumps to mind. Even the incident with the boy didn't seem to distract you—and that after you'd been the target of a gunman! Whatever the reason for your intense concentration, it must have been an extremely compelling one."

Feeling her face grow warm under his inquisitive gaze, Kathryn looked away. She saw that without her realizing it, they had walked onto a small finger of land pointing into the harbor and uncommonly free of wharves. The threat of rain had passed and the sky was clearing of clouds. Noise from the waterfront sounded strangely muted, as though the Army of the Potomac's flotilla was slowly sinking of its own weight beneath its own river. A less fanciful explanation being that the last ships of the day had been launched, Kathryn decided with an uncontrollable shiver at the memory of *Alhambra*'s departure.

Dr. Travis abruptly indicated that she should seat herself on a nearby fallen birch, and appeared about to remove his coat. She guessed he intended to spread it over the log.

"No, please," she said, hurrying to seat herself before his intention could be carried out. "This isn't in the least dirty—I've noticed that birch logs rarely are."

She had never noticed any such thing, and inwardly cringed at the speed with which she had learned to improvise—lie—so glibly. It had been only a white lie, though, she tried to convince herself, because she knew that the flannel cloth of his dark blue coat and trousers would make the birch shavings cling like lint—and she did not want to be any more indebted to him. She also feared that she would be forced to lie to him again, and that it might need to be a darker one.

He stepped forward to plant one of his boots up on the log, then rested his forearm on his raised thigh and leaned toward her. "The boy back there," he said, "had every intention of stealing your purse, and you obviously recognized it. So why did you give him money?"

The question was so unexpected, and its answer so obvious, that Kathryn looked up to see if he was again being sarcastic. The odd smile was absent.

"Because I assumed the boy needed it," she answered. "Why else would he steal?" She did not add that she had also wanted to prevent the wretched lad from being charged with thievery.

His responding frown seemed to be a puzzled one, as if this would never have occurred to him. He remained silent and gazed off to where the river lapped against the land, while for something to occupy her hands, Kathryn brushed at the dust on her cape, relieved that he hadn't asked a more probing question.

Her relief was short-lived.

"Who were you searching for on the steamship?" he asked. "With the opera glasses."

"Ah . . . I wanted to see if anyone had been hit by a bullet."

"The gunman fired only once."

"Yes, well . . . I'm afraid I wasn't keeping count."

Kathryn held her breath, waiting to see if this would satisfy him and wondering how she might gracefully leave. She had first seen Dr. Travis at Frederick Olmsted's office, which meant the doctor could be associated with the Sanitary Commission. Which also meant that if she offended him she could stand to lose her new position. In any case, he had behaved gallantly, and she could not appear so ungrateful as to just rudely walk off. But how could she continue to dodge his questions?

To her mounting distress, he would not let the subject drop, and asked, "What made you think that gunman had a specific target? You cried out something—something that sounded as if you knew exactly whom he intended to shoot."

"Why would you think that?" Kathryn protested, sounding disingenuous even to herself.

"Because we're in Virginia! I doubt that has escaped your notice. And since Alexandria is a strongly pro-Southern city, the natural reaction on your part would have been to assume the man was probably an enraged secessionist. Who decided, on the spur of the moment, to bag himself a naval officer. *Any* naval officer."

"Or perhaps he was simply deranged," she suggested evasively.

"He may have been deranged, but not necessarily," came the swift reply. "War does peculiar things to people's judgment. No, yours was not the normal response, especially since by confronting him, you risked being shot yourself."

Kathryn, who had been watching his face while he put forth this unassailable logic, quickly looked away.

His next comment was another unexpected one. "I was

told by Frederick Olmsted that he had enlisted you for the Sanitary Commission. He said you've more qualifications than any woman he had interviewed. But is Olmsted aware," he added, "that you are also remarkably composed under fire? As I have so recently seen, and may still be seeing. That's a highly useful attribute in a field nurse. One I wouldn't have thought a woman capable of possessing."

Kathryn started to object, then paused to consider what he had said. "I guess that might be true," she conceded. "I've been told before that in a crisis I behave more calmly than might be expected, but—"

He was watching her closely. "Go on."

"But I can't really believe that," she murmured, shaking her head, "because I've always been . . . well, plainly speaking, I'm very shy."

Why on earth had she said that? What did he care about her personal shortcomings? Worse still, she had just heard what sounded like a skeptical opinion of women as nurses, or perhaps even of women in general.

"Shyness is not a character defect," he responded. "But duplicity—that's a defect."

Kathryn rose quickly to her feet. "Sir, I must leave now."

"Because I implied you've been lying?"

She gathered the cape around herself, determined to escape regardless the possible consequences, but he stepped away from the log and took hold of her wrist.

"Kindly release me, Dr. Travis."

"Not until I have some answers that make sense."

"And who are you to demand answers from me?" she said, startled by the coldness of her voice, but more startled by her cold surge of anger. She had never thought herself capable of such an ill-mannered response, but this man had gone beyond the bounds of civility. Although, unfortunately, she was nearly as guilty as charged.

"Who am I?" he said, the arrogant smile again in place. "Well, I will tell you, Miss Llyr. The United States Army, in its occasionally questionable wisdom, has seen fit to loan me to your Sanitary Commission—officially to act as liaison, but in reality to advise the Medical Bureau of what you eager volunteers plan to meddle into next. And I like to know who I'm dealing with. For example, those who might practice deception. Is that answer enough?"

He released her wrist so suddenly she nearly staggered backward. Kathryn had never felt such anger, but she had to control it, or she would betray her sister.

Since she was finding it difficult to think straight, she took a deep breath. Then another, before she said, "Dr. Travis, I have not willingly lied to you. Rather than do that, I have tried—admittedly with little skill—to deflect your questions, which I am not at liberty to answer. And which, in any event, are none of your concern!"

"I think they are. If men will be shooting at you, I have—"

"As you said yourself," she interrupted, "that gunman back there was likely an angry or deranged secessionist."

"I don't believe that."

"So now it is you who have practiced deceit."

His lips parted in obvious surprise, and as if he would object, but then closed firmly.

Kathryn, wondering where she had found the boldness to say such a thing, turned and walked rapidly toward the road.

He caught up with her in a few long strides. "I don't think, young woman, that I've been spoken to like that in some time. I doubt even my former governess would have dared."

"Then we are far from being even, sir, because I have *never* been spoken to the way *you* have!" she said, and was instantly sorry she had said anything at all. And "young woman," indeed! He didn't look all that much older than she. Eight or ten years at most.

"Then why," he retorted, lightly grasping her shoulder and slowing her pace, "didn't you simply say you were—as you phrased it—not at liberty to answer?"

"Because," she answered, shrugging off his hand, but not

quite brave enough to face him squarely, "I am not experienced in being interrogated by a total stranger."

She broke off, reminded again that even though his manner was unforgivably overbearing, he had, after all, put his own life in jeopardy for hers.

"Very well," she amended, raising her eyes slightly from the road, "an *almost* total stranger."

To her astonishment, Kathryn heard a soft laugh. She resumed walking as rapidly as the long, swinging skirt and petticoats would allow without tripping, but to her distress, he simply shortened his strides to match hers. At least he said nothing more.

When they neared the road, Kathryn glanced at the sky, clear of clouds and with perhaps an hour of daylight left. She should have small trouble crossing back over Long Bridge to Washington. If necessary, she would walk as far as needed to find a carriage for hire. Anything to get away from this man.

"Are you returning to Washington?" he asked her. His voice was not nearly as harsh as it once had been, but she was too wary to trust him, or her own temper. She refused to answer.

Several phaetons were parked along the roadside. One had three passengers with a driver evidently waiting for a fourth, so she hurried toward it, but Dr. Travis went ahead of her and she saw him speaking to the driver.

When she reached the carriage, he told her, "This one will take you back to the city."

Kathryn didn't reply as she raised the hems of her skirt and cape to climb into the phaeton, but his hands were suddenly at her waist, and he lifted her without effort onto the empty seat behind the grizzled driver.

"I have one more question," he said to her in a surprisingly civil voice, while he extracted several coins from a trouser pocket and handed them up to the driver. "What brought you here to the wharves today?"

Kathryn touched the driver's shoulder, saying, "I will pay my own way. Please return that gentleman's money." She had already begun pawing through her purse for coins.

The driver shrugged and scratched his untidy beard before glancing back at her. Then he looked down at Dr. Travis, who was shaking his head.

"Look 'ere, miss," the driver said, in a not unkindly voice, "I don't keer beans who pays me. But I shure ain't goin' to set here all day while's yerself and yer officer fights a duel over it."

Kathryn felt her face flush and heard one of her fellow passengers chuckle, while the other two made sounds that indicated impatience. She bent forward to touch the driver's shoulder again, murmuring, "Very well. Please just leave."

But to her further embarrassment, Dr. Travis now held the horse's bridle. "You haven't answered my question," he said to Kathryn, who wanted to burrow under the floorboards. "Why were you here? Or aren't you," he chided, "at liberty to say?"

The sardonic smile had reappeared. Kathryn, sensing the irritation of the other passengers, answered him shortly. "I was seeing off someone dear to me."

His smile might have wavered, but if so, it steadied so swiftly that Kathryn couldn't be certain she had truly seen anything. As she was turning her face from him, Dr. Travis released the bridle, saying only, "I see."

He stepped back, and the driver gave the horse a flick of the whip. The carriage lurched forward a few times before it began to clatter down the rutted, hard-packed dirt road. Determinedly, Kathryn stared straight ahead.

15

A ministering angel shall my sister be.

—Shakespeare

Washington City

Kathryn avoided looking at her fellow passengers, but was uncomfortably aware of their sideways glances. They were three well-fed, well-dressed men of middle age, whose satisfied faces might have been those of merchants who had just sold their entire supply of grain and livestock to the United States Army. She supposed it natural that they were curious about her. They could hardly have failed to note Dr. Travis's uniform and the bright green medical sash, or to hear his demanding, too-familiar questions: *Why were you here? Aren't you at liberty to say?* Lord only knew what these men were thinking.

Twilight had come, bringing with it a light wind, and Kathryn rose slightly from the carriage seat to free the cape which had bunched beneath her. She looked back at the gleaming, silvery river and suddenly glimpsed a figure, some distance behind the carriage, darting into the underbrush beside the road. It gave her a start, and although the figure did not seem large enough to be a man, and was more likely a large dog or a deer, she felt uneasy and continued to look back from time to time. Whatever, or whoever, it had been, it did not reappear.

After the carriage left Alexandria and crossed the Potomac by way of the Long Bridge to Washington, the driver pulled the horse to a stop. The three men climbed down, and when one of them turned back and, with a highly suggestive smile, offered Kathryn his hand, she seized the driver's shoulder, asking him to please take her directly to the Treasury Building.

By the time the carriage drew up before Treasury's south wing, she doubted whether the coins Dr. Travis had given the driver were sufficient. "How much do I owe you?" she asked him, loosing the drawstrings of her purse.

He shook his head. "Way I figger it, miss—seein' yerself and yer officer spat was 'nough pay."

Grinning at her, he added, "Fer a lil' whip of a gal, yer did yerself right proud back thar. Kept yer dig-ni-tee, yer did. And hisself so high-'n'-mighty! Don't take no more a' his guff, y'hear?"

Kathryn insisted on pressing a coin into his callused palm, hoping the gathering dark would conceal her renewed embarrassment. "Thank you for your kind words," she whispered before climbing down.

Rhys Bevan had requested that she come by after Bronwen's ship had departed. Inside Treasury's spacious, ornately detailed entrance hall, a guard found her name on a list and escorted her up the stairs to the chief detective's office.

Kathryn was lowering herself into the chair Rhys held out for her, when he asked, "I presume *Alhambra*'s launch was without difficulties? You're later than I expected, so I guessed there was a delay—not surprising given the number of ships in that harbor—but otherwise there were no problems?"

As he made his way around the desk to seat himself, Kathryn could only stare at him, wondering what on earth this man *would* consider a problem, if not an attempt on the life of her sister?

"Miss Llyr? You look pale. Are you feeling faint?"

"Not faint, but certainly a little stunned. I'm not accustomed to a gun being leveled at a member of my family."

"What? *What* did you say?"

"I said—" she paused at the incredulous look she was receiving "—but surely, Mr. Bevan, you have heard what happened? You had other agents at Alexandria."

"I've heard nothing about guns! The two agents I sent reported back, stating they left the wharves shortly after your sister went up the gangplank."

Kathryn intended her moan to be inaudible, but evidently it was not. Rhys rose quickly from his chair, went to the office door and locked it, after which he went to a corner cabinet and withdrew a wine bottle. While splashing a goodly amount of sherry into two stemmed glasses, he said, "I'm assuming that, since you are here, your sister is on the ship and in . . . good health?"

"I believe so. The last I saw of her, she was standing near the stern of the *Alhambra*." She took the glass he handed her, shivering at the first swallow.

"Tell me," was all he said.

He did not interrupt while she recounted what she could remember. Although she explained the intervention of Dr. Travis, she saw no need to include what had followed it; with only limited success she had been trying to forget that conversation. And what possible bearing could the doctor's interrogation, and her own clumsy sidestepping of it, have on the gunman incident?

"When your sister was waiting to board," Rhys asked, "did she, or you, observe anyone watching or following you?"

"I did not, and if Bronwen saw someone following us, she didn't tell me. Mr. Bevan, you mentioned that you sent two agents, but I recall Bronwen pointing out four . . . or possibly five."

His brows lifted, and his voice was tight when he asked, "What were their names?"

It occurred to Kathryn that perhaps Bronwen should not

have brought notice to these people, even to her sister. And, too, since Rhys had said his agents left before the gunman's appearance, Kathryn decided she must have been mistaken in thinking she had seen one of them later.

"I can't remember their names—Bronwen didn't introduce those agents to me," Kathryn told him, "and she concluded they had probably just come to 'see the show,' as she phrased it. It was worth seeing," she added.

"Perhaps, but I sent only two. Was one of those she pointed out named O'Hara?"

"Yes, him I remember."

"That doesn't surprise me." Having said this, however, Rhys leaned forward and scribbled something on a sheet of foolscap. "Your sister's usually alert to her surroundings— was she this afternoon?"

"Mr. Bevan, there was so much commotion there, keeping track of anyone or anything would have been next to impossible."

"I know. I was there yesterday. This gunman—you said you've never seen him before. Are you certain of that?"

"Yes," Kathryn answered, "and he had a hat pulled down over his forehead, so I doubt I would recognize him even if I saw him again, but . . ." She left her thought unfinished while she considered it.

"But what?" he urged.

"I'm trying to recall something. About the man. It all happened so fast that I'm not confident of my recollection, but it seemed to me that he had some peculiarity. I can't remember what it was, or perhaps I just imagined it. I don't know as I was thinking clearly just then."

She felt rather foolish bringing it up, since her memory was so faulty, but Rhys, after again writing something on the foolscap, said, "It may be that you'll remember later, and if so, please contact me immediately." He paused, glanced off, and then asked, "Is it possible this gunman saw you with your sister?"

"I wouldn't think so. We said our good-byes some distance from the ship's wharf."

"So there would probably be no reason for him to associate you with her?"

Something started to come to mind, but whatever it was got lost in the fog of weariness. Kathryn shook her head, and passed a hand over her eyes, which seemed to be swimming in grit. If Rhys saw her gesture, he didn't acknowledge it, although he did lift his wine glass and ask if she wanted more sherry. She declined, thinking it would put her to sleep.

He sat for a minute as if lost in thought, rolling the bowl of his glass between his palms, before he said, "Miss Llyr, I don't want to alarm you, but you should be aware that there may be a situation here that could result in some . . . let us say, risk."

"Well, yes, Bronwen often seems to be at risk, and given the gunman—"

He broke in, "For you, I meant."

Kathryn drew in her breath as he continued, "Some weeks ago, your sister was on assignment in Baltimore, where at the home of a rather prominent doctor she uncovered some incriminating material. It disclosed that this doctor is an active secessionist with ties to the Confederate intelligence service. We must assume—because of later unfortunate events—that members of this organization know of her discovery. And may know her identity. What they do *not* know is that she was interrupted before she could finish her search."

Kathryn, who had been staring fixedly at the puddle of butter-colored light made by his desk lamp, looked up and asked, "You mean these people might think she knows more than she actually does?"

He didn't immediately answer, but looked as if he were taking her measure. "Since you don't seem terribly surprised by this, Miss Llyr, can I assume your sister told you about the assignment?"

Bronwen's warning leapt to mind: *Don't say anything to*

anyone! But Rhys Bevan was Bronwen's superior, so surely she had not meant to include him in her "anyone."

"I don't suppose she should have told me, and frankly, Mr. Bevan, I would be happier if she hadn't, but she did. She also cautioned me over and over not to repeat a word of it. Which I will not."

Rhys replied, "No, she shouldn't have, but we both know she doesn't always . . . shall we say, agree with, or follow standard policy."

In response, Kathryn managed a faint smile.

"Your sister's creative approach," he went on, "has distinct advantages, but, in this case, she has provided an example of why certain policies are in place. Although I'm sure you will be discreet, Miss Llyr, and that your sister was confident that you would be, I hope we don't have reason to regret her disclosures."

"Mr. Bevan, I'm confused as to why you're suggesting that I might be at risk."

"Because the stakes for the other side could be high. Did your sister, for instance, also happen to mention the navy's ironclad ship the *Monitor*?"

"Oh, Lord," Kathryn exclaimed, "I knew she shouldn't have said anything about that!"

Rhys Bevan's expression indicated agreement. "All right, what did she tell you?"

"Nothing specific, although I gathered—reluctantly—that Bronwen had concern for the *Monitor*'s security, because of some recent incident. She didn't say what it was, though," she added in Bronwen's defense.

She then recalled that Rhys had not been in Alexandria this afternoon because of an emergency meeting called by some navy secretary. Had Bronwen's concern about the *Monitor* been justified? Kathryn did not want to know.

Rhys said nothing more about this, and she didn't expect him to, but she saw with uneasiness that he was again studying her, much as he might a moth circling dangerously close to a flame.

"I have just a few more questions," he finally said.

Her responding expression apparently prompted him to open a desk drawer, taking out a large gold-foil box which proved to hold chocolates. When he handed the box to her, Kathryn very nearly dived into it.

"Let's go on," he said, after jotting something on his foolscap. "You said that you had met this Dr. Travis before?"

"It was a very brief encounter. I ran into him—literally ran into him—just outside of Frederick Olmsted's office. Do you know Mr. Olmsted?"

"I know who he is. His office is here in this building. Your sister said you'd been interviewed by him and accepted as a Sanitary Commission nurse."

Kathryn nodded. "It was right after that interview with Mr. Olmsted that I collided with Dr. Travis."

Rhys abruptly leaned forward over the desktop. "You said this Travis had been just outside Olmsted's office. Do you mean he was standing behind the door?"

"I don't know. I had pulled it open and just rushed out."

"And ran into him?"

"Yes, but why do you ask?"

"Could Travis have deliberately . . . overheard your conversation with Olmsted?"

"I have no idea. But why should he eavesdrop? He would be informed shortly by Mr. Olmsted of my interview—and, in fact, Dr. Travis said he was—because he's acting as liaison between Sanitary and the Army Medical Bureau."

"That's what he told you?"

"Yes."

"But you have only his word for it?"

Kathryn shifted uncomfortably in the chair, then slowly nodded. "But why would he say that, if it weren't true?"

Rhys steepled his fingers under his chin. "I don't know why," he answered, "but I intend to find out if it *is* true. I am not a great believer in coincidence, Miss Llyr. In this work one can't afford to be."

"What coincidence?" But as soon as she had said it, she realized what he had in mind.

It must have been obvious to him, because he immediately asked, "Has it occurred to you that the doctor's appearance today at that particular wharf was, at the very least, markedly serendipitous? What with all the military there in Alexandria, and the tumult involved in loading those ships, don't you think it's extraordinary—one might even say suspicious—that he showed up exactly where and when he did?"

"I hadn't considered it, not until now," Kathryn answered, wondering if she would have, had it not been for what followed the shooting.

"Think about it," Rhys told her. "You haven't been in Washington for long. How many people have you met here?"

"Not many," she answered, again shifting uneasily, since she could guess what he meant by this question.

"Not many," he repeated. "Yet despite that fact, one of those people pops up today, right before your very eyes, in Alexandria, Virginia."

"It is odd," Kathryn agreed, unhappily.

"From what you said a minute ago, this Travis suddenly appeared in the midst of all those people, rather like a sorcerer materializing in a puff of smoke. Now, is that simply an uncanny coincidence?"

Kathryn didn't reply. What was there to say?

"As I mentioned, I don't trust coincidence," Rhys continued. "It's almost as if Travis knew in advance what would occur, right there on that spot. And if he did know, it means that either he *is* a sorcerer—or he is something else."

"He said he's a doctor," Kathryn protested, although she was not sure why.

"Miss Llyr, if I told you I had earned a degree in literature from Harvard College, would you believe me?"

"Why should I not?"

"Exactly. And that's my point. You have no reason not to believe me. Except that it doesn't happen to be true."

"I know it isn't," Kathryn admitted, "because the degree you earned was in history. I confess that I'm usually trusting to a fault—or at least I used to be until I met up with you Treasury people—but in this case I was playing your game. Aunt Glynis, you see, had told me of your academic background."

"Did she, now?" For the first time that evening, he almost smiled.

"And that's *my* point, Mr. Bevan. An academic record can be verified—in your case a letter to Harvard should be sufficient—and surely Dr. Travis's medical degree can be verified. Or not."

"Oh, I plan to verify it, or not."

"But if he lied to me," Kathryn persisted, "he must also have lied to the Army Medical Bureau and, necessarily, I would think, to any number of others. Does that seem reasonable to accept?"

"Perhaps not. But as we have recently been reminded, even if Travis is a doctor, it doesn't mean he's not also something else as well."

He smiled faintly when he added, "Of course, there could be a less troubling explanation. Travis may simply have been following *you*. For the same age-old reasons that any man might trail after a lovely woman."

Rhys Bevan could not know how wrong he was. Kathryn only shook her head, twisting the drawstrings of her purse around her fingers, which all at once reminded her of the ragged pickpocket in Alexandria. It seemed curious the boy had even been there, because she did not recall seeing any other youngsters at the wharves.

They left Treasury shortly after that, Rhys hailing a carriage and accompanying her to the boardinghouse.

"Here's the address of my residence," he said at the door, handing her a card. "It's only two blocks from here, around the corner from the Red Horse Tavern. And I have a house-keeper, so you can leave a message for me at any time." He added offhandedly, "Just in case you should remember something else about today."

His casual manner did not deceive her. He was troubled by the day's events, and Kathryn would have been more troubled herself if she had not been so exhausted. But perhaps there had been enough worrying for one day.

For want of Bronwen, the attic room in the boardinghouse seemed drab and dreary and much enlarged. Her transport ship was probably somewhere in the lower Potomac, or had even by now reached the Chesapeake, Kathryn guessed as she turned down the wick of a kerosene lamp. She had fallen asleep in the rocking chair for what had been several hours, but still felt so tired, she immediately made up the daybed. After taking off her shoes and petticoats, she went to open the single, tall dormer window.

The room must have been recently painted, or at least after the cold weather had set in, because the window frame was stuck fast to the adjacent molding, as if glued with cream-colored paint. Kathryn absently wondered if the window in the opposite attic room was likewise sealed shut.

She glanced at the clock on the bureau and decided the hour was too late to ask the landlord to take care of it. It would have to wait until morning. Which was disappointing, because the clouds of the day, while not bringing much rain, had brought a change of weather; it had become an unseasonably warm night, almost like that of late spring. A perfect evening for thousands of Union troops, and her sister, to steam down the Chesapeake.

This made her recall the gunman at the Alexandria wharf. And Dr. Gregg Travis. Finding herself now too unsettled to sleep, she pulled up the rocking chair before the window; although the glass was wavy and thick, she could still look out. Under a moon three-quarters full, gas lamps blinked in the distance like fireflies, and Washington looked deceptively peaceful, what with much of the army afloat. Too much of it, she had heard her fellow passengers in the carriage that afternoon complain, concerned that the city might be vulnerable to attack by the Confederate troops in the Shenandoah Valley.

Kathryn bent forward to gaze down at the road fronting the boardinghouse, now all but deserted. Once in a while a single carriage would clatter past, and she could hear sporadic bursts of shouting, even some trumpet blasts, from the nearby Red Horse Tavern, but otherwise she felt completely alone in this volatile city. Since, as Rhys Bevan had pointed out, she knew practically no one, she might as well be a newly arrived immigrant.

She was disturbed that she had not mentioned to him the unpleasant scene with Dr. Travis. The Treasury detective had succeeded in making her uneasy about the doctor's timely appearance at the wharf, and too, she wondered about the gunman. Who had gotten away, or so Dr. Travis had said.

Coincidence did seem too far-fetched to explain his arrival there. Since Kathryn did not believe in sorcerers any more than Rhys Bevan did, there could, she thought, be another explanation that was considerably more ominous. What if Dr. Travis had performed not as a sorcerer but as a guardian angel? What better way to gain her confidence than by appearing to rescue her and her sister?

That would be so fiendish she could nearly imagine him in the role.

Role. Kathryn had been rocking as she thought, and now stopped, and searched her memory. It was exactly what he had said—that he had been playing a role. That of an officer and a gentleman.

She laid her head back against the chair, wondering if she were becoming as cynical and suspicious as Rhys Bevan and, increasingly, Bronwen. Could Dr. Travis truly be capable of such underhanded treachery? Contrary to what had seemed his forceful directness? Arrogance did not make one a criminal. Although what if he were involved in espionage—after all, her own sister was . . .

What was that sound?

Finding herself slumped in the chair, Kathryn came bolt upright, for a moment not knowing where she was. She must have drifted off to sleep and been wakened by that strange rattling noise. Since it had not come from outside the sealed window, she cocked her ear toward the door, listening, while she reached for the lamp; although she had turned its wick down, a dim glow remained.

There was the sound again. This time it was accompanied by a clicking noise that mimicked a mouse running over a bare floor, except that it seemed to come from the hallway. Still muddled by sleep, Kathryn could not remember whether she had locked the door.

She slid from the chair, picked up the lamp, and crept toward the door. With profound relief, she saw the key lying on the bureau, and now recalled having taken it from her purse to open and then relock the door behind her. Somebody must simply be having trouble unlocking the other one across the short, narrow hallway that led to the second, attic room.

But as Kathryn started back toward the bed, she recalled that several days ago the young married couple living in the other room had moved out. And there were only the two rooms on this attic floor.

There it was again!

She spun back toward the door. Someone was trying to unlock it, searching with skeleton keys to find one that fit, and making the rattling and scraping noises she had heard. There was no mistaking now the chatter of loose keys, and the sound of one being inserted into the lock.

Willing her pulse to slow, she took a deep breath and made herself think. The landlord lived in the basement, four flights down, but if she screamed for help, it would take time for him, or anyone else, to respond—if she could even be heard. Not only that, she remembered, with sinking hope, the ancient man who lived directly below was as deaf as a post.

She rushed to the window and pressed her forehead to the glass, knowing before she looked that the street below would be empty.

After taking several deep breaths, she forced herself to tiptoe back to the door. She should not just stand there awaiting whoever it was like a helpless child. *But what could she do?*

An answer came, though it must be the oldest trick in the world. But it might work.

To her surprise her fingers were fairly steady as she turned the lamp wick all the way up, then held the lamp down at her side, trusting its light could be seen under the door. At the same time she backed away, calling, "John! John, wake up! There's someone trying to break into our room!" She waited, made herself count to five, and then exclaimed, "Yes, yes, of course I'm certain! Where's the *pistol?*"

Waiting again, she held her breath. Silence. She moved closer to the door, rapping her key hard, six times on the brass handles of the bureau, making a metallic clicking she hoped might sound like bullets dropping into chambers. "Do you have the *gun,* John? And it's *loaded?* Oh, thank heavens!"

She heard the scrape of a key in the lock being withdrawn, followed by rapidly fading footsteps; they were not as heavy as she would have expected the footfalls of someone fleeing to sound. Allowing herself to breathe again, she remained by the door as long as she could bear it, then went to the window. Standing to one side of it, she cautiously peered down.

The road was still deserted. She wouldn't hear through the glass any sound from the alleyways that ran to either side of the house, but she listened for noise overhead on the roof. She heard nothing.

Lifting up the lamp, she peered at the clock. Its hands read a little after one. She stood there, breathing in and out with the clock's steady ticking until she felt less shaky, but her fear was being replaced by a confused anger.

Twice, in less than twelve hours, she had been put in danger, unquestionably due to the activities of Bronwen and Rhys Bevan. Who were not acting in their own selfish interests, but in behalf of their country—so how could she be angry with them?

What truly puzzled her about this second incident was that she was a stranger here. No one could know who she was. And then, suddenly, she remembered what had eluded her earlier in Rhys Bevan's office: At the wharf she had cried to the gunman, "That's my *sister!*"

Could someone believe that she, too, was with Treasury, and would therefore know everything that Bronwen knew? But how would anyone, how *could* anyone, know where she was staying? That was impossible. She was only terrifying herself with these wild imaginings. Perhaps she had jumped to an unwarranted conclusion, and this last had nothing whatever to do with Bronwen.

While pushing the near-empty bureau to stand in front of the door, Kathryn attempted to convince herself that whoever had been trying to break in was a common cat burglar. He had entered through the window of the other room, reasoning that the occupants of the house would be asleep. Which at this hour they undoubtedly were. The fact that he had picked this particular night to burgle, following the shooting incident in Alexandria and her own later visit to the office of the Treasury's chief detective, was nothing more than an astonishing coincidence.

As she placed the lamp on the floor in front of the bureau, Kathryn discovered that, like Rhys Bevan, she was not a great believer in coincidence.

What if the threatening person returned?

It would now be impossible to stay on at this boarding-house, but she obviously could not go traipsing about alone at this hour. She would have to wait until dawn—four or five hours away. Since she would never sleep tonight, anyway, she might as well pack her valise with her few belongings. If nothing else it would keep her occupied.

Frowning, she sniffed at the air, then drew in a longer breath. What was that faint, rather acrid smell? It hadn't been noticeable before. She started toward the window to raise it, before remembering that she could not. Which was just as well—why accommodate potential cat burglars? The odor likely came from the warm air lying over Washington's swamps and woodlands, since it carried a trace of something like pine resin.

Kathryn tried to ignore her fear and concentrate on packing her valise. Once she thought she heard rustling noises in the hall, and froze in place before she made herself creep to the door to listen, and was confronted with total silence. The sounds must have been made by her own overwrought imagination. Finally, she put on her shoes, and while she was lacing them, found herself perspiring, which seemed odd because her efforts hadn't been strenuous. On the other hand, the room did feel warmer.

When she was dragging the chair to the door, having decided to add another obstacle to the bureau already there, one of its rockers caught on a hooked rug. As she bent over to free it, she realized that the smell had become much stronger. And then she heard, coming from the hallway, a soft hissing and crackling.

An unspeakable thought crossed her mind, and she rushed to the door. The odor there was pungent, and with a surge of terror she identified it: the smell of turpentine. And with it, burning wood.

Her heart pounding, Kathryn shoved the ungainly bureau aside, then remembered the key, and reached for it on top of the bureau. It was not there. Maybe it had slid off when she moved the furniture, and going down on her hands and knees she searched frantically. Her fingers at last touched metal; it had been snagged in the rug.

When she crawled to the door, there were tendrils of smoke swirling over the sill. She turned the key in the lock and had started to push the door open, before it occurred to her that this could be exactly what she was meant to do; there was no doubt in her mind that the fire had been deliberately set. Scrambling to her feet, she hauled her skirt up over her nose and mouth, then cracked the door open just enough to see out. And was met by a carpet of leaping flames and black smoke.

Her knees nearly gave way and she gripped the door to steady herself. Was it worse to be burned alive in this room than to face whoever might be out there? The kind of person who would set a torch to a wooden building?

She slammed the door and ran to the window, pounding her fists against the frame, but couldn't move it any more than she could earlier. If only she had Bronwen's stiletto. Beginning to cough, she glanced back at the door to see smoke pouring under it in billows. She could hear flames seething, and from somewhere below the floor came a muffled shouting. But no one would be able to reach her now, and the room itself was growing hotter by the second. She tried the window again, tugging and pushing at it, but it refused to move. And the air was thickening with smoke.

Casting a desperate glance about her, she spotted her valise. She snatched it up, and grasping it with both hands, she stepped back and flung it at the window. The leather case bounced off the frame as if it were made of rubber, leaving only a spidery crack in the thick pane.

Every time she inhaled, she coughed, and her eyes were tearing so she could barely see. She would suffocate before the flames even reached her. The window was her only hope. The worst that could happen in breaking the glass would be slicing an artery, but at least bleeding to death would be faster than suffocating or burning alive.

She grabbed the valise, and moving to one side of the window, planted her feet and swung the case hard. The pane shattered with a burst of glass and a shower of slivers. Ignoring the ones lodged in her skin, she yanked a cotton sheet off the daybed to wind around her fist and began knocking off the jagged shards remaining in the frame. She couldn't avoid inhaling the smoke as she took great gulps of air, tears streaming down her face.

A volley of shouts was coming from below, and she thrust her head through the opening. The landlord was standing in the road with his hands cupped like a megaphone around his mouth, yelling at her, as other men carrying lanterns and pails were running toward the house.

"Jump, miss!" he yelled. "Jump! It's your only chance!"

The fire was crackling fiercely behind her as Kathryn looked down at the road, three tall stories below. Snatching her valise again, she heaved it through the opening to watch it hurtle downward. When it struck the road, the leather case split open like an overripe melon; if she jumped, she would break her every bone in her body, if not her neck.

"A ladder! Get a ladder!" she screamed at the men below, tossing out her purse for no other reason than that it held some identification. Because if she were to die up here alone . . .

"You gotta jump!" shouted the landlord. "No time for a ladder—the whole building's ablaze! Jump!"

Seconds later the howl of the fire drowned any other sound. Others below looked to have joined in the shouting, but she could tell only by their gaping mouths.

Paralyzed by indecision she looked down at the road again. It was too far. She could not do it. She slumped against the window frame, hopeless panic overwhelming her. Then came a memory, made long ago, of her sister.

Bronwen, having been banished once again to her second-floor bedroom for some transgression, had climbed out of a window and crawled down a rope to the ground, while Kathryn, transfixed by her sister's boldness, watched from her own bedroom window.

And now it would be better to risk something that might work, than to jump in panic, which, if it didn't kill her, could cripple her for life. With a quick prayer asking for some of her sister's daring, Kathryn rushed to the daybed, and tore off its remaining sheet even while she was shoving the metal frame toward the window. She stripped the sheets from Bronwen's bed and tore off the bloody one wrapped around her hand.

Don't think about the fire, she told herself over and over. *Concentrate only on what needs to be done.* Her hands were slick with sweat, and she clamped her wildly chattering teeth to make herself take only shallow breaths, as she knotted the ends of the sheets together. While she was yanking them tight, she heard a thunderous crash. Even over the fire she could hear a great moan rising from the road below.

Don't think about it.

Her bloodied fingers fumbled with an end of the sheeting as she threaded it twice around the metal bedframe and tied it. An explosive burst of sound behind her made her whirl to see the blazing door and bureau collapsing. Flames came leaping at her across the floorboards.

Don't think.

She thrust the length of sheeting through the window opening, and it fluttered downward. It would fall short of the road, but by now there were so many people below she prayed someone would catch her. Barely able to see through the thick, roiling smoke, she could give the sheeting only one last hard tug. With flames nearly at her heels, there was no more time.

She scrambled onto the windowsill.

The roar of the fire blanketed the shouts from the crowd, but over them she could hear a clang of fire bells. She scanned the housetops and roads, but failed to see the fire brigade. And she could not wait.

The flames were sweeping into the dormer as she turned on the sill. She looped her skirt over her forearm, and lowered herself to straddle the twisted cotton rope, gripping it between her bent knees as she had watched Bronwen do that night. One of her hands clutched the sheeting, but her other hand was clinging to the sill as if it were nailed there. She couldn't let go.

Don't think. Just let go!

The entire room was ablaze, with flames shooting through the roof, and still she could not loosen her death grip. Then another crash, followed by a violent tremor that shook the outer wall, jerked her hand from the sill. Clawing at the sheeting, she felt herself dropping straight down. A desperate grab gave her a handful of taut, stretched fabric, and she closed her eyes, knowing the sheet would split and she would plunge to the road. But with a shoulder-wrenching jolt, she stopped, and hung swinging just inches from the smoking wall. Her eyes flew open and above her she saw the daybed's upended frame tilted across the window opening.

Then she heard in terror a sharp ripping sound. How long could the sheets hold her suspended on their flimsy lifeline?

The shouts of those below were urging her down, but the sheets would surely tear apart if she moved. When a flame shot out of the trembling wall, licking at her shoes, she had no choice. Hand over hand, she began to inch downward, squeezing the cotton rope between her knees.

Suddenly the wall of the building shifted. She lost her grip, the rope running through her palms, searing the inside of her knees and her hands. She couldn't hold on . . .

A blur of upturned faces rushed at her, and she felt hands grabbing her, breaking her fall before she hit the road. Then she was being dragged forward.

"No!" she cried. "My hands—no, don't touch my hands!"

She lay sprawled in the dirt, aware of people jumping away from her as the heat of the fire drove them back across the road. Her palms were raw, and she pushed herself up on her elbows, shoulders aching while she struggled to keep her balance until she was kneeling. She thought she could faintly hear someone calling her name . . . it must be Bronwen. No, Bronwen was on a ship.

There it was again, her name, but no one here knew her. She must be hearing something that wasn't there. The heat was scorching, like the fire itself closing in on her, and she had to get up, get away from the building before it collapsed. The pain of her burned palms was making her light-headed, but she pushed her knuckles against the road, struggling to her feet.

"Kath-ryn!" The voice again, clearer now, calling her to come to it. "Kathryn, this way!"

She tried to take a step forward but her legs wouldn't hold her. Heat was bursting her lungs, and over the raging flames, and the clanging bells and the shouting voices, she kept hearing her name. And now there seemed to be two voices yelling, "Kathryn!"

Jostled by the people around her, she staggered forward a few steps. Her legs refused to carry her farther, and she stood there, swaying, while through a blur of tears she tried to find who it was calling her.

And then she saw them. Two men running toward her, shoving people aside as they sprinted in and out of the crowd, one of them now racing ahead of the other. Kathryn wanted to wave her arms so he would see her, but she couldn't lift them.

From behind her came a series of ground-shaking explosions, followed by a withering blast of heat that made her stumble forward. An instant before she pitched headlong to the road, she was caught by Gregg Travis. Directly behind him was Rhys Bevan.

16

I was learning that one of the best methods of fitting oneself to be a nurse in a hospital, is to be a patient there.

—Louisa May Alcott, *Hospital Sketches*

Washington City

Kathryn tried to free herself, but Dr. Travis gripped her tightly against his chest, shouting to her over the clamor, "Stop struggling! I'll have to carry you, so stop fighting me."

Since her hands were useless, and she could not stop coughing long enough to protest, she gave up her feeble resistance. Bells were clanging with deafening urgency, and he swept her up just before the first horses of the fire brigade thundered past. Waves of heat and noise swirled around them, coupled with the pulsating brilliance of towering flames, and Kathryn's head throbbed with each heartbeat. She saw with dispassion that blood was dripping from her arm onto his coat. Each drop was instantly swallowed by the wool flannel.

Dr. Travis, elbowing people aside, moved with ruthless determination through the gawking crowd, and Kathryn felt her stomach begin to churn.

"Please put me down," she cried through a spasm of coughing. "I'm going to be sick. Please!"

"Then be sick!" he shouted to her. "We've got to get clear of this crowd."

Kathryn clamped her teeth together, convinced she was about to vomit, and heard Rhys Bevan shout, "The back entrance of Chesterton's Inn—it's around that next corner."

They swerved into a narrow alley, and over Dr. Travis's shoulder she could see Rhys Bevan striding alongside, his fair skin made ruddy by the unnatural reddish orange light.

Bile rose into her throat, and struggling against what seemed imminent humiliation, Kathryn found herself abruptly deposited on a stone step. She lowered her head and at the same time felt something warm being dropped around her shoulders. Nausea rose in waves, and she fought it back, barely conscious of the fierce light and raucous noise in the background.

Her left arm was raised, and there was a sensation of something being pressed against it, but she had no strength to look up, and although her stomach had begun to calm, she kept her head down because it felt too heavy to lift. Something was being done with her hands, too, and she wished whoever was doing it would just leave her be. Even the clamor of fire bells scarcely penetrated the wall of fatigue. She thought she had never been so tired.

"Miss Llyr . . . Kathryn?" It was Rhys Bevan's voice. "Kathryn!"

It took effort to raise her head. Rhys was crouched on a step below her, illuminated in the pale light of a lantern he held and in the suffused red glow surrounding them. The light above them, she assumed came from the inn's gas lamps.

She couldn't see Gregg Travis and hoped that meant he had left; her indebtedness to him felt too great to bear. How did he keep appearing at these acutely dangerous moments? It could not be coincidence. Almost as baffling was his arrival in the company of Rhys Bevan. But she should probably stop trying to think. It made her nauseous.

"Kathryn? Kathryn, can you hear me?" Rhys asked.

"Yes, I can hear you," she answered with some surprise. Did he believe fleeing a fire made one deaf?

"Do you know who I am? Rhys Bevan?"

"Mr. Bevan, who else would you be?"

His sudden smile was one of relief.

From somewhere close by, she heard Dr. Travis say, "Good, she's not in shock. Make certain she is kept warm. I'll go to the inn entrance and flag a carriage." He then said in a harsh tone, "No, you cannot talk to her!"

Kathryn looked around, moving her head slowly so the nausea wouldn't return, and saw him striding off in a pall of smoke. To whom had he been speaking? The only one there other than Rhys Bevan was a rail-thin, sharp-featured boy slouched against the side of the opposite building. She narrowed her eyes and thought she recognized him.

"Mr. Bevan," she said, her voice sounding as if her throat were packed with cotton instead of smoke, "I think I know that boy. Would you ask him to come here, please?"

Because Rhys looked about to refuse, she started to raise her hand and gesture to the boy, but felt a jab of pain along her forearm. She gasped at the surprise of it, and looked to see that her left arm was somehow immobilized, but was still dripping blood, although much more slowly than before. It had not hurt much until she moved. Her hands, all but her fingers, were bound in what looked like strips of her cotton sheets. She also saw a dark, wool-flannel army coat draped around her shoulders. It smelled of pipe tobacco and soap, and a trace of vinegar. How apt, the vinegar, because perhaps the doctor drank it, which could explain a great deal, she thought, restraining a bizarre impulse to giggle.

"Travis said you weren't to move either of your arms until he'd had a chance to look at them," Rhys told her. "You might have injured your shoulders climbing from the building, to say nothing of hitting the ground. And you're still bleeding. So I doubt you want to speak to this street urchin."

"I ain't no urchin!" came a startlingly clear voice. "Just tryin' to do the lady a favor-like."

"It's all right," Kathryn told Rhys, grateful that the coughing and pain in her throat had eased. To the boy she said, "Please come here so I can see you."

The boy stepped toward her. Kathryn saw that he clutched an object in his hand and was dragging something else behind him by a strap.

When he moved closer, she recognized both objects. "My valise, and my purse too! However did you retrieve them?"

The boy advanced until he stood in front of her, then thrust the purse at her.

Rhys Bevan muttered, "The artful dodger."

"I ain't no dodger neither," the boy growled.

Kathryn tried to take the purse from him, but her bandaged hands were too clumsy. He took a step forward and laid it in her lap.

"I'm very grateful to you," Kathryn told him, "but what are you doing here?"

Rhys inserted, "You said you know this boy?"

"Yes, he was at the Alexandria wharves."

With this the boy began to back away, and Rhys's hand shot out and grasped his arm. The boy squirmed in his grip, glaring up at him, and Kathryn said quickly, "No, don't leave—you must have some payment for what you did."

The boy stopped struggling, and said, "That'd be fine by me."

A sudden gust of wind brought down cinders in a gritty rain, and fire no longer lit the sky. The clanging bells had mercifully quieted, and the crowd noise had dwindled.

Rhys seemed to be waiting to speak until several people had passed, then asked Kathryn, "You saw this youngster at the wharves? When the ships were launching?"

The boy began squirming again, and gave Kathryn a dark look, as if his predicament were her fault, but she sensed that despite his bravado he was afraid. Although she didn't have the strength to figure out why, she could ignore the question. "Mr. Bevan, would you please take some money out of my purse? I can't manage to do it myself."

Still gripping the boy's arm, Rhys said, "Why don't we wait a little for that."

Kathryn, fearing that at any minute she would fall asleep, said, "No, he was good enough to rescue my belongings."

"That's assuming they're all there," Rhys commented dryly.

"Hey, mister!" the boy yelped. "I didn't have to bring 'em here, did I now?"

"No, so why did you? Expecting a substantial reward, I imagine."

"I only done it 'cause the lady, she were nice to me 'fore."

"Tell me what your name is," she asked him, afraid that if Rhys persisted in frightening the boy so that he ran off, she might be unable to find him later.

The boy shook his head. "You don't hafta know."

"She may not, but I do," Rhys responded, giving the boy a shake.

Kathryn wanted to protest, but couldn't get the words out because her teeth were chattering, and she had started to shiver.

"Natty," the boy said sullenly. "My name's Natty. Leave go of my arm!"

"Natty what?" Rhys said. "What's your family name?"

The boy ducked his head and then gave a short laugh. "Ain't got one."

"A name or a family?"

"Neither. What's it to you?"

They all turned at the sound of footsteps. Dr. Travis was rounding the corner of the alley.

"Had a hell of a time finding a carriage," he told them. "Roads have been barricaded because of the fire, but I have a buggy waiting at the hotel entrance."

Kathryn inwardly groaned at the thought of having to

move anywhere. "Can't I stay here longer?" she asked.

"This is no place for a woman," Travis replied shortly, but then asked, "How are you?"

"I'm tired. I just want to sleep."

"Well, you can't do it here. You need care. There are glass fragments in your hands, a wound in your left forearm, you've possibly dislocated a shoulder, and you're bleeding. Or hadn't you noticed?"

His diagnosis presented an impressive array of injuries, but they didn't seem to belong to her. She answered, "No, I hadn't much noticed. Perhaps I'm in shock. I just want to sleep," she repeated.

"He's still here?" she heard Dr. Travis ask Rhys. "What does he want? Money?"

"Please," Kathryn said, "let the boy be. He was trying to help." She did wonder how he happened to be there—how they *all* happened to be there—but she was too tired to ask.

"Just a minute," Dr. Travis was saying to the boy, "Haven't I seen you before? Yes, in Alexandria! So what the devil are you doing here?"

He turned to Rhys saying, "This rascal tried to steal her purse. Right after the shooting episode."

The boy was again squirming in Rhys's grip, and Kathryn tried to struggle to her feet. Her eyes held dull spots of light wavering like dancing gas lamps. The lights dimmed and disappeared, followed by a soft darkness. She was barely aware of being lifted and carried.

Kathryn thought that if her left shoulder hadn't been dislocated before the buggy ride, it surely was after it. Her right hand was now wrapped in a cotton bandage that left her thumb and fingers free, so she carefully reached for the mug of coffee on a low table beside her and took a grateful swallow. Then grimaced at the added dash of brandy.

"Don't fidget," came the command.

She sat propped on a wooden straight chair in a small drab

room with rather dingy walls but with numerous lamps, while Dr. Travis, seated on a low stool, bent over her left hand, removing glass splinters. She winced as the tweezers nipped her flesh, but it was not as painful a process as she had feared. It had been a different matter when he had cleaned her arm.

"Must have been slashed with a shard of glass," he had muttered. "You're fortunate it didn't do permanent damage. Do you need more brandy?"

"I need to sleep," she had repeated, determined not to so much as whimper. While he was unquestionably skilled, she decided that Gregg Travis lacked much in the way of a bedside manner—which hardly came as a surprise. Perhaps lack of sympathy was a requirement for an army surgeon. Her mind wandered as she watched with detached interest while he sutured the edges of the wound. The brandy worked wonders as an anesthetic. And she had to concede he worked swiftly and surely.

"You have a high tolerance for pain," he had commented.

Kathryn had refrained from explaining that pride often overrode pain.

And now, as he bent over her hand, probing at it, she thought he resembled a large malevolent bird, the rumpled black hair swinging over his forehead as shiny as raven feathers.

Her mind wandered again, and she murmured, " 'Take thy beak from out my heart and take thy form from off my door—' "

" 'Quoth the Raven, Nevermore,' " he finished, not pausing in his work.

Had he really said that, or had it been the brandy?

She straightened her spine and asked, "Did Mr. Bevan say when he would be back from Treasury?"

"He's back now."

"I'd like to see him—and the boy. Where are they?"

"In a room across the hall. I thought you wanted to sleep."

"I'd like to see Rhys Bevan," she persisted.

He made an exasperated sound. "Not yet! You know, I fail to understand, Miss Llyr, how one rather fragile-looking female can so frequently find herself in so much peril. First you are shot at, then you are forced to abandon, by acrobatics, a burning building. Were you born under an evil star, or . . . ?"

His voice broke off as he extracted another sliver of glass.

Kathryn knew she was gaping at him, but she had never been asked such a thing. Was he, in his sarcastic manner, making fun of her? Or did he, by some wild stretch of the imagination, think he was being humorous? *An evil star?* The brandy had undoubtedly made her light-headed—wine was the strongest spirits she had ever drank—and she supposed she shouldn't say anything at all, but it seemed impossible to stop herself. Mimicking the actor Edwin Booth, whom she had seen in New York, she quoted gravely, "The fault, Dr. Travis, lies not in our stars but in ourselves."

His head came up with a start, and he was smiling. It was a handsome, non-sardonic, genuine-looking smile. He had very white teeth.

"Calling on Shakespeare and Poe, and both in one night?" he said, still smiling.

"It's the influence of my evil star," she replied. "Or too much brandy, and I shouldn't have any more. I still want to see Mr. Bevan and the boy. Do I need to scream?"

His smile vanished, and he got to his feet. "That won't be necessary," he said curtly. "Since you had said you were shy, I was trying to spare you embarrassment. I had thought, mistakenly, that you might prefer undergoing this discomfort without an audience. I'll fetch them—just don't tell me again that you are shy!"

He was gone before Kathryn could respond. But what would she have said? He was, after all, partly correct; she did respond to him very differently from anyone else she could recall. Perhaps he and she were one of those unfortunate combinations that brought out the worst in each other.

When Rhys Bevan entered the room, he was pulling the clearly reluctant boy after him. Dr. Travis, without a word, returned to the stool, picked up his forceps and resumed probing.

"Lady," said the boy immediately, "would ya tell this here gorilla to lemme go?"

Kathryn swallowed hard against laughter. It must be the brandy. Or gathering hysteria. She had to collect herself, because in the past hour she had given much thought to the boy's unexpected appearance in Washington, and she had some questions. Drawing a deep breath—which brought a scowl from Dr. Travis—she concentrated on what she wanted to know.

"Mr. Bevan does not in the least resemble a gorilla," she said. "Now . . . Natty, is it?"

When the boy grudgingly nodded, she went on, "Natty, how did you come to be in the street outside the boarding-house?"

"I've asked him that repeatedly," Rhys said. "He won't answer, at least not truthfully."

Natty sent him a glowering look and folded his arms imperiously across his thin chest.

"Are you all right?" Rhys added, gesturing toward her arm.

"Yes, I'm fine," she answered, receiving a sharp glance from the doctor. "Mr. Bevan, did you give Natty some money as I asked?"

"No!" Natty answered with vigor. "He didn't give me nothin' but questions."

"I promise you will have your reward," Kathryn told him, "but Natty, I hope you can shed some light on a few things. For example, someone deliberately set that boardinghouse fire."

This statement was greeted by three incredulous stares.

But she saw that their incredulity did not stem from the same source.

Rhys Bevan recovered first, saying, "Are you certain?"

At least he did not look disbelieving, as did Dr. Travis, and after Natty's initial reaction, he didn't continue to exhibit surprise.

"I'm absolutely certain," she answered, aware the boy was glancing sideways at her. What did he know? Something, she was almost sure.

Rhys asked, "How can you be sure it was deliberate?"

Kathryn related the incidents leading up to her discovery of the flames in the hallway. "Although I can't think why *I* would be the object of something like that," she finished, looking straight at Rhys Bevan to let him know she would say nothing about Bronwen's activities.

Dr. Travis had stopped what he was doing. "You said you didn't know why someone would want to shoot you, either," he commented. "Which, incidentally, I still don't believe."

"Dr. Travis," Kathryn said, deciding it was brandy that allowed her to be so bold, "why were you at the Alexandria wharves? And why were you at the fire?"

This was met by silence until Rhys Bevan said, "I can answer the second part of that. After I left you at the boardinghouse last night, I went back to Treasury, and traced the doctor through the War Department's Medical Bureau records."

He gave Kathryn a long look, and she nodded. So Rhys was satisfied that Gregg Travis was indeed a *bona fide* doctor. By this time she could have told him that herself. Dr. Travis obviously knew now that Rhys was with Treasury, but with its detective unit?

"I sent word that I wanted to see him," Rhys continued, "and we met shortly after that at the Red Horse Tavern."

Kathryn glanced at Dr. Travis, who had apparently at last completed his surgery. He got off the stool and went to a small cabinet, while Rhys went on, "When we heard the fire

bells, we went outside with everyone else. Of course I recognized it was your boardinghouse blazing. We arrived there
as you were coming out of the window. Reminding me of
your intrepid sister," he said with a smile.

"I am not in the least intrepid, Mr. Bevan. Unlike my
sister, I terrify easily. And I doubt I would be here now if
she hadn't shown me the way by escaping from her bedroom
on a rope one night."

"Gawd almighty, there's 'nother of you?" said Natty, who
had been staring at her with green-flecked hazel eyes from
under a mop of dirty blond hair that resembled a helmet with
ragged edges. "I seen you comin' down that buildin', Lady,
and it was better'n the circus. 'Ceptin' I thought you was a
goner."

"I did, too," agreed Kathryn, then flinched as Dr. Travis
swabbed something on her hand that smelled like carbolic.

The boy had stepped closer to watch, his expression suggesting that he was fascinated. "Don't that hurt?" he asked
her.

"Something fierce," she answered, batting with a bandaged
hand at her tearing eyes. "Why did you do that?" she asked
Dr. Travis. "I hope it was for good reason."

He gave her one of his sardonic smiles. "No, I just enjoy
torturing patients. Of course it was for a reason. If you're
interested, I'll tell you later."

He seemed less intense now that there were others around,
although he had not answered the question regarding the Alexandria wharves.

Rhys Bevan at present seemed more interested in the boy.
"So what's your excuse?" he said to Natty.

" 'Scuse fer what?"

"You know very well for what. Why were you at the fire
scene?"

The boy glared at him, and again settled his arms across
his chest, and while Kathryn saw his gesture as a defensive

one, he sounded belligerent. "I don't hafta tell you nothin'! An' I gotta a right to be anywhere I wants."

"Fine," Rhys said. "Then you won't mind being jailed for arson."

"What'd you say?" Natty yelped. "You a copper or somethin'?"

Kathryn objected, "You're scaring the boy—"

"I ain't *scared!*"

"—and I doubt it will have the results you want."

To her surprise, Gregg Travis nodded in agreement. He reached into his trouser pocket and extracted a gold coin, then held it out to Natty, saying, "Miss Llyr wants you compensated for saving her belongings, so here's a dollar."

Natty's hand shot out to snatch it, his eyes gleaming brighter than the coin, but Dr. Travis raised his hand above the boy's reach, saying, "Not so fast."

Kathryn started to object, but decided that she wanted the information more than she wanted to interfere. It was selfish, and cruel, too, but she had been attacked twice.

Meantime Natty was sending her a look that said she should be defending his right to the coin.

Dr. Travis said, "If you tell us what you know about the fire, lad, and the shooting at the wharves, too, there are two more coins where this one came from. I would wager that you've never had three dollars—honestly acquired dollars—in your pocket at one time in your entire life, have you?"

Natty did not immediately answer. Instead he turned to glare at Rhys Bevan. Rhys and Gregg Travis exchanged a look, and Rhys said, "All right, young man. Give us the truth and I won't have charges pressed. But understand it has to *be* the truth! If I discover that you've lied, I'll have you clapped into prison so fast you won't know what hit you."

Kathryn thought the threat was excessive, and since she had seen Natty's shoulders hitch, it was probably even a hindrance. She murmured, "Natty, please. I'll be very grateful if you can help us." And sent him a look of silent appeal.

The boy shrugged, "O.K., Lady. But first you gotta spit-'n'-swear you won't let these here thugs put me away."

Kathryn was astonished when amusement crossed Dr. Travis's face. When he saw that she had noticed, the look vanished.

"I give you my word," she told Natty, "that I will try to stop any thugs who attempt to jail you."

The boy looked doubtful, but shrugged again. "Can't hurt none, I guess," he said, then demanded of Gregg Travis, "and I gets the three dollars too, right, mate?"

The doctor nodded soberly, but his facial muscles twitched.

"O.K.," Natty said, "here's the skinny. Yesterday, this hoity-toit lady—only she weren't no lady—gets outta a big carriage on the road, and she comes up to me and says how some other lady stole her purse. The hoity-toit wants me to get the purse back fer her, and says how she'll pay plenty fer it. So's she walks me to the wharves and she points to you," he told Kathryn.

"Natty, I hope you know that wasn't true. I don't steal."

"Don't matter none to me. You wanta hear this or no?"

"Yes, I'm sorry for interrupting."

"So's she gets back in the carriage, and I follows after you. When you goes to stand under the tree, I starts to come up to you, but then I sees that thug with the gun. I thinks I don't want no part of *that,* but by then the gun's already shot off an' you drops the purse and this here gent's got you covered up."

Natty indicated Dr. Travis who, Kathryn noted, had been promoted from thug to mate to gent.

"Go on," prodded Rhys.

"The hoity-toit, she tells me to go fer the purse anyways. So I do. That's it."

"What did this woman look like?" Rhys asked him.

"Like a woman, what else?"

"Can you describe her—for instance, how she was dressed?" Kathryn said. "And was she tall, short, large, small?"

"Nope. Regular. Big huge hat and one a' them stupid skirts that stick out like a beehive."

"A hoop skirt."

When the boy shrugged, she told Rhys, "There were very few hoop skirts at the wharves. I just happened to notice that, because my Cousin Emma—"

"The one who owns a dress shop?" Rhys interrupted.

"Yes," she answered, surprised.

"This cousin came up a few days ago. When your sister and I were . . . we saw a woman with a very large hat and even larger hoop skirt."

Kathryn thought she understood what he was implying. Clearly, given their expressions, Dr. Travis and Natty did not.

"Keep going," Rhys again prodded Natty.

Kathryn listened with growing concern while Natty told of being bribed to follow her back to Washington, and to then report her whereabouts to the woman. So *he* had been the figure she had glimpsed behind the carriage from Alexandria. He had waited outside Treasury until Rhys and she had left, then followed them to the boardinghouse.

"Where did the woman tell you to report to her?" Rhys asked.

"A hotel."

"Which hotel?" his audience chorused.

"I dunno. It's a big one, on the street that's got a number six."

"The National, on Sixth Street?" Rhys asked.

Kathryn realized the boy apparently couldn't read, but he knew his numbers—no doubt learned from the necessity of counting ill-gotten coins.

"Yep, that could be it," he agreed. He went on to say that the woman had refused to pay him what she had promised.

"Made me right mad," he said, scowling. "She tosses me a cent and says 'Go away.' And after I'd a-done all that runnin' to keep up with you," he told Kathryn.

"What did you do then?" she asked.

"Well, I was powerful put out. So's I went back to yer place there, and I was gonna tell you 'bout what she did— 'cause I dint think you was the kind of lady to steal a purse, nohow. And you gives me money when you sure don't had to. Then I sees the fire. I feels kinda bad, 'cause I'm wonderin' if that hoity-toit didn't have somethin' to do with it."

Gregg Travis, who had been leaning against his cabinet during this recital, now said, "Can you describe the woman any better? Beside the hat and the hoop skirt, was there anything else about her you noticed?"

Before Natty could reply, Rhys asked, "Did she happen to walk with a limp?"

"You mean was she lame? Yeah, she was."

Kathryn felt a distinct chill, recalling the woman she had seen at the wharves, the one who had presumably been waving good-bye to a soldier. Her hoop skirt had swung unevenly, and Kathryn assumed she had simply been stumbling with grief. And she had gone to a large carriage.

She suddenly felt exhausted again, and her arm was beginning to ache as the effects of the brandy wore off.

Dr. Travis, with surprising perception, said, "Miss Llyr needs rest. We can cover anything else tomorrow."

"Yes," said Rhys, "and I need to get some men to the National Hotel right away. Miss Llyr, you'll need a place to stay—"

"I have taken care of that," interrupted Dr. Travis, his tone preemptive. "She'll stay here tonight."

"Where's here?" Kathryn asked, although she was too tired to much care. "And what about the boy? He can't be allowed to traipse around at this hour."

"I kin take care of myself just dandy!" Natty announced, also preemptively. "But I want my money!"

Dr. Travis handed him the coins, which the boy seized without thanks. He did turn and nod at Kathryn as if she were solely responsible for his windfall, and it struck her that she had yet to see him smile.

"I need an address for you," Rhys told him.

"Address? You mean where I stays? I ain't got one. But I don't wanna see you no more nohow."

Rhys looked about to respond unpleasantly, but Kathryn sent him a pleading look, and said, "Natty, there are several more things I'd like to know. It's too late tonight, but would you come back here tomorrow? Please?"

The boy shrugged. "S'pect mebbe I kin. Lest I got somethin' more important to do."

He suddenly darted to the door, flung it open, and disappeared. Rhys did not even try to catch him. "I doubt we'll ever see him again," he said to Kathryn before he left himself.

"Where am I?" she asked Dr. Travis, mostly because she was unwilling to leave the chair. She would crumple if she tried to walk.

"My hospital wing. The room next to this one has a bed. You'll stay there so I can keep an eye on that arm."

"Do you think it will become infected?"

"How healthy are you? In general, I mean."

"I'm rarely ever sick," she answered, knowing that the chances of infection were lower for more robust people. "Except," she added, "when being carried through crowds."

He seemed not to have heard and was gazing at her with an odd, detached expression. He unexpectedly asked, "Have you had the chicken pox?"

"Yes, I have," she answered in puzzlement.

"Measles?"

"Yes."

"Diphtheria?"

"Yes, when I was an infant, my mother said. But why?"

"It will take time for you to heal. And Olmsted can't use

an injured woman in the Sanitary Commission."

Kathryn closed her eyes against a spurt of tears. Until now, she had kept herself from thinking about Mr. Olmsted's assignment. She brushed at her eyes with the bandaged hand, and glanced up to find Dr. Travis studying her closely.

He appeared to be ignoring her fight against tears, and said, "Sanitary is converting a few excursion boats to use as hospital ships. Olmsted plans to take them to the Virginia peninsula, in expectation of casualties during McClellan's campaign. Those ships won't be ready for several weeks, though, and by then you may be healed sufficiently to serve as a nurse on one. In the meantime, you can be of help here."

Kathryn's hopes soared, then swiftly plummeted. "I'm afraid not, Dr. Travis," she said, the profound disappointment in her voice apparent even to her. "I have already applied to Miss Dix for a hospital position, and she refused my application."

"I'm not surprised. I couldn't imagine her accepting you."

"Why?" Kathryn asked in confusion. "Oh, my age . . ." She stopped because of his bemused look.

"Was that question sincere?" he said. But without waiting for a reply, he went on, "According to Olmsted, your letters of recommendation are excellent. And you've had experience in hospitals. For my purposes, you have already had the usual diseases—and we know they don't usually revisit their victims. I'm attempting something new here to see if by separating men who are sick from those who are not, we can keep the diseases confined to single wards. Since we don't know the origins of them, it will be a trial-and-error approach, but I think it's worth trying."

His face, while he had been talking, lost the slightly dangerous, guarded look it carried, and Kathryn thought how open and unforced he sounded. The difference was striking.

"Tomorrow," he went on, "you can move to the Willard Hotel—"

"Oh, no," Kathryn protested, dismayed that he would think

she had the money for such lavish quarters. "I . . . I couldn't possibly afford that."

His forehead creased, as if in confusion, and as if her response was something he had never considered. It was, Kathryn recalled, the same way he had reacted at the wharves when she explained why she had given Natty money. She also recalled that he had made mention of a governess. But if he was from wealth, why was he here in this mean setting? In the midst of a war? Why not in one of the sanitariums or health resorts that catered to the rich?

"In that case," he now said, rather briskly as though he had regained his footing, "arrangements can possibly be made for you to stay here. We'll discuss that further in the morning. Are you agreeable, then?"

"Yes. Yes, I am. I'm grateful to be of some use. But Miss Dix—"

"Miss Dix has no authority in this wing. You can learn a great deal here, and God knows we're going to need experience. I should tell you, frankly, that I have been opposed to women as nurses—I don't think most of them have the needed temperament. But I've witnessed your determination, and you also . . ." He stopped, then said as though it were a liability, "You have courage."

He would be disappointed if he believed that was true of her, she thought uneasily. He must be confusing self-preservation with bravery.

"The rules of Miss Dix, as I have said, hold no sway here," Dr. Travis added, his eyes dark with some inscrutable meaning. "Therefore, if you prove you are competent, I am willing to overlook your beauty."

17

It is a double pleasure to deceive the deceiver.

—Jean de La Fontaine

Northern Virginia

Joseph Maddox poured himself another small measure of bourbon and glanced at the seated Bluebell and Vandyke, who were undoubtedly almost as restless as he while they waited for Major Norris. He took a swallow of his drink, and wandered to a window of the otherwise deserted tavern room. It was too dark to see anything but his own reflection.

"It's almost three in the morning," said Bluebell, her tone irritable. "How long does Norris expect us to just sit idly?"

"Until he gets here," retorted Maddox, his temper becoming shorter as the wait became longer. What had prompted the head of Confederate intelligence to summon them to this godforsaken place? What could have gone wrong?

Vandyke was grinding his knuckles in his eyes when he said, "I still can't get over the size of McClellan's operation—he's shipping 120,000 men to Fort Monroe! How does Jefferson Davis think he can defeat an army that big with half the number of troops?"

"With intelligence," Bluebell answered, and Maddox gave her a swift look to see if she was indulging in wordplay. He doubted it; humor was not in Bluebell's makeup.

"In that case," he ventured, "how is the *Monitor* affair proceeding?"

Bluebell shot him a narrow look, answering, "You'll have to ask Shadow Man that question."

"He's not here," observed Maddox gratuitously, and imagined she was nettled by not knowing the man's identity. Or did she know?

"Naturally he's not here," the woman responded. "*He* at least is engaged in doing something useful!"

"And what is that?"

Before she could reply, the door swung open and Major Norris entered. His face appeared strained, but he would have endured a long journey by train and stagecoach. He glanced around, nodding to the three of them before he rounded the bar and its stools to reach the liquor supply.

While pouring himself a whiskey, he asked, "Colonel de Warde hasn't arrived?"

"Not yet," said Vandyke.

He who makes others wait, Maddox thought, maintains the upper hand.

"All right," Norris said, taking a chair. "I have some things to cover before he comes. I assume you have all been to Alexandria and seen the number of troops and weaponry that McClellan is sending to the peninsula. Which means you must be aware that we have our work cut out for us."

"And then some," agreed Vandyke.

"In the meantime," Norris continued, "the *Merrimack* has been reduced to skulking around the Norfolk naval base. Which means the James River is protected for the moment, but we don't know when the *Monitor* will strike again. *It must be dealt with soon.* When we destroy that ironclad, we also destroy the opportunity for McClellan to use the James in his campaign. He'll be forced to supply his troops from the York River, which limits his ability to maneuver freely, and both President Davis and his adviser General Lee agree that, whatever the cost, McClellan cannot be allowed to move within reach of Richmond. For that reason, holding Norfolk and the James, and protecting the *Merrimack,* are essential."

"I thought the *Monitor* was being handled," Maddox said, "by our absent friend."

"As you know," Norris told him, seeming to sidestep the question, "sabotage attempts at the Brooklyn Navy Yard were thwarted. But they alerted the U.S. War Department, and their navy, so we must contend with increased security in disposing of the *Monitor.* Also, I am reasonably certain that Colonel de Warde, and his colleagues at British Intelligence, have not been impressed by our efforts so far, which may be why we are—"

He broke off as the door opened again and Colonel Dorian de Warde came into the room. Norris, Maddox, and Vandyke rose to their feet; the woman remained seated. De Warde glanced around, gave Norris a brief, but courteous nod, then removed his impeccably tailored overcoat and went to stand at a window. What he might find in the darkness beyond his reflection was an enigma, but perhaps like the hawk, which the slim, elegant man's features resembled, he had acutely developed vision.

The tension in the room rose several notches, which was undoubtedly de Warde's intent.

Norris cleared his throat, but before he could speak, de Warde glanced at the clock hanging above the bar, saying, "I apologize for the late hour." His back was to the room and his voice bore not a trace of contrition. "However, the situation required immediate attention. And I do not trust the telegraph."

Maddox was watching Norris, whose patience was clearly wearing thin.

"Colonel, the hour is indeed very late," Norris said. "Your communiqué indicated that a matter of urgency needed to be addressed. I suggest that we address it."

"Quite right," agreed de Warde, pivoting to face those in

the room. "Are you aware, Major Norris, that at the Alexandria wharves an attempt was made on the life of a Union
naval officer? Or, I should rather say, it was ostensibly a
naval officer who appeared to be targeted. While the attempt
was unsuccessful, it seriously endangered a nearby civilian
woman."

Norris's eyes widened slightly, but he kept his gaze focused on de Warde. "I did not know that, Colonel, but I fail
to understand, sir, how this concerns us?"

"It was one of your agents who made the attempt," answered de Warde. "I know, because I was there."

Maddox stiffened, feeling a trickle of sweat inch down his
back. The stiff postures of Vandyke and Bluebell indicated
that they, like Maddox himself, had not spotted de Warde
on the waterfront.

Norris said only, "Unfortunate as it may be, one must fight
war with war."

"But fight it silently," replied de Warde, whose eyes glittered with an unconcealed cunning that Maddox found unnerving. "When you draw attention to yourself, Major, it can
only alert the enemy to your presence and your purpose.
Espionage must be conducted with subtle stealth and a velvet
touch, not with a sledgehammer."

Maddox gave a short laugh, more from tenseness than
amusement, saying, "Well, Colonel, you should know."

De Warde responded with a disarming smile. "Indeed, Mr.
Maddox, spies have been with us and among us for many
long centuries, and the British, if I may say so, have been
major players in this game for much longer than your young
Confederacy. The stakes here are high for you, and I can
only hope that you are prepared to wager wisely."

Maddox had become aware that de Warde said little which
did not contain some underlying message, and here it was
transparently clear. Britain's recognition of the Confederacy
was essential, as was its military aid, and if this man sensed

a lack of discipline, or an excess of ineptitude, the likelihood of that recognition could be jeopardized.

"Colonel de Warde," said Major Norris, "we have had to accomplish a great deal in a very short time—"

"Forgive me," de Warde interrupted, "but that is precisely my point. Impatience is dangerous. You have already committed several unnecessary blunders due to excessive haste and negligence. For example, the ill-advised murder of two U.S. Treasury agents in Baltimore, stemming from the regrettable Dr. Worth's careless—"

Norris interjected, "Worth is no longer in Baltimore, and will have little opportunity to repeat his error."

"Indeed," said de Warde, his brows lifting.

Maddox saw Bluebell shift slightly on her chair and look at Norris, who sent her an almost imperceptible nod.

"Nonetheless," De Warde continued, "there were also the unsuccessful attempts on the Union ironclad at the Brooklyn Navy Yard. More can be learned by infiltrating the enemy— and you have admittedly made some progress there—than by attacking him. The object of espionage is to acquire information. Allow your military to do the killing.

"But naturally," he added, "there are times when this is unavoidable, as in the case of Pinkerton spy Timothy Webster. When an enemy agent hoists his flag in the air, it may be desirable to cut it down."

Maddox watched Norris as he nodded curtly. What de Warde said was true—if one had the luxury of time. But while Britain had waged wars that lasted decades, the Confederacy would not survive for a single decade if bold action was not taken.

"And now, having said that," de Warde went on, "what is the current situation concerning your ironclad warship *Merrimack*? I understand the Union *Monitor* is roaming the Chesapeake at will. Your friends abroad are watching this situation with interest, as I am certain you can appreciate."

Maddox almost smiled at the man's thinly veiled warning.

In other words, if the Confederates could not remove the *Monitor*'s threat, why should European powers risk their own wooden ships against it? Thus the odd-looking little ironclad had suddenly acquired a strategic importance all out of proportion to its unassuming appearance.

It was sometime later that Maddox followed Vandyke and Bluebell out of the tavern, but he did it with de Warde's insistence on stealth in mind. He did not trust Bluebell, whose inclination for ignoring the long term in favor of immediate action had proven dangerous. Thus he slipped behind the door as she and Vandyke lingered at the tavern entrance.

"De Warde is typically British," she was saying. "Too cautious and conventional by far. He is also contradictory. He talks about subtlety when his countrymen are still waging war in brilliant red coats, for God's sake!"

Maddox heard Vandyke chuckle as he told the woman, "Norris knows that, but he has to appear to play along. We need the British. And events have already been set in motion, so it's too late to stop them now, no matter what de Warde says."

There was a pause before Bluebell remarked, "That Treasury wench is still a danger, however. She can recognize me and must be—"

"You needn't further concern yourself with her," Vandyke interrupted emphatically. "In fact, I've taken steps to ensure that, even as we speak, her threat is being . . . eliminated."

18

Wherever his fleet can be brought no opposition to his landing can be made except within range of our fixed batteries.

—General Robert E. Lee, 1862

Chesapeake Bay

From the minute Bronwen had first entered it, she felt uneasy in the ship's cabin, so close and cramped that it gave her a sense of impending doom as certain as that of a rat caught in the jaws of a terrier. Adding to her unease were the entirely too many unknown persons who had recently boarded the *Alhambra*. At five bells, a contingent of navy men had arrived in several dinghies and headed directly for the main cabin and poker tables; by her labored computation the time would have been 10:30 P.M. Why couldn't ships simply use commonplace, everyday clocks and join the rest of the world in the nineteenth century?

Most of the ship's crew were already bunked, other than those on the first watch, so despite the new arrivals, there appeared to be little activity on the upper deck. This only served to make her more edgy. A small, inner whisper kept telling her that something was wrong, and while she couldn't put her finger on exactly what, she didn't dare ignore the warning. Rhys Bevan had called it a "sixth sense," which was as good a label as any.

Now crouched at the edge of her bunk, Bronwen tried to convince herself it was only natural for her to be somewhat tense, since she was the sole woman aboard a ship composed entirely of men. With the back of her hand she wiped perspiration from her forehead, as the small cabin was becoming intolerably hot. Her erstwhile bodyguards, after consuming numerous bottles of Dutch beer, had long since been sprawled on the floor, snoring loudly. These fine specimens of manhood deeply resented, as she had heard one tell the other, having "to play nursemaid to a scrawny female." As far as she was concerned, she would have been better off without them. Where had Rhys Bevan unearthed these characters? They had probably been rejected by the military.

She felt too restless to sleep here, but what were the alternatives? The ship was lying at anchor one and a half nautical miles above Fort Monroe.

The *Alhambra* was one of three steamers clustered together more for fellowship than protection. They were surrounded by scores of other vessels in the Union flotilla, so many of them that during daylight hours this part of the Chesapeake Bay resembled a floating forest. Before darkness had fallen, dinghies and other small craft had been darting on its surface like water bugs, landing the last of the troops arriving from Alexandria, and ferrying officers from ship to ship. Rumor had it that McClellan was even now advancing on Yorktown.

The day prior to launch, the *Alhambra*'s captain had been informed by Rhys Bevan, in only the sketchiest of terms, that Bronwen was carrying documents to General Wool at Fort Monroe. Captain Pieter Van Lyttle—a misnomer of massive proportions for the more than six-foot, three-hundred-plus-pound seaman—had assigned Bronwen and her bodyguards this cabin near his own. His assignment had been made on the now-proved-to-be-dubious theory that the crew, berthed in the forecastle, would not have access to this section of the ship. But if that were the case, who was parading outside in the gangway? Granted the numbers had dwindled considerably in the past hour.

The *Alhambra*'s Van Lyttle was not a naval officer, but the civilian owner of a Hudson River excursion boat commandeered by the War Department for transport duty. As such, he seemed a trifle vexed at being ordered about like some dockhand by the navy men aboard. Other than this, Bronwen found him to be quite an amiable fellow, and she wished she knew where he was right now. Or for that matter, she would gladly take Lieutenant Commander Farrar, whom she had briefly seen when boarding in Alexandria. She hadn't noticed the lieutenant or his aide since then, but she had kept herself concealed, and assumed that Farrar either had not come aboard at Alexandria or, if he had, was by this hour already landed at Fort Monroe.

She reached for a braid of hair to chew on, before she remembered the awful truth. There were no braids.

In light of the previous day's shooting attempt at the launch wharf, she had been forced, with extreme reluctance, to reach a painful conclusion; the one Rhys Bevan had reached some time ago. How other than by her hair could the gunman have identified her? By stubbornly resisting what now appeared to have been inevitable, she had put her sister in danger. It had been simply chance that while she was scanning the waterfront with her field glasses, she had spotted the man kneeling like a marksman, with the side of his overcoat hanging down suspiciously, as if he had a large pistol in his pocket. Which it turned out he did. When she had blinked and looked again, the gunman was gone. But Kathryn, after responding to Bronwen's frantic gestures, had nearly been shot.

Thus, early on the previous evening, while steaming around the last bend of the Potomac, she had sought out Captain Van Lyttle for advice. He had been highly indignant at the notion that someone had tried to shoot at his boat, and might even do so again.

"My God, we can't have that!" he had thundered.

The captain should have been in the military, because the man had a veritable cannon for a voice. Even when he meant it to be restrained, it sounded like a twenty-one-gun salute. Bronwen, having seen the startled looks cast her way during this conversation, regretted ever starting it. Her instinct was to trust the captain, but she knew this instinct might have become rusty with disuse.

Nonetheless, she had soon found herself with the ship's muscular barber, whose native tongue was French, and with a flamboyant swoop the scissors had descended. Bronwen refused to watch.

When she had finally raised her eyes to the mirror, the first glance told her that she closely resembled the barber's poodle. A second glance told her that it could have been worse. Her hair, deprived of its heavy length, and as if shrinking from the scissors, had recoiled into curls ending midway between her ears and her chin.

The barber, telling her to wait, had gone off in search of a goat. So he had said. Bronwen, assuming she may not have translated this correctly, sat in stunned silence, staring into a mirror that mocked her with the image of an unfamiliar self.

Suddenly, she had the unpleasant impression that she was being observed. Drawing the stiletto from her boot, she slipped off the chair, then crept to the only partially closed door. When she flung it open, there had been the sound of rapid steps down the gangway. She hadn't noticed the door had been left ajar, so concerned had she been with her hair. Another good reason to have done with it.

She had stood by the door until, some minutes later, the barber reappeared, carrying a bucket in which a pale white liquid sloshed. Perhaps the Warren Hair Dye people had in mind locks more amenable to dye than hers—or perhaps they meant milk of the cow rather than of the goat—because the final result looked less brown than it did dark auburn. But the goal had been achieved. She did look . . . different.

Now, as she tentatively fingered what hair remained, an explosive snort from one of the sleeping men on the cabin floor brought her to her feet. Looking different meant she ought to be able to sneak up on deck for a breath of fresh air. Besides, there had been no footsteps out in the gangway for some minutes.

A minuscule porthole opened onto a narrow strip of deck lit by lanterns hung every ten or twelve feet, and its dim light allowed her to find her cap. She clamped it on her head, but since it no longer had to cover a braided mound, it settled over her ears and forehead. After slipping into her oversized pea jacket, she took a few short steps to the sliding cabin door. When she began to slide it open to peer down the murky gangway, lit only by a single lantern swinging beside the companionway ladder, she heard a stealthy pad of footsteps.

She quickly slid the door shut. There was probably nothing to worry about, but the whisper of warning in her head made her cautious. Earlier she had seen that the door latch was inadequate, more for show than to bar entrance, nor did the door slide tightly against its frame. It would not take a genius to lift the latch from the outside with nothing more than a probing length of wire.

She dropped it into place anyway, and stood listening. Once the footsteps had passed the door, and she began to let out her breath, she realized the steps had stopped. And remained stopped. She then heard only a faint click of metal, but it was enough.

Leaping over the two sprawled men, she stripped the blanket from her bunk and threw it over the porthole, plunging the cabin into darkness. She was fumbling her way back toward the door when she heard the latch rattle.

Though it was too dark to see, she assumed the latch had been lifted, and that this was no mistaken entry by someone simply coming upon the wrong cabin. She bent over and withdrew the stiletto, groping around on the floor until she found her duffel bag.

After pulling the loops of its drawstrings over her head, she twisted the bag until it hung down her back; if she managed to get out of here in one piece, she was not returning. She positioned herself next to the stationary side of the door, and gave the nearest prone body a sharp kick in the ribs.

The man let out a groan. She kicked him again.

"Sonofabitch!" he cursed, grunting loudly as he struggled to his feet.

She flattened herself against the wall, and gave him another hard kick, while at the same time stretching out her arm and yanking back the door. She relied on the darkness of the cabin to momentarily blind the intruder, and on the lantern light in the gangway to illuminate him for the infuriated guard.

As she had hoped, the guard lurched forward to grab the figure just outside the doorway, yelling, "What the hell do you think you're—"

His words must have been cut off by a blow, and he staggered backward, grappling with the intruder. Bronwen inched sideways as they wrestled, waiting for an opportunity to slip past them. By now the second guard was on his feet, and the intruder was being drawn into the cabin, making Bronwen jump aside as the bodies merged in a brawling mass. The cabin was alive with movement, and so crowded she feared the walls would give way before she could escape.

A crashing slam of bodies against the porthole wall brought the blanket down over a swirling heap. Bronwen saw her chance, and shoved past them. She hesitated only a split second when she saw something flash in the lantern light, which she guessed was a knife blade, and went stumbling into the gangway.

Her fear had been finding an accomplice there. It seemed to be empty, but the light was too dim to see the far end. She dashed to the companionway ladder and was clambering to the upper deck when a bloodcurdling scream erupted from the cabin.

She cringed, scanning the deck area rapidly to orient herself. When boarding yesterday, she had made note of several lifeboats stowed along the port side near the stern, and, glancing about her with every step, she stealthily prowled aft. Finally ahead of her were the small boats.

Hearing no outcry, she paused to see which one would best conceal her from the deck. A veiling of mist floated around her, and the damp air against her skin felt warm for April. It also seemed eerily quiet, except for a periodic clang of fog bells.

The *Alhambra,* riding at anchor, creaked softly as it rocked on a flood tide, and the water, moving inexorably toward the shore, slapped against the windward hull. Seeing no one, she climbed into a lifeboat that had been lashed several feet above the deck and behind several tall mounds of neatly coiled line. She might be safe there for long enough to decide what to do next.

Off the *Alhambra*'s bow and stern there would be white lights signaling the ship was at anchor, but here, with only a few lanterns, it was fairly dark. She could see nearby ships bearing the same white lights, and through the wispy fog, she spotted in the distance a large block of light, almost certainly the vast citadel that was Fort Monroe.

And out there in the Bay somewhere, too, was the *Monitor.*

When Bronwen had earlier asked Captain Van Lyttle about the ironclad, he told her he had wanted to go aboard for a look at the ship—as did every other seaman—but the *Monitor*'s security had been tightened. It docked for fuel and supplies at night, and other than its trained crew, only naval officers had been allowed to board it for sight-seeing purposes.

Now the men's voices coming from the main cabin were barely audible, and Bronwen could hear an occasional order given, along with the fog warning bells. But close by, a new sound made her cautiously peer over the lifeboat's gunwale to see a shadowed figure walking across the deck. She crouched down in the boat and waited until she could no longer bear the suspense, then rose slightly, the stiletto ready.

The figure, about average height, had paused near the starboard stern, and she saw the red glow of a cigar or cigarette. A minute or two later, a sparking glow soared over the ship's rail and into the water as the figure turned and walked forward. He ducked as he passed briefly under a lantern, and Bronwen glimpsed only a dark, double-breasted frock coat, the long sleeves throwing off a glimmer that must have been gold lace stripes. Something about the sleeves and the fit of the coat bothered her, but she couldn't place it. The *Alhambra* had been boarded by naval officers, so why shouldn't this particular officer have simply come on deck for a smoke? It did not mean that he was looking for her. At this point she began to wonder what had happened in the cabin after her escape; the two guards had been inept and lazy, but she did not wish them ill. It seemed strange that all had been so quiet after that one scream.

With another quick look around her, she sat cross-legged on the floor of the dinghy, and leaned back against the duffel bag wedged between her and the boat, the stiletto gripped in her hand. Staring up at the black sky through tendrils of mist, she tried to figure the time. If close to midnight, the watch would soon change, and that might reveal what had taken place below.

She reflexively reached for a braid, remembered, and felt a sadness remarkable in its intensity. Moreover, if she had been marked *after* her session with the barber, losing her hair would have been for naught. Maybe that was not the case, though; Captain Van Lyttle had made the cabin assignment before her shearing. But there had been the unseen presence while she was in the barber chair. Still, who could have known she was aboard the *Alhambra*? The gunman at the wharf. Who might well have had an accomplice. Or someone either already on the ship, or who had come aboard after dropping anchor here in the Bay.

She jumped at a sudden noise, then recognized the clanging as the watch bell striking the hour, and she counted eight bells. Which meant midnight, the end of the first watch. It should not be long now.

Within minutes she heard the first muffled shouts.

Gradually she gathered the gist of what had apparently been stumbled over in the vicinity of a forward cabin; a male corpse, stabbed a number of times.

Given the knife she had seen, this news did not overly surprise her. The question was, which one of three men had been the victim? Until she knew that, she was not moving an inch.

As shouted bits of information began to filter aft, she was also not surprised when, upon hearing a description of the corpse, it unfortunately more or less tallied with one of her guards. And now she could hear it being relayed that a second male had gone missing. Guess who? thought Bronwen, managing only with effort to restrain herself from plunging headlong into the Chesapeake. If she did that, she would lose her duffel bag. And it was early April, which meant very cold water.

Clearly, she had to disembark this death trap. Hadn't Rhys Bevan mentioned something about not placing her in "excessive peril"? A misleading statement if ever she'd heard one. If she had thought it would lessen her chances of becoming the next bloodied corpse, she would resign. Retroactively. It was just too bad about abandoning her country and her president. Neither country nor president were at the moment in the unenviable position of a sitting duck.

The voices were becoming more distinct. She peered over the lifeboat gunwale to see a handful of lanterns bobbing at the bow of the ship. Undoubtedly a search had begun for the man missing; perhaps he was suspected to be one and the same as the killer. Evidently the whole ship had not yet been alerted, which must have been the way Captain Van Lyttle had ordered it. Surely he could not be in league with the killer. Absolutely not! Probably not. Possibly . . . It was possible.

She grasped at the hope that it was also possible Van Lyttle had deliberately not raised a general alarm, because he was giving her time to flee. But how could she get off this floating coffin? She could see the search lanterns sweeping aft, and whether she wanted to or not, she had to move fast.

Frequently the best course was the simplest one. If Captain Van Lyttle was truly trying to help her, and without exposing her, she might succeed. Otherwise, she could probably count on becoming Chesapeake crab bait.

Glancing around to reassure herself that no one had yet come too close, and trusting that she would still be hidden by the mountains of coiled line, she climbed out of the boat. The duffel bag felt like a hump on her back and was definitely a hindrance, but given its contents, it was a necessary one. Keeping herself low to the deck, and clutching the stiletto, she inched along the leeward side of the ship.

At last she spotted below the dark shapes of the dinghies which had brought the most recent boarders. Tethered to the *Alhambra* with towlines, the smaller boats bobbed gently on the light waves. She crouched down, glanced around her, then tested the strength of the nearest manila rope lashed around a cleat. She might get wet, but that was preferable to the alternatives.

When she cautiously dropped her duffel bag, it made barely a dull thud when it hit the floor of the dinghy. After another quick glance at the lanterns moving slowly aft, she crept back to the starboard stern, and succeeded in gathering up some of the coiled line. It was much heavier than she would have guessed, but the heavier the better to create a diversion. She managed to shove it over the side, and didn't wait for its resounding splash before sprinting back to port.

As she scrambled over the rail, the shouts now coming from the bow told her the searchers were indeed diverted, and she started down the manila line, hand over hand. It wasn't difficult, and she had done this often from trees with her brothers, as well as once from her own bedroom.

For no earthly reason, she had a sudden image of Kathryn standing in her bedroom window, staring down at her sister, her expression one of terror. And Bronwen, for the first time since leaving the cabin, shivered with fear.

She shook off the image and continued on down the rope. The dinghy must be just below her now, riding the water that lapped against the ship. And then, from somewhere above her, a voice came with chilling clarity.

"I think there's something over here!" he called. "Here to port!"

Bronwen, expecting at any second to be caught in lantern light, dropped to the dinghy in the same semi-darkness. While pulling the stiletto out of her boot, she heard a familiar voice booming like a cannon. "No! To *starboard!* Be quick! There's something's *here!*"

Bless Captain Van Lyttle, she thought as the stiletto's razor-sharp blade sliced through the line. Then she and the dinghy were free. After grabbing the oars stowed under the seat, she shoved them into the oarlocks, and began to pull hard toward the shoreline, and the lights of Fort Monroe.

As she moved steadily away from *Alhambra,* she saw more lantern light sweeping its upper deck. The dinghy, though, would be difficult to see with the naked eye. And by the time someone discovered the severed manila rope, even field glasses wouldn't find her, not when she was cam-ouflaged by the other ships at anchor. And if she *were* spot-ted now, she doubted that even the Union navy could persuade Captain Van Lyttle to weigh anchor and steam after something the size of a water bug.

There had been no way to avoid her would-be assailant's

learning that she had slipped away. He would figure it out. She could only hope that he had heard of the cabin assignment before she metamorphosed, tracking her to the location rather than to her shorn self.

But why was someone, or, given the past weeks' events, obviously more than *one,* trying to kill her? To whom was she threatening? The answer must be that she was suspected of knowing something dangerous. Since these attacks had started after her foray into Dr. Worth's Baltimore library, it had to be connected to that, and to what she had found in his files. That was long past, though, and surely the Confederate intelligence network—if it were behind these attempts on her life—must have learned of it by now, and have moved on.

For the present, however, and with no strenuous effort on her part, the flood tide was carrying her rapidly toward the Virginia peninsula.

19

*I will stake my life, my reputation on the result—
more than that, I will stake upon it the success of
our cause.*

—General George B. McClellan, 1862

Fort Monroe

The closer Bronwen had come to it by night, the larger it
had loomed. Now, as daybreak came to the Chesapeake's
western shore and Old Point Comfort, she woke from a light
sleep inside the dinghy to see the massive fortress rearing
over her like a dragon's keep.

She had pulled the dinghy ashore behind a clump of trees,
too tired to worry much about encountering pickets on the
Bay side of the fort. What was there to guard, when the
Chesapeake itself was awash in Union vessels?

It proved impossible to see all of the squatting, masonry
fort from where she was now crouched; it sprawled a third
of a mile over Old Point Comfort. On a lofty pole atop a
central, square structure that might be General Wool's headquarters, the Stars and Stripes had just been hoisted. From a
distance, as the flag fluttered limply in the near-windless air,
it might have been any red, white, and blue combination—
even the Confederacy's Stars and Bars banner—a situation
which had already created dangerous confusion on the bat-
tlefields.

Shining on this flag now with ever growing brilliance, the morning sun rolled upward through the mist like a plaything; the dragon's silver ball.

Bronwen grabbed the duffel bag, relieved that she had kept enough of her wits last night to take it from the ship's cabin, despite the nuisance it had been, and pulled from it her military disguise: expansive fatigue blouse, Federal infantryman's dark blue, single-breasted frock coat, blue kersey trousers, and a forage cap. Not that the cap would conceal much, perched as it would be on top of her head.

She glanced around, seeing no one close enough to observe her, and stripped off the dockhand's garb, one garment at a time, replacing it with the uniform. Shivering in the April cold, she buttoned the trousers that had been taken in but were still too large and which, as she buttoned the suspenders, made her long for food. All she had eaten for hours were a few biscuits of hardtack. Even that small supply was now gone.

The outer belt would conveniently hold her sheathed stiletto. Finally, she hauled the cap down as far as it would go, then stuffed her hair up under it with disgust, as it was just as much trouble, if not more so, than the braids had been. But since the first order of business was to disguise herself, she supposed it provided at least a variation. She should have changed when she had first beached the dinghy, but she had been too cold and exhausted.

After she rolled up her wool blanket, and before stuffing it back into the bag, she pulled out her sheaf of maps, continuing to glance about uneasily, although she assumed that she couldn't be spotted unless someone on the fort was using field glasses and specifically looking for her. Otherwise the trees should conceal her. Most troubling was the thought that whoever had tried to attack her on the *Alhambra* might by now have reached shore. Her assailant could have been almost anyone.

She stood holding the map of the fort in front of her, and

decided that in spite of her hunger, she first needed to find General Wool and the telegraph room. Before starting off for the fort, she looked around again to make sure she had left nothing behind to betray her.

Well, almost nothing. A last backward glance told her she owed Captain Van Lyttle, or some Union naval officers, one small dinghy.

She climbed to the top of an isolated, outside flight of stairs leading to what should be General Wool's quarters, having gotten by the sentry at its foot without a snag. Her disguise must be effective, although security was clearly not an over-riding interest here; for all the ease with which she had passed the drowsing guard, who had merely grunted at her, she could have been Jefferson Davis.

When she had mounted the top step, Bronwen paused to look south-southeast at Hampton Roads, the heavily traf-ficked channel of water running between the mouth of the James River and the Chesapeake. Beyond it lay Norfolk. Three days after Virginia had seceded, a panic-stricken Union navy commander had ordered its strategically located naval yard to be evacuated and burned, a disastrous mistake made starkly evident when the Virginia militia promptly marched in to occupy it. One of the scuttled Union ships had been the wooden *Merrimack,* now risen like an ironclad phoenix to wreak vengeance on its betrayers. Bronwen had learned most of this from Rhys Bevan's peculiar Mr. White, but she never did discover what had since happened to that feckless naval commander. Perhaps he was now sailing the amber waves of Nebraska.

She wondered where the *Monitor* was at present. Rhys Bevan had said to keep her ears open, but so far there had been nothing to hear.

As she moved off the step, a pair of gloved hands reached out and grabbed her.

One hand covered her nose and mouth and because she'd

had less than a moment's warning, the only thing she could use for defense was her brain. The useless thought whipped through her mind that whoever had seized her was good; she had barely felt a brush of air before he struck. Although now she noticed a bizarre, out-of-place odor.

She instantly went limp, and felt his hold on her relax slightly. She lunged forward and kicked backward so hard that when her abrupt release came, she staggered several steps. Without conscious thought, she had already yanked the stiletto out of its sheath, when a sound came from her former captor that sounded like "Sheeshhhhh!"

Even so the voice was all too familiar, as was the smell of chocolate. She whirled around to face him, snapping, "Dammit to hell!"

"So how y'all doin,' Red?"

"O'Hara, you rotten scum!"

"Still think that sweet-talk will get you somewhere with me, don't you? Don't look so agitated—nobody's around yet. I almost forgot what an early bird you are."

To Bronwen's satisfaction, he was vigorously rubbing his shin, but the turquoise eyes were brimming with their usual mischief. She backed up against the outer wall, saying, "Don't come near me, O'Hara. And don't talk. Don't say one single word, you lunatic."

"Red, I regret that your better nature has not yet emerged."

"Don't call me Red!"

"From the looks of things, it's no longer accurate, anyhow. What the hell did you do to your hair . . . sir?"

Bronwen folded her arms, glaring at him with disgust. "That was some smart trick, O'Hara. You almost got served a stiletto for breakfast. What did you think you were doing, coming up behind me . . . how did you know it was me?"

"Now, sir—"

"Stop saying that!"

"Yes, sir! To answer your question, I didn't get to be this

old by not recognizing a body when I see one. Especially a nice one. Sir."

"O Hara, I swear to—"

"You really have to quit that swearing, Red. 'Tain't ladylike." He walked around her with his head cocked, grinning like a blue-eyed baboon, then darted forward and snatched off her cap.

"Actually," he said, taking chin in hand as if he were appraising a horse at auction, "the hair still has some red, and I have to say, it looks good short! Real good. But if you're trying to pass yourself off to me as a member of the opposite gender, my girl, you haven't got a prayer. Granted that I was expecting you." He gestured to the field glasses hanging from a strap around his neck, and twisted his face into a suggestive leer. "Been spying on you."

"What are you doing here, O'Hara? Counting the number of seashells?"

"An unfair gibe. And I'm doing the same thing you are."

"Which is?"

O'Hara peered at her closely. "You still don't trust me, do you? Think I'm Johnny Reb in sheep's clothing?"

"I don't know what you are."

"In that case, let me tell you. I'm Rhys Bevan's surprise."

Bronwen felt herself gaping at him. "No!"

"Yes! Assigned to welcome you to Fort Monroe."

"I can't believe Rhys Bevan sent you down here."

"Oh, you think this fort is your own personal property? Can you afford the upkeep?"

They heard the footsteps at the same moment.

O'Hara clapped the forage cap back on her head, then hooked his thumbs over his belt and leaned casually against the wall as several men came up the steps. Bronwen, as she planted her feet and assumed a masculine stance, briefly wondered what O'Hara's outfit was supposed to convey; set at a rakish angle was a dark-green felt slouch hat sporting a saucy feather, accompanied by fringed doeskin jacket and trousers, and intricately tooled leather boots. He looked as if he were attempting a composite of Robin Hood and Sam Houston.

She had an unpleasant moment when she recognized the approaching men as naval officers, and then a further discomfort when she didn't know, as an army private, whether or not to salute. Better to err on the side of vanity, she decided, averting her head to shadow her face, and touching her hand to her cap brim. The men passed without seeming to notice her.

O'Hara was grinning broadly. "If only they knew," he whispered, "what's under that private's uniform."

Bronwen decided the most insulting response would be to ignore this. When the officers were well beyond earshot, she said scornfully, "And who are you impersonating in that get-up? Davy Crockett?"

"Close," answered O'Hara, as ever refusing to take offense. "River scout."

"Why?"

"You never know when the *Merrimack*'s captain will maybe need guidance up the James. In which case, I am honor-bound to tell him that his draft is way too deep. That he'll find himself beached without a chance of avoiding the *Monitor*'s tender mercies."

"Isn't that a little too far-fetched, O'Hara, even for you?" Without waiting for a sassy response, she asked, "Where's General Wool's quarters? Or don't you concern yourself with anything that practical?"

"As a matter of fact, you're almost there," O'Hara said cheerfully. "Follow me, Private Llyr." He turned and went through a set of doors.

"This is probably the biggest mistake of my life," Bronwen muttered as she reluctantly trailed him, her right hand resting on the grip of the stiletto.

A few turns brought them to another door, which O'Hara pulled open, motioning her inside. A uniformed aide seated behind a desk barely looked up when they entered.

"State your purpose," he said in a flat voice.

Bronwen started to reply, but was interrupted by O'Hara's, "We'd like permission to burn the fort."

The aide was halfway to his feet before he began to laugh. "You again, Clancy?"

Clancy? At least O'Hara's choice of name was consistent, thought Bronwen, questioning, not for the first time, whether his surname was really O'Hara, but determined to say nothing that might associate her in any way with this character.

"I'm here to see General Wool," she said briskly to the aide. "I believe I'm expected." She had already pulled a short document from her trouser pocket, and now handed it over the desk to the aide with the raised Treasury seal toward him.

The aide glanced at it with lifted brows, looking at her, and then at O'Hara.

"It's the genuine article," O'Hara replied to the aide's unspoken question. "Now tell me—don't we have the best-looking privates in this war?"

Sending a ripple of alarm down Bronwen's spine.

She somehow kept her stiletto in its sheath, and avoided looking at O'Hara. What was he doing, trying to expose her? The obviousness of his ploy was undoubtedly an effort to mislead her, and instead it increased her distrust of him two-fold.

The aide answered with a smile, "You'll get no argument on that." He pushed back the desk chair and got to his feet. "I'll tell General Wool you're here."

When he went into an adjoining room, he left the document lying on his desk, and Bronwen snatched it up, murmuring under her breath, "That was brilliant, O'Hara. Why don't you have me announced from the roof of the fort? Or, as they say, just run it up the flagpole?"

He leaned toward her saying, "That aide's name is O'Toole, one of me own blood. And almost as important, he's been cleared by the War Department and Treasury."

"As have you," Bronwen retorted angrily, but with lowered voice, "so I don't care if he's been cleared by God
Almighty! You keep your flapping mouth shut about—"

She broke off as the door swung open, and the aide
O'Toole nodded to her. Before she could protest, O'Hara
moved ahead of her through the door. She looked in frustration at the aide, but his response was a shrug.

When she followed O'Hara into the rather small neat
room, the first thing she saw was a slender but imposing-
looking man standing sideways before the window, his hands
clasped behind his back. His features in profile were sharply
etched and patrician, and despite his years he held himself
erect. Brigadier General John Wool was seventy-eight years
old and the Federal army's senior officer.

He turned slowly—a slowness born not of age but of dignity and self-control—and when his deep-set eyes spotted
Bronwen, their color was that of forged steel.

"Young man," he said, the voice commanding in its control, "have you not learned to salute senior officers? Do so
immediately, Private!"

"Ah . . . yes sir," Bronwen said, flustered as she raised her
hand. She did not often fluster, but she was somewhat awed
by the man. She wasn't often awed either. She noted that
even O'Hara for once was silenced.

"Private, what is your name?"

She took a deep breath, by now realizing that General
Wool must not have been alerted to her coming. "Sir, my
name is Bronwen Llyr, and I am not a private. I am not even
a man." She wondered if that sounded too apologetic.

"Indeed," said General Wool. "If not a soldier or a man,
then what, may I ask, are you?"

And now Bronwen caught it; the very faintest trace of
humor in the level gaze.

"I'm in the employ of a special unit of the Treasury Department, sir," she answered, adding, "for intelligence."

"Has Treasury run out of men with intelligence? I would have thought that was more true of the War Department."

She nearly smiled. "I should have said for intelligence-gathering purposes, General."

"Very well, Miss . . . it is 'Miss'?"

"Yes, sir, it is."

O'Hara took a step forward, saying, "Excuse me, sir, but Miss Llyr—"

"Is apparently capable of speaking for herself," General Wool interrupted, giving O'Hara a look that would have sunk the *Merrimack*. "Young man, you are excused. By that I mean you are dismissed."

Bronwen hoped she was successful in concealing her satisfaction.

O'Hara had sense enough not to argue. He nodded politely to the general and walked from the room, leaving the door ajar. Bronwen looked at it, and then with appeal at General Wool. He indicated with a gesture that she could close it, which she did quickly and with gratitude. "Thank you, sir. Were you informed by my superior at Treasury, Rhys Bevan, of my purpose?"

"I was informed. I prefer, however, to make my own determinations," he said, his eyes narrowing. "What do you require, Miss Llyr?"

"I would like to use the telegraph, sir. I need to report an unfortunate incident—one that involved two men sent with me from Alexandria. We were aboard a transport ship."

"How unfortunate was this incident?"

"One might say as unfortunate as it could possibly be, sir."

The white brows rose. "Indeed. Where were you when this occurred?"

"To be truthful, I left the premises as fast as possible, so I can't tell you exactly what happened. I'm not sure I know. But one of those men is dead, and the other, last I heard, had gone missing. Which I didn't think looked promising for my own future."

"That seems a sensible assessment. Be seated, Miss Llyr."

She took the chair indicated, and while General Wool low-ered himself into one behind his desk, Bronwen had oppor-tunity for a quick glance around the spartan room. The walls were covered with maps of the Chesapeake—in fact, the en-tire eastern coastline.

"This incident," said General Wool, "was aboard a trans-port? Was it a navy ship?"

"No, sir." She gave her account as succinctly as she could. His face was impassive, so she could not read his reaction, but while he was clearly scrutinizing her, he did not interrupt. "And this morning," she finished, "I came straight here."

"You rowed to shore in a dinghy?" He had folded his hands on the desktop and still seemed to be studying her intently.

"Yes, sir."

"When did you last eat?" came the perceptive inquiry. Trust a soldier to bear in mind the basics.

"I really don't remember," Bronwen answered candidly, She felt less intimidated, as hunger did after all provide some common ground. "It's been some time, sir."

General Wool rose and went to the outer office. She couldn't catch all of what he said to the aide, but she was quite certain she heard the word "food." Remarkably, she did not hear O'Hara's voice.

When he returned, the general told her, "I have had steak and eggs sent to the telegraph room. The operator there can transmit your message."

Since he remained standing, Bronwen also got to her feet, trying to keep her mind off the forthcoming steak and eggs. "Thank you, sir, I'm very grateful. But with your permission, I would like to transmit the wire myself."

Again the brows went up. "You are capable of operating the telegraph?"

"Yes, sir. I don't mean to imply that your facility is not secure, but the message needs to be encoded. And I'd rather not . . . ah . . . share that code. With anyone," she added, fairly confident by now that he would comprehend her meaning. Whether he would permit her use of his military telegraph was another matter.

He gave a short nod. "I have no objection. Do I understand that you are proceeding from here to Richmond?"

So he *had* known what to expect. She smiled without thinking, but withdrew it quickly.

"It is permissible to smile, Miss Llyr. Just don't do it too often. And yes, I received a wire about you, from someone with rather more rank than Mr. Bevan."

Lincoln, Bronwen instantly surmised, recalling now that the president was said to frequent the War Department telegraph office. No wonder General Wool had admitted her so swiftly.

He said, "I'm to issue you a pass, is that correct?"

"Yes, sir, if you would. I assume I'll have to cross the path of the army—which I believe is advancing on Yorktown."

"That is the rumor, although I myself would not use the term 'advancing.' I am certain the Army of the Potomac will find itself in siege before Yorktown for some time to come, building elaborately engineered fortifications that would be commendable were they not so unnecessary. Thus you will undoubtedly reach Richmond, Miss Llyr, long before the army does. *If* it does."

She found herself staring at General Wool, astonished at his implication until she recalled that by reason of his seniority, he had been due for command of the army himself. And had been passed over in favor of McClellan. Rhys Bevan had said that Wool then somehow finagled to have Fort Monroe exempted from McClellan's authority. Given Wool's age and rank, Bronwen supposed the man could say anything he chose. She decided she quite liked him.

The general reached for a quill pen, thrust it into an inkwell, and began to write, while Bronwen stood pondering the imponderable politics of men.

"Here you are," he said, handing her the document after he had stamped it. "How do you plan to reach the city?"

"I intended to go to West Point to reach the Richmond and York Railroad terminus there. I calculate it's about thirty-five miles up the York River."

"That's close enough. Do you need a mount? I assume you can ride?"

"Yes, sir, and I'd be grateful for a horse."

General Wool eyed her speculatively for a moment, then walked to one of the maps. Although not bearing a great amount of detail, it charted the Virginia peninsula. "Let me show you something, young woman."

He took a long-handled pointer from his desktop.

"Your intended route is here," he said, running the tip of the pointer parallel to the York River. "If I were to make this trip myself, I would go up the center of the peninsula to avoid both the York and James Rivers. Thereby preventing possible . . . interference. I would then reach White House Landing, here," he pointed, "where the York River Railroad crosses the Pamunkey River. From there the rail line runs straight west into Richmond."

Before he had finished, Bronwen was pulling her maps from the duffel bag. General Wool waited until she'd found the appropriate one, took it from her, and went with it to his desk. After a quick stab with his pen into the inkwell, he firmly marked his proposed route.

"This course has several advantages," he said as he handed her the map. "Primarily, that no one who has prior knowl-edge of your intentions will anticipate it. Nor does anyone need to know. It can be arranged for you to depart the fort . . . shall we say, in solitude?"

He fixed her with a long look that told her he recognized her concern about those involved in the *Alhambra* incident, which might even include O'Hara. A shrewd gentleman, she thought appreciatively, and nodded to him.

"An added attraction," he went on, "if you are interested in such things, is that at White House Landing you will go past the house where George Washington courted Martha Custis. Be aware that one of Mrs. Washington's descendants is now in residence there—the wife of Jefferson Davis's chief military adviser, General Lee."

Again Bronwen caught the hint of humor in Wool's eyes. He was probably amused at the prospect of a Union intelligence agent passing this particular house—given what had been Washington's own attention to espionage.

"I thank you sincerely, General Wool," Bronwen said as she folded the map and replaced it in her duffel bag. "I trust I will not get too lost traveling the Virginia countryside."

"Young woman," came the crusty reply, "you appear to be a canny and resourceful lass, and Richmond is not all that difficult to find. The only one apt to lose his way is the Army of the Potomac's commanding general."

20

―――ᗰ―――

Soon after our arrival in front of Yorktown, malarial and typhoid fevers again appeared. . . . I took measures to send to the north those too ill to move with us.

—Dr. Charles Tripler, Surgeon,
Army of the Potomac, April 1862

Washington City

Kathryn, holding an armful of blankets, stood just inside the doorway of a long, low-roofed structure, one of three sheds radiating like spokes of a wheel from Waterford House. The large mansion had recently been pressed into service as a hospital.

At the outbreak of war and the arrival in Washington of thousands of men, the city had one hospital, and since no preparation by the Army Medical Bureau had been made for what would quickly become a mushrooming number of sick soldiers, stopgap quarters had hastily been contrived. Not only privately owned mansions had been donated, or appropriated. So too had churches, hotels, schools, warehouses, and government buildings, including City Hall and the Patent Office.

Most of the soldiers in Washington's makeshift hospitals were casualties not of battle but of disease.

Kathryn was watching young Natty weave his way down the narrow, artificial corridor created by two rows of beds placed with their heads against the wall; all of the beds held diphtheria patients. Dr. Travis seemed convinced the disease was passed by handling articles used by those infected, or by some invisible agent in the air, or possibly both, and Kathryn worried that the boy might contract it. But after several weeks of exposure, he appeared healthier than when she'd first seen him at the Alexandria wharves. He had lost the gray circles under his eyes and was gaining weight, although he needed to gain much more before he looked other than gaunt. She had just sent him to the main house for additional blankets, because the nights were still cooler than usual for April.

When she began counting those she had prematurely stored on shelves, she glanced at her hands, grateful that they had mended so quickly after the boardinghouse fire. She must be in good health because the sheet-rope burns on her palms had fully healed, and so had the scratches from the window glass. The only visible souvenir of that night was the arm wound, still protected by strips of cotton but almost healed. Dr. Travis had said she would always bear a scar, and over time it would become merely a white line. He had seemed rather pleased with his handiwork.

She heard a noise behind her and turned to see Dr. Rosen coming through the doorway. He had arrived from his medical practice in Boston three days before, at the request of Dr. Travis.

"Afternoon, Miss Llyr."

As Kathryn returned his greeting, she saw his gaze go to Natty, just now passing through a door at the far end of the shed, one that opened onto a covered passageway to Waterford House.

"You look uneasy, Miss Llyr. The boy's not in trouble again, is he?"

He had been there only three days, Kathryn thought

bleakly, and already he had heard about Natty. Among other misdemeanors, the boy had stolen food from the kitchen, cursed the hospital stewards, and "collected" money from the soldiers; whenever he went to buy such things as cigarettes for them, he took his "cut," as he called it, off the top of any money given him for purchases. Kathryn found this practice distasteful in the extreme, but the soldiers didn't appear to mind. Unfortunately, some of them even found it humorous.

Natty, when informed by Dr. Travis that he must bathe and be inoculated against smallpox, had refused both; he had then been ordered to leave the premises. Even after Kathryn had begged the boy to submit, he'd loosed hair-raising oaths while the relatively painless inoculation was being given. Only after being wrestled to the ground had he been bathed by several large male stewards, and he now made these men's lives as miserable as possible. Solely because of Kathryn's constant pleas had he temporarily been allowed to remain. Even so, he was on probation.

"No, he's not in trouble today," Kathryn sighed. "At least not yet."

"Well, the day's still young," said Dr. Rosen, smiling. "Do you know where Dr. Travis is?"

"Yes, he was called to the surgery wing a short time ago. For an appendectomy, I believe."

In reality, the surgery wing was a large former master bedroom on the mansion's second story. Dr. Travis had so far been unsuccessful in his attempts to have the surgery relocated on the first floor, nearer to a source of hot water. In the meantime he had improvised a pulley system that lifted buckets to the windows of the second-story room.

"In that case," Dr. Rosen told her, "I think I'll wait a while after he finishes to approach him. He's probably none too happy about being interrupted by something as ordinary as an operation devised a century ago, while he's doing surgery that's more innovative."

As he spoke, he peered around the door of Dr. Travis's

office. The desk inside was covered with papers and books and journals, most of which were lying open, and the bare floor around the desk was likewise cluttered. Dr. Rosen went into the room and stood looking down at the desktop, muttering, "Place looks like a library—wonder if the man ever takes time to sleep."

This was something that almost everyone at Waterford wondered.

As he walked out of the office, Dr. Rosen asked, "Do you read German or French, Miss Llyr?"

"I can manage French, but not German. I know Dr. Travis reads both, as well as Latin."

He nodded, saying, "Gregg reads everything. That hasn't changed since I first met him. Did you know we attended the same medical college in Boston?"

"No," she answered, surprised he would ask. Dr. Travis did not volunteer personal information, at least not to her. He'd barely spoken to her since she had been here, except to deliver crisp orders concerning what he wanted done. Which admittedly was more tolerable than his rudeness in Alexandria.

"I guess you wouldn't know," Dr. Rosen said. "Gregg's never been very sociable, except with his patients. We used to joke in medical school that if you wanted to talk to him, the best way to do it—usually the only way—was to get sick."

Kathryn smiled faintly and supposed she should be reassured by this. Apparently it was not just herself that Dr. Travis spoke to in such a clipped manner, when he didn't avoid her altogether.

"I would imagine he was a good student?" she asked Dr. Rosen.

The man nodded thoughtfully, saying, "Oh, the best. The professors all thought he had a brilliant future in surgery, but as you've likely observed, he prefers diseases. God only knows why."

"Perhaps because they affect far more men than those wounded in battle."

The doctor gave her a searching look, then laughed softly. "You sound just like him. I hope he doesn't have you scrubbing the floor twice a day, since he's become a fanatic about dirt. Thinks there are little creatures scurrying around, just waiting their chance to prey on some unsuspecting human."

"It might explain the constant outbreak of diseases, though," Kathryn murmured, telling herself that she was not defending Dr. Travis, but merely voicing his theory. "Even men who are brought in here wounded become diseased when they're placed in close proximity to others."

Dr. Rosen gave her a reluctant nod. "I have to confess that when I arrived here, the first thing I thought of was a medieval city swept by plague. In those days people just shut their doors and didn't come out until the danger passed."

"And those cities were much smaller than the population that's suddenly been thrust upon Washington," Kathryn quietly pointed out.

"Oh, I believe Gregg's thinking has merit," he said, again nodding. "Here we've been months without a single large campaign and yet a third of the army's sick. It's a mystery to me, though, why the man labors like a demon—he comes from money, so Lord knows he doesn't have to work. He himself paid for the construction of what he calls these 'quarantine sheds' when the army wouldn't do it—did you know that?"

Kathryn had not known.

"Well, I must be off," said Dr. Rosen cheerfully. "Tell Travis I'd like to see him, will you? Nothing urgent, so— what is *that*?"

From one of the beds came the reedy sound of an oboe ascending a scale.

Kathryn smiled. "We have some musicians here."

"From one of the military bands?"

"Yes, they're all from the same regiment."

"And all have diphtheria?" When Kathryn nodded, he smiled. "Gregg must think he's in heaven—bet he's asking them hundreds of questions about what they ate, how often they bathe, was their water clean, where they've crapped . . . begging your pardon, Miss Llyr."

It was, however crudely put, the truth. She had herself written down many of the men's case histories, as Dr. Travis termed them, and they were a large portion of the clutter in his office.

After Dr. Rosen left, Kathryn moved down the center aisle, talking to the men and checking each of them while the oboe piped softly in the background. She all at once had the peculiar sensation of being watched, and glanced around to see Dr. Travis, his arms crossed over his chest, leaning back against the door jamb. She had no idea how long he had been there, or why he was looking at her with an expression she could not have described.

He held her eyes for a long moment before a flush rose in her face, and she looked away. Then, walking past her without a word, he went into his office and closed the door.

Natty rushed in, dumped the blankets on a bed, and stood before Kathryn, rocking on his feet with impatience. "Lady, I gotta talk to you!"

"Why?" Kathryn braced herself for more trouble, and she was unsettled by the intense gaze of Dr. Travis.

"Can't tell you here," Natty whispered. "Come on outside. And hurry up!"

What had he done now? Since he looked so agitated, Kathryn followed him through the doorway. He avoided the covered walkway to the main house and struck out over the grass.

"Natty, what *is* it? What's happened?"

He shook his head and kept walking with determination around the mansion.

"This is far enough," Kathryn said, stopping. "I can't go any farther. What if one of the men needs something?"

"Your chum the doc's back," Natty retorted, "and this is important!"

"What is?"

Natty finally stood still long enough to say, "Lady, that one I told you about? I seen her!"

"*Saw* her."

"That's what I said."

"Whom do you mean, Natty?"

"Her! That hoity-toit—the one hired me to steal your purse."

"What . . . *where* did you see her?"

"Here! Right here! She was lookin' in a window of the big house."

"Natty, you must be mistaken. Rhys Bevan said he went to the National Hotel to question her, and the manager told him she'd checked out."

"How the hell would he know?"

"Please don't curse," Kathryn said, now a mechanical response born of repetition. "Mr. Bevan described the woman to the manager, who said she had registered as a Mrs. Bleuette. And that she'd given her address as Baltimore."

"I don't care what he says, I seen her!"

"I *saw* her—"

"You did too?"

"No, I meant . . . Natty, are you sure?"

"Sure I'm sure! And doncha think it's kinda queer fer a hoity-toit to be lookin' in a window like she was at a peep show?"

Kathryn studied his face, deciding that she should probably not dismiss this. Natty was remarkably observant, undoubtedly a reason he had survived on his own. On the other hand, he occasionally did bizarre things—such as contorting his face like a circus clown—for reasons she'd guessed were to gain her attention. But she had not yet caught him in a blatant lie.

"Natty, exactly where was this woman when you saw her looking in a window?"

"Round the other side of the big house," he gestured, swinging his arm in the general direction, "where some of the regular docs work. You know, like the old geezer who's always gawkin' at you?"

She did know. One of the doctors kept appearing in her wing, and his attention to her was disturbing. "I assume you mean *civilian* doctors?" she asked.

"That's what I said."

Kathryn eyed him suspiciously. "Natty, I had asked you to fetch me blankets, but the store rooms are not anywhere near that side of the house, so why were you there?"

To her surprise, he responded by looking untypically flustered, and gazed down at the grass he was scuffing with the toe of a boot. A new one, she noted. Heaven only knew how he had gotten new boots.

"You haven't answered me," she said.

"Doncha even want to see if she's still there?" he evaded, starting to move away in the direction he had indicated.

"All right," Kathryn agreed, falling into step beside him only because he was so insistent. "But tell me," she said as they walked, "why you were on a part of the grounds where you're not supposed to be, and know you aren't. Natty, I want an answer."

" 'Cause of the flowers," he mumbled.

"What flowers?"

"The yellow ones. They look kinda like one of them musician's horns," he said defensively.

"Horn . . . oh, you mean daffodils?"

He shrugged. "There's 'bout a million of 'em growin' all over that bank. I was goin' to bring you some, is all."

"Natty, that was thoughtful of you."

He looked so uncomfortable she did not say more.

"There's the window," he told her, pointing, "right there. And she's gone! On account of," he said, fixing Kathryn with an accusing stare, "it took us so long to get here."

Kathryn tried to imagine what might lie on the other side of the window, one that looked like many others on the mansion's ground floor. She could see burgundy draperies that were partially drawn, probably because of the bright sunlight. Suddenly Natty dashed toward it.

"No, come back," Kathryn called, fearing the boy would be in more trouble if he were seen. "Natty, you're not going to—" She stopped because it was obvious he was indeed going to peer inside.

As she hurried toward him, he went up on his toes, craning his neck and cupping his hands around his eyes. Then he seemed to stumble backward, which was odd because he was so agile. When she reached him, she saw that his face had paled.

"Natty? What is it?"

He shook his head, and stretched to look in the window again, while Kathryn glanced anxiously about. A cluster of men stood some distance away, but they appeared too engrossed in conversation to notice the boy.

Natty at last said in a hushed voice, "If this don't beat all. It's 'nough to make you fall off the pisspot."

"*What* is?" Kathryn asked, trying without success to pull him away.

When he was silent, she stepped forward to see for herself, but his hand shot out and grabbed her sleeve. "Lady, I don't think you oughta look."

"Why not?"

" 'Cause it ain't a pretty sight."

"*What* ain—isn't?"

"There's a man in there, and he's got what looks like a bullet hole in his noggin. It's that gawkin' doctor—and I s'pect he's a goner."

She had sent Natty for Rhys Bevan, because she did not know what else to do. And since the mysterious woman, who seemed to grow more sinister every time she surfaced, might somehow be involved in the death, Kathryn had thought Rhys should know.

Now, several hours later, he nodded to the men departing with the body, and said to the police chief, "Make sure the corpse is kept on ice until we have an identification."

"You telling me how to do my job, Mr. Treasury Hot-shot?" Chief Duffy said, smiling good-naturedly.

"Naturally," Rhys replied, also smiling. "We have a suspicious death here, and it's very likely murder, since there is no indication he shot himself. It's peculiar there's no next of kin listed on this Dr. Worthington's medical records—which, by the way, I've seen and they appear to be in order. They also give the address of his Washington residence, so that's the first place to look for a relative. The boy here saw a woman outside on the grounds, looking in the window of the room in which the dead man was later found. Of course, she will need to be located and questioned."

While Rhys did not mention the previous episode involving the woman and Natty, to Kathryn's alarm Chief Duffy was beginning to scrutinize the boy with what appeared to be more than idle curiosity.

And now he said, "Hey, haven't I seen you somewhere before?"

"Who, me?" Natty replied, his expression angelic.

The chief's eyes narrowed. "Didn't we pick you a couple times for purse snatching? Shoplifting?"

Kathryn glanced at Rhys. His expression was impassive.

"Nope, couldn't 'a' been me," Natty denied with practiced nonchalance.

"Well, I think maybe it was," said Duffy to Rhys. "Both times the kid wriggled out of our—"

"Officer," Kathryn interrupted, "I'm sure there must be some mistake. The boy lives here at the hospital."

"Yeah," Natty agreed eagerly, "and this lady's my dear old auntie."

"Guardian," Kathryn said. "Also his guardian."

She glanced furtively at Rhys, waiting for him to expose them both, and horrified at herself for becoming a willing accomplice to Natty's . . . misrepresentation.

Rhys, though, said nothing to the police chief other than, "You have anything to add? If not," he went on without waiting for an answer, "I'll begin an investigation of this death straightaway. Any problem there?"

While it was phrased as a question, Kathryn thought that anyone watching Rhys's face would know it was not.

"Listen, Bevan," the chief said, "I got enough on my hands in this town to keep me busy without taking on some doc's murder. You're welcome to it. And to my ice house, too."

He gave Natty one more narrow-eyed glance, nodded to Rhys, and walked off.

As Rhys had instructed, when they followed the litter outside, Kathryn and Natty said nothing while they watched the body being loaded onto a wagon.

When it had clattered off, Rhys said, "We'll go back to the diphtheria ward. Your Dr. Travis seemed disgruntled that you've been 'detained without due cause,' as he phrased it. Very cordial, very accommodating fellow, that Travis. If possible, even more unpleasant than the first night I met him."

Natty snickered, and Kathryn sent him a cautionary look.

"I'm hungry," he announced as they walked past the knots of men gathered to discuss their colleague's untimely demise.

"I'll find something for you to eat," Kathryn told him, although still upset by his fabrication. Natty seemed blithely unaware of anything save his stomach, but she couldn't imagine it was every day he discovered a corpse.

When they neared the shed, the boy said to Rhys, "I bet the hoity-toit drilled that hole in the doc with one of them little muff pistols. I reckon she kept it stashed under that big skirt."

"And I reckon," Rhys replied, "that you'd better watch your step, young man. Lying to the police about your own affairs—such as they are—is bad enough, but now you've involved Miss Llyr. So any more trouble from you, and I'll take action myself. Do you understand?"

"How come she—"

"Do you understand?"

"Sure. How come she'd kill him, though?"

Rhys shot Kathryn a why-are-we-putting-up-with-him look, then answered, "We don't know that she did kill him."

"Yeah, it were her. She's a bad one."

"So you know the difference between good and bad?"

"Sometimes. Maybe she's an ass—"

"Watch it!" Rhys growled.

"Lemme finish. It's somethin' that starts with 'ass' and it ain't my idea nohow. Means somebody who gets paid fer knockin' people off."

Kathryn stopped walking and stared at him. "Do you mean 'assassin'?"

"That's it! Maybe the hoity-toit does this all the time. Could be her proper business fer all we know."

"Now there's an unsettling theory," said Rhys Bevan, and he gave Kathryn a look before adding, "I think you need to be extremely careful. And the boy, too."

21

---

*My entire force is undoubtedly considerably inferior
to that of the Rebels.*

—General George B. McClellan, 1862

Virginia Peninsula

The rainclouds at last seemed spent, and although late-afternoon sunlight filtered through a canopy of trees, Bronwen relied on her compass to assure her that she was still heading west.

Twice, certain she had heard gunfire, she had reined in the bay gelding. The cold rain that had been falling day after day was flooding the peninsula's network of tidal creeks and marshes, and turning the dirt roads into quagmires, thus she had been forced to higher ground. Now she worried that she might have passed beyond the Union army's position. If that were true, she could be heading straight into the enemy lines.

She had assumed that passing the Confederate fortifications along the Warwick River, which cut across the peninsula, would be the most hazardous part of the trip, and while she was now dressed as a farmgirl—despite the gelding from Fort Monroe that only a city boy would take for a farm animal—she had planned to change into Confederate uniform once she had ridden beyond the Union's Yorktown lines. According to General Wool, though, "lines" was not an adequate description of the extensive fortifications and trenches that McClellan had engineered, reinforced by the huge siege guns he had ordered hauled from Fort Monroe. The mud might have slowed that project down, Bronwen guessed, and any trenches must now be knee-deep in rainwater.

For some time she had been riding through a heavily wooded area, and now the noise came again; the crack of rifles. Recently she had also begun to hear what could only be the whistle of shells.

She should stop and take another good look at her map, since there seemed to be more artillery here than General Wool had predicted. With luck, it might be only pickets of both sides firing randomly at each other to fend off boredom. After reining in the horse beside a thicket of pine, she dismounted and stood against a tree trunk to study her map, keeping one hand curled around the four-inch derringer nestled in her skirt pocket.

She had stayed an extra day at Fort Monroe, learning how to use the little Remington pistol with its pearl-handled grip. Both General Wool and O'Hara had insisted that her stiletto was not sufficient. Rhys Bevan had frequently said the same thing and likely assumed she had taken his word for it, but the Treasury-issued revolvers were heavy, bulky things, a bigger trouble than they were worth for a woman; one could hardly wear a holster over a skirt. Not and play the role of Virginia farmgirl, one couldn't.

"I can't figure Wool giving that to you," O'Hara had commented when he saw the derringer.

"It's probably because he's from central New York," she had answered, "and the pistols, a pair of them, were given to him by one of the Remington sons. The general said he had never used them, and couldn't imagine he ever would, but they're deadly little things for their size. Not accurate at much of a distance, although Wool says I'm an excellent shot, O'Hara, so you're forewarned. Keep your distance!"

To her surprise, she had found herself sorry to take leave of crusty old General Wool, but not of O'Hara, of whom she remained suspicious. Rhys Bevan wanted him there at the fort to act, if need be, as a courier.

The faintest whisper of leaves made her glance up from the map. She had been so engrossed in studying it that if the threat of Confederate scouts hadn't heightened her senses she might not even have caught the sound. She tossed the reins over a tree branch and pulled the derringer from her pocket, cautiously creeping forward, and keeping close to the thick pine. A sudden flash of light pulled her up short, and she edged farther into the branches.

Several hundred yards away stood an oak tree, its trunk thick enough to conceal someone, so the flash might have come from field glasses. Whoever held them had just moved slightly, because she saw a swinging fringe of buckskin, and felt a spurt of anger. It was probably O'Hara and, if so, it meant he had been following her all the way from the fort. Worse still was the fact that she hadn't spotted him before now. But it might not be O'Hara.

She dropped to a crouch, and looked around her. If she were stealthy enough, she might be able to circle around and come up behind the man. On horseback it would be impossible to sneak past him, so she had small choice.

She turned and cautiously retraced her steps, then made a wide arc, darting from tree to tree and treading so as to not make any sound, a tracking skill she had learned from the same half-Iroquois man, Jacques Sundown, who had taught her to throw the stiletto. Her greatest concern was that this man might not be alone, but the fringed jacket spoke of a scout, unlikely to have a companion.

And now she caught a glimpse of him, back turned toward her, some distance ahead. He was scanning with field glasses the road she would have taken if it hadn't been mired in mud with ruts the depth of wagon wheels. She moved closer, and then stopped dead in her tracks.

The man was hatless, his glossy black hair falling to wide shoulders. She would know that hair, those shoulders, that stance, anywhere. But it couldn't be Sundown. Not here.

Just as she was deciding she must be mistaken, she spied a black-and-white paint tethered to a nearby tree; it didn't have the same markings as the horse he usually rode, but it was similar. He had always preferred paints.

Bronwen was so stunned, it took her a moment to recognize that she could be in danger.

This man was fast. So fast he would turn and whip a gun from its holster before she could even aim the derringer, not reliable at that distance anyway. He could throw a knife even faster.

Whatever she did, it had to be the right thing the first time out.

She flung her arms wide, and in the most feminine voice she could muster, called, "Sundown! It's me, Bronwen!"

He whirled, at the same time dropping to a crouch, the knife ready to leave his hand.

"It's Bronwen," she quickly repeated. "My hair's different, but it's still me."

She saw Jacques Sundown scan around and behind her, and only then did his knife descend. As she walked up to him, the realization that she had actually, successfully, taken him unawares gave her a jolt of pride.

"Jacques, I almost shot you." She raised the little pistol, unable to refrain from showing him how thoroughly she had learned his lessons.

He stared down at her with flat brown eyes. "Since when're you using a gun?"

"Since I started meeting up with men in woods!"

She cocked her head to get a good look at him. When she had first met him, she'd been very young, and to her brother Seth's profound disgust, she had called Sundown the most beautiful man she had ever seen. Eight years later, he still was. Half-French, half-Iroquois, his high cheekbones and features were clean and strong, the smooth skin copper-sheened.

"Since you're not in the army, Jacques, what are you doing here? Scouting for McClellan?" He had done this in the past when the general had been president of the Ohio and Mississippi Railroad.

Jacques rarely responded to direct questions, so she was surprised when he said, "No."

"No? Then why are you here?"

"Looking for you."

There would be no point in asking how he knew she was riding near Yorktown that particular day; it could be any answer that he might choose to give, reasonable or not, or no answer at all.

"Well, you've found me," Bronwen said, "and since you're so forthcoming, why aren't you with McClellan?"

"You eaten today?"

"That's an answer? No, as a matter of fact, I haven't had anything but biscuits since this morning. Why, do you have some real food?"

"Army does."

"I thought you said you weren't with McCl—"

"I'm not. He doesn't believe it. You can't get through the Rebel lines. Not today."

"How did you know . . . never mind. And I have to get through. Since you always know everything, you must know I need to reach Richmond."

"Can't get through. Ask your friend Lowe."

"Professor Lowe is here?"

"Go get your gelding."

"My geld—how did you know I had a gelding? Sundown, did you know all along that I was circling you?"

He did not answer.

∙ ∙ ∙

It would have been hard to miss the Union army. There were, after all, close to a hundred thousand men encamped. Once she and Jacques had ridden out of the trees to the edge of a huge cleared area—cleared if one excepted an ocean of mud—there were tents as far as she could see. From the looks of the lowering sun, it would soon be twilight, and the men were gathering into their various companies. When Jacques led her along the very fringes of the camp, she kept her straw hat tilted over her face; a woman parading through an army camp was not a smart idea.

They dismounted some distance from the tents, but close enough to one campfire for her to smell coffee and roasting meat. "Jacques, is McClellan here?"

"He's never here. He's at field headquarters. You want to see Lowe?" He walked on before she could answer. The York River appeared straight ahead and due north, and she could see the small village of Yorktown sitting on a rounded hill to her left. Almost directly across the river from the village lay Confederate-held, heavily fortified Gloucester Point.

The Union's huge, nine-ton seacoast mortars had been placed southeast of Yorktown, the batteries manned by soldiers who ambled back and forth companionably behind the guns. Occasionally a shell would come whistling over the water, but other than making the men glance up, the shells did not seem to gather much attention. One had the sense, Bronwen thought, that both armies had settled in, resigned to being here for some time.

She saw the grounded balloon *Intrepid* before she spotted Professor Lowe. A portable gas generator freed him from city gas sources, and the generated hydrogen had even greater lifting power than the coal gas he had used when Bronwen had ridden with him a year before.

Lowe was poking the balloon, probably testing the amount of gas in it, when she walked up to him. As usual, he looked elegant in high cavalry boots and long, light-colored smock coat. His hair was a sleek dark cap, and his blue, deep-set eyes glittered when she hailed him.

"My dear Miss Llyr, a pleasure to see you again. I had heard you were coming. As always you are most beautiful," he said, smiling and bending over her extended hand.

"How did you hear I was arriving?" Bronwen asked, deciding her shorn hair must be a total failure as disguise.

"A wire from Fort Monroe. Your friend Mr. Sundown told me."

She sent Jacques a black look. So he *had* known to expect her.

"Have you been aloft?" she asked, gesturing to the *Intrepid.*

"Alas, the rain has so far prevented all but two ascensions," he answered. "And the trees make it difficult to see for any distance, so it has been impossible to estimate the enemy's numbers. I believe they are fewer than the general fears, but once we move forward it may be easier to see."

Lowe was such an optimist. Even if she told him that her maps indicated still more woods ahead, it wouldn't discourage him.

The smell of roasting meat was making her mouth water, and she took leave of Lowe to follow Sundown toward the horses. "Jacques, is there somewhere I can change my clothes?"

"No. Stay the way you are."

"Why?"

"You won't be here long. As soon as it's dark enough, we leave."

"Leave for where? How?"

"The river, but don't talk about it. Not to anyone." He turned to stare at her as if sensing her bewilderment. "You hear me?"

"Yes, not to anyone."

It would be futile to press him for more explanation, but did he think McClellan would try to keep him from leaving?

Surely even the general could not interfere with a civilian scout.

Then he volunteered, "There's someone here wants to see you."

"Was an announcement that I was coming made with Lowe's megaphone?" she asked irritably. "Is there anyone who *doesn't* know I'm here?"

"Everyone you're worried about knows it."

"Meaning Allan Pinkerton?"

"Meaning him."

"How—oh, the telegraph. I need to avoid Pinkerton."

"He's not in camp now. Get some food."

They rode for some time in the gathering twilight before Bronwen saw a large farmhouse. It must be headquarters, she decided, as Jacques rode toward it, and then reined in behind a clump of river birches, saying to her again, "Don't talk about leaving here tonight. Not to anyone."

"I think we went through this earlier, Jacques, and I heard you then. What are you worried about?"

"You're the one needs to worry. Stay here."

He left her and went toward the house, passing a wide front porch where several officers sat smoking, then climbed steps to reach another, smaller porch. This porch held two wooden reels of telegraph wire. The reels resembled enormous spools of thread, usually moved by wagon, or on the backs of mules, while the wire unwound behind the marching army like a trailing black snake.

Jacques emerged a few minutes later with a man in a private's uniform. Neither of them said a word until they had almost reached her.

"Welcome to Camp Muddy," the private said with a smile, his voice little more than a whisper. Despite his uniform, Bronwen recognized Treasury Agent Ward Nolls.

"What a place to see someone familiar! I didn't know you were down here, Ward."

"I didn't know you were," Nolls said, "until the wire from Fort Monroe came in. Bevan likes to keep us all in the dark."

"He thinks it's safer."

"Well, safe or not, General Wool sent a telegram that he'd given you a pass, and that you weren't to be . . . I believe the words he used were 'detained or molested.' That made certain people a mite irked, as you can guess, but Wool likes to nettle some folks." Ward glanced back, then said with a smile, "Young Napoleon thinks you've come to spy on him for Lincoln."

"And I wager Pinkerton also had a few choice words to offer," Bronwen replied. "Have you been here long?"

"A few days. Sent to keep track of the front lines, and Bevan maneuvered me into position as a relief telegraph operator—smart of him to make us learn to operate that gadget. And by the way, nobody here is supposed to know I'm connected to Treasury. Although obviously Sundown does."

Jacques had gone to lean against one of the birches. He appeared to be gazing toward the river, but Bronwen had every confidence that he was far more alert than he looked.

"That's right," she said, "you and Sundown know each other. I almost forgot, Ward, that last year you were involved in the Oswego River raid. Remember that?"

Ward gave a soft chuckle. "I'll never forget it! You and Lowe bobbing overhead in that balloon—and being used for target practice—while Sundown's riding for the river hell-bent-for-leather with us Treasury city boys trying to keep up with him."

He glanced at Jacques and received a flat stare.

"So now," Ward said to her, "I expect you are on your way to Richmond. Well, good luck! You leaving tomorrow?"

"Have to wait and see," Bronwen answered. If Jacques wanted to keep his exit secret, she wouldn't betray him. "I only hope," she added, "that it doesn't rain again."

"Why do you think we call it Camp Muddy?" said Ward with a quiet laugh. "O.K., girl, I'd better return to my post.

Watch your back in Richmond, and if I don't see you to-morrow—again, good luck!"

He turned and trotted toward the house, and Bronwen felt a wash of relief; she wasn't completely alone, not with Ward manning the telegraph line.

Jacques strode to the horses. "We ride back to the far side of camp, and we wait," was all he would tell her.

The dark had been gathering for some time when Jacques abruptly disappeared. Bronwen felt the night close in, the men and guns quiet other than launching the occasional shell for no reason that she could discover. The swollen York River made barely a sound; it was eerie, the relative silence, considering there were several cities' worth of men on these riverbanks. Her hand was around the derringer in her pocket, and she found the curve and the weight of it reassuring.

Her eyes had grown accustomed to the dark by the time Jacques returned, and she saw in his outstretched hand Seville lumps that looked like charred wood or coal.

"What are these for?" she asked as she took them.

"For you, paleface."

Bronwen laughed softly, rubbing the black dust on her cheeks and forehead until he was satisfied.

"You got trousers in your duffel bag?"

"Yes, Confederate uniform trousers," she whispered.

"Good. Put them on."

While she wriggled into the trousers, he went to untie and unbridle the horses, then prodded them off toward the camp. The air was chill, but not frost-laden, and she managed to button the trousers without much fumbling, stuffing the skirt into her bag, as he motioned her forward. At the edge of the river, and between the trunks of several trees, the canoe was nearly invisible. Jacques scanned the area, telling her, "We wait, but not long."

He lowered himself to the bank beside her, silent as the dark water.

"Jacques, do you really think we can paddle past Confederate troops on both sides of this river?"

"Their lines are stretched thin. They won't be watching the York. It's their Warwick River line they're worried about."

"But some time ago General Wool sent out a man, supposedly a Union deserter, who enlisted in a Southern regiment. And when this man came back to Fort Monroe, he said there were fifteen to eighteen thousand Confederate troops standing between the York and the James River."

Jacques made a soft noise that astonished Bronwen, because it sounded like a short laugh. Since Sundown rarely if ever laughed, she could only assume that the figure was so hilariously low that he had broken precedent.

"I guess that's not accurate?" she asked uneasily, suddenly envisioning millions in gray behind the trees.

"It's close enough," Jacques said, further astonishing her. "Lowe's first estimate came in about there, too. McClellan doesn't believe it."

"He thinks there are less?"

"He thinks there are more. Twice more. He plans to sit here safe for a good long time."

"I doubt Lincoln will be happy about that."

"Richmond and the Confederate troops will be."

"Is that why you're leaving?"

"By the time McClellan maybe gets a fire built in his belly," he said, "there'll be almost as many Confederate troops down here as he guesses there are now."

"And you know that there aren't?"

"Watched a Confederate general march the same men in a circle through the trees, back and forth in front of the Union army for a couple days. McClellan thinks he's outnumbered two to one."

Jacques gazed out at the water, and Bronwen could hear bitterness when he said, "War might have been over in a month. Now it won't. South will figure if McClellan can't take Richmond with all this force, they can hold out and beat him. Maybe they can. Before that, lot of men are going to die who don't need to. On both sides. Why stay and watch that."

Since it had not been a question, Bronwen said nothing. What Jacques had said scared her. It had not seriously occurred to her that the North could lose this fight. Jacques must be wrong.

"So where are you going now?" she asked him.

"West. Maybe find some good men in the army out there."

"Why the army, Jacques? Why not just stay out of this?"

"I don't like slavery."

She thought a minute, then said, "I would guess you'll go back to Seneca Falls before you leave for the West. Please don't tell Aunt Glynis what I'm involved in, O.K.? She'll only worry. Just tell her I'm all right?"

"I'll tell her. Might even be true."

The number of campfires up the river had dwindled to only a few when Jacques said, "Time to leave."

He got to his feet and told her, "We've got a ways to go, up the York to where it forks. South fork is the Pamunkey River. West Point's there. Railroad's there too, and it goes into Richmond."

He waited until Bronwen nodded. Her map indicated that West Point was close to thirty miles northwest, and a long pull by canoe. Longer, she figured, if it rained again.

"O.K.," Jacques said. "Don't talk. Sound travels over water."

She crawled into the bow of the canoe and stowed her duffel bag before she picked up a paddle. After Jacques pushed the canoe into the water, he leaped lightly into it, and they glided out into the river.

He didn't need to tell her not to talk, Bronwen thought, because she was too nervous to open her mouth. All those Confederate troops were just ahead, and the dark water flow-ing toward the Chesapeake would work against the canoe's passage.

For a time she wondered if they were making any headway, but then saw dots of light on the elevated Confederate outpost at Gloucester Point. This would be the most dangerous part, because the York narrowed here, and both shores were clearly visible. But although batteries of heavy guns stood above, who of the gunners could see one small canoe? Who would even be looking for it? No one could know she was here, but she remembered she had thought that before.

Her sense of foreboding was strong as a pale moon slipped from the clouds, outlining the rounded hills of Yorktown and the Confederate camps. Then she heard the whistle of a shell.

It sounded like a bee buzzing, and Jacques obviously heard it too, because when she turned to look at him, the paddle was motionless in his hands. Bronwen heard a report, then a splash, almost at the same time—she could hardly have said which came first. And it might have been just a random shot.

Jacques had resumed paddling almost immediately, the flat blade dipping and swinging rhythmically with his powerful strokes. Bronwen shivered, then bent to her own paddle. A minute or two later, the same sounds repeated. The most unnerving aspect, after hearing the buzz, was waiting for the shell to land.

Jacques was not paddling any harder, so he must not be too concerned. It then occurred to Bronwen that Jacques never seemed concerned. The entire Confederate army could be standing on either York shore, firing directly at the canoe, and he would not even flinch. A fact that did not ease her fear.

Another buzzing shell struck what must have been a tree at land's edge, because for a few moments the explosion illuminated the shoreline. This random lobbing of shells with the hope that one just might happen to hit a target made it even more chilling to Bronwen. It was so impersonal, a matter of chance alone if she and Jacques were killed. But then, some argued that impersonal was exactly what war had become during the last decades.

"Jacques," she whispered, "can they see us?"

"Quiet."

For the next minutes—at least Bronwen thought they were minutes, although they felt like hours—the shells whistled. As the night became darker, and the river wider, the shelling finally stopped.

The canoe continued upriver, farther and deeper into the heart of Confederate Virginia.

22

—⁓—

Organizations of women for the relief of sick and wounded soldiers, and for the care of soldiers' families, were formed with great spontaneity at the very beginning of the war.

—Mary Livermore, *My Story of the War*

Washington City

Kathryn sat opposite Dr. Travis's desk, waiting for him to finish what he was writing, although he had admitted her to his office readily enough. She fingered the paper on which was scrawled the message delivered to her several minutes earlier from Rhys Bevan's office at Treasury; he had information about Dr. Worthington's death, the message said, and there was new word of Bronwen. Rhys had emphasized that she should not speak to anyone about her sister's assignment, and that it was urgent she meet him at Treasury as soon as possible.

Dr. Travis now looked up at her, put his pen back in the inkwell, and nodded. "What can I do for you, Miss Llyr?"

"I need to leave Waterford House for a short time."

"Of course; you're not a prisoner here; but why?"

She watched his jaw tighten as she told him.

"No, I think not," he said immediately after she finished. "You shouldn't become any more involved in the Worthington matter. It was a tragic incident, but one that isn't your concern. If Bevan wants to speak with you, he can come here, and I'll send him word to that effect."

"I'm sorry you think you can speak for me, Dr. Travis," she replied, finding the courage to confront him only because, as far as she knew, Rhys Bevan had received nothing else from Bronwen since she had arrived at Fort Monroe. She felt a flush rising into her face and didn't know if its source was embarrassment or anger. It sometimes seemed that she had been angry more often than not since first meeting Dr. Gregg Travis. And now this.

"You are in my employ," he said.

"Forgive me," Kathryn persisted, "but I had thought I was employed by the Sanitary Commission."

"You thought wrong. That's a voluntary organization, and as such does not employ nurses. I assumed responsibility for you, because your injuries prevented you from leaving on the first hospital ships bound for Virginia. Plus I though you might be useful here."

Kathryn knew she must be gawking at him like a simpleton. The money she believed she had been earning from Sanitary had come instead from his pocket?

"I . . . I didn't know," she finally managed to stammer.

"Know what?"

"That I was a charity case."

The legs of his chair scraped across the bare floor as he rose abruptly and went to stand at a small window. His hands gripped the sill as if he were trying to compose himself, and his back was to her when he said, "Miss Llyr, are you always so difficult?"

"Difficult?"

"Yes, difficult!" He turned to face her. "Why do you insist on interpreting everything I say as an insult? I admit that I'm not the most gracious of men, nor do I—unlike your glib Mr. Bevan—have a talent for words, but I've never known anyone else to consistently ascribe to me the worst possible motives."

It took Kathryn some moments to recover her wits. While it was true that she avoided conversation with him, her effort seemed to have been reciprocated, and was not, at least on her part, some form of reproach.

"Dr. Travis, I don't mean to appear ungrateful, but I do not care to be in your debt. I would never have taken money had I known it was coming from you."

"Why not?"

"Because . . . because . . . well, it isn't right."

He raised his hands into the air, a gesture more spontaneous, and demonstrative, than she would have thought him capable of.

"Miss Llyr, you are truly exasperating! I might have thought—I *did* think—that a woman who behaved with such composure in two crises which would have challenged the resources of many a man, would not be so . . . so conventional. Not only that, but you have chosen to enter a field that is traditionally male, presumably knowing that your choice would be unacceptable to most men—especially to physicians, who are notoriously conservative. And now you are protesting because you've been paid for your work?"

Presented that way it did sound ludicrous, Kathryn had to agree, though she wondered why he kept comparing her to a man? She was hardly the only woman who met crises without hysteria, and not the only one to make nursing a choice. Was he really so ignorant about women?

Instinctively she backed toward the door that she had left ajar, realizing that the entire ward behind her might be hearing this. In any event she needed time to think it through. When she turned to leave, Dr. Travis brushed past her and slammed the door shut, then stood in front of it with his arms crossed over his chest.

"No," he said, "you're not running away again. Not until we have this out."

"What out?"

"The reason you persist in thinking ill of me."

"Dr. Travis, I don't think this is an appropriate time or place to discuss something like—"

"Damn the time and place! I want an answer."

"I . . . I can't give you one. But I feel as if you're bullying me, now and in the past. Is that answer enough?"

She paused, waiting for another barrage of words, but he had fallen strangely silent, looking at her with what appeared to be genuine bewilderment. Once again she was trapped by the knowledge that because of Bronwen she could not truthfully explain anything to him. Admittedly, he was not to blame for that.

He suddenly said, "Yes, I was probably too brusque with you in Alexandria. I've thought about it, and believe you had cause to be offended, and for that I apologize. But you must admit the circumstances were, to say the least, peculiar. It was only later that I realized you were undoubtedly distressed over the departure of your . . . your betrothed."

"My *betrothed*?" Kathryn repeated in astonishment. What on earth was he talking about?

"You said you were seeing off—"

"Oh, *that*!" And then, too late, she remembered what she had specifically said that day, and feared her blurted dismissal would only make things worse.

"Yes, that," he repeated. "What you said exactly was that you were seeing off someone 'dear to you.' "

"Oh, Lord," breathed Kathryn, at a loss for words. Curse Rhys Bevan and Bronwen, and the deceptions they practiced with such apparent ease, while expecting others to do the same. She was not good at deception—nor did she want to be. Worse yet, Dr. Travis was clearly making an attempt at amends, and awkward as it was, she could not even accept his apology without engaging in still more deception.

She edged closer to his office window to gaze out, far more disturbed than she had imagined she could have been;

never in her life had she responded to anyone in such adversarial fashion. She thought of herself as being rather passive, and did not understand why she and Gregg Travis produced such heated exchanges. The blame for it couldn't all be hers. He seemed to regard her as a curiosity, as if she were something under his microscope that he had never before seen. Was he simply naive about women—perhaps he'd had no sisters, or his mother had died young? Or did his attitude possibly reflect some bitter memory?

And then there was the matter of Rhys Bevan's continued distrust of this man. She couldn't help but be wary.

But this must not continue. If Rhys Bevan had suspicions about Dr. Travis, *he* should address them, prove or disprove them, without any participation on her part, and without her complicity.

"Dr. Travis," she began, "if I have appeared to be difficult, it's because of circumstances—as I told you before—which I am simply not at liberty to discuss. I don't like the position this has put me in, and it is not of my choosing, but there it is."

"Do these mysterious 'circumstances' as you put it, involve Rhys Bevan?"

"I'm not free to say. You should take it up with Mr. Bevan."

"I intend to do that."

"I must still keep the appointment, however."

"Are you aware, Miss Llyr, that your Mr. Bevan—"

"Forgive me, Dr. Travis, but that is the second time you have referred to *'your'* Mr. Bevan. He is not mine."

He gave her a dubious look, when he retorted, "Bevan has been checking my background with much more than casual interest. I received a wire from a medical school professor saying that he had been questioned. A colleague has been queried about his and my time spent working in the Crimea. Can you think of any reason why I should be subjected to such intense scrutiny?"

Her hands clenched, and Kathryn experienced an irrational urge to pound his desk. This was unfair. She was not in the service of Treasury. "Yes, I can think of a reason. But I'm not—"

"Free to say," he finished, his dark eyes flashing with what had to be anger. And she could hardly blame him.

"Yes!" she answered. "Why don't you ask Rhys Bevan that question?"

"I'm asking you."

"I can't answer."

"Why?"

"Please, Dr. Travis, there are things at work here over which I have no control. And if you dislike intense scrutiny, how do you suppose I feel right now?"

He looked startled.

"Again," Kathryn said, taking advantage of his apparent confusion, "I need to go to Treasury. The patients are settled for the morning, and shouldn't miss me for an hour. I hope I won't be gone any longer."

"Oh, they'll miss you, all right," he muttered. Then unexpectedly he said, "Very well, since you're obviously determined to ignore my wishes—"

"Damnation!" exclaimed Kathryn, and was immediately stricken. "I'm terrible sorry, Dr. Travis," she apologized with abject embarrassment. "I can't imagine what came over me, other than frustration, but please believe I am not at all in the habit of cursing."

She was barely able to credit her eyes, because the man had begun to smile. "I know you're not, Kathryn."

She did not know what to say then, but he added, "Go fetch your cloak. I'll take you to Treasury myself."

"But Mr. Bevan—"

"Hang Mr. Bevan!"

Outside the Treasury detective's office, Kathryn was seated uncomfortably, while Gregg Travis paced the floor.

When the door finally opened, Rhys looked taken aback at the doctor's presence. "Good day, Miss Llyr," he said. "Dr. Travis, thank you for escorting the lady, if that explains your being here."

"Not entirely, Bevan."

When he said no more, Rhys glanced at Kathryn, who could give him nothing more communicative than a slight shake of the head. What could she say that would not possibly jeopardize her sister?

When Rhys gestured that she should enter his office, Dr. Travis said, "I'm coming in too, Bevan. If you want to speak to Miss Llyr in private, you can do it after my questions."

Kathryn watched anxiously as the two men eyed each other, each presumably sizing up the other's resolve. She felt like a deer trapped between two hunters, and would have turned and fled had it not been for her worry about Bronwen.

"Mr. Bevan," she asked, in an attempt to compose herself as well as to break this deadlock, "can you please give me some reassurance that all is well with . . . with our mutual acquaintance?"

"I have heard that the journey begun was completed with the destination reached."

Kathryn sighed with the first real relief she had felt in days, although on second thought, she was not sure she should be relieved. Rhys Bevan must mean that Bronwen was in Richmond, far from a safe haven, and he wore a look of concern. What else had he heard?

"If this arcane dialogue is for my benefit," Dr. Travis stated, "I'll ask my questions, take my answers, and wait outside. I have no desire to see Miss Llyr made more ill at ease than she clearly already is. So, Bevan, why have you been contacting my medical colleagues, my professors, and even my few remaining family members in Boston?"

Rhys gave Kathryn a quick, cryptic glance.

"I have told Dr. Travis that he should address his questions to you," she told him, hoping she would not be drawn into this any further, "since I'm not at liberty to answer them. It has become more and more difficult to keep my silence, and I'm uncomfortable being forced into this circumstance. It is also jeopardizing my position with my . . . my employer," she added lamely, but was at least satisfied that she had managed to say what she meant.

She could sense both men's surprise.

"Please be seated," Rhys finally said, gesturing to several chairs.

"I'll stand if you don't mind, Bevan. And I'd like those answers."

Rhys looked at Kathryn, saying, "You've told him nothing?"

As she shook her head, Dr. Travis agreed, "No, she's said nothing. If this was some test of Miss Llyr's will, or of her loyalty—which is what I have begun to suspect—she has passed it with flying colors. And you, sir, deserve a thrashing."

Kathryn stiffened, but, to her astonishment, Rhys Bevan smiled. She recalled, though, that Bronwen had always portrayed him as being unflappable and almost incapable of being provoked. And Bronwen should know.

"You're absolutely right, doctor," Rhys said, his smile disarming. "I'm afraid I gave little thought to the position of Miss Llyr in this. And you are also correct in saying I've been investigating your background, but you gave me cause—"

"I did not!"

"Perhaps not deliberately. Now, I'm tired of standing here, so I'm sitting even if you don't."

He rounded his desk and seated himself in his desk chair, and Kathryn sank into an opposite one.

"To begin, Dr. Travis," Rhys said, "the night you and I met at the tavern, we had just started to talk when the fire bells sounded. I'm sure we all remember what followed that."

"Go on."

Rhys looked at Kathryn. "What does he know about your sister?"

"Nothing," she answered, "at least not from me."

"Bevan, let's forget the small talk and get on with it," Dr. Travis demanded.

"It is not small talk," Kathryn protested. "It's really the crux of the matter."

"What the devil does your sister have to do with it?"

"Miss Llyr's sister works for Treasury," Rhys stated. "Which means for me."

The doctor's expression changed, a deep line forming between his brows, although whether it was from concentration or from anger, Kathryn couldn't tell.

"Again," he said, "how is that circumstance related to your investigation of me?"

"Dr. Travis, from all I've been able to learn, you're an intelligent man," Rhys said, "and if you would put aside your personal irritation, I'm sure you'll arrive at the connection."

"I'm not here to play guessing games, Bevan, so why don't you just spell it out? If Miss Llyr has a sister employed by Treasury, how does that . . ."

His voice trailed off, the frown deepening. Then, "How is she employed? As what?"

"As a Treasury agent."

"You mean in counterfeit investigation?"

Rhys nodded. "And she's an undercover agent, which means—"

"I know what that means! But since I've never engaged in counterfeiting, I still don't understand your interest in me. Although, I can see now why Miss Llyr—Kathryn Llyr— has been sworn to secrecy."

He swung to look at her with unmistakable reproach. "Why didn't you just tell me?"

"It's more complicated than that," Rhys answered him. "You appeared at those Alexandria wharves at a very crucial time, and while everything else about you checks out, doctor, I still haven't determined why you were there that day. And at that particular moment—"

"Is that a serious question, Bevan? I was checking the medical supplies leaving on two of the transports, that's why!"

Kathryn looked at Rhys Bevan, praying he would explain further, so this issue could be laid to rest.

Rhys said to him, "You were there when someone tried to kill Kathryn's sister."

"Kill her sister? What the devil are you talking about? If you mean that deranged character with the gun, I saw no sister. I saw no other woman at all!"

"Which may be another matter, doctor," Rhys said dryly. "Aside from your being unaware of anyone other than Kathryn—which isn't too hard to believe—the fact is that someone intended to shoot Bronwen Llyr after she boarded the transport ship *Alhambra*. And it was no random attempt, believe me. Although the 'deranged character,' as you so interestingly phrased it, may or may not have been at all deranged."

Dr. Travis jumped on the words, saying harshly, "And are you now insinuating that I hire inmates of the local insane asylum for assassinations?"

Kathryn must have made her distress evident, because Dr. Travis, his tone suddenly much less strident, said to her, "Surely you can't believe I was in any way involved in that incident?"

Kathryn did not believe it.

Before she could answer, Rhys Bevan said, "I was the one who thought you might be. And I suggested to Kathryn that it might be wise to look into your background. It's my business to do that, Travis." Rhys was no longer smiling when he added, "Especially when one of my agents is threatened."

"I had nothing to do with it," Travis again stated, but when he spoke he was looking at Kathryn.

"So far I'm reasonably satisfied that you didn't," Rhys conceded. "But how did you come to be in such an auspicious spot that day, doctor?"

For some reason, Dr. Travis again looked annoyed. "I've said all I intend to say, Bevan. You finish your investigation, and you let me know what you've unearthed. Miss Llyr, I'll wait for you outside."

As he turned to go, Rhys said, "It's not quite that simple, Travis. If you'll stay another minute, you can take Miss Llyr back to Waterford House. First I need to ask her something."

Dr. Travis paused with his hand on the door handle.

Rhys said to her, "Do you recall telling me that you noticed something peculiar about the gunman?"

She nodded. "I couldn't put my finger on what it was."

"Please try again. While I think we may have an explanation soon, in the meantime you might temporarily toss aside any preconceived beliefs as to how a gunman should look."

Kathryn could not imagine what he meant, but before she could ask for more explanation, Rhys said, "I'll need to see you again within the next few days. And you, too, doctor. But not here."

"Where?" Kathryn asked him, by now thoroughly bewildered.

"At Old Capitol Prison."

23

—w—

How joyful was I to be put in communication with what to me was most sacred—Federal soldiers in prison and in distress!

—Elizabeth Van Lew, 1862

Richmond, Virginia

 *B*ronwen paced around the foot of a graceful elm standing at the rear of Elizabeth Van Lew's property on Church Hill. Where the devil was Marsh? According to the note she had extracted from a hollow in the elm, he should have been here by now. She stopped pacing long enough to stretch her arms and flex her fingers, still vaguely sore from the upriver canoe journey of several days ago.

Some distance below Church Hill, which rose in a slope from a bank of the James River, the lanterns of ships on the water glowed as the dusk gathered, as did the gas lamps of Richmond. Bronwen felt a sudden sharp pang of longing for the lights of home. The longing wouldn't last if she could distract herself, but for the moment the ache was fierce.

Where was Marsh?

When Bronwen had reached Richmond, Elizabeth Van Lew had directed her to the attic room of a nearby tavern, where she found Marsh happily ensconced with the pigeons, as well as a plentiful supply of the tavern's ale. They had then sent winging home to Rhys Bevan the first messages with word of her arrival and of the ongoing siege of York-town. Although Rhys was surely already aware of that stale-mate, perhaps he and Lincoln did not know how sparse the lines of Confederate troops were rumored to be, as reported by General Wool's infiltrating scout and further confirmed by Jacques Sundown, and by Bronwen's own observations.

Yesterday, she and Marsh had sent another message, this one regarding the impending execution of Timothy Webster. Which now reminded Bronwen; where also was Miss Van Lew? She should have returned from Castle Godwin prison by this time. Or, if she had been denied access to Timothy Webster, then from General Winder's office.

Suddenly something grazed Bronwen's ankle. Startled, she snatched the derringer from her pocket, preparing to fire, until she realized it had been one of the dozens of cats shar-ing Miss Van Lew's mansion. And now two more cats streaked past her; hunters vanishing like dusky shadows into the advancing night. She drew a breath to steady herself, repocketed the derringer, and again began to pace.

This assignment seemed cursed from the start. Remarka-bly, she had traveled to Richmond by train without mishap, but it could well have been Jacques Sundown's presence at the West Point railroad depot that had thwarted an attack there. Her stalker, whoever he—or they—might be, must have decided to wait until she reached Richmond to strike. Thus since her arrival, her wariness had become an exhaust-ing vigil, and she feared that she would grow careless from sheer fatigue.

This stalker knew too much about her movements. Despite her efforts to ignore common sense, it persisted in telling her that he was no stranger. She had racked her brain for possible clues to his identity; some detail, some small telling thing she might have missed over the past weeks. Despite Rhys Bevan's assertions to the contrary, her suspicion kept return-ing to Kerry O'Hara.

Unfortunately, Sundown was by now on his way west. Bronwen had tried to dissuade him, arguing and finally even pleading, something that didn't come naturally to her and clearly didn't do well, because her attempts had failed.

These had taken place while they waited for a decrepit old train to wheeze into the West Point depot. The last she had seen Sundown, he was striding in the direction of a livery stable where, she would willingly wager, he had found another black-and-white paint horse.

Now a rustle, from somewhere down the long slope to the river, made her drop to a crouch behind the tree.

"It's only me," whispered Marsh, appearing on the slope. "Don't shoot. And don't toss that stiletto either."

"Why are you coming from that direction?"

"Because the city's under curfew and the main roads aren't safe," he answered. "People are already coming into Camp Lee for Timothy Webster's hanging there tomorrow. It will be a party for some of those ghouls."

"No! I'm still hoping that Jefferson Davis will offer to exchange him."

"Don't bother with hope. Davis is making an example of Webster. Wants to be sure any Northern spies get the message—and that includes us, in case you've forgotten. Besides, the scaffold's been built and I don't think they plan to waste that wood."

Bronwen kicked the foot of the tree, and immediately heard a responding snarl. Marsh had yanked a hunting knife from its sheath on his belt, before Bronwen said, "It's just a cat. Look," she gestured to a branch above, where two luminous green, unblinking ovals stared down at them.

"Damn cats!" Marsh cursed. "I'll end up stabbing one yet."

"You do that, and Miss Van Lew will have you run out of Richmond faster than General Winder could," Bronwen warned, only half-joking.

As Marsh returned the knife to its sheath, he said, "Think we should send off another pigeon to Bevan? About Webster?"

"There's nothing new to report. You didn't chance to see Miss Van Lew, did you?"

"She's not back yet?"

"No, and she may be our last chance to find out who that fifth Pinkerton agent is . . . or was."

Marsh, leaning up against the elm, said, "You think maybe he's dead?"

Bronwen shrugged. "If he weren't dead, wouldn't we know it by now? Unless he—" She stopped and looked off toward the river, pondering what she'd been about to say.

"Unless what?" Marsh asked.

"Unless that agent doesn't want to be found. And just why do you suppose that might be?"

"He's scared. Gone into hiding."

"Or maybe," Bronwen said slowly, reluctant to put it into words, although the idea had been with her before she had left Washington, "he could be a double agent."

"That's crazy. Webster's supposed to have hired that agent himself. Why would he—"

"Obviously he wouldn't if he had known!" she broke in.

"But you said yourself that Webster was careful," Marsh argued, and in the dim light Bronwen saw his stubborn expression. She didn't blame him for not wanting to credit this nasty theory.

Yet whenever she had considered it further, it made a terrible kind of sense. "Marsh, think about it. No one knows the name of that agent, not even Allan Pinkerton, because according to Rhys Bevan, Pinkerton has only the initials 'H.J.K.' That is strange in and of itself. Since Webster was too cautious to have hired just anyone, I think it must have been someone he already knew, or a person whose credentials appeared to be irrefutable. Or maybe it was both. I've never been able to accept that Webster was caught because he was careless. The other agents, maybe, but not Webster."

"He was sick. That can make anybody careless."

Bronwen nodded, saying, "But he also might have been betrayed."

Marsh stared at her through the gloom, finally saying, "Well, then, who?"

"If I knew that . . . but I don't."

That wasn't all she did not know. She had been able to accomplish only part of what Rhys Bevan and Mr. Lincoln had assigned her. It appeared that the president's friend Jim Quiller had left the country. If so, his most likely destination would have been France; Lincoln, after all, wanted to know where the French stood on recognizing the Confederacy. Chantal Dupont, her Aunt Glynis's friend who lived a short distance down the James, was acquainted with a tobacco merchant who knew Quiller, and who was fairly certain that Paris had been his destination. Which was better news than the other possible reason for Quiller's mysterious disappearance.

In addition, Bronwen had learned that British agent Colonel Dorian de Warde was now in residence at Richmond's Spotswood Hotel. He unquestionably was dangling before Jefferson Davis the prospect of England recognizing the Confederacy, and promising aid in breaking the Union navy's blockade of Southern ports in exchange for cotton and tobacco and God only knew what else.

She also, not surprisingly, had learned little about the ironclads, other than that the Virginians thought they had a knight in their *Merrimack*'s not-so-shining armor. While there was apprehension in almost all quarters about McClellan's campaign, the general feeling seemed to be that so long as the James River was protected by their ironclad at Norfolk, Richmond was safe. The *Monitor* was rarely mentioned, except for disparaging comments in the newspapers about its humble appearance.

Interrupting her thoughts, Marsh said, "Listen! Hear a buggy coming?"

"Yes, and we better pray it's Elizabeth Van Lew."

They rounded the mansion at a sprint to see Miss Van Lew's black buggy, driven at a fast clip by the woman herself, rolling up the drive toward the carriage house.

Her stocky servant, Jim, a former slave who had been freed by Van Lew upon her father's death, came out of the carriage house to meet the buggy. The small-framed woman grasped his hand and alighted, telling him to go to bed after he had stabled the horse; the horse that Elizabeth said had been kept for a time in her front parlor to avoid seizure by Richmond's militia.

Despite this, and a few other eccentricities, it astonished Bronwen that Elizabeth had succeeded in convincing her Richmond neighbors that she was deranged: "Crazy Bet" they called her. Crazy like a fox, Bronwen thought, and it was on Van Lew's part a highly useful charade.

In the lantern light, Bronwen could see that Elizabeth's face looked drawn, her expression tight with distress.

As Bronwen and Marsh reached her, Elizabeth told them bleakly, "Jefferson Davis refuses to stay the execution. At sunrise tomorrow, Timothy Webster will hang."

Marsh muttered an oath, and Bronwen's hands balled into fists at her sides.

"Did you manage to see Webster?" she asked.

"Yes, my dear, I received permission to see him briefly. I had taken General Winder some of my lemon cakes," she explained with a wry smile. The smile was gone by the time she added, "Poor Mr. Webster's health is shattered and he is in pain, which is not helped by that damp, dark cell he's been kept in. He was feverish, so how much of what he said can be relied upon as truth I don't know. And, too, General

Winder insisted that two of the guards be present the entire time."

She shook her head, making its pale blond corkscrew curls quiver, and then glanced over the dark grounds, saying, "Best come into the house. I'm chilled through and through."

They followed her as she walked briskly to the large stucco mansion, purchased by her father in more placid and affluent days. All three looked cautiously about while climbing the stone stairs to the back entrance, and again before entering the kitchen, wending their way around scores of reclining cats. Bronwen sent Marsh a warning scowl when he looked about to remove one from his path with his boot. His growing distaste for cats must stem from his current post as pigeon-protector.

After requesting hot tea from another servant, Elizabeth led them into the front parlor, where a fire flickered weakly over its meager supply of wood. She gestured to a large sofa that had obviously at one time been resplendent, its velvet nap now worn thin. It reflected the rest of the room, sorely in need of refurbishing and unlikely to receive it in a city whose inflated prices had made paupers of the once wealthy.

Bronwen found it difficult to sit still, but she had learned that Elizabeth would not be rushed. The woman carefully unfolded a red cashmere shawl, shot through with moth holes that made it look as if bullets had passed through it, and wrapped it around her shoulders before seating herself in a rocking chair before the fireplace. She gazed into the flames while Bronwen tapped her fingers on the arm of the sofa in what she knew was ill-disguised impatience.

Finally, after several sips of tea, Elizabeth asked Bronwen, "Does the letter *K* mean something to you?"

Bronwen frowned in concentration. "*K*? As in . . . *killer*, for instance?"

"Yes, I believe so. Poor Mr. Webster, as I told you, appeared to be feverish, but he persisted in mumbling what sounded like 'K,' over and over. He also kept repeating 'money,' as if it were tormenting him, the wretched soul."

"Was this in response to your questions?" Bronwen said, baffled by the two references. But then, suddenly, came a glimmer of understanding.

"At first, I thought so," replied Elizabeth. "As you had directed, I inquired as to the name of the agent whom he had recently hired."

"And?" Bronwen prodded, attempting to veil her eagerness. She did not want to color the woman's recollection, because her memory could be faulty.

But Elizabeth seemed definite when she said, "Mr. Webster became distraught, and I thought he was stuttering when he mumbled something that sounded like 'kay,' and then 'hay, jay, kay.' At last I guessed that he might mean the initials H.J.K."

Undoubtedly Pinkerton's elusive H.J.K.! thought Bronwen in excitement, aware that the others were looking at her expectantly, but she still wanted to avoid swaying Elizabeth's memory.

"Nothing comes clearly to mind," Bronwen told them, also worried that Webster's reason might have fled with his hope of rescue. "Did he say anything else that could bear on this?"

"He did keep talking of money," Elizabeth answered. "I assumed that he meant ransom money, as if he thought that payment of some kind to the Confederacy might win his release."

Bronwen frowned in thought, before saying, "But Webster must have known that money wasn't the issue here, unless he was grasping at any straw. Still, it does seem odd. Did he actually use the words 'ransom' or 'payment?"

"No," Elizabeth said slowly, her forehead furrowed as if trying to remember something vital. "Although . . ."

Her voice trailed off for a moment, while Bronwen felt sure she would jump out of her skin with impatience. She glanced with exasperation at Marsh. He only looked puzzled.

Elizabeth suddenly sat forward in the rocker. "Ah, yes,

now I recall. At one point, Webster did repeat several times, 'pieces of silver, pieces of silver.' "

She had seemed satisfied that her recollection was correct, but then, when she turned to Bronwen, her expression turned doubtful.

She needn't have doubted.

"Pieces of silver!" Bronwen echoed, for the first time in her life grateful for that long-ago, mandated Sunday school attendance. "In the Bible, Christ was betrayed by Judas for thirty pieces of silver. *Betrayed!*"

Marsh jerked forward. "If Webster thought he'd been betrayed, why not just say so?"

"Because, as I surely mentioned, there were two guards in the cell with us," Elizabeth stated with some irritation. "I believe you're right, my dear," she said to Bronwen. "Now do calm down, young man."

Marsh muttered as he sat back, eyeing an approaching cat with a warning scowl, "Or, Webster could have simply meant rich, if he kept repeating 'money.' "

Elizabeth gazed into the fire, and Bronwen wondered if the woman was reminiscing about her father's flown fortune. How reliable was her memory, and could she have been mistaken about Webster's words? But what else did they have?

Unexpectedly Elizabeth offered, "The man did say 'money' many times. In fact, he became terribly distressed at one point, and as if gathering his last ounce of strength, he nearly shouted at me something that sounded like 'hills of money.' "

Bronwen's mind raced furiously, trying to find a connection. Had Timothy Webster, still rational enough to know he was overheard by General Winder's guards, tried to convey something other than betrayal? Or something in addition to betrayal?

Money. The simplest explanation was that he meant money as payment for betraying him to General Winder and the Confederate authorities. But payment to whom? Could it have been to H.J.K.? Surely the other Pinkerton agents would not have been rewarded for something they were forced to disclose under interrogation. It made no sense.

"Miss Van Lew, do you know if since her arrest Hattie Lawton has been allowed to see Webster?"

"General Winder told me that she had come twice. But on both occasions she became so disturbed—and had fainted the second time—that Winder allowed her no more visits. I saw her this evening," Elizabeth added off-handedly.

"You *saw* her? Tonight?"

"Yes, my dear, that's why I was so late. General Winder himself took me by carriage to Castle Godwin prison."

Bronwen felt rather than saw Marsh's startled look, and she guessed what he was speculating about the peculiar alliance between this aging yet attractive woman and the provost marshal of Richmond. Bronwen thought it far more likely, and preferred to believe, that General Winder simply had an unusually keen taste for lemon cakes.

"When I saw her, Mrs. Lawton was severely distressed," Elizabeth said now. "I do fear for that poor woman's sanity. She behaved more like Timothy Webster's lover than his colleague—but she is married, you know, to another of the Pinkerton operatives."

Bronwen knew, and wondered if Elizabeth Van Lew, who was not naive about most things, might actually believe that the one state totally precluded the other. She thought it prudent not to inquire.

"Miss Van Lew," she said, sitting at the edge of the sofa, "did Hattie Lawton know what Timothy Webster might have meant?"

"Oh, my dear, the woman was severely disturbed and not in command of herself, so with General Winder there in the room, I wouldn't even ask."

Bronwen slumped back against the sofa.

Elizabeth, her voice beginning to sound weary, said, "I did receive the impression that Mrs. Lawton believed they had been caught because of betrayal by the two other agents arrested earlier."

"And Webster theoretically should have believed the same thing," Bronwen protested. "So why would he go on and on about something else? His repeated reference to money doesn't make sense in that context."

Both Marsh and Elizabeth were shaking their heads, and Bronwen had to admit that the words of a sick man on the eve of his execution might not be the most reliable. But she knew Webster. He had been too lucid, too intelligent to rave wild gibberish, no matter how ill he was. If he could not be saved from the gallows, someone should at least try to find the meaning of his words—which were possibly among his last.

"Miss Van Lew," she began, "it's been a long evening, and I'm sure you are tired, but could I ask one more thing?"

Elizabeth said graciously, "Yes, my dear, ask away."

"Of the things that Timothy Webster said, was 'money' the most frequent one?"

"Oh, unquestionably."

Bronwen stood up to leave, with the word *money* spinning in her head like the silver coins in the biblical passage of which Webster had spoken. She had to believe that his was not senseless raving, but an allusion made by a sane man.

A signpost pointing to his betrayer.

24

_~m~_

The Shadow cloak'd from head to foot
Who keeps the keys of all the creeds.

—Tennyson, _In Memoriam_

Richmond, Virginia

_T_here was nothing more certain to draw a good crowd than
a public hanging. Particularly the hanging of a Yankee spy.

So reasoned the man who stood at the edge of an impatient
throng milling over the grounds of Camp Lee. The road into
the camp was filled to overflowing, and even the threat of
cold rain couldn't keep away these spectators. The man supposed, with an inner smile, that the Confederate government
believed this spectacle would discourage other potential foes.
Which was nonsense. There had been spies since the first
man walking upright had suspected his neighbors of knowing
something that he did not.

Still, a well-timed execution would be good for public
morale. Reassure the citizens that their mayor, their provost
marshal, and their police chief were earning their wages. It
would also divert attention from drunkenness in the streets,
and from food scarcities and exorbitant prices which fleeced
alike the rich and the poor. And from the much more potent
threat of the Union army, a mere few days' march from the
gates of Richmond.

Now a stir among those closest to the scaffold brought a gradual hush in which could be heard the rattle of a wagon jouncing over a rutted path. This was heralded by shouts of "Here comes the swine!" "Gallows bird!" "Death to the Yankee spy!"

The usual cogent observations, the man thought, still keeping to the crowd's edge, but moving forward to better view the final result of what had been a tedious and occasionally unsafe assignment.

The shackled Timothy Webster gripped the sides of the wagon, swaying on his feet as the tumbrel neared the scaffold. Webster's impassioned request for a firing squad had been denied.

Word on the street had it that Pinkerton himself, together with a member of General McClellan's staff, had traveled here under a flag of truce to sue for Webster's release. A communiqué from General Wool at Fort Monroe had offered generous terms for a prisoner exchange. All had been rebuffed by Jefferson Davis.

The man drew back as the wagon clattered past. Did Webster know who had betrayed him? His own handpicked, experienced agent, for good reason listed by Webster in Pinkerton's records only as H.J.K.?

"Hey, buy some flowers, mister?" came a shrillish voice at his elbow. "Fer a cent I'll getcha a piece of the rope."

The ragged child tugged at his coat sleeve. The man shoved her roughly away, reflexively checking his pockets. He needn't have bothered; Major William Norris's message outlining the destruction of the Union *Monitor* was secreted in an inside pocket of his shirt. And as its courier, he had encoded the message himself. He would leave Richmond shortly, as soon as he finished one last item of business.

He had noted Webster's weakened state, the deterioration of a once-sturdy man hastened by a cold, filthy cell, and his head shook slightly at the folly of engaging in such a perilous calling as Webster's. Ironically, it was his own calling, notwithstanding a somewhat more complicated twist.

Webster under interrogation had not broken. Two of his contacts had, thus saving their own necks by incriminating him. They had not, however, known his whereabouts. Finding him had been the work of this man and the reason for the coin of the realm—the British spy de Warde having quietly added to the prize—which now jingled so lightly in his pocket.

The Lawton woman had not talked, it was said, but she would not hang. For the time being the death of Webster should quiet the most bloodthirsty. Still, the Lawton woman had received a prison sentence that she might not survive, and woe be to any other woman who might venture into the treacherous shoals of the wartime Confederate capital.

The man now scanned the crowd for another such woman—more resourceful and better trained than Lawton. This one had already caused considerable trouble, and the man would attend to her soon, but it needed to be in private. Colonel de Warde was correct about stealth. It wouldn't do to have a beautiful young woman arrested; she would scatter names and knowledge all over the landscape. Arranging an accident could also be risky; she just might escape, as she had done before, which could sever his own tenuous tightrope strung between the two camps. It was a shame that she had to die, because he liked her. But curiosity had killed more than one green-eyed cat.

Now, amid taunts from the crowd, a hood was being placed over Webster's head by a black-robed executioner, a rope then looped around his neck. As the man had expected, the condemned bore himself with a dignity that would have put to shame a less vengeful rabble than the one gathered here. There would be no pleading, no groveling. Not from this Yankee.

The man moved into the fringe of the crowd, keeping his face averted and shadowed by his black slouch hat. He had just spotted his target.

She should not have reached Richmond, but one just could not rely on others to do a job right, he sighed. She had not yet figured out his role—if she had, he would certainly have heard—but she would before long. They had both, after all, been sent South by the same man. She needed to be silenced before he left for the Chesapeake with Norris's message. There was enough time.

Now, with a sharp report, the trap under Webster was sprung. The knot around his neck slipped. When he dropped to the ground, the crowd gasped, then muttered to itself while the condemned man was hauled upright and hurriedly marched again up the steps. Webster's groan was audible, as were his words, "I suffer a double death."

The rope was made shorter. Too short in the opinion voiced by one of those officiating, and Webster answered, "So you are going to choke me this time."

The trap was sprung again. This time the attempt proved successful.

Marsh gripped her arm so tightly that his fingers must be meeting bone, Bronwen thought abstractly, too consumed by rage to feel physical pain.

"You can't stay here," Marsh insisted under his breath as he tried to drag her from a spot near the scaffolding. "It won't do Webster any good now, and it's dangerous."

She stood looking up at Timothy Webster's limp body, left to dangle there, turning slowly in the morning sunlight.

"C'mon," Marsh whispered to her. "Someone might recognize you."

"I don't care."

Marsh said quietly, "I've never heard anything like that from you before."

"I've never witnessed the deliberate, cold-blooded killing of a good man before."

"Don't let it make you reckless. Rhys Bevan would say

you can't get personally involved. You want to end up
there?" Marsh gestured at the gallows.

"Leave me be!" she snapped, and was instantly sorry. The
man swaying at the end of the rope was not Marsh's doing,
and he was right. She was being careless. It had been risky
enough to come, but she could not have stayed away. This
had become personal, and if Rhys Bevan didn't like it, that
was just too bad.

"C'mon," Marsh urged again, and this time she let him
draw her away, with one last glance over her shoulder. How
long did they intend to leave Webster there?

They walked in bleak silence to where Elizabeth Van
Lew's servant Jim waited with the buggy.

Sometime later, on the way to Church Hill, Bronwen
tapped Jim's shoulder. "Please stop the horse."

Marsh began to shake his head, but must have taken note
of her expression and gave Jim a nod. The horse had barely
been reined in when Bronwen jumped from the buggy.
Marsh followed her.

"I want to be alone so I can think," she told him, hitching
up her trousers, but barely slowing her furious pace. She
could not shake the bone-deep rage. It was making her head
pound.

"Can't let you," Marsh objected. "Bevan would have my
hide if you ran into trouble."

"I can take care of myself!"

At least he had the good sense not to respond in kind to
that childish remark, she thought, her gait so fast she was
jogging. The James River was beyond and maybe the sight
of it would cool her head. It throbbed so, she could not think
straight, and something at the edge of her mind, ominous but
elusive, kept slithering away.

They had gone some distance down a path beside the water before she slowed to watch the boats. The slopes across
the river were misted green from the endless rain, and Bronwen turned to look at the hills of Richmond, a city her aunt

had said was one of the most beautiful she had ever seen. It was not so beautiful now, soaked as she saw it in blood.

Marsh cleared his throat, saying in a transparent effort to distract her, "See those smokestacks over there, on that group of buildings across the river? It's the Tredegar Iron Works."

Bronwen, only half-listening, recalled Lincoln's comment about his spy Quiller's "eyesight failing" whenever he scouted around those iron foundries.

"I've heard," Marsh went on, "that Tredegar manufactures half the cannons of the Confederate army. There are more mills and machine shops in those valleys and knolls across the river, but Tredegar is supposed to be the largest. They don't have the equipment yet to forge steel, so the cannons are made of pig iron or bronze. I think the plates for the *Merrimack* were made there and—"

He broke off, because Bronwen had stopped short and now stared at him in alarm.

"What's wrong?" he said to her. "You look like you've seen a ghost."

"What did you just say?" she asked him slowly, her hands clenched in her pockets, her eyes fixed on the far shore.

"I said the *Merrimack*'s iron plates were manufactured over there at Tredegar. Why?"

Bronwen shook her head, a chill creeping through her, and the idea taking shape in her mind making her legs rubbery.

"Just be quiet a minute," she told him, squatting to one side on the path and gazing across the water.

The scattered pieces of the puzzle blurred before they gradually came together. She thought it through at length, before being forced to conclude that she could be right.

If so, she knew who had betrayed the four Pinkerton spies. The one most responsible for Timothy Webster's death, and the murders of the two Baltimore Treasury agents, even if those deaths had not been by his own hand. She did not believe that he could have been acting alone, but his treachery was by far the most despicable. And for her he was the most dangerous.

25

〰️

Come, let's away to prison . . .
And take upon's the mystery of things,
As if we were God's spies.

—Shakespeare

Washington City

"Yep, it's her alright," Natty said. "That's the ole hoity-toit."

Kathryn noticed that his glance, having rested only briefly on the woman, was now darting over the yard of Old Capitol Prison. This woman, whom Rhys Bevan called Mrs. Bleuette, was seated on a bench some yards away, near a handful of men playing what appeared to be bluff poker.

"Take another look," directed Rhys, gripping the boy's shoulder to prevent him inching closer to the poker game. "Are you sure that is her?"

"Sure I'm sure. I knows that hoity-toit when I sees her. She's got eyes like a dead fish, ain't she?"

"*Hasn't* she," murmured Kathryn without thinking.

"You think so, too?" said Natty, giving her a conspiratorial wink.

The boy was knowing, sometimes far beyond his years—whatever they might be, since Natty claimed he didn't know his birthdate—and Kathryn reluctantly conceded that his cleverness was undoubtedly what had allowed him to survive on his own.

The prison's atmosphere, even here in the open, was so foul that Kathryn found it difficult to concentrate on anything other than the surroundings. The smell alone, of unwashed bodies and stinking open sinks dug behind the greasy cook-house, made her think the only way to treat this place would be to flood it with several thousand gallons of vinegar and lye soap.

The Old Capitol had become a makeshift jail, originally meant to house only prisoners of war. It now held a vast variety of inmates, from Confederate soldiers, smugglers, blockade-runners, and spies to Union military deserters and destitute former slaves, and Kathryn found the latter's presence here more grievous than anything she had seen so far in this city. She had heard, too, that Rose Greenhow, before her recent trial and deportation to Richmond, had been imprisoned here, and another notorious Confederate spy, Belle Boyd, had also been a resident.

Although Kathryn had protested when Rhys first insisted on Natty's attendance today, she now decided it might be a good lesson for the boy. If he were disturbed enough by what he saw, it might make him think twice before he blithely went on pilfering.

"Kathryn, do you recognize the woman?" Rhys now asked.

"I can't say. That day in Alexandria, I wasn't close enough to see the woman on the road clearly. I assumed at the time that her uneven gait was caused by grief, but it might have been from an injury."

Dr. Travis, who had been standing beside her, stepped forward, presumably for a better look at Mrs. Bleuette. "I can't tell from this distance either," he said to Rhys, "but didn't you say you found a walking stick and ankle strap in her belongings?"

When Rhys nodded, Dr. Travis added, "If I could get a

closer look at her ankle, I might be able to confirm a prior injury."

"We'll have to go inside for that," Rhys told him, "and I had hoped to spare Kathryn that experience."

"No, she shouldn't be exposed to the cell portion of the prison," said Dr. Travis firmly, and Kathryn was again disturbed by his assumption that he could speak for her. Moreover, from what Rhys had implied, and Natty had insisted, this woman might have been involved in the boardinghouse fire, and in the attempt on her sister's life. In which case, Kathryn would do whatever was necessary.

"I'm willing to go inside," she told Rhys. "And I think it should be done now, because I'm to leave soon for Virginia."

Rhys nodded, his expression grave ever since they had met him, and it made her doubly uneasy. Was he for some particular reason worried about Bronwen?

"Who knows?" he now told her. "It might be useful for the boy to see, because if he keeps to his present course, he can expect to reside here."

"Hey, c'mon," Natty protested indignantly, while edging closer to Kathryn, "I ain't no common thief or somethin', an' I ain't never done nothin' bad 'nough to land me in this rat trap!"

While Rhys gestured to a guard, apparently signaling him to take Mrs. Bleuette inside, Kathryn watched Natty with concern. Was he learning anything? She obviously could not continue to protect the boy after she departed Washington, and if left to his own devices, she worried that Rhys Bevan's prediction would become fact.

They entered the dilapidated building through a set of creaking doors, then passed what appeared to be some sort of holding cell. Its numerous, noisy occupants were confined in this filthy compartment faced with vertical bars. There was little light available, as wooden boards had been nailed over the windows, although a few lanterns had been strung overhead in the passageway. The smell of urine and vomit was nearly overpowering, and Kathryn had hurried past before realizing that Natty was no longer beside her.

She turned around in the hallway to see him standing in front of the holding cell.

"Natty!" she called, although he probably would not hear her over the din. She had forgotten what sharp ears he owned until he half-turned and made a hand gesture for her to go on ahead. Not without you, she thought, hurrying toward him.

When Kathryn reached him, she saw that he was speaking to someone inside the cell. She resisted the urge to turn and flee from the wave of catcalls and whistles her appearance had brought, and grasped Natty by the arm.

"Come along," she said, her voice trembling under the caterwauling.

"Jest a minute," he replied, trying to pull from her grip.

"No, now!" she insisted, tugging him down the hall.

Dr. Travis was standing by an open doorway ahead, apparently waiting for them, and before they reached him, Kathryn dragged Natty to a halt.

"What was that about?" she asked him, knowing she sounded upset, which rarely got her anywhere with this boy. She saw, though, that his slender face had gone white, and his eyes were wide.

"I knows them," he whispered to her.

"Whom do you know?"

"That man back there," he said, jerking his thumb over his shoulder. "And two of them kids, somethin' like my age, I guess. They was dodgers, and good at it, so's I can't think they really got tumbled—but they must've. Gawd, what a rum thing. What if they can't get outta here?"

"I don't know, Natty." She had seen by now that his eyes were filling, and having never seen tears from him before, she had to stop herself from drawing him to her. It would embarrass him and might make him furious. There was also no point in reassuring him that all would be fine, when he could see the truth of it for himself.

"What'll happen to 'em?" he persisted.

Kathryn, without knowing what he wanted to hear, and without a ready answer in any event, was searching for something to say when Dr. Travis suddenly appeared beside them. She shook her head at him, worried that he might try to lecture the boy on the wages of sin, and Natty would run off.

She had misjudged the man. He simply slung his arm over Natty's thin shoulders and, without a word, guided the boy down the hall. Kathryn stood there for a moment watching them, wondering how she could feel such a lift of heart in such a terrible place.

This morning she had been delivered a message from Rhys Bevan, which said to meet him here at noon. The message had also said that the previous evening Dr. Travis had gone to Treasury and had satisfactorily explained his presence that day at the Alexandria Wharf. While Rhys had not included the explanation in his note, he had said he no longer suspected the doctor of complicity in the attack on Bronwen.

Kathryn now followed them into a small room that must be someone's office. The smell was even worse, if possible, than in the yard; added now was the reek of rotting cabbage and pork, and even Natty, apparently somewhat recovered, wrinkled his nose as he inched closer to her.

A man who Kathryn guessed was prison superintendent William Woods came through the door, saying to Rhys, "I've questioned the woman and can't get a thing out of her. She's stubborn as a mule, but you're welcome to try your hand."

He turned and motioned to a guard, who gave the attractive, black-haired woman whose arm he grasped a slight push into the room. She did not look familiar to Kathryn.

"Let me know when you're done," Wood said before he and the guard left. "One of us will be right outside."

Natty sucked in his breath. "That's her!" he said to Kathryn. He motioned that she should bend down, and then whispered in her ear, "She can't finger me, can she—I mean, fer trying to steal yer purse? You won't let 'em keep me here?"

"You needn't worry about that," she told him, not as sure as she sounded. She turned in question to Dr. Travis, but he was studying Mrs. Bleuette, his gaze dark and thoughtful. He then gave Rhys a brief nod, which Kathryn assumed was a prearranged signal between the two men.

Rhys gestured to several chairs. The woman, saying nothing, moved to one, and without a limp. When Kathryn seated herself in another, Natty quickly came to stand behind her.

"You had no right to bring me here," the woman stated, "and no right to keep me here now. I have demanded that bail be set, and I have friends who will gladly post it. I don't have anything to say to you, Mr. Bevan."

Her voice had a husky quality, and she was, Kathryn thought, very handsome until one saw the expression in the cold, whitish blue eyes. She had to agree with Natty's earlier description.

"I doubt you'll be going anywhere soon," Rhys said to her amiably.

"I need to look at your ankle, madam," said Dr. Travis, and moved to crouch in front of her chair. Mrs. Bleuette looked irritated, but didn't resist, Kathryn saw with relief, as she had been expecting resistance from this frightening woman.

Earlier, when they had met Rhys at the prison gate, he told them that papers—found when Dr. Worthington's residential hotel suite had been searched—identified the deceased as a Dr. Elias Worth of Baltimore. Kathryn had been stunned. Bronwen had spoken of her surveillance of Dr. Worth, and of the incriminating evidence she had uncovered in his library.

Rhys had said he then instructed two Baltimore Treasury agents—a Harriet King and Dan Morrow—to question Dr. Worth's wife. Mrs. Worth told these agents that her husband had disappeared shortly after the body of their manservant had been found in the carriage house. She also admitted having learned some months before—so it had been reported to Rhys—that her husband kept a mistress in the house next door to their own. Mrs. Worth had not confronted her husband, because she had been afraid Worth would divorce her, thus leaving her penniless.

The agents had obtained an arrest warrant. The police and the train stations had been alerted, and Mrs. Bleuette was apprehended when she arrived in Baltimore. After which Mrs. Worth tearfully identified the woman as her husband's mistress. Two days ago, Mrs. Bleuette—whose name, and byname of Bluebell, had appeared, tellingly, in the files Bronwen had copied in Dr. Worth's study—had been charged with espionage and extradited to Washington.

"You actually face several more charges," Rhys now said to her.

He glanced at Dr. Travis who had straightened and said, "There's still some inflammation of the ankle."

If surprised by either of these comments, Mrs. Bleuette did not show it. "And just what charges are those?" she asked in a disdainful tone.

Rhys answered bluntly, "I think you killed your lover Elias Worth."

Kathryn, dumbfounded, felt Natty pressing hard against the back of her chair.

"That's absurd," the woman said. "Naturally I deny it. I also deny even knowing anyone named Worth."

"I expected you would," Rhys said. "I'll get to your affair with Worth later, but meantime let me say that I have two witnesses who place you here in Washington at the time of his murder. Two witnesses who can identify you as being here, even though you have sworn you never left Baltimore. I also saw you in Washington, the day you followed one of my agents and myself after we left the president's office."

Kathryn, as Rhys had requested, attempted to keep her

face expressionless. While the murder disclosure had been shocking enough, she had an uneasy sense of something even more unpleasant approaching. She was certain, from past experience with Natty, that he would also be capable of maintaining a straight face. Especially since he appeared worried about being detained here.

But then Rhys said, "I think you attempted to kill that same agent, madam. *My Treasury agent,* which I take even more seriously than the death of a traitor."

Kathryn half-rose as she grasped his meaning. This woman had tried to kill Bronwen? Worse yet, it appeared that she now was starting to smile about it.

"You must be a dreamer, Mr. Bevan, if you think such an outrageous idea could ever be proved."

"You are wrong," said Dr. Travis. "You were at the Alexandria wharf that day. Disguised as a man." Kathryn couldn't restrain a quick intake of breath, and found herself nodding. The gunman had been slight, and moved like a dancer when he . . . she rose with the gun clutched in both hands. She had noticed that, but it had not fully registered, because how often did women take the role of assassin?

"After the gun discharged," Dr. Travis went on, "I was distracted before chasing you, but I had a look at your face just as you fired, and again just before you disappeared into that warehouse. My concern for Miss Llyr made me give up the chase, but I did see an old discarded overcoat and slouch hat on the ground just outside the building." He turned to Rhys, saying, "As I told you last night, at the time I didn't think much of it, just assumed they belonged to a hobo."

Kathryn was still trying to absorb the fact that this woman had planned to kill her sister. With Natty now so close she could feel his breath on her neck, she said to Mrs. Bleuette, "I remember that large carriage. You went to it sometime before the shooting, and now I can guess that is where you put on the overcoat and hat. And Nat—" Kathryn paused because she felt a finger jab her back "—that is, a witness also places you in a position to start the fire outside my room. But why? Did you think I could identify you? That I saw you clearly at the wharf?"

"How imaginative of you," the woman said to Kathryn, her face revealing nothing, and she turned again to Rhys saying, "Mr. Bevan, this is a very poor farce. Surely you don't need me to tell you that if you persist in these charges, which are entirely circumstantial, you will be made a laughingstock from here to Richmond."

"I don't think so," Rhys told her. "For one thing, several days ago an acquaintance of yours positively identified Worth's body."

Kathryn saw the woman shift almost imperceptibly.

Rhys continued, "This same acquaintance also informed me that one night, after a strategy meeting, he overheard you and one Major William Norris briefly discuss the merits of the doctor's early demise. I'm certain you will recognize the acquaintance to whom I'm referring here. His name is Joseph Maddox."

The woman's reaction was instant, and while she quickly brought the look of fear under control, Kathryn could see that Rhys had hit the mark.

"Yes, I thought you knew Maddox," Rhys said to her. "We know him, too. He plays both ends against the middle, depending on who's paying him the most today."

"Maddox is one of yours?" she snapped, then bit her lip, obviously regretting the question.

"For the moment," Rhys replied. "And long enough to know of your association with Major Norris." He turned to the others to say, "Norris heads the Confederate espionage network that Maddox successfully infiltrated."

He turned back to the woman, saying, "I would guess you had already decided that Worth needed to go, because he was careless and egotistical, and therefore a dangerous man. His habit of leaving incriminating evidence lying around made him a liability. I would also guess you were intent on ingratiating yourself with the new director of Confederate intelligence. But I am afraid, madam, that you are now in deep trouble. Deeper than you know."

When the woman did not respond, Rhys said in a tight voice, "I have just received word that Pinkerton agent Timothy Webster was hanged in Richmond."

The look of fear again leapt into the woman's eyes and this time it did not retreat, while her fingers opened and closed on themselves.

"I see you understand the implications of that, Mrs. Bleuette," Rhys went on. "And that's good, because it will spare me having to describe how bitter Webster's death has made us here in Washington. Retaliation for his execution is on many minds. So if you think there's no chance of *you* hanging for murder, and attempted murder, and treason—think again!"

"Gawd . . . the hoity-toit's gonna swing?" Natty whispered to Kathryn. She motioned him to quiet, while she stared at Mrs. Bleuette with growing fury. The terror of the fire was still vivid, and her sister might have died by this woman's hand.

"Very well, Mr. Bevan," the woman said, and although her voice was less sharp, it still carried contempt. "I suppose you want to bargain, is that it?"

"Depends on what you have to bargain with," Rhys replied.

"In return for a promise of clemency, I can quite possibly assist you. Otherwise, you have no hope at all of saving that agent of yours from death. Although it may already be too late for her—"

"Bronwen!" Kathryn was on her feet before she realized it. "Is it my sister whose life you are so lightly dismissing? How dare you!"

Natty was tugging at her skirt, and she felt Dr. Travis's hands grip her shoulders. She pulled away from them both and went to stand over the woman. "Answer me!"

"Your sister?" said Mrs. Bleuette, her face blanching.

"My sister! What do you know about her?"

The room was very quiet. Kathryn was aware that Rhys
Bevan had not moved, but he couldn't be as furious or as
stricken as she. "Let me promise you, Mrs. Bleuette," she
said with a rage barely checked, "that I will see you hanged
in that yard out there, if you know something about my sister
that you're not telling us!"

"Actually, I'm quite certain that promise can be kept,"
Rhys added. "Especially since Agent Llyr is such a particular
favorite of the president's."

The woman's breath hissed, and she shifted in the chair.
"I know very little, but—"

"Hanged!" Kathryn repeated.

"Yes, well . . . Maddox may be a viper in our nest," said
Mrs. Bleuette, shifting again to avoid Kathryn's glare, "but
of recent you have a viper or two in your own nest, Mr.
Bevan."

Color drained from his face. Then, his voice eerily steady,
he said, "I want names, not just some vague accusation."

"I don't know the names," she answered, and Kathryn
watched her closely, trying to see a lie. "At least not their
real names. One has a beard, and because he's a double
agent, all I have is his code name. Vandyke."

Kathryn spun to Rhys, who now, his eyes narrowed, stared
at the ceiling. She could nearly see the agents parading
through his mind as he sifted the bearded from the clean-
shaven. *How many have beards?* she wanted to shout.

Rhys leveled his gaze on the woman, nodded, and asked
her brusquely, "Where is he now?"

"Virginia," she answered sullenly.

"Not good enough," said Rhys. "Is he in Richmond?"

"He may be, or he will be soon."

"Another name."

She shook her head, saying, "I know there's someone else
who has recently been recruited. He was at one of our meet-

ings—but no name was given—and he kept to the shadows, presumably so he couldn't be seen or identified. Why don't you ask your friend Maddox?"

Only from an angry flash of his eyes could Kathryn tell that Rhys expected nothing more from this Maddox.

"Is the new man in Treasury?" he asked, then added, "Let me remind you, madam, that your fate is riding on these answers."

"I don't know who he's with," she said quickly, "but he spoke with some authority about military matters."

"Where is he now?"

The woman gave a dismissive jerk of her shoulders. "He could be anywhere—but possibly in Virginia."

Rhys walked to the window, and stood staring out at the yard. The woman's revelation had obviously disturbed him, but how surprised had he been? Or had she confirmed a suspicion?

He turned back to the room abruptly, saying, "What did you people have to do with the attempt made on Agent Llyr? Aboard the transport *Alhambra,* and after the ship reached the Chesapeake?"

"I don't know."

Kathryn bit her lip and sank back into her chair. Natty bent down and whispered, "Lady, the gent said the *attempt.* Means they didn't get 'er."

Kathryn brushed away a spurt of tears, saying to Natty under her breath, "Thank you for pointing out that distinction."

"Mrs. Bleuette," Rhys persisted, "I questioned Van Lyttle, the captain of the *Alhambra,* when the ship returned to Alexandria. One of the men I hired had been stabbed, the other probably tossed overboard. The captain said his roster showed that those on board that night were his seamen, a civilian barber, and three cooks. All of them had been with Captain Van Lyttle for a number of years. The rest were ostensibly members of the Union military. Who is the Confederate agent among those I've named?"

"It could be anyone—a Southern loyalist, a paid informant, even a double agent like Maddox. I don't have a name. But . . ." She hesitated, then said, "I have your word on clemency, Mr. Bevan?"

"Mine, yes," he replied curtly. "I can't speak for others."

She seemed to measure him briefly, then responded, "Norris has been planning something big. I don't know what it is, because I will play no part. But I think this new man is involved in it, and I also think your redhead may suspect who he is. Or Norris has reason to believe she suspects. Which is why she's been marked."

In revulsion, Kathryn shrank back in the chair, her eyes going to Rhys Bevan. "Do something," she told him.

An hour later she stood gazing at the slate gray Potomac, mirroring a sky of low-sailing clouds. Gregg Travis, standing beside her, said, "What the devil is the lad up to now?"

"What?" responded Kathryn absently, her thoughts on Bronwen. "Oh, Natty . . . where is he?" She looked around her, hearing only the muffled sound of hammering and sawing. The final Sanitary Commission ship was nearly ready, converted from excursion boat to floating hospital.

It was this ship that she was scheduled to take to Virginia a few days hence. Dr. Travis had persuaded her to look at it, although Kathryn suspected it was an attempt to distract her. Natty had insisted on tagging along, and if anything good had come from the nightmare of Old Capitol Prison, it had been the change in the boy. If it lasted.

"I got to get outta here," he had said to her as they approached the outer doors. He had run on ahead, bursting to the outside as if chased by demons.

A few minutes later, as the three of them walked toward the river, he said, "I think I hafta leave the city."

Kathryn stopped to ask, "Why?"

"Bad air," responded Natty soberly.

Kathryn heard Dr. Travis make a choking sound. She glanced up to see him forcing back a smile. It occurred to her that it was only the second genuine one she had ever seen from him.

"Now, that's 'zactly what I mean," Natty said, pointing at the doctor. "Gotta get outta here 'fore I catch my death."

"Does this sudden urge of yours," Dr. Travis asked, "have anything to do with the prison?"

" 'Course not!" Natty scoffed. "You think I'm a sissy? 'Fraid to go to jail?"

Now Kathryn forced back a smile. Until she remembered the woman's words "Which is why she's been marked."

Now, as she glanced about for Natty, she felt again the uncontrollable fear.

She shivered, and felt Gregg Travis raise her shawl around her shoulders, saying, "Don't think about it."

"How can I not?"

"From what Bevan said, your sister isn't alone. That she has another agent with her there in Richmond. And given what I've learned today, if anyone can take care of herself, your sister can."

"You don't understand," Kathryn told him. "Bronwen is nearly fearless. And because she assumes nothing can happen to her, she tends to be reckless. A dangerous quality anytime, but in these circumstances . . ."

Her voice trailed off, not wanting to think about 'these circumstances.'

"It's probably her lack of fear—or more likely her high tolerance for it—that makes her an effective agent. Although I can't picture a woman in that role."

Kathryn did not ask what he *could* picture, since he had apparently now added espionage to the work he had just learned women were performing. It was as though he had recently been dropped here from the moon. Which, she admitted, was not being fair to him. He *had* hired her as a nurse.

"Why did you hire me?" she said now, surprised at herself for asking, but wanting to know. "Why not hire another male nurse? Especially since I know you don't much like the idea of women nurses and—" she paused, but felt compelled to say it "—and perhaps don't much like women, period."

Another man, more schooled in manners, or more superficial, would have quickly denied it from sheer habit. He looked down at her with his dark eyes, his expression unreadable, and she thought he wouldn't answer.

"You may be right," he said, finally. "But don't judge a man too harshly until you know the reasons why he is . . . the way he is. And perhaps one day I will tell you. As to why I hired you? After I finished medical school, I went to the Crimea. The war was nearly over—and no, I did not meet Florence Nightingale. I did, however, meet another admirable British woman, as competent and caring as any doctor there. Her name was Hester Latterly, and because I haven't forgotten her, I was willing to chance it with you. You also, of course, had excellent recommendations, and experience, and . . ."

He did not finish the sentence. Instead, he changed the subject. "This sister of yours sounded to me very little like you, until you became enraged—justifiably—in the prison back there. Then, I imagine, you resembled each other."

"Dr. Travis, I have been angry more often in the past several weeks than all the other times in my life combined."

She didn't add that much of it had to do with him.

Apparently she didn't have to say it.

"I'm aware of that," he told her. "I'm also aware that I've often been the cause. But as I told you yesterday, I am not glib, or gracious, or any of the other qualities that supposedly belong to a gentleman."

"It's as if you deliberately avoid owning them," Kathryn said, and was then appalled at herself.

"Why are you flushing?"

"Because I shouldn't have said that. It was rude, and I apologize. Perhaps it's Natty's bad air."

He laughed, a deep rich sound that she had never before heard. It sent a pleasant sensation down her spine.

Since he might tell her now, she asked, "Dr. Travis, why *were* you at the *Alhambra*'s wharf that day?"

"Because you were there."

She changed the subject, because he was looking at her intently . . . and Natty might be watching them. "Do you know when I'm to leave for Virginia?" she asked.

"You, and the others, leave at the beginning of next week."

"Others?"

"You didn't think I'd let you go down there alone?"

"Dr. Travis, I do not need a guardian or a chaperone. I am a grown woman and I'm capable—"

"Kathryn!" he interrupted. "I know you are capable and most assuredly know you are a woman—but that has nothing to do with it."

"Why do you insist on treating me like a child?"

"Where is home to you and your sister?" he suddenly asked, making Kathryn stop in her tracks at the total irrelevance of this question.

"Why on earth does it matter where our home is?"

"I was just wondering if there's something alarming in the water there."

Kathryn caught the flash of his smile. She felt in herself an odd shift, like the colored pieces of a kaleidoscope rearranging themselves in a different pattern, and she smiled up at him, holding his gaze as he drew her to him. His mouth had barely brushed hers, when, "Lady!" yelled Natty. "Hey Lady, come 'ere!"

Kathryn jerked back, but Gregg Travis smiled, and his hands still firmly at her waist, he called, "Don't shout, lad. And don't order Miss Llyr around."

By the time the boy came running up to them, Kathryn had been released, but Natty, skidding to a halt, eyed them skeptically. "What're you two doin'? It don't look good."

Flustered, Kathryn could say nothing but *"Doesn't* look good."

"Yeah, that's right, it don't."

"What is it, Natty?" she asked, placing her palms against her hot cheeks.

"Capt'n of that boat there says he can use a cabin boy," Natty told her, " 'cause I'm related to you and all."

"What did you say?"

"I told him you was my ol' auntie."

Kathryn sighed, as Natty continued, "It's so's I can get outta this here city and go to the Virgin's place with you. But," he rushed on as Kathryn tried to interrupt, "I need a reck-. . . uh . . . It's somethin' from you, doc."

"Young man," said Gregg, "are you asking me for a recommendation? After you've pilfered your way through my hospital?"

"Yeah, I'm askin'."

"We'll see. Why don't you write down . . . can you write?"

"Nope. How am I s'posed to do that?"

"All right, then in your head make a list of what you think the duties of a cabin boy are. And why integrity might be important."

"I already knows the duties. Capt'n told me. But I dunno what inte-grity is."

"That's fairly clear."

"What is?"

"Natty," Kathryn inserted, "do you understand why that ship is going to Virginia?"

"I don't care why."

"It's not a place for a young boy."

"And is the city of Washington?" Gregg asked her in apparent seriousness. "I doubt it."

"Yeah," Natty chimed in agreement, "fer once he's right. O.K., doc, I'll tell the capt'n you'll give 'em the . . . thing."

He was running toward the dock before either Kathryn or Gregg Travis had time to stop him.

"It will be dangerous for him," Kathryn said.

"It won't be any less dangerous for him here. His instincts about that are sound. Sooner or later he will end up in Old Capitol Prison. Besides, if he's determined to go with you, do you think anything short of a cannon will stop him? He'll figure out something—probably will stow away, and then you'll be saddled with an outlaw instead of a cabin boy."

"I think I'm already saddled with an outlaw." Kathryn began to smile, but at once sobered. "I used to call Bronwen that, because she was always in some kind of trouble. And now, I'd give anything to make her safe."

"You can't do that, Kathryn—"

"Wait, I've just remembered something!" she broke in. "After the shooting at Alexandria, I thought I saw a Treasury agent come from one of the warehouses. Oh, dear Lord, do you suppose he might have been an accomplice of that woman's? Perhaps he was even retrieving the overcoat and hat you saw there. And if not in league with her, why didn't he report it to Rhys Bevan?"

"We'll tell Bevan that. Kathryn, try to stop worrying—he told you he was sending another agent on to Richmond immediately."

But which agent? wondered Kathryn. Rhys had said he was not sure he knew who the traitor was. And would Bronwen know, before it was too late?

She barely noticed that Gregg Travis had taken her hand and was leading her toward the hospital ship.

26

Secret guilt by silence is betrayed.

—John Dryden

Richmond, Virginia

He was out there, prowling somewhere beyond St. John's cemetery, and he was looking for her.

Bronwen, crouched behind a tall, upright tombstone, knew this with absolute certainty, and she also knew, with nearly as much certainty, that he was the deadly H.J.K., recruited by an unwitting Timothy Webster, and betrayer not only of Webster but of colleagues and country.

And he must suspect she knew his identity.

She passed a hand over her eyes, anger and fatigue grinding her between them like millstones. It had been shortly after Webster's hanging that she realized she had a stalker. The stalking had been relentless. So far, the anger had kept her alert and one step ahead of her pursuer. She had hoped against hope, given Rhys Bevan's secrecy regarding his pigeons, that this man hadn't known of Marsh's involvement.

But yesterday, a bullet had come winging through a tavern window and nearly struck the owner's wife. Since then, Bronwen had been constantly on the move, because she would not slink out of Richmond on her belly, or in a coffin either. What she needed was a way to strike back.

Her roaming had yielded one positive result: she had learned a great deal about the tense anxiety which had at last begun to grip the Confederate capital. Its citizens had become well aware that McClellan and a hundred thousand Union troops were readying to advance up the peninsula, and a pall of fear hung over the city. The very air reeked of it.

St. John's Church and its cemetery stood on Grace Street, diagonally across the road from Elizabeth Van Lew's mansion. Bronwen had checked the place periodically, but hadn't dared go directly to Elizabeth, because the woman was under surveillance by the Richmond police. Then two hours ago, just at twilight, she had seen two burning candles in a third upstairs window: a signal that Elizabeth had urgent information.

Bronwen had been forcing herself to wait until darkness would cover her. The May night was warm, the only piece of good luck given her lately, and now, she decided, it was dark enough. She crept cautiously by way of a roundabout route through the graveyard, then darted across the road, backtracking to the rear entrance of the mansion.

Elizabeth must have been watching, because Bronwen found her at the open back door.

While she sat gulping lukewarm coffee and devouring lemon cake in the woman's unlit kitchen, Bronwen tried to calculate what her chances were of safely reaching the tavern. The information Elizabeth had just received from her contacts in eastern Virginia was urgent in the extreme, so Washington had to be alerted quickly. And pigeons would fly at night.

"I'll provide a distraction," Elizabeth said from her chair at the kitchen table.

"No," Bronwen protested, "Police Chief McCubbin's men are almost certainly watching the house, especially if they know what's now planned at Norfolk. They're also—courtesy of the informer—surely looking for me. It will be dangerous to draw attention to yourself."

"General Winder won't allow harm to come to me," Elizabeth declared, and Bronwen half-believed her. "We have no choice," the woman went on, "because Lincoln must have this information! If you're willing to take the risk, I'm only too glad to assist you."

Without waiting for a response, she turned on her heel and headed for the front entrance. Bronwen braced herself to leave by the rear.

Only a minute or two passed before a series of hair-raising screeches and yowls issued from the mansion's main entrance. Once Bronwen figured out what they were, she nearly found the heart to smile at the service rendered by the Van Lew cats. Whatever it was the woman had incited, several agitated male voices—likely McCubbin's men—could be heard cursing loudly as Bronwen crept out into the night.

She dashed toward the road, feeling confident that while torch light flickered near the front door, the remainder of the grounds was dark. But without warning, a shadowed figure burst from behind a clump of trees.

Bronwen leapt into some bushes, cocked the derringer, and could hardly believe her luck when the shadow raced past, presumably also on the way to the road. She hadn't been spotted, she decided. And readied herself for another dash to the graveyard.

As she again moved cautiously forward, she suddenly heard the pounding of footsteps coming up behind her. She ducked behind a tree as another shadowed figure passed.

Dear God, were there *two* of them after her? If so, shouldn't she have known it sooner? Or had fatigue so completely dulled her senses?

She darted to the cemetery and stopped to catch her breath, trusting she was concealed behind the same tall tombstone. One block away was the tavern. Bronwen glanced around swiftly, got to her feet and, dodging gravestones, raced toward it. Haste was now more crucial than caution.

When she reached the dim light thrown by the tavern's

lanterns, she slowed her pace and scanned its periphery. Voices rumbled from the inside, and a couple of men stood smoking beside the hitching post. Keeping a wide path between herself and the tavern, she made her way around it, and when another quick scan showed no one nearby, she dashed to the rear door and cautiously drew it open.

Noise, heat, and smoke hit her, but the stairs leading to the upper floor and attic rose directly in front of her. She started up the steps, taking them two at a time, and stopped abruptly. From somewhere above her, a muffled report sounded. Had it been a gunshot?

She crouched on the step to peer over the railing. No one came out to investigate, so the noise in the tavern room must have been loud enough to cover the report. She continued to creep up the steps, listening with her every nerve strung tight. When she reached the landing, she stopped again to listen. Hearing nothing but an odd, high-pitched squawking, she slowly inched open the heavy door leading to the attic.

She was met by a flurry of feathers and the shrill cries of frightened pigeons, and she could hear their wings beating against the wooden crates. Her breath caught in her throat, but while knowing that something was terribly wrong, she couldn't see anyone moving above the open stairwell. Hugging the side of the slanting wall, her derringer poised, she moved cautiously upward.

Over the noise of the pigeons, she heard a stunningly familiar voice shouting, "You rotten bastard! Why'd you do it?"

Another familiar voice answered, "Don't move—just stay where you are until she arrives. Stop shouting, and drop the gun."

"And let you shoot me, too? I don't think so. In fact, I'd say we have a standoff. And what makes you think she'll come? With you hunting her, she may have left Richmond. She's not stupid!"

"No, but she's loyal. News from Norfolk has just reached

Van Lew—I made certain of it—and Llyr won't leave Richmond until she sends word to Bevan and Lincoln."

Bronwen leaned against the wall, her heart pounding so noisily they must hear it. A third voice that she expected to hear had been ominously silent—or silenced. The pigeons still sounded frightened, but now footsteps moved away from the stairwell, so Bronwen kept her head ducked and went up one more step from where she could see the attic floor.

Ahead of her, motionless in front of the pigeon crates, lay Marsh, blood seeping from the side of his head. Shock made her lightheaded, before a surge of rage sent her racing up the remaining steps. The two men spun toward her. Both held raised revolvers.

"He's right," she shouted at the one farthest from the stairs. "You're a bastard!"

The closer man drawled, "Red, what the hell took you so long? Were you sight-seeing along the way?"

"Be quiet, O'Hara!" Her voice barely under control, she said to the first man, "Notice it's not a standoff anymore? That you now have two guns trained on you? And, as you know, we're both very good shots."

"You're right," he responded affably, the revolver lowering, "but since I'm also a good shot, I can likely manage to take at least one of you with me."

Over the past few days, when recalling the trace of British accent in his speech, she had wondered if he was linked to Colonel Dorian de Warde; although that man, while treacherous, wasn't known to encourage murder.

"Well, I don't know about Red, here," O'Hara told him, "but I'm willing to kill you right now."

"No!" said Bronwen vehemently. "First we need some answers. Watch him," she told O'Hara, while she risked a sideways glance at Marsh. He hadn't moved, and if he were dead, she would shoot his killer herself.

"Did Rhys Bevan figure it out?" she asked O'Hara, and

now did not move her eyes from the other man. "Is that why you're here?"

"That's it. Bevan sent a wire to Fort Monroe, telling me to hightail it to Richmond. Had the devil's own time getting here, Red, circling all those troops, so you might show a little appreciation."

The other revolver raised slightly, and both Bronwen and O'Hara hitched theirs higher.

The other revolver lowered again. "How did *you* know?" he asked Bronwen.

"O'Hara, stop the comedy and watch him!"

"I'll do that, sir!"

The man smiled, asking again, "How?"

"In the end, it was your initials," Bronwen answered, in hope that by talking she could take him off guard. There was no question in her mind that given a chance he would kill both her and O'Hara.

"Would you repeat that?" O'Hara said to her. "Maybe provide a little more detail, 'cause nobody ever tells me anything. All I know is Bevan sent me here to find you. This bastard followed you to Van Lew's, where I'd gone figuring to catch up with you. Instead I find not only you but a traitor skulking in the bushes—two for the price of one!"

"So you were the second person who ran past me?"

"That was me," O'Hara said, grinning, but closely watching the other man. "Gets confusing, doesn't it, with everybody following everybody else. Now, what about those initials?"

"There were other signs pointing in his direction," Bronwen answered, "but I didn't recognize them until the day of Webster's hanging. Marsh and I were looking across the river at Tredegar Iron Works, and he said something about valleys and knolls."

"That's sure clear as mud," commented O'Hara.

Bronwen went on, "I realized then that I'd never seen his name written out, and had assumed it was spelled the way it sounds, *N-o-l-l-s*. Once I found that silent *K*, the shortened Ward for Howard became obvious. *H* and *K*. And what does the middle initial *J* stand for, Knolls? Judas?"

"James, like the river," he answered, still smiling, still holding the threatening revolver at his thigh.

"When Van Lew saw Webster," she said, "he mentioned thirty pieces of silver. Symbolic of betrayal. But he also— because guards were listening—kept repeating 'money' to her. It took me a while to realize that he meant money lit- erally. And just what has money, Knolls?"

The man smiled more broadly and nodded.

O'Hara said, "Can I play this game, too? 'Cause I would guess the best place to find money is in a *treasury*! Red, it's indeed an honor to know you."

"It was an unfortunate mistake, meeting you at Yorktown, wasn't it?" Knolls said. "After I intercepted General Wool's wire from Fort Monroe, I wanted to make certain you were going on to Richmond. And were going alone. After all, you'd managed several times to evade my . . . my confeder- ates," he said, smiling again, and casually raising his left hand to finger his short beard.

"I finally connected your beard, Knolls," Bronwen said, "with the name—or byname—of Vandyke. I may have done it almost unknowingly after I saw you at Yorktown, because the name Vandyke had figured prominently in the papers I found in your colleague Dr. Worth's library."

"Another unfortunate mistake—Worth, himself, that is. You may be pleased to know he's no longer with us, also quite literally. *I'm* certainly pleased."

"We're glad you're happy, Knolls," O'Hara said, "but you want to go over that last again?"

"I hadn't planned to speak with you at Yorktown," Knolls said to Bronwen, "but Sundown said you knew I was there. Did you?"

"No, I didn't," Bronwen said. "But it was a mistake, all right, because it made me recall that you'd spent time in

Virginia—even in Richmond—before this war started. Is that when your double-dealing began?" When he merely smiled, she snapped, "It was also a mistake to let Sundown find you at Yorktown, when he could recognize you from the Oswego raid a year ago."

Ward shrugged slightly. "I had no choice. It was bad luck he just sauntered into McClellan's headquarters, where I had so carefully placed myself—how better to keep track of the Union army? Ironically, the Indian had come to tell General Napoleon that he was quitting."

"Sundown thought it was peculiar," she said, "for a Treasury agent to be at McClellan's headquarters, especially since Allan Pinkerton was also there and he's no friend of Rhys Bevan's detective unit. Pinkerton hadn't ever met you, though, had he?"

Knolls only smiled.

"Sundown made sure I saw you there, Knolls, so I was uneasy myself. Since I figured he was heading north after he left me at West Point, I asked him to contact Rhys Bevan, questioning the fact that you were down here. Obviously I couldn't send a wire myself from Richmond."

"Smart thinking, Red," O'Hara inserted. "Damn distrustful of you, though, I must say."

"But there's more, isn't there, Knolls," she said. "Because someone else has to be—"

Bronwen broke off at the sound of a groan. Although she reflexively glanced toward Marsh, she still caught Knolls in the act of whipping up his revolver.

She fired the derringer at his gun hand, just as O'Hara fired at his chest, two shots in rapid succession.

Knolls's revolver went skittering across the floor, and O'Hara was about to fire again.

"No!" yelled Bronwen.

Knolls fell forward heavily, and jerked several times before he lay still.

"O'Hara, you fool! You've probably killed him!"

"That was the intention," said O'Hara. "He who shoots first with the most lives longest."

"We *needed* him, O'Hara! Go see if he's still alive."

She hurried to kneel beside Marsh, trying to locate a pulse in his neck. She found it, and it was fairly steady. When she examined his head wound, it appeared that the bullet had tunneled through his forehead and exited beside his left eye. The bleeding had all but stopped.

"Marsh, can you hear me? Marsh?"

He groaned softly, and Bronwen felt her heart begin to recede from her throat.

"O'Hara, what about Knolls?"

"He's dead. Very. Why are you so riled up, Red? I fired because I thought he was going to kill you!"

"Maybe."

"Listen to me, Bronwen!" O'Hara said. "Listen! Rhys Bevan knew he hadn't sent Knolls here. He was supposed to be in Fredericksburg checking on Stuart and our other Rebel chums there. When Bevan got Sundown's wire, as well as hearing something from some woman prisoner, he put two and two together. The telegram he sent to Fort Monroe stated—explicitly stated—that I was to use any means necessary to stop this bastard."

She got to her feet, eyeing him narrowly. He might, just possibly, be telling the truth.

"O'Hara, we needed more from Knolls."

"Like what?"

"Have you forgotten those two men Bevan hired—the ones I told you were killed on the transport ship *Alhambra*? Ward Knolls was not on that ship! He was already here on the peninsula."

Bronwen decided her vague suspicion that O'Hara had deliberately silenced Knolls might be overreaching. It didn't feel quite right. Her sixth sense—and what else did she have to trust?—told her to believe his explanation, at least for now. He could easily have shot her when he killed Knolls, because he knew very well the derringer held only one bullet. But he could have reasons for wanting her alive.

"I need to go to Fort Monroe," she now said.

"Not alone, you don't."

She shrugged. "Marsh obviously won't be taking care of the pigeons, so they will need to be loosed. I'll stay here with him while you go to Van Lew's and get her driver, Sam, and the buggy. And tell her we need a Confederate uniform."

"What for? You signing on with the Rebels? I'd hate to have to shoot you, Red, after all we've meant to each other."

"Stop clowning! Marsh needs medical attention, and the new Chimborazo Hospital is right up this same road. It's a military hospital, so clearly he has to be taken there as a wounded Confederate soldier."

"Good thinking! What'll we do with Knolls?"

After considering this for a minute, Bronwen answered, "I'd say a quiet burial in the river would be a fitting end for Howard James Knolls."

"Brilliant stroke! Dump him in the James!"

Bronwen flinched, but then, remembering Timothy Webster's terrible death, she decided O'Hara's callous response might be right after all.

"We want Knolls's associates to think he's still working with them," she said. "By the time they realize he's disappeared, McClellan may be here in Richmond."

"You want to bet on that?"

"O'Hara, just go and get Sam."

"Very good, sir!"

After he had left, Bronwen went to look at Marsh, who seemed to be breathing more easily, and then knelt beside the body of Howard James Knolls. Like it or not, she needed to go through his clothing. Nothing could be left to identify him, not if Confederate intelligence was to believe he had simply gone to ground, temporarily, as Webster and Pinkerton had previously believed.

She tore the label out of Knolls's frock coat and his shirt collar, and checked the waistband of his trousers before turning the pockets inside out. With increasing dislike for the job, she removed his boots and, before putting them aside to be dropped into the river separately, checked the soles and heels. Satisfied she had found everything, she was just beginning to rise when she suddenly remembered the pocket; the inner one that all the male Treasury agents had sewn into their shirts. She began to unbutton the cotton fabric, flinching as her fingers touched his cooling skin, and then she heard a faint crackle. Instantly forgetting her queasiness, she ripped the shirt open, and withdrew a folded piece of paper from the inner pocket.

The message was written in code. But it was one of the same codes that Treasury used; she had memorized it some months back in the company of Knolls himself.

Since she was still wary of O'Hara, and since he would be back shortly, she would wait to decode the message until after he and Van Lew's carriage took Knolls to the river.

She couldn't resist taking a closer look now. One series of letters was a date, or two dates, that much she could tell almost immediately. Another short, seven-letter sequence interested her because she could quickly see that it carried three vowels.

She heard the sound of O'Hara's whistle, and stuffed the paper into her own inside pocket.

One of the last two pigeons Bronwen released into the pre-dawn sky bore a message which when decoded would read:

BEVAN: HJK permanently indisposed. Marshall at Chimborazo Hospital. All pigeons on return flight. Operatives O'Hara and Llyr bound Fort Monroe. Urgent: Confederate evacuation Norfolk naval base anticipated within week.
BL

A few minutes later she watched the last pigeon lift into a clear, navy blue sky, and circle above the tavern. Then, as the first rays of sun touched its shining wings, the bird made a final turn and flew to the north as true as an arrow. The coded message this pigeon carried read:

FOX: Your presence Fort Monroe urgent four days hence. Re: Monitor
BL

27

~m~

Fort Monroe

Headquarters, Army of the Potomac
May 4, 1862

PRESIDENT LINCOLN: Yorktown is in our posses-
sion. Our success is brilliant.
G. B. McCLELLAN

War Department, Washington
May 5, 1862

MAJOR-GENERAL McCLELLAN: Capture of York-
town welcome news. Reports indicate possible Con-
federate evacuation of Norfolk naval base. Please
advise your plans for seizure and occupation of
same.
A. LINCOLN

Headquarters, Army of the Potomac
May 5, 1862

PRESIDENT LINCOLN: Your telegram re: Norfolk
acknowledged. No plans to seize and occupy same.

Am greatly outnumbered as have repeatedly stated.
Have no troops to spare. My sole objective is capture
of Richmond.
G. B. McCLELLAN

War Department, Washington
May 5, 1862

MAJOR-GENERAL McCLELLAN: Arriving Fort
Monroe tomorrow evening. Would like to meet with
you there to discuss the matter of Norfolk.
A. LINCOLN

Headquarters, Army of the Potomac
May 5, 1862

PRESIDENT LINCOLN: Unable to meet at Fort
Monroe. My army has need of me here in the field.
After brilliant success at Yorktown we now march
forward to capture Richmond. Please advise when I
can expect additional troops necessary to achieve
victory.
G. B. McCLELLAN

Bronwen stood on a lower fort rampart and watched through her field glasses as the *Miami*, a Treasury revenue cutter, drew nearer to the fort. Its passenger list included President Lincoln, War Secretary Edwin Stanton, and Treasury Secretary Salmon Chase. On the shore to meet them was General Wool and his staff and color guard. General McClellan was conspicuously absent, and the rumor mill had it that he had declared himself too busy to see his commander in chief.

This gossip had been flying over Fort Monroe several hours ago when she and O'Hara had arrived. She found it inconceivable that General McClellan would ignore the pres-

ident. O'Hara, of course, found it hilarious. He found everything about McClellan hilarious.

In disgust, Bronwen had left him chortling to himself,
while she went in search of clean dockhand's overalls and
shirt. After leaving Richmond cautiously but uneventfully at
early dawn, she and O'Hara, dressed in the guise of Virginia
farmers, had first taken a skiff down the James River, with
O'Hara constantly peering over the side to see if a body
might have surfaced and moved downstream since its recent
watery interment. It had not. They had spent the remaining
time avoiding troops on the lower peninsula. She felt as if
the red soil of Virginia was permanently embedded in her
skin.

By now the *Miami* had docked, and she spotted the president's tall figure, dressed in his customary black suit and
top hat, coming down the gangplank. He was closely followed by Stanton and Chase. There was no ceremonial
pomp, although two columns of naval officers stood facing
one another, forming a pathway through which the president
passed, and after an exceedingly brief greeting, the president
and General Wool started for the fort, again trailed by the
two secretaries.

With her field glasses, Bronwen took a long look around
her, alarmed by the lack of security afforded Lincoln, the
alarm prompted by memories of the preinaugural assassina-
tion attempt in Baltimore. She dashed off the rampart and
down a series of stairs, meeting no guards at all until she
reached the bottom. There a guard finally did step forward,
but she flashed her pass from General Wool and the soldier
moved aside.

She stopped as Lincoln approached, and when he had
nearly reached the steps she heard him say to General Wool,
"With the fall of Yorktown, and the Confederate retreat toward Richmond, Norfolk appears to be increasingly isolated."

"However, the *Merrimack* is still there," responded General Wool.

"Then she should be drawn out to where the *Monitor* can reach her," the president said firmly. "A gunboat squadron should also be dispatched across Hampton Roads to discover if there *is* an evacuation of Norfolk in progress as reported. Who is the ranking naval officer here?"

When General Wool signaled to one of the navy men and ordered him to locate Flag Officer Goldsborough, Bronwen all but smiled. The commander in chief apparently intended to command.

She slipped through the small crowd and sprinted down to the far wharves, scanning the water with her glasses for an approaching small vessel. A wire from Rhys Bevan had been waiting when she arrived at the fort, stating that a cutter bearing Assistant Navy Secretary Fox would dock some thirty minutes after the president; Fox wanted to make his presence unobtrusive. Bronwen was to meet the secretary at the wharves.

It was nearly an hour before the cutter arrived. When Fox came down the gangplank, Bronwen, her cap in hand, waited a short distance away. There were not many others nearby, and she assumed the secretary would not recognize her, since she probably looked significantly different from when she had first met him outside the president's office.

To her surprise he came directly toward her, and he looked very much the same. Dressed in gray frock coat, with white shirt and collar gleaming, he looked every inch the businessman.

"I thought it likely we should meet again," he said to her quietly by way of greeting. "I was here at the fort in March, but found the place to be a maze, so would you be so kind as to lead me to the telegraph office? We shall talk further there."

Those were the only words spoken until they reached the telegraph room. Fox dismissed the young operator, who at first protested being ousted by a civilian, but he moved quickly enough when the secretary identified himself.

Fox waited until the door closed behind him before taking a chair and gesturing for Bronwen to seat herself. "I understand you have been busy, Miss Llyr."

She smiled at the dry understatement.

"I am here as you requested," said Fox. "And as Mr. Bevan and the president insisted."

"Yes, sir. Just a moment please." She turned slightly to reach into the neck of her shirt and withdraw two by now rather crumpled pieces of paper, Knolls's original message and her own decoded copy, from where they lay tucked between her chemise and her breasts. They were still warm when she handed them to Fox, and it crossed her mind that the navy secretary probably did not receive much correspondence this way. Confederate spy Rose Greenhow, however, would undoubtedly approve of the method.

She waited, trying to contain her impatience while he read her version. His eyes moved back and forth, and up and down over the page several times, his expression changing from grave to grim, and when he refolded the papers and placed them in his inside coat pocket, he gazed soberly at her.

"I believe, Miss Llyr, given all that has preceded it, we need to treat this as a genuine threat to the *Monitor.*"

She nodded. "But I can understand why you might have doubts," she answered.

"No, Mr. Bevan gave me reason to think it would be worthwhile to interview you. I trust his judgment. It was extremely wise of you to keep it . . . out of the public eye, so to speak. Thus I trust no one else has seen this?"

"None that I know. Since I found it, no one else has had access to—"

She broke off in embarrassment. Why didn't she stop and think before blurting out such indelicate things?

But Fox's mouth twitched in a wry smile, and he nodded,

saying, "It was also wise of you not to send something so valuable by bird."

Bronwen smiled, too, although she was more amused by his use of the word "wise." It was one not often applied to her.

"Although no recipient is named on this communiqué, the sender of it," Fox said, "is indicated with an *N*. I think we can assume it is the work of the head of Confederate intelligence, Major Norris."

Bronwen nodded, and told him quickly how she had acquired it. By the time she was done, his brows had nearly lifted into his receding hairline.

"Mr. Fox, I have some thoughts about who might be the intended recipient of that message. But before I discussed them with you, I'd hoped to have a wire from Rhys Bevan with answer to a question I asked him several weeks ago. I telegraphed him about it again today, soon after I arrived from Richmond, but haven't received a reply."

Fox reached into another coat pocket. "I have your reply. Mr. Bevan had intended to wire it, but instead gave it to me just before I left Washington."

Bronwen took it eagerly, and read, "Agent Llyr—No record exists of three captured Baltimore gunmen arriving Washington or Alexandria—RB"

"Are you satisfied with that answer?" Fox asked her.

"Yes, it confirms my—"

"Before we talk of that," Fox interrupted, "one thing needs to made clear. This is a matter for the U.S. Navy. And for no other. Notwithstanding Norris's message's referring to the advance of General McClellan, and to the proposed movement of the Confederate *Merrimack* from the James to the York River to disrupt his supply lines—after having removed the threat of the *Monitor*. Again, this is *solely* a navy matter. It's essential that you understand that."

"I do," Bronwen answered, guessing that Fox's concern was not only the threatened *Monitor*—and the repercussions

further indicated in the message if the ship was destroyed—
but the future reputation of the navy and its other ironclads
now ready to be deployed. And this was to say nothing of
the casualties of *Monitor*'s command and crew if the directives of Norris's communiqué were carried out.

"Good," Fox responded. "From the dates given in this"—
he waved the decoded message—"we need to move quickly.
The timetable here suggests that the Confederate evacuation
of Norfolk was anticipated by Norris at least a week ago."

"That was my impression, too," Bronwen agreed.

Fox nodded. "I'll order the *Monitor*'s security to be dou-
bled."

"Excuse me, sir, but doing that might well reveal your
knowledge of the message, and considering the dates in it,
you have twenty-four hours before tipping your hand. The
one intended to receive Norris's message must be waiting for
it as a signal to proceed. Wouldn't it be better to discover
who he is?"

Fox did not respond immediately, and Bronwen feared she
had been too forward, until he replied, "Rhys Bevan thought
your question of him indicated that you have suspicions.
True?"

Bronwen answered, but hesitantly, "Ah, yes, I have some.
They're only circumstantial, though, and I may be wrong on
several counts." She watched his face for an expression of
dismissal. When she saw none, she ventured, "Mr. Fox, I
think there is a way to test my suspicions, but you would
need to be the one to set it up."

"I am listening, Miss Llyr."

Bronwen anxiously paced the floor of the telegraph room,
waiting for a reply from Rhys Bevan to her last wire. She
had been checking for it these past twelve hours, in between
dashes to the ramparts with her field glasses, where she
scanned the *Monitor*'s new position. This move of the ironclad to a location close to Norfolk had been ordered by Sec-

retary Fox. She also watched another ship, a navy gunboat which would soon be leaving Fort Monroe for Norfolk, or so she hoped. The trap had been set. Would a rat take the bait?

Even from inside the fort she could hear the thumps and explosions of the Union naval bombardment of the last remaining Confederate batteries defending Norfolk. Lincoln himself had ordered the attack after a loyalist tugboat captain, having deserted the Confederate navy, confirmed the troop evacuation of the naval base at the mouth of the James. Given the overall importance of this operation, she thought, vital information was surely coming from the most modest of sources.

To the dismay of Bronwen and almost everyone else, Lincoln and Secretaries Stanton and Chase had set off across Hampton Roads in a tugboat, determined to locate a landing site on the Norfolk beaches for General Wool's troops. At this point, Bronwen had to agree with O'Hara's unflattering assessment of McClellan; it was the general's indifference to the strategic importance of Norfolk that had forced the president into this dangerous activity. Admittedly, when she had watched Lincoln leave Old Point Comfort, he had seemed more than eager to take charge.

Her greatest concern now was the disappearance of Kerry O'Hara. She hadn't seen him since yesterday, nor had anyone else she had asked, including General Wool's aide.

"Saw him night before last, hunched over a pint of ale," O'Toole had said, "but not since then."

Where was he? And why didn't Rhys reply to her wire? Bronwen wondered with increasing impatience. How long did it take a chief detective of Treasury to finally admit he had made a mistake with O'Hara? The question now became, What was O'Hara doing? Sabotaging the *Monitor* himself?

"Are you sure the telegraph is working?" she asked the young operator for probably the tenth time.

"It's working," he repeated, also for the tenth time. "Unless there's a break in the cable, but that's unlikely, because David Bates—he's in the Washington War Department's telegraph office—has already sent three messages through today."

Could her wire to Rhys not have been clear? She reached into her pocket and began to pull out the original she had drafted before wiring it to Washington, but the operator stopped her by saying, "Here comes something."

And indeed the machine had begun to chatter.

"From Washington?" she asked, peering over his shoulder.

"Hey, you're not supposed to see everything that comes in here," the young man protested as he wrote. But then added immediately, "Yeah, it's yours, all right. Can't make heads nor tails of this garble."

Bronwen assumed it would be useless to ask him to move and let her take over, so she fairly danced with impatience while she waited.

"Short message for all the trouble you've given me," grumbled the operator, handing her the sheet of yellow foolscap. "Here it is."

Bronwen snatched it from him and leapt to a table to decipher it.

War Department, Washington
May 10, 1862

LLYR: Your telegram re: Urgent Query is acknowledged. Operative in question on assignment. Forget him. Repeat: Forget him.
BEVAN

28

The evacuation of Norfolk ... came upon the unsuspecting inhabitants of that city with the effect of a tornado from a cloudless sky.

—Sallie Brock Putnam, *Richmond during the War*, 1862

Norfolk, Virginia

It was not over yet, thought Bronwen, although against the steel gray sky she could see the Stars and Stripes flying above Norfolk. She was huddled anxiously under a tarpaulin on the deck of a navy gunboat, and as it neared the harbor, she watched people fleeing the town. Many hundreds had undoubtedly already fled. These were not Confederate troops but ordinary townsfolk, and she could hear fragments of their muted, frightened cries: "They're coming! The Yankees ... run!"

Did these civilians really believe they were in danger? That they would be cut down in their own streets?

She realized, viewing them through her field glasses, that she had not put faces on those living in the path of the Union army. Even in Richmond she had never looked around without thinking she saw the enemy everywhere. But these terrified people weren't the enemy. They were commonplace, everyday families clutching their children and a few belongings, and running.

She felt a stab of pity, but she could not give into it, surely not now. Her stomach was roiling, and she knew it was from fear and not seasickness.

She still wondered where O'Hara had run. His absence was now as damning as his attitude. Bevan might be wrong; he had been about Knolls. And then he and she might just be even, she thought with a distress close to despair. How could she have made such a dangerous blunder?

Back at Fort Monroe, when she had seen signs that the gunboat was preparing to load, she had checked her overall straps, pulled her cap down over her forehead, and headed for the wharves, arriving in time to see the president indulging in a rare show of temper. He had looked like a black windmill, flapping his long arms and gesturing vigorously at the transport ships, while scores of uniformed men milled helter-skelter over the docks.

"I just got here," she had said to a sailor, obviously waiting to board ship. "What's wrong with Mr. Lincoln?"

"He's havin' a fit, that's what," the sailor had responded, grinning. "He comes a-hurryin' down here and he sees us all just lollygaggin' around, so he asks us what we're doin'. 'Waitin' for orders,' we tells him. 'Whose orders?' says Abe. 'Dunno,' says we."

"But General Wool and Secretary Chase are already on their way to Norfolk," Bronwen said, "so why are we just standing here without orders?"

The sailor shrugged. "Foul-up by the big brass, it is. But we got us some marchin' orders now, 'cause Old Abe there hollers, 'Get me a body who kin write.' So's we did, and right then and there he spews out an order. Sendin' all of us over there to Norfolk as re-in-forcements, he is."

Bronwen could see the president's large hands gripping a railing, his face reflecting a deep frustration, as though he would like to shove every man there onto the waiting ships. Rain began to drizzle down, but Lincoln did not move from his post.

Still grinning broadly, the sailor told her, "Poor feller, he's findin' out it ain't no fun bein' mucked about by them in charge!"

Bronwen had nodded and moved away, weaving in and around the clumps of dockhands and waiting uniformed men, marking time until the gunboat cast off. She had already recognized that Major Norris had shrewdly counted on the confusion that would accompany an unanticipated Union occupation of Norfolk. With such a massive jumble of bodies and boats, who would be expecting, or watching for, a saboteur to strike?

Fox had taken every precaution in ensuring the *Monitor*'s security, but Hampton Roads was deluged with ships, large and small, and there was always the danger of someone's inadvertent negligence. Also, to be certain an injustice was not committed, Bronwen herself had suggested that Fox station two trusted officers at Norfolk; ones that could instantly recognize the suspected saboteur, and would follow him.

Fox thought that, given the ironclad's present position, the suspected man would head for the wharves on a small peninsula pointing north into the Chesapeake, the wharves closest to the *Monitor*. The reason why the ironclad's position had been changed. Once there, where the man had no possible reason to be, he would be apprehended. There would be little doubt then that he had swallowed the bait.

The gunboat had begun to load, and as Bronwen had been scanning the crowded dock, her gaze had abruptly come to rest on a single figure, who had been standing slightly apart from the other men and only a few yards from the gunboat's gangplank. He had been attempting to light a cigarette.

It had been his stance and his vaguely familiar motions that had caught her attention, because her recent memory was clouded by having seen in the past days so many hundreds of men. But when this man had turned away from the wind, hunching his shoulders and cupping his hands around a match, then, suddenly, she had felt the blood drain from her head.

She had made a mistake. A terrible, dangerous mistake. So had Secretary Fox, but he had followed her lead. She had backed up and leaned against a post, trying to think her way out of this rapidly descending nightmare. An earlier conversation with Fox had gone streaking through her mind.

"It is difficult to conceive of this man being suicidal," Fox had reasoned, "because surely he intends to enjoy the large amount of money he will be paid."

"So he'll employ a means that allows him to escape," she had agreed. "The *Monitor* plans! The set that temporarily disappeared from the shipyard—that's why they were 'borrowed.' He must have been looking for the location of something like . . . like the gunpowder magazine?"

Fox had nodded slowly. "A long fuse could be set to reach the magazine, giving him enough time to escape."

"If he remembers to bring a match," she had muttered absently.

That, right there, should have warned her.

Straightening, she had glanced toward the fort. If only there were some way to signal Fox, who was surely watching this launch through glasses from the fort's ramparts. But there was no means to gain his attention without also gaining the attention of others, and there was no time to climb to the ramparts herself. The gunboat was almost ready to cast off.

She had taken a deep breath, made the only decision possible, and started for the gangplank.

As the figure strode onto the ship, she kept him in sight and insinuated herself into the column of men trooping aboard. Only a few minutes later, when she had looked up at the bridge, Lieutenant Commander Farrar had been standing there. She had expected it. Fox had maneuvered Farrar's command of this gunboat, and he had also purposefully waited until the last minute to announce it; protocol was subject to the will of the Assistant Secretary of the Navy.

Fox had said that when Farrar was told, he had been de-
lighted.

"He comes from a wealthy family, did splendidly at Annapolis, and has shown great promise as an officer," Fox had
told her. "We must be sure, very sure, before we ruin an
innocent man."

That conversation should also have waved a red flag at
her; Farrar did not need money.

Her guilt now felt all the greater because it had taken her
so long to figure this out. She should have pressed Rhys
Bevan sooner about the Baltimore gunmen. The last she had
seen of them, they were being hustled to the brig of a frigate
to sail down the Chesapeake. It became perfectly obvious
why they had never reached Washington or Alexandria: they
had been released, that was why. And the frigate had been
under Farrar's command. But Farrar was rarely alone.

Now the gunboat was steaming into a Norfolk wharf, and
Bronwen tried desperately with her field glasses to find two
naval officers who looked as if they might be waiting for
Farrar. Which was plainly absurd of her, because Fox's men
would hardly stand there with a sign that said: *Monitor* this
way.

Good—if she could manage humor, she might be all right.
She wedged herself behind coils of line in order to watch the
unloading, and wait. The noise and confusion here were even
worse than at the fort, with men running up and down gangplanks and shells still bursting over the now nearly abandoned Confederate positions. The air reeked of gunpowder.
She began to fear that when he finally appeared, she would
lose her man in the melee.

At last she saw Farrar and his aide striding down the gangplank. She scrambled over the coiled rope to follow, but was
again forced to weave around others, at the same time watching the officer and the ensign and still trying to spot the
planted navy men.

She stopped short, bumping into a soldier ahead of her,

because Farrar had paused to say something to Ensign Evans. She craned her neck, attempting to see around several artillery wagons just left to stand there. When a group of men walked between her and her marks, she lost sight of Farrar. She pushed forward, her nervousness so great she nearly stumbled headlong into an admiral.

She saw him. He was headed off with quick strides west along the waterfront. He looked to be alone, and she could see no one trailing him, but it was difficult to tell with so many men moving in all directions. She glanced anxiously around her, realizing that Farrar was alone. Where was the ensign? *Where was he?*

Whirling to her left, then to her right, she found him, already some distance beyond her. He was heading east toward the Chesapeake. It was an inconvenient time, she thought as she went forward with her gaze locked on him, to question whether she could have been wrong about both Farrar and Evans.

Evans, the perfect ensign, always at Farrar's heels, doing and knowing everything Farrar did. Even reading messages strategically placed in Farrar's quarters, designed to lure a lieutenant commander, but instead snagging his aide.

Her mind spun frantically; what could she do to stop him? *How* could she stop him? And where was he now headed?

She smiled grimly as she recalled Fox telling her—when she had requested to go over to Norfolk and possibly see the *Monitor*—that he could not allow her to be placed in any peril. At that moment, Bronwen fervently wished that men like Rhys Bevan and Gustavus Fox would cease their disastrous, backfiring efforts to spare her from danger!

It soon became evident, as she cautiously trailed her man through a nearly deserted area of small houses and sheds and warehouses, that Norfolk was indeed again in Union hands. The mayor had already met with General Wool and Secretary Chase to turn over the symbolic key. Which meant the James

River would be open for the navy to support McClellan's advance on Richmond.

It appeared that President Lincoln's first field command— to all appearances a bloodless one—had been successful. Unless he lost the Union's first ironclad. She suddenly wondered where the *Merrimack* was anchored, lurking in the shadows, waiting for the permanent removal of the *Monitor.*

The rain was still a heavy mist rather than droplets, which Bronwen thought would help to conceal her, but the sky seemed to be clearing. She hung back to put more distance between herself and Evans when she realized he was approaching a telegraph office. As he was about to enter it, the ensign stopped abruptly to glance around, a move that sent her diving into a doorway. She waited for several minutes, her little derringer long since out of her pocket and held ready. When she finally peered around the doorway, the man had disappeared, presumably into the office. While it seemed somewhat reckless for her to move much closer, she had to make certain.

She wondered if, like Treasury-unit agents, he knew how to operate the telegraph. This was answered when she crept alongside the small structure and heard, coming through a window, a male voice saying, "Yes, go ahead and shut down the line, but do it after you've transmitted my message. I've written it out, so send it now!"

Another voice murmured something she couldn't make out, and then all was silent. Bronwen inched away, intending to wait at a safe distance. She had no trouble clearing the dirt road in front of the office, but then a metallic crash sounded behind her.

She jumped, and spun to see a feral cat streaking away from the rolling ash can it had overturned. The door to the telegraph office burst open, and the navy ensign coming through it held a revolver.

Her derringer was of no use at this great a distance. She turned, and was racing toward a group of warehouses when she heard behind her the sharp thud of a bullet striking the ground. Zigzagging as she ran, she prayed that the navy did not pay much attention to marksmanship. And it was small consolation now to know that she had the right man.

Dodging around the first warehouse, she raced through the open door of another, her heart pounding as she ran toward the opposite door to the outside. With luck, Evans might figure she had hidden herself inside the building and would stop to search it.

She tore around the corner of a small structure, avoiding bales of straw to approach a door that was standing ajar, and skidded to a stop. Facing her was the barrel of a shotgun.

"Stop right where you are, you blasted Yankee, or I'll blow yer head off!"

Bronwen squinted into the mist to see a long-bearded, aged man holding the shotgun, and a small, curly-haired child clinging to his tattered coattails. The little girl was about two, three at the most, and she looked terrified.

"Yes, sir," Bronwen said quietly, raising her hands and speculating how accurate the wavering shotgun might be. And how close the revolver might also be by now.

"Ah, sir?" she tried, "sir, I'm not a soldier. And I'm a woman, see?" She took a chance and reached up to whip off her cap, hoping to summon the legendary Southern gallantry.

The barrel inched higher, occasionally aiming at her hair as it still wavered dangerously.

"Sir, I'm just a . . . a newspaper reporter," she tried again, "traveling with the troops. I don't mean any harm to you or your . . . your granddaughter?" she guessed.

"I s'pect a Yankee's a Yankee," said the old man, "so's you jest get yerself a-ready to—"

His arm went up and the shotgun flew as he staggered backward, dragging the child with him.

A split-second earlier Bronwen had heard the whine of a bullet. She saw the eyes of the little girl grow wide and her lower lip tremble.

These people were not the enemy.

Bronwen threw herself at the child, rolling them both up against the building's wall. Not daring to look around, she scrambled to her feet and, snatching up the girl, ran inside. After lowering the child, she pulled the door shut and crouched next to it.

The little girl gave a soft whimper. Bronwen reached out and drew the child to her side, whispering, "Try not to be scared. I'll get us out of here somehow, but you have to be quiet, O.K.?"

Even in the dim light Bronwen could see the large blue eyes glittering with tears. As she distractedly patted the child's cheeks, she looked around. Overhead there seemed to be some kind of loft with a ladder leading to it.

She crept to the nearest window and, flattening herself against the wall, peered out. The old man was hobbling toward the door, his right arm bleeding and held at a peculiar angle. His shotgun still lay on the ground where it had landed. Bronwen could see no one else from where she stood, and wished she could retrieve the gun, but couldn't justify the risk; not with the man holding the revolver expecting her to do something just that stupid.

While she waited for the child's grandfather to reach the door, she tried to recall how many of the revolver's bullets had been fired. Her quick glance, as Evans had stood in the telegraph doorway, told her that his revolver was a Colt, so it had either five or six chambers. Did he carry more ammunition? Probably. So drawing his fire to empty the gun would also not be worth the risk.

Bronwen sidled to the door, opening it just enough for the child's grandfather to come through, then quickly closed it again. No revolver had sounded. Did that mean the ammunition was low, or gone?

"Where's the child?" the old man wheezed.

"Over there," Bronwen said, jerking her thumb. "Did you see the one doing the shooting?"

"Sure 'nough didn't see much." The old man spat. "But he's one of y'all."

"Not mine," Bronwen said. "How's your arm?"

The old man spat again and said nothing as he stumbled to his granddaughter.

"I have to get out of here," Bronwen told him, "but I'll send someone back to help you."

"Don't need help from no Yankees!"

If *his* stubbornness was the prevailing attitude, Bronwen thought, this would be a very long war indeed.

"Where was the gunman when you came in?" she asked him.

"Now jest how in tarnation would I know that? If I had've known, I would 'a' grabbed thet shotgun and blown both yer heads off."

After Bronwen checked the door and window, she inspected the interior of the structure. It smelled of horses, and although it was now vacant, the stalls indicated use as a livery stable. A dilapidated buggy leaned against one of the stalls, decaying bales of hay were piled against a far wall, and the floor was littered with straw.

Fear coursed through her as she suddenly remembered the match that had lit a cigarette, and could as easily light a fuse leading to a powder magazine. She could not rule out the possibility of a desperate act by Evans—he was, after all, a gambler. A stable in flames would not be considered suspicious in the confusion of the Union takeover, and while she might manage to get out in time, maybe even without being shot, it could sacrifice the other two here.

Before she went to the ladder she had seen, she said to the old man, "You'd better stay here, sir. And be quiet about it, because that man out there could shoot you without a glimmer of conscience. Since I'm your best bet right now, I hope you believe what I'm saying."

She didn't wait for an answer and ran toward the ladder, climbing it rapidly to reach the loft. Its window, as she had assumed, overlooked the road below. Directly under the window were more bales of straw. Where was the ensign? How long would he wait before trying to smoke her out, or before leaving to do what he had originally intended? Not long, Bronwen guessed.

She took another glance out the window to see the Chesapeake Bay, not far to the north. Scores of ships rode its waters, and among them was the *Monitor*. Accessible only to navy men, as Evans would well know.

Taking a deep breath, she launched herself out the window, dropping easily to the straw below. Whipping the derringer from her pocket, she scrambled down the far side of the bales, expecting at any second to hear the crack of a revolver.

Hearing nothing, she edged around the bales, and again noticed the shotgun lying in the dirt some yards away. If she could just get to it—and then she saw him.

He was coming around the side of the livery, and if he had not seen her jump, he wouldn't have spotted her yet. His revolver was held ready, but he might not have much left in the way of ammunition; even if he did, it took time to reload. She waited with impatience, heart again pounding, but he still wasn't close enough for her to use the derringer. Then, for some reason he stopped, looked at the livery door, and took a step toward it. She could not chance the old man or the child wandering through it.

Bronwen stepped out into the road. "You really want to see who's the better shot?" she shouted. "If I were you, I wouldn't bet on myself!"

He stopped short with the revolver aimed straight at her. When he fired, she was already leaping back behind the straw. As he started forward, nearly into the derringer's range, the livery door swung open. Before Bronwen could even scream a warning, the child toddled out into the road. She stopped, her expression bewildered, between the drawn guns.

Dear Lord, now what? Bronwen could feel sweat on her forehead, threatening to roll into her eyes, but resisted the urge to wipe it off.

"Put down the gun," she yelled, not even remotely believing he would do it. The object was to gain time. Time to somehow remove the child. Where was the grandfather, passed out from the bleeding arm?

"You know," she went on, desperate to hold his attention until she could think of something, "Pinkerton always used to say 'get rid of bad habits.' And that's a very bad habit you have there, my treacherous friend. Smoking on the deck of the *Alhambra* that night, you had on one of the lieutenant's coats—which was too big and didn't fit well—because your own coat was covered with blood, wasn't it? Remember, back in Baltimore when Farrar told me smoke made him cough? Well, you weren't coughing! Weren't even breathing hard after killing two men, Evans!"

She watched the ensign's head shift slightly to his left. Trying to see how he could move past the child to get a clear shot at her. He still was not quite close enough for her derringer to be reliable, but evidently he didn't yet realize that. He would know she'd have only one shot.

Distract him, she told herself, racking her brain for a way out of this without further endangering the child. The little girl was just standing there, fingers of one hand in her mouth, the other hand twisting the hem of her skirt, eyes huge in her small white face.

Bronwen had a sudden and eerie vision of this fragile child imposed over the powerful bulk of the ironclad ship. *Please Lord, don't force me to choose.*

"You know something else, Evans?" she shouted, hoping against hope that someone would appear—where *were* the Union troops? Still down at the wharves? "That's a mighty unsavory bunch of characters you chummed around with. A female assassin who's probably due to hang, and a gone-rotten U.S. Treasury agent who's now residing at the bottom of the James River. Your inside contact, Evans, is as dead as a doornail."

Bull's-eye! His expression showed that he hadn't heard about Howard Knolls's "disappearance." It must have jarred him, because he finally spoke.

"I'll kill the girl if I have to, Llyr. Throw down the pistol, and do it now!"

At his harsh bark, the girl looked even more frightened, and Bronwen's heart sank as the child turned and began to stumble toward her.

"I mean it, Llyr! Put down the pistol!" He had drawn a bead on the child as a sure way to make Bronwen comply. She saw only one path open. And only one chance to take it.

"O.K., you win," Bronwen shouted, "I'll get rid of it. Here!"

She crouched down and stretched out her arm, tossing the derringer just far enough to take the child out of the line of fire. Evans's eyes were fixed on the gun, and as he jumped toward it, she yanked the stiletto from her shoe, rose on her haunches and flung it.

The knife hit Evans in the right shoulder so hard he stumbled backward before he fell. His Colt discharged into the air, but he was still very much alive. Bronwen raced to grab the revolver before he could fire again, but at the same time, coming from a different direction, she heard the crack of another gun. She hurled herself to the ground, and her scrabbling fingers had just touched metal when a voice somewhere above her said, "Please do not trouble yourself further, Miss Llyr. It is not at all necessary."

For a terrible, split second she thought Howard Knolls had risen from his watery grave, because the voice bore a British accent. She tensed, lunged forward and snatched the revolver, then rolled and jumped to her feet, where she looked straight into the sharp black eyes of Colonel Dorian de Warde.

"Do you recall our first meeting, Miss Llyr? he said languidly, then blew on the end of his lethal and smoking walking cane.

With movements so deliberate she could not mistake his intention, he replaced the cane's silver ferrule, saying, "I believe it was in Alabama, was it not? Wretchedly hot place, Alabama."

Bronwen looked down at the corpse of the ensign; Evans would not be firing anything again, owing to de Warde's deadly intervention. The threat to the *Monitor* was over, unless de Warde planned . . . no. He would have killed her if the ironclad's destruction were his scheme.

"Such a sorry business," de Warde sighed. He walked some steps toward the livery and patted the child's head. The little girl looked up at him and smiled shyly.

"All right, de Warde," Bronwen said. "What's the story here? I trust you won't tell me you killed Evans to keep him from shooting me."

"Why else?" The black eyes snapped with humor.

"To silence him. Prevent him from talking. Of recent there's been a plague of that tactic."

"My dear young lady, you are too cynical and long before your time. Let us just say that I deplore the violence that men like Mr. Evans insist on inflicting on us all."

"De Warde!"

"Very well, then let us also say that occasionally even friends need to be taught a lesson."

"Thou shalt not kill without my permission?" Bronwen said mockingly.

"Precisely. Mr. Evans was quite prepared to sacrifice this innocent child, simply because she stood in the way of an ill-advised plan to destroy a ship. Beware a man who will sell his country for a few pieces of silver."

Bronwen stared at him, dumbfounded, but nonetheless disbelieving. "Why are you here in Norfolk?"

"Simply protecting my business interests. Ironically for Mr. Evans, I have been concerned about my tobacco investments."

This was the one thing he had said that Bronwen could believe.

"I fear I must leave you now," de Warde announced, twirling his cane with a flourish and managing to sound regretful. "However, Miss Llyr, I am rather certain we shall meet again."

"Is that a not-so-subtle suggestion that I owe you something, de Warde?"

He smiled charmingly and as he turned to leave, said over his shoulder, "Do give my fondest regards to your lovely aunt."

Bronwen half-believed he might vanish in a cloud of smoke. Instead, she watched him walk sedately back the way he had apparently come. She eyed the revolver, annoyed he had known she couldn't shoot him in the back.

Flinching as she bent over Evans to withdraw her stiletto, she felt something grab her, and looked down to see the little girl clinging to her legs. Bronwen snatched the derringer, scooped up the child and took her to the livery where the old man stood swaying in the doorway.

"Here she is, sir," Bronwen said. "I'll tell someone to come take care of your arm."

As he started to protest, she interrupted him, saying, "You might not like hearing this, sir, but we Yankees aren't a whole lot different from you. There's a few rotten apples in our barrel for sure, but believe me, you've got some rotten ones of your own. Now, you take good care of your granddaughter."

She gave him a brisk salute, then turned and loped toward the telegraph office.

When she emerged from the office a few minutes later, she held a piece of yellow foolscap.

May 10, 1862
N: Union occupying Norfolk. Your directive re: Monitor to be executed this night.
SHADOW MAN

As she stood looking off toward the Bay, Bronwen thought she heard someone whistling. She looked up the road, expecting to see Union soldiers, and instead saw Kerry O'Hara strolling toward her.

"What the devil are you doing here?" she asked.

"Checking to see that the telegraph line is closed to Richmond. And I've just been on the James, reporting to the *Merrimack* flag officer, in my capacity as river scout, that he would be unable to take his deep-draft ship up the river more than a few miles. Thus leaving *Merrimack* entirely at the mercy of the Union shore batteries, or of capture by Union troops. The poor fellow just doesn't know what to do now. I'm afraid I couldn't have you tagging along, Red, which was a shame, since you missed all the excite—"

He broke off as he looked up the road, apparently seeing the body of Ensign Oliver Evans. He walked a few yards, and turned to stare at her before saying, "And just what the hell have *you* been doing?"

"Nothing much."

"You want to tell me about it?"

"Not particularly," Bronwen said, tucking the foolscap into her pocket before walking past him.

She headed back toward the wharves, but not before taking one last look at the Bay and its ships. With her field glasses, she skimmed the water and found it at last. The gallant little *Monitor,* plowing through the waves instead of riding them; an ugly iron duckling among graceful wooden swans.

29

—∽∞∽—

*Last evening, as we entered the Chesapeake, we saw
the crimson glow of a great fire in the direction of
Fortress Monroe or Norfolk; and this morning early
we heard the dull, heavy sound of an explosion or
brief cannonading in the same direction.*

—Katherine Prescott Wormeley, May 11, 1862

The floating hospital *Daniel Webster* was steaming steadily up the York River, and Kathryn, standing on an upper deck, had been told the ship would soon anchor off Yorktown. There were sick men to be brought aboard. In the past few hours, surgeons from shore had been hailing the steamship, rowing out in smaller boats to request lemons and brandy and any kind of soup available. She had heard them say their fever patients on shore were suffering dreadfully.

Nurses were needed, but whether women nurses would be welcomed by the surgeons remained to be seen.

She glanced around her, wondering what trouble Natty was brewing now. He had run past her a few minutes ago, and every step had made his bulging pockets clank suspiciously. She sighed, assuming it would not be long before the complaints began. Gregg Travis wasn't here to answer them. He had embarked on another ship, leaving Washington so suddenly that Kathryn had not even known he was gone, or where he was bound. If General McClellan's campaign was successful, the war would be over soon, and she wondered when, or even if she might see the doctor again. She had been fretting over it and should not be; there were too many other more serious things to occupy her. Mostly she worried about her sister and brother.

Where was Bronwen? That she might be at Fort Monroe, as Rhys Bevan had said, didn't comfort Kathryn in the least. Not after the sky-splitting explosion early this morning, which everyone aboard the *Daniel Webster* agreed came from either the vicinity of the fort or from Norfolk.

There was also the letter she had received before leaving Washington, saying that their brother Seth's New York regiment might now be on the peninsula. How could three members of one family be strangers in Virginia, with not one of them knowing where the others were?

She looked across the water at the riverbanks, so densely overgrown that the land beyond could not be seen, and scolded herself for ingratitude. This was what she had wanted to do, and she should concentrate only on what needed to be done.

Kathryn took a breath, squared her shoulders, and gave an answering wave to another small boat approaching the steamship.

Joseph Maddox gazed out a window overlooking the James River as he remarked, "Well, Norris, it's been a bleak several days for our side, wouldn't you say?"

Major William Norris, seated behind a desk, said nothing.

Maddox turned and waited for a response. Finally the grim-faced Norris sent him a reluctant nod. "Yes, I'd say that."

"It's hard to understand, the Confederate navy destroying the *Merrimack* last night. Someone's head should roll," Maddox commented.

"The flag officer exercised poor judgment," Norris agreed. "He grew distraught when the river scouts told him he couldn't go upriver more than a few miles. Thought he would be at the mercy of Union batteries. So he ran *Merrimack* aground, took off the crew, and set her afire, he claimed, to prevent her capture."

"Heard it created quite an explosion when the flames hit the powder magazine," Maddox remarked. He was unable to resist reminding Norris of the irony involved in the *Merrimack*'s destruction, since he had learned it was precisely what the major had planned for the *Monitor*. "But with your U.S. Navy connection lost," Maddox added, "we'll likely never get the full story."

"There are always other connections," Norris answered cryptically. "And young Evans was becoming expensive, what with his gambling and his debts. I understand he bet half a year's wages on a single poker hand in a Baltimore tavern. He was fast becoming a liability."

"But we've also lost Bluebell, and Howard Knolls seems to have disappeared," Maddox said carefully. "Can they be replaced?"

"Oh, I don't think we have necessarily seen the last of Bluebell," Norris said, apparently at last finding something to smile about. "But yes, Maddox, anyone can be replaced."

Bronwen stood in the telegraph room of Fort Monroe, waiting for a reply to her wire. She supposed that Rhys Bevan had already been informed of events by Secretaries Chase and Fox, but orders were to report herself.

After a transport had returned her to the fort, she had received a message that the president wanted to see her. She had found Mr. Lincoln standing on a stone parapet, gazing out across Hampton Roads.

"I hear you've had yourself an adventure," he had said.

"Yes, sir. I hear that you had one, too."

He had smiled, but the furrows beside his eyes and mouth had deepened. Every time she saw him, he had aged markedly.

"I reckoned you might like a piece of news," he had told her. "Seems you were right about my friend Quiller. Had a letter from him the other day. Said his eyesight is mighty fine now, and he's enjoying the French cuisine—gettin' fat as a summer porcupine. But he's decided to mosey on home. When he does, I'd like you to meet Jimmy. Have him tell you all about his travels. Think you might want to do that?"

"Of course, sir," Bronwen had responded quickly, but then held her breath anxiously after she had asked, "When Mr. Quiller leaves Paris, would he be coming back to . . . to Richmond?"

"I s'pect so."

She had succeeded in restraining a heart-sinking sigh.

Now her head jerked toward the telegraph as it began to chatter, and she grabbed a pencil.

War Department, Washington
May 11, 1862

LLYR: Applause for cleaning Navy dirty linen. Your sister aboard hospital ship Daniel Webster. *Arriving Yorktown today. Permission granted to meet her there.*
BEVAN

Bronwen tore off the sheet of paper from the pad and slipped it into her pocket. After picking up her cap, she started to set it on her head with its usual rakish tilt, but stopped, thought of what lay behind and before her, and then straightened it.

When she stepped out of the telegraph room, it was to walk briskly along the parapet and down the steps to the wharves.

HISTORICAL NOTES

—ɯɯ—

Bates, David Homer

(b. 1842) Bates was just eighteen or nineteen when the Civil War began. One year later he was made the manager and cipher-operator of the U.S. Military Telegraph Office located in the War Department, and he remained in this position until after the war. His wartime diary was published in book form in 1907 under the title *Lincoln in the Telegraph Office*. In his diary Bates recalls, among other things, Lincoln's fondness for Shakespeare.

Dix, Dorothea

(1802–1887) The sign in Miss Dix's office stating her requirements for female nurses was authentic but not complete, as she had additional rigid dictates. However, Dix had no guidelines, and no precedents, since at the beginning of the war there were no recognized, professional female nurses in America; by the war's end, approximately 20 percent of the nurses were women. Dix proved to be an ineffective administrator, and was eventually removed from her superintendent position, but her earlier work to reform insane asylums remains a significant and lasting legacy.

Ericsson, John

(1803–1889) Ericsson was a Swedish-born inventor who designed and named the *Monitor* and supervised its construction. The ironclad was built at a shipyard on Long Island for $275,000. While under construction it was the subject of an article in *Scientific American,* and drew mocking derision as "the cheese box on a raft," and "Ericsson's folly." The *Monitor* effectively made all wooden ships of war obsolete, and its name is still used to classify certain ships. In January of 1863, the first gallant little *Monitor* was struck by a violent storm and lost at sea.

H.J.K.

Edwin C. Fishel, in *The Secret War for the Union* (Boston: Houghton Mifflin, 1996), says in regard to this shadowy figure: "an agent listed in the records only as H.J.K. who apparently joined Pinkerton's only a short time before leaving for Virginia. HJK disappears from the records after five months of payroll entries. . . . no reports from him are in McClellan's or Pinkerton's records."

Lawton, Hattie

Lawton was one of the first female private detectives, hired after Kate Warne (see *The Stalking-Horse*) and in the employ of Allan Pinkerton's agency. She was arrested in Richmond along with **Timothy Webster**, with whom she was frequently paired. (She may have been married to another agent.) Source material indicates that she served a prison term in Richmond, and when released in 1863, she reported back to Pinkerton. She then disappeared, and there seems to be no further trace of her.

Lloyd, William

Lloyd was used as a model on which to base the fictitious Jim Quiller. The information on Lloyd is scant, because the most successful spies are rarely ever known, but there is indication that Lincoln received information from this man, as the president did from other sources outside governmental circles. Lloyd was a New York and Baltimore businessman, a well-known publisher of railroad and steamship guides and maps of the South. At some point General Winder became suspicious of Lloyd and had him watched closely, diluting his usefulness. Given Lincoln's serious concern about intelligence information, it should not be surprising that the president had his own "personal spies."

Maddox, Joseph H.

A smuggler-spy about whom there is also limited information. Maddox was well educated, served in the Mexican War, and became owner-editor of the *New Orleans Crescent*. After moving to his wife's property in Maryland, the mysterious Maddox may have been, at least early in the war, a double agent. Eventually he did provide the Union with some valuable intelligence information. He was imprisoned at Fort Monroe (Federal) for three months during 1864, apparently due to a misunderstanding over a tobacco investment in Richmond, leading Maddox to file suit against Secretary of War Edwin Stanton. Maddox ultimately recovered his tobacco—by then worthless—and was given a substantial sum of money for damages.

McCubbin, Samuel

Richmond police chief in 1862.

Norris, William

A resident of Baltimore, Major William Norris was the head of the Confederate Signal Corps and Secret Service Bureau and established the "Secret Line," a swift and efficient intelligence operation with contacts as far north as Quebec.

Olmsted, Frederick Law

(1822–1903) Olmsted is considered to be America's first landscape architect. Before his work on New York City's Central Park and other significant projects, he traveled widely in the South. His reports to the *New York Times* from 1852 to 1855 were later published as *The Cotton Kingdom*, a book reflecting Olmsted's opposition to slavery. In 1861, he became the highly effective executive secretary of the newly organized U.S. Sanitary Commission.

Pigeons

These ubiquitous birds have a long and noble history as trustworthy messengers. They were kept by the ancient Egyptians, Greeks and Romans, the Crusaders, and the European explorers. Pigeons can fly at sustained speeds of forty to fifty miles an hour, are able to travel at night, and have been used for centuries by military forces to carry messages. Indeed, during the twentieth century's World War II, the U.S. Army used pigeons to carry messages from intelligence agents behind enemy lines—some three dozen pigeons received medals for their brave service! Pigeon-racing remains today as one of the oldest documented, worldwide sports.

Pinkerton Agents

(or the lack thereof) In February of 1862, detective Allan Pinkerton was unaware that Timothy Webster had been stricken in Richmond with inflammatory rheumatism and was being nursed by another agent, Hattie Lawton. Pinkerton sent agents Lewis and Scully to investigate why Webster hadn't reported, and all of these agents were subsequently arrested. However, an agent recently hired by Webster, and known to history only as a genderless H.J.K., disappeared completely. Nothing further is known of this agent. As regards the loss of Timothy Webster (see **Webster**), and Pinkerton's other Richmond operatives, Edwin C. Fishel in *The Secret War for the Union* writes: "The most remarkable fact about intelligence in McClellan's Peninsula campaign, his grand effort to win the war, is that during the last four months of the five-month campaign Pinkerton had not even one agent at work in Richmond or anywhere else behind Confederate lines."

33rd New York Regiment

Composed of men mainly from Seneca Falls and Waterloo, the 33rd saw continuous action during McClellan's 1862 Virginia Peninsula Campaign. It participated in the battles at Yorktown, Williamsburg, Mechanicsville, Golding's Farm, and Savage's Station.

Spies

One of the great spymasters of any time and place was George Washington. After Washington's time, though, the United States espionage structure that he had so vigorously built began to deteriorate. It revived briefly during the War of 1812, but was then allowed to disintegrate. Thus, at the beginning of the Civil War, the Federal government was relying on the privately owned and operated Pinkerton firm.

U.S. Treasury Building

The present, neo-classic building on 15th Street in Washington, D.C., was begun in 1836 to replace an earlier one destroyed by fire. (Its architect, Robert Mills, had previously designed the Washington Monument.) The west, north, and south wings were added between 1855 and 1869; this time span accounted for primarily by the reasons given in Chapter Two. The office of the Sanitary Commission's executive secretary Frederick Olmsted was originally located in this building. Treasury Secretary Salmon Chase's offices have been restored to their Civil War–era splendor. It remains as unquestionably one of the most beautiful and impressive structures in our present-day capital city. But a word to the wise: since its security measures have vastly improved since Bronwen's day, don't attempt a spontaneous, self-guided tour.

Van Lew, Elizabeth

(1818–1900) This woman, according to Ulysses S. Grant, was the most effective Union spy in Richmond. Before the war she sheltered runaway slaves, and during it she worked tirelessly to provide food and comfort to Union prisoners. Not only did she manage to ingratiate herself with General Winder, but she and her servants organized relay stations between Richmond and Union headquarters on the James River. Her house was condemned and demolished in 1911, and the Bellevue School now occupies the site, which is at the corner of 24th and E. Grace Street in the Church Hill Historic District of Richmond. The American elm tree that Bronwen and Marsh used for messages still lives there on a corner of the property behind the school. Given its now mammoth size, the elm is undoubtedly several centuries old, an ancient, battle-scarred witness to turbulent Richmond history.

Webster, Timothy

(1821–1862) Considered by Allan Pinkerton to be his best agent, Webster was one of numerous casualties on both sides during the war's battle for intelligence information. Webster's arrest, imprisonment, and death were as they appear in the novel. The site of his capture varies slightly from one source to another; although it is usually given as the Monument Hotel, there is one account that places it at a Union sympathizer's home in Virginia where Webster may have temporarily stayed. **Hattie Lawton** was the only sympathetic witness to this event. Allan Pinkerton eventually brought Webster's remains back to Chicago, where they were buried in Graceland Cemetery. Pinkerton himself is buried there, as well as a number of other employees of the detective firm, including the country's first professional female detective, Kate Warne.

Winder, John Henry

(1800–1865) In 1862, Winder was the commandant of all prisons in Richmond, and thus in charge of all federal prisoners of war there. Then, in 1864, he was placed in charge of all prisons in Georgia (including the notorious Andersonville) and Alabama, and shortly after that became commissary general in charge of all the prisons east of the Mississippi.

Wormeley, Katherine Prescott

(1830–1908) After working at the beginning of the war with her Rhode Island Women's Union Aid Society, Wormeley volunteered for the Hospital Transport ships, operated under the auspices of the U.S. Sanitary

Commission during the 1862 Peninsula Campaign. After the war, she compiled the letters she had written to family and friends during the campaign: *The Other Side of War; On the Hospital Transports with the Army of the Potomac* was originally published in 1889. It is a well-written and often surprisingly "modern"-sounding account of the first major effort of the commission.